THE FAMILY

A Reed & Billie Novel, Book 11

DUSTIN STEVENS

The Ghost
A Reed & Billie Novel
Copyright © 2022, Dustin Stevens
Cover Art and Design: Jun Ares

*Revenge is a luscious fruit which you
must leave to ripen.*
—Emile Gaboriau

*It is difficult to fight against anger;
for a man will revenge with his soul.*
—Heraclitus

Prologue

"They got her," the sheriff whispered, the three words coming out as little more than a wheeze. A sentence forced out along with all the air in his lungs, managing to convey a host of emotions.

Shock, at what he was just forced to witness.

Shame, for the fact that he was too late in arriving.

Frustration and fear and no doubt a handful of others, all mixed into a cocktail that stripped the man of any ability to formulate much more than that. A state of being that his prior years of service had never prepared him for. Reed able to envision the man standing outside the house forty miles away, weight shifting to either foot as he stared out, bordering on catatonia.

A position Reed himself might have found himself in years before, the same competing thoughts and reactions all festering inside him as well. Reflexive responses that time and experience had managed to mold in a way that shifted their respective percentages greatly, meaning that instead of finding himself slipping into a stupor, rage was the predominant thing to well within him.

Unbridled vitriol that rose like bile in the back of his throat, causing his molars to clamp down and his eyes to narrow. A full-body

1

clench that brought veins to the surface along his exposed forearms and sweat to his features.

The first time he'd seen either in weeks, the hatred filling him stronger than whatever cold the month of November could throw at him.

Latent hostility that his partner picked up on instantly, shoving her muzzle up through the front seats of the sedan. Amped up on the same energy pulsating through him, she took in deep breaths through her open mouth, hints of pink tongue flashing behind the rows of exposed teeth.

An exaggerated stance letting Reed know that she too felt what he did.

"Sweet Jesus," the sheriff muttered, his voice trailing away. "They got Ava, too."

Knowing better than to even try to reply, Reed ended the call there. A single press of a button cutting off the conversation, plunging the interior of the car back into silence as they tore north through the night.

Quiet that did nothing to stop the final words the man uttered from resonating throughout the vehicle.

They *had* gotten Ava, too.

And if Reed and Billie didn't get there in time, they would likely get two more as well.

Chapter One

The instructions The Artist gave were beyond refute. Ironclad directives that allowed her brothers – or, more aptly, just the one – to do at least some of what they wanted to while still giving her the space to do what she must.

A clean canvas for her to work with.

The opening application of what had been months in planning and design. Years in waiting before that, fighting against every internal desire before finally being given the greenlight.

The first and foremost of the two rules she had handed to her brothers before sending them off was to not get caught. Not to so much as even be seen.

An order that meant they had to be as meticulous in their actions as she was in hers. A continuation of the months of preparation that now covered the basement wall in the homestead they shared.

Work that would be proven worthless if they were to get careless now, when it mattered most.

The second order was that, within reason, they could do what they wanted from the neck down. No weapons of any kind could be used. No guns or knives or anything that would take a life, but using fists or feet or knees or elbows, they could begin to start unpacking some of the angst she knew them both to be carrying.

Seven long years of rage that had not dissipated in the slightest, instead slowly simmering.

Pressure in need of a release, the first signs of such already dappling the bare torso of the man before her. The guy firmly in his sixties with a thick shock of graying hair and deep creases around his mouth and eyes, no amount of money able to obscure the passage of well over half a century.

A figure who could not help but spur the same repulsion in The Artist that had driven her brothers' actions, even if her way of showing it was to be of a vastly different nature.

Stripped bare from the waist up, the man was sprawled out on the white sheet spread across the concrete floor. Arms and legs splayed in a starfish pattern, his head lolled to the side, his eyes closed tight.

Mouth gaping, loud breaths passed between his lips, products of the trauma tormenting his body and the chemical sedation keeping him asleep.

A state he would remain in for at least the next twelve hours. Long enough for The Artist to do what she must and all three of them to scrub the place clean before departing. A location that was not ideal, far from the ultimate intrusion they had hoped to inflict upon him, but was necessary due to his unique living situation.

The mansion tucked away in the midst of a gated community, making any hope they had of getting in and slipping away undetected impossible. Protections that months of reconnaissance had proven weren't impenetrable, but were deterrent enough to keep them from going any further.

Safeguards afforded by the very wealth that had landed him on their list to begin with.

Items they were wise enough to sidestep, knowing they had so much more to do, this just the start of things.

"Bastard is still getting off easy if you ask me," The Angel muttered, his voice threaded in between the pounding of his boots just

4

behind The Artist. Constant pacing she was able to follow by the sound of his heels clicking against concrete.

A reversion to the state he had been in for much of the last six months. Unbridled energy and hostility threatening to burst from any available opening, not needing the slightest provocation, but only a direction to be pointed.

Somewhere to aim before exploding outward, The Artist knowing fully well that the early bruising dappling the man before her was but the start. An initial taste that would soon leave her brother hungry for more.

"Were you seen?" The Artist asked, not wanting to entertain The Angel's comment. The beginning of a back-and-forth they'd been through many times before, his notion of fair and equal retribution of a much different nature than hers.

Something carrying a heightened sense of finality.

A worldview shaped through his own unique circumstances and experiences, decidedly at odds with the task that was handed down to them.

"No," The Tall Boy answered from his post against the wall beside her. Assuming one of his trademark stances, his overly long legs were folded into a crouch, his backside resting against the exposed studs of the garage.

A standard pose, as if trying to hide his elongated dimensions from view. A way to make himself smaller, drawing less attention.

A force of habit so ingrained it was done even while in the presence of his siblings, the closest other conscious human being miles away.

"Of course not," The Angel snapped. The polar opposite of The Tall Boy in every way, the two shared a birthday and nothing else. Twins who had been on divergent paths since leaving the womb, evident in everything from their physical makeup to their respective demeanors.

A pair of contradictions that The Artist had been tiptoeing between for decades, becoming even more pronounced in the last six months.

"You think those rich assholes pay any attention to what's going on around them?" The Angel continued. "All other people are to them are servants meant to carry out their orders."

The start of a tirade The Artist had heard too many times to count, she left her brother to ramble as she did one last check over the items laid out beside her. Tools similar to what she'd been using for years, while at the same time very different.

A variation of her chosen vocation, meaning that while each piece looked and felt familiar, they were also foreign. Utensils and applications that had never been attempted for real before.

A start to something she had envisioned a thousand times, finally at hand after waiting for so long.

"Quiet," The Artist hissed, the order enough to cause The Tall Boy to raise his gaze from the man sprawled on the floor between them, but did nothing to cease the ongoing monologue rolling out of The Angel.

Continued rambling that The Artist was in no mood for, feeling her pulse already beginning to thrum through her temples.

"Enough!"

Her focus aimed straight ahead, The Artist waited long enough to ensure that the message was received. There would be no further complaint from The Angel. Not even the steady patter of his boots thumping against the floor.

Total quiet, allowing her to reach out and take up the closest object from the floor beside her. Flipping the switch along the side, she closed her fingers tight around the base of it, letting the resulting vibrations travel the length of her arm.

A steady buzzing that she used to steady herself, steeling her nerves before exhaling slowly.

"Alright boys, here we go."

Chapter Two

The suit Reed Mattox was forced to wear felt like it weighed nearly half as much as he did. A bulbous monstrosity that resembled one of the oversized sumo suits he'd seen people put on at carnivals and fairs. Inflatables that folks could squeeze into before rolling around with one another, each attempting to wrestle the other into submission while their friends and family cheered them on.

A scene of well-meaning frivolity that was about as far from what Reed was now doing as could be, this a case of necessary evil and nothing more.

A sacrifice he was glad to make on behalf of his partner, though there would be no joy in it. No smile elicited from him or cheers from the handful of people standing nearby.

"Okay," Sergeant Jed Traeger said as he cinched the Velcro straps on the back of the suit into place. "When I give the word, I want you to start off across the field here. I know it'll be awkward, but just do your best."

Despite the cool temperature of early November, the sky the color of milk overhead, Reed could feel sweat in the small of his back. A condition of the enormous heft of the suit he was wearing, no matter that he was only donning a pair of gym shorts and t-shirt underneath.

Clothing chosen in anticipation of this moment, knowing how stifling the garment could be.

"Got it," Reed said.

"Once you get a ways out, his handler will give the command and Kona will take off," Traeger continued, circling around Reed's arms extended straight out to either side, the thick padding inhibiting him from putting them down. "Your natural inclination will be to try and brace yourself, but just try to stay relaxed.

"When he hits you, don't jam him up, just let him take you to the ground."

As the training officer for Reed and the handful of other K-9 handlers gathered today, Traeger had already been through the directions a couple of times. Instructions that had been received with varying levels of effectiveness, a couple of the younger guys donning the suit for the first time giving in to human nature.

Self-preservation, the strongest of all desires.

"Got it," Reed repeated, already playing the next few moments out in his mind. His turn to wear the suit and play the role of the fleeing bad guy, just as one of the other K-9 officers had for him and his partner Billie earlier.

An initial run that had seen Billie completely knock the slighter man from his feet, blasting him like a linebacker hitting an unsuspecting receiver in the open field.

A sequence that again flashed across Reed's mind, causing his pulse to pick up slightly, the briny taste of sweat crossing his lips.

Outcroppings from the fact that Kona was a German Shepherd to Billie's Belgian Malinois, outweighing her by at least ten pounds or more.

"Alright," Traeger said, reaching out and slapping Reed on the shoulder. An open-handed swat that sounded hollow against the thick padding, the sound lingering for a moment as he spun out of sight.

A retreat that lasted just long enough to put some distance between them, clearly establishing which was the target, before he shouted, "Go!"

Anticipating the order, Reed took off as best he could within the encumbering confines of the suit. A start from a dead standstill that took a few paces to get going. The combined effects of the recently healed bullet wound to his calf and the girth of the suit pulling him from side to side.

An exaggerated penguin waddle that made it feel as if he was moving in diagonals before finally he was able to raise his pace.

Speed enough to let him elongate his strides, moving across the open ground of the training lot. Momentum aided by the additional weight he carried, propelling him forward.

"Attack!"

Delivered more than fifty yards in his wake, it felt like the handler was speaking directly into his ear. A single word that sent a jolt through Reed's system, just as he had seen happen to his partner so many times before.

A visible charge that surged through her as she took off, eager to carry out whatever task was just handed down.

His arms stuck out wide to either side, it felt as if Reed was a mash of two distinct halves. His lower body, free from the excessive bulk, able to move easily in the gym shorts, offset by the heft of his top half. Weight that caused him to list to either side as he pounded forward, trying his best to extend the chase a few extra moments.

Give Kona and her handler an experience as close to the real thing as possible.

Feeling the lactic acid beginning to burn in his thighs, Reed pushed himself onward. Long strides through the center of the grass clipped short, most of it already dead or dying, prepared to lay dormant for the winter season.

Open ground that gave no resistance as he gulped in precious oxygen, pushing ahead a final few strides. Extended steps with his focus pinned in the distance, fixed on the chain link fence encircling the facility.

A point to strive for, even as he heard the impending sounds of Kona behind him. The deep braying of his bark. The guttural sigh of his breathing.

The heavy thump of his footsteps hitting the ground, chewing up the distance between them.

A full enactment of what every perpetrator Reed had ever sent Billie after must have gone through, ending in the same exact way.

Precursors that told Reed contact was imminent, but still didn't fully prepare him for the blast of Kona slamming into him from behind. A launching of his enormous body at Reed's outstretched arm, clamping his jaws around the padded sleeve.

A vise there was no escape from, twisting Reed to the side, leaving his back and side fully exposed to the rest of Kona's weight and momentum. Almost seventy pounds of coiled muscle that mashed into him, popping every vertebra the length of his back.

An unholy collision of padding and brown fur that sent Reed toppling to the ground, the sky above twirling by as he rolled through, eventually coming to a stop face down on the grass.

A prone position with Kona still locked on tight, tugging at his sleeve, doing his best to carry out his instructions.

Chapter Three

Billie, Kona, and their two training classmates Sheba and Barty, were lined outside of the sports bar like sentries. Enormous statues ranging from Billie's solid black to Sheba's almost complete coat of burnt sienna, the other two falling somewhere in between.

A color palate unto themselves, each lowered to their haunches and staring out at the street, as if daring visitors to come close.

A formidable wall lined shoulder to shoulder, each just a few inches past the imaginary threshold between the rolltop door along the front standing open and the sidewalk outside.

"How many people you think have driven by or gotten as far as the corner and saw those four sitting there and thought, 'Oh, hell naw,'?" Jim Stanson asked. A detective out of the 7th precinct across town from Reed and Billie's home in the 8th, he was partnered up with Barty, the pair serving as the elder statesmen of the group.

The one who suggested everybody stop by the sports bar after the day's training was complete, commenting that the Bengals were set to kick off in just a few minutes.

A game Reed didn't have the least interest in – his own collegiate rooting interests having played the previous afternoon – though he wasn't about to turn down the opportunity. Not the camaraderie or the chance for a couple of beers, the repeated shots from Kona earlier leaving his entire body feeling as if it was slightly out of alignment.

"At least a dozen," Traeger agreed, leaning out from his post on the end of the table to peer at the line of dogs perched nearby.

"Which is still way less than the number of times the owners have probably wanted to say something, but didn't have the heart," Reed added.

"Or balls!" Stanson quipped, slapping his hand down on the table and laughing loudly. A shot hard enough to send droplets of beer up over the edge of his glass.

A guffaw with enough force to cause a few glances from the patrons lining the bar nearby.

In response to the outburst, all four animals turned in unison. A twist that looked almost choreographed, each of them peering back for several seconds before resuming their watch over the street, content that everything within was as it should be.

A move Reed matched in reverse as he turned back to the table before him, most of the available space filled with a pair of pitchers of amber brew and a handful of plates of appetizers. Items Stanson had ordered without needing to see a menu, reminding the waitress that they had made it just in time for the half-price happy hour special before rattling off a list of items.

Things that had appeared within minutes, ranging from the familiar nachos and potato skins to something Reed had never encountered before, known as buffalo cauliflower wings.

An offering he still hadn't brought himself to try yet.

A shying away shared by the two remaining men at the table with them - Parker Burke and Teddy Walsh - both patrol officers with the downtown precincts. Young guys who hadn't been out of the academy more than a year or so, both almost as tall as Reed though quite a bit leaner.

Each in their mid-twenties, they were discernible mostly by their color of hair, Burke a brunette, Walsh a strawberry blonde.

Combined, the two guys hadn't said more than a handful of words since leaving the training grounds, Reed getting the distinct feeling that they had been pulled along out of a sense of obligation and nothing more. Desires not to turn down an offer from ranking officers, or maybe even the chance to glean away a stray bit of knowledge shared around the table.

Notions he considered trying to aid them with, about to ask how long they had been working K-9 or if they had encountered any incidents yet. An exploratory start that was cut short by Traeger at the head of the table turning his way and asking, "To what do we owe the pleasure of seeing you and Billie out with us today?"

Leaving behind the questions he was about to pose to Burke and Walsh, Reed rotated his focus back in the opposite direction. A blur of food and drink offerings on the table, matched by the assorted broadcasts from around the country covering the bank of television monitors lining the wall beside them.

"Long overdue," Reed admitted. "After what happened down along the river a couple months ago, I wasn't exactly in any shape to be putting on the suit."

Nearly three months prior, Reed had taken a round through his left calf. A shot fired by the suspect he and Billie and an assisting detective from the Cincinnati Police Department were chasing that had gone through and through the muscle belly, forcing him into a quick procedure to close things up and eight miserable weeks of physical therapy to get things back to some semblance of normal.

A period of time during which he and Billie were put on a reduced schedule, back to mostly working graveyard shifts. Walking patrols that had doubled as extra therapy and had them both feeling a bit antsy, each for their own respective reasons.

Bottled energy that today was meant to be a first step in helping to alleviate, though Reed was already suspecting it was more a matter of swapping one form of stiffness for another.

"Between that and being pulled over with the state..." Reed continued, letting his voice trail away.

The start of a diatribe that he had already been through many times regarding the new hybrid role he and Billie had been forced into. A special position seeing them pass between the CPD and the

Ohio Bureau of Criminal Investigation that neither had asked for or wanted.

Were only now, the better part of a year later, starting to make peace with.

"Yeah, that's actually more what I was alluding to," Traeger said. Lifting his eyebrows, he raised his beer, taking a long pull before asking, "How is that going?"

"Being on the governor's speed dial?" Reed asked, making no attempt to hide the disdain he still felt for the setup. A design that the Chief of the CPD had done her best to aid him in crafting, though was still far from ideal. "Just wonderful."

His beer still held a few inches from his chin, Traeger snorted loudly. A sound of derision that looked to be the start of something more, overwhelmed by the crowd at the bar erupting in cheers. A boisterous outburst fueled by excitement and alcohol that drew the attention of the table up toward the screen in time to see the running back for the Bengals burst into some sort of celebratory dance.

A mixture of shimmy and shuffle that they watched nearly to completion, Stanson the first to look away and continue, "I don't know how you do it. No way I could always be on call like that."

Gaze still lifted to the screen, Reed waited long enough to see the full replay of the score before lowering his focus to the older man at the end of the table. Opening his mouth to respond, he thought of pointing out that they were basically all always on call. An inherent part of the job that was now a bit more heightened for him and Billie, required a touch more travel, but wasn't that different from when they were exclusively with CPD.

A reply he was still in the act of crafting when he felt the familiar vibration of his phone coming to life in the rear pocket of the jeans he'd changed into after training.

One pulse after another that caused him to lean to the side and extract the device, needing only a quick glance at the screen to know that any chance of answering Stanson was gone. Same for eating more food or even finishing the beer in front of him.

A brief respite from the grind that had been abruptly brought to an end.

"Speak of the devil," Reed said, wagging the screen at Stanson. Pushing back his chair, he nodded to Traeger and said, "Excuse me."

A graceful retreat the training officer acknowledged with a nod, allowing Reed to spin out from the table and pass by the row of dogs lining the rolltop doorway along the front. A quick exit that was matched by Billie as she fell in beside him, the two going just far enough to escape the noise of the bar before accepting the incoming call.

"Mattox."

"Are you familiar with the governor's residence?" Eleanor Brandt, Chief of the Columbus Police Department asked. A question without formal greeting or even lead in, immediately alerting Reed that whatever she had was bad.

An assumption Billie picked up on beside him, moving closer and pressing tight to the twin scars hidden beneath the leg of his jeans.

"I mean, I know where it is," Reed replied. "Don't really get over to Bexley very often."

"No," Brandt replied. "Not that residence. The other one."

Chapter Four

The official governor's residence that Reed alluded to on the call with Chief Brandt was located in the suburb of Bexley in the southeast corner of Columbus. A two-story mansion in the heart of the town taking up the equivalent of a couple of square blocks, with an expansive home and even larger spread of gardens and assorted outbuildings around it.

A botanical wonder unto itself, meant to demonstrate all the various foliage the state had to offer.

Or so Reed had read in a pamphlet one time, having not once been to – or even by – the place. Working out of the 8th Precinct in a part of town known as The Bottoms – a chunk of urban blight about as different from Bexley as imaginable – there had never been any call for him to be over that way.

Not even with the new role he and Billie had taken on with the governor's office, the task of security falling exclusively on the Ohio Highway Patrol.

While listed as the official domicile of the state's ranking official, whether or not the governor chose to stay there was completely up to them. A choice that had been a mixed bag since the turn of the century, the last few splitting their decision between residing there and simply using it as a showplace.

Options that current Governor Thomas Cowan seemed to be using in equal measure, spending some of his time there in Bexley, the remainder at his sprawling estate north of the outer belt encircling the greater metropolitan area. A chunk of land that had the size and scope of a farm, though to Reed's knowledge nothing was planted there.

Nothing but hundreds of acres of lush grass and landscaping, every bit of it tended to with meticulous care.

All on the state taxpayer dime.

An expenditure that Reed couldn't help but shake his head at as they drove past almost a full mile of rolling meadow framed by white board fencing. Slats recently painted, so bright they nearly glowed beneath the gathering darkness of early evening.

A sight that normally Reed wouldn't mind in the slightest. A call-back to his growing up on the outskirts of Oklahoma City and the small town a couple of hours from there where his parents still resided.

Even to the farmhouse he and Billie now called home west of Columbus.

Hallmarks of a different form of life that seemed woefully out of place encircling the homestead of Thomas Cowan. A man who liked to fashion himself something of a modern cowboy, right down to the hand-tooled boots he always wore and the bolo ties that he so often donned in front of the cameras.

Indicators all of a man woefully short on self-awareness. Someone who believed that the people in the state weren't mindful of what he really did for a living before going into politics, his fortunes built on the backs of others going back decades.

A modus operandi Reed couldn't help but think the man was still utilizing now, him and his partner the latest targets, called away from the sports bar after a long day of training to chase down whatever personal peeve the governor had.

The fact that it was Sunday night be damned.

Doing his best to keep signs of such frustration from his features, Reed dropped his blinker to give the OHP officers serving as guards warning of his arrival. A moment later, he did as indicated, turning into the main drive for the spread and coming to a stop upon the raked gravel in front of an expansive gate.

His foot resting on the brake, he extended a hand in either direction. With his right, he grabbed up the badge that was stowed in the middle console, letting the silver chain usually employed for draping it around his neck hang free over the back of his wrist.

His left he used to roll down the driver's side window as a man not much older than Parker Burke or Teddy Walsh stepped out of the small guard stand that had been installed at the corner of the gate. Both thumbs hooked into the belt of his uniform, he glanced to the offered badge before flicking his gaze up to Reed.

"Mattox?"

"Yes, sir," Reed replied, lowering the badge to his lap. Tilting his head backward, he added, "My K-9 partner, Billie. We got a call a little while ago telling us to come by."

Making it no closer than five feet from the sedan, the guard took a step back in retreat. "Yeah, they've been expecting you. Seemed kind of urgent, so I'll let you guys head on up."

Who all exactly was expecting them, Reed couldn't be certain. Same for what the reason was for their being summoned or why it was so urgent.

Questions he was certain the young man wouldn't have answers to, let go with a simple wave as the guard disappeared inside. A moment later, the heavy wrought iron gate parted through the middle, pushed to either side on heavy rollers resting just a few inches above the ground.

A slow opening that Reed watched with growing impatience, his thumbs tapping at the top of the steering wheel. Anticipation that had started the instant his conversation at the bar was interrupted, cresting with the comment made just a moment before.

Validation of what Jim Stanson said earlier about them essentially being on-call detectives.

Waiting just until the gate was past the edge of his front bumper on either side, Reed nudged the gas, pushing them forward. A straight shot of more than two hundred yards, framed on either side by towering pin oak trees, dead leaves still clinging to their branches.

Under the tires of the sedan, the sound of gravel crunching could be heard through the open window. A soundtrack that caused the feelings within Reed to rise a bit more, in turn pulling Billie up through the front seats. A quick check to see what was happening before resting her muzzle against his shoulder.

Silent assurance that she was near.

Leaning back into her, Reed kept the vehicle aimed straight ahead, pulling them up in front of a sprawling structure that was a mixture of mountain lodge and southern plantation. A place with brick and columns comprising the center, with wings made of stone and log sweeping outward in either direction. Framing all of it were mulch beds more than a dozen feet across, their interiors filled with mums and junipers and assorted other plants.

A spread worthy of the sorts of magazines Reed's mother still subscribed to, confirming most every working assumption Reed had about the man who called it home.

A manifestation of excess that Reed expected nothing less than, giving it nominally more than a single sweep before settling his attention on the two vehicles already parked in front of the main entrance. Twin SUVs that were alike in classification and color, though any similarities ended there.

On the far right sat a boxy Mercedes that looked like it had just rolled off the showroom floor, the only thing missing being the sticker on the windshield advertising it at somewhere in the low six-figure range.

A sight Reed figured had something to do with their being summoned at such an hour, especially when sitting next to the dented Subaru belonging to Chief Eleanor Brandt. A woman who exited as they pulled up and came to a stop, waiting on the sidewalk lining the edge of the drive as they climbed out and made their way toward her.

A slight woman by any discernible metric, she was made to appear even more so by the jeans and oversized fleece jacket she was wearing.

Attire that seemed to envelope her narrow frame, further accentuating her sharp features and dishwater blonde hair pulled straight back.

One of the few times Reed had ever seen her in civilian attire, normally sporting the full department uniform.

"If you're here, this must be even worse than I thought," Reed said, bypassing any sort of greeting, much like she had in their conversation earlier.

An opening that Brandt seemed in agreement with, raising her brows in resignation. "Truthfully, I have no idea why the hell either one of us are here."

To say that Reed's relationship with Brandt had been rocky in the past would be a massive understatement. Another casualty of the difficult period in the wake of Reed's former partner passing that hadn't begun to be repaired until he and Billie were able to save the life of Brandt and her nephew.

The start of a rehabilitation process that had improved greatly since the new role was created by Cowan, both of them now having a shared enemy to aim their ire toward.

"But if I had to guess, I'd say it has something to do with that monstrosity I'm parked beside," Brandt added, putting to words exactly what Reed was thinking just moments before.

Chapter Five

Given the size of the home and the grounds beyond, Reed surmised that it must take a team of at least a dozen to keep things looking the way they did. A number that probably swelled whenever the governor was in residence, assorted staff and security personnel making the trip north to join him.

A traveling circus that could easily double in size, making the fact that outside of the patrolman manning the front gate Reed had not seen another soul all the more unnerving.

Not an assistant or some such staffer to answer the front door. Not a secretary to ask to take the chief's jacket or to offer them a beverage as they passed through the front doors and crossed a massive foyer with gleaming hardwood floors.

Not even a housekeeper or Cowan's wife glimpsed moving about the hallways as the governor led them through the heart of the sprawling home, pulling up just shy of a pair of oak pocket doors pulled closed. An entry into a den or study of some sort, the man pausing just long enough to turn and give both Reed and Brandt a look.

A solemn stare with his mouth pulled into a tight line, as if trying to impart again what he had said after pulling the front door open to greet them personally. An admonishment that what they were about to see and hear was not to be shared with anyone who wasn't present tonight.

A warning matching everything about Reed and Billie's new position, all of it seeming to have been pulled from some old television procedural. An alternate reality where making statements such as that or fixing them with the look he now wore was really necessary.

A glance that was mixed of equal parts threat and entreaty, the full weight of it something Reed was not the least bit interested in unpacking, matching the man's gaze.

A pointed stare, making no effort to hide the growing confusion he was feeling. Uncertainty, mixed with more than a little annoyance. A continuation of what Jim Stanson had mentioned earlier, the fact that he and his partner were essentially concierge detectives bad enough, this being the first time they had been summoned directly to Cowan's personal home.

Something that Reed refused to ever let become a pattern, no matter what damn office the man before him held.

Opening his mouth twice, as if about to repeat what was stated outside, perhaps even add to it, Cowan let it go with a sigh. An audible exhalation paired with his features sagging slightly.

Exhaustion of his own, hinting for the first time that whatever this was, it wasn't his idea.

A surprise visit from whoever was driving the Mercedes outside, catching him at home in jeans and a plaid shirt, without even time to fix the few errant hairs on his head or change out of the loafers on his feet. Shoes that took at least two inches off his already shortened stature, as compared to the lift provided by the boots he was never seen in public without.

Turning back, Cowan slipped his fingers into the crack between the doors and pulled them wide. Spreading his arms to either side, he let the momentum of the doors carry them beyond his outstretched fingertips, disappearing from view.

The big reveal, showing the interior of the room to be a private library. A space with enough volumes along the walls to make any neighborhood institution envious, shelves lined both sides, with books filling every available nook.

Displays that gave the room the feeling of being inside a tunnel, winnowing everything toward the far end of the room. A rear wall with matching French doors to either side providing direct access to the backyard, framing a stone fireplace comprising any remaining space.

River rock of various shades of gray rising clear to the ceiling, the open hearth blazing bright, tendrils of orange and red causing shadows to flicker across the floor.

All of it serving as an elaborate backdrop for a pair of high-backed armchairs positioned directly in front of the flames. Matching over-stuffed pieces that had been dragged over, one of them – presumably Cowan's – sitting empty, while a pair of feet created long shadows beneath the other.

Thus far, the sole thing save the SUV in the driveway to denote that someone else was even present.

"I'd like to introduce you both to a friend of mine," Cowan said as he stepped forward, letting his hands fall to his sides. An unceremonious drop that ended with them smacking loudly against his thighs.

Another unspoken acknowledgement that he wasn't any happier about this than Reed or Brandt.

A fact that could make their being summoned better or worse, depending on how one wanted to look at it.

Serving as the point person for the small procession, Cowan cut a diagonal path across the area rug covering the center of the room. An enormous piece that stretched from the door to just shy of the fireplace, with loop fibers that swallowed any sound from their footfalls.

Circling around the side of the empty chair, Cowan swung out in front of the fireplace and extended a hand before him.

"Chief Brandt, detectives, this is Dean Morgan," Cowan said. His lips parting as if there was more he wanted to add, he got as far as drawing in a short breath before thinking better of it.

A pause to allow Brandt and Reed to both fill in beside him, Billie bringing up the rear. The final steps of a journey that had started more than an hour earlier, every moment since fraught with questions.

Inquiries that nobody seemed to have answers to, the reason for that delivered in an instant.

A single glimpse at the man sitting at an angle in the chair, his eyes glassy, his gaze fixed on the flickering flames before him. A faraway stare that Reed was content to leave him to for the time being, his own focus resting on the thick block letters etched into the man's forehead.

A tattoo so fresh that the tips of lank hairs hanging down from his scalp stuck to it, siphoning away bits of black ink.

A recent acquisition that – based on the red and puffy nature of the skin surrounding it - Reed would bet every last penny he possessed wasn't obtained voluntarily.

A single word, done in block letters, stretching the entire length of his brow.

PRIDE.

"As you can see," Cowan added, his voice barely more than a whisper, "he needs our help."

Chapter Six

Whenever there was more than one of the siblings together in a vehicle, The Tall Boy was always the driver. A spot to accommodate both his extreme dimensions and the strain it had put on his joints over the years. A frame that was stretched beyond what the human body was ergonomically designed for, already starting to break down in just his late twenties.

A result of too many years of playing basketball inside small country gyms just like the one framed within the front windshield. Countless games and practices, all endured with the promise that there was some reward at the end of it for him.

A new school or a new town or a new life, the first two coming about a couple of times, the third forever elusive.

An ethereal goal he had thrown himself whole-heartedly into, believing the empty promises and weak praise that was tossed his way. Empty grandstanding and posturing, offered by people who had their best interests at heart, not his.

Never his.

To this day, the only people who had ever been in his corner could be counted on less than one hand. A number that had diminished even further in the last couple of years, dwindling from several fingers down to just the one person sharing the front seat of the vehicle with him.

The Artist, sitting stone still in the passenger seat. Her boots removed, one stockinged foot was pressed against the front dash. The opposite elbow rested on the windowsill, her arm bent back as she gnawed on her thumbnail.

The same exact pose she had been in since they got on the highway and headed west hours before, the only change being the digit she was attacking furiously.

A methodical progression that already had her down to the last finger, the other four on that hand stripped to the quick, rimmed with blood.

Three years older than The Tall Boy, it was a habit he had been staring at for as long as he could remember. A disgusting tic in direct correlation to whatever stress or nerves she was feeling, today being easily the worst case The Tall Boy could remember since it all began.

Not six-months-ago began, but way back at the beginning. The incident that changed things for all of them forever, setting up what they knew would one day transpire.

Even if none of them could have foreseen that it would eventually have them sitting here like this.

"Jesus Christ, how long are they going to go for?" The Angel asked from the backseat. No less than the fifth time he had lodged such a question, this one was paired with him clasping either of the front seats and pulling himself forward.

A move so he could see better from his spot in the rear, The Tall Boy feeling the chairback of his seat strain slightly beneath the extra weight.

For nearly six solid months now, his brother had been nothing short of thrumming. A daily battle between what they were trying to accomplish and his own wants and needs, constantly having to put his baser desires at arm's length.

An ongoing struggle to try and stay the course, following what they had all agreed to. The best possible path for fulfilling the charge that had been handed down to them.

A final favor not just to the one asking, but also to those who had gone before. Quite possibly the only thing strong enough to keep The Angel in line, even now as it was visibly threatening to consume him from within.

A junkie who had finally gotten a taste after so long, now dying to immediately get back to it. A continuation of what they had started with the older man the night before.

Anticipation maximized by the second target just out of sight and the impending encounter they all knew was a mere hours away.

"Open gyms never end on time," The Tall Boy replied, glancing to his side before turning his attention back to face forward. "This time of year, everybody's trying to make a good impression."

Snorting loudly, The Angel kept himself perched between the front seats, his gaze aimed straight ahead. Cherubic features that were the source of his nickname, their mother having dubbed him as such when they were all still children.

On-the-nose naming that The Tall Boy couldn't help but wonder was mixed with wishful thinking, their mother identifying at an early age the proclivities underlying the rounded bone structure and rosy complexion.

Camouflage to mask his true demeanor, worn throughout the assorted travails of the last decade.

"Good impression, huh?" The Angel repeated. "You mean like getting everybody to focus on you being tall, rather than being uncoordinated?"

Sliding his gaze to the side, The Angel settled his stare on The Tall Boy's profile. A pointed glare that almost burned as it rested on his skin.

"Or the fact that you didn't have a lick of aggression?" he added. "No killer instinct?"

One at a time, The Angel lobbed the barbs. Low whispers that needed to only travel a few inches, arriving at the same time as his hot breath on The Tall Boy's cheek.

More of the unending goading that had marked the last fifteen years. An ongoing escalation that had gotten so much worse in recent months.

A problem The Tall Boy hoped to soon be rid of for good, like so many other things in his life.

"Couldn't protect the rim, or anything else for that matter."

"Okay, that's enough," The Artist said, her voice piercing the air for the first time in more than an hour.

An order The Angel seemed to ignore for a few moments, his gaze remaining in The Tall Boy's periphery, before eventually he smirked. Flush lips peeled back over bright teeth as he retreated between the seats.

"Why aren't I surprised you're jumping in to protect him?" he spat. "Just like mama used to."

"I'm not protecting anybody," The Artist replied. "Look."

Jutting a finger out before her, she motioned to the plain metal door on the side of the gymnasium. A portal into the interior that had at last opened, sending bright light spilling across the cold asphalt.

A sight The Tall Boy had been waiting on, practically aching for, just moments prior, all but pushed aside by being the target of The Angel's ire. Animosity that was nothing short of palpable, causing prickly heat to run the length of The Tall Boy's neck, bringing a veneer of sweat to his features as he fought to draw in air.

"Come on," The Artist said, glancing over at him from the passenger seat. "Let's go. Time to get into position."

Chapter Seven

Even after several months in their new role as liaisons with the state Bureau of Criminal Investigations, there were still some kinks to be worked out. A few items Reed was actively working to change, a handful more that he had already accepted were going to be things he just had to learn to deal with.

None more so than a lot of the cases he and Billie were given being loaded with extraneous motivations. Governor Cowan's own on-demand investigators, there whenever he decided to cherry pick a particular matter, hoping to glean something from it for himself.

A gateway to a policy change he was in favor of. A partnership with an agency or department that could later be exploited.

The chance to call another press conference and preen in front of the cameras about the great work the BCI was doing under his leader-ship while Reed and Billie and even Chief Brandt lingered offscreen.

A way of doing things that Reed was beginning to find increasingly unnerving, each successful case he and his partner worked managing to embolden the governor a bit more. A list of high-profile victories that seemed to have him believing he was in some way a part of law enforcement himself, his growing hubris what Reed originally suspected the night was going to be about.

A private summons to the man's home, Reed assuming after hanging up the phone with Brandt earlier that this was just the latest in an escalation pattern. A slow transition from the arrangement the two sides originally agreed to, trending much closer to what Cowan actually envisioned when putting this together.

His own private police force, falling somewhere between a modern dictator and a character from some show on a streaming network.

Suppositions that were proven woefully wrong by the sight of Dean Morgan sitting before them, any annoyance Reed felt upon first arriving at the home already gone. Instant dissipation, along with whatever soreness he might have felt after the day spent in training with the other K-9 teams.

Even whatever stiffness might exist in his calf, gone in an instant.

A complete system shift, everything winnowing to the broken man cowering in the armchair in front of the fire. Someone who had likely not been so much as talked back to in a long time, beaten down in a manner that had him visibly cracking.

Humiliation personified, before even considering the still-damp ink etched into his forehead.

Twin assaults to both his mind and body, the resulting devastation enveloping him like a cloak.

Having not yet so much as even glanced up from staring into the fire, Morgan seemed oblivious to anyone else having entered the room. Eyes glazed, he seemed lost deep within himself, failing to notice even as Reed stepped forward to the vacant chair and settled onto the edge of it.

A seat chosen to put the two of them at eye level. A way for Reed to have a conversation with the man without feeling like there was someone looming over him.

A return of the threat that had just violated him in such a way.

"Mr. Morgan?" Reed began. A question that just barely penetrated, a flicker registering behind Morgan's eyes, though nothing more.

"Mr. Morgan?" he repeated a second time, raising his voice a bit louder. Volume enough to bring Billie in a little closer, brushing against Reed's leg before moving into the gap between the two chairs.

A combination of sound and movement that just managed to get through, Morgan grunting softly as he turned their way, his brows rising at the sight of them.

Further still as he slid his gaze upward, taking in Cowan and Brandt standing on the edge of the firelight, the unexpected sight causing him to draw in a sharp breath.

"Oh," he managed as he pulled his attention back toward Reed. "I, uh, sorry..."

Skipping past the apology and whatever explanation was likely to follow it, Reed replied, "Mr. Morgan, my name is Detective Reed Mattox, and this is my K-9 partner Billie. We are liaisons between the Columbus Police Department and the state Bureau of Criminal Investigations.

"Governor Cowan called and asked us here this evening."

Again, Morgan's gaze shifted to the side. A look that this time wasn't as much exploration as accusation, his focus settling on the governor.

Eyes narrowing, he said nothing, merely staring until Cowan replied, "Dean, they have already been fully briefed on how delicate this matter is. Not a word of anything they see or hear tonight makes it to the press.

"You have my word."

For just an instant, Reed couldn't help but allow those lingering feelings to rise back to the surface. A renewed form of every misgiving he had with the existing relationship and the repeated oversteps, each becoming a bit more egregious in nature.

Cowan inserting himself into investigations in a manner that now included promising what could or couldn't reach the airwaves, without having the first clue of what they were up against.

Self-importance and preservation of a friend taking precedent over whatever a case may require. A thought that Reed could see tense Brandt's expression also as he flicked his gaze to her, letting it linger for only a moment before moving back to Morgan beside him.

A return to the more pressing matter, the rest to be addressed when – and if – it needed to be.

"Mr. Morgan, can you please tell us what happened?" Reed asked, leaving the question purposely vague. An invitation for the man to start wherever and however he felt best, any additional details to be gleaned out later with further inquiries. "How you ended up here this evening?"

Shifting his gaze a few degrees at a time, Morgan moved his focus back to the rug in front of his feet. A slow reversion back to the position where they originally found him. Lips pulled into a line so tight they nearly disappeared, he exhaled loudly, his nostrils flaring.

"No," he muttered after several moments. A single syllable that he let linger long enough that Reed nearly jumped in, affirming what the governor had said just a moment before.

Further confirmation that the story would be kept confidential, if that would help to get things moving.

Again, the veracity of such a thing left to be dealt with later.

"Because I really don't know," Morgan eventually added. "One minute, I'm leaving the Buckeye watch party at Holman Brothers Steakhouse, everything fine. The next, I wake up in my car parked behind an elementary school, my ribs beat to hell."

Pausing just long enough to grab at the tail of his shirt, he lifted it up, revealing most of his torso. A move not just to prove the veracity of the last statement, but to also put on display the smaller block letters stretched across his stomach.

RICH BASTARD.

"Magic marker clear across my stomach..." Morgan said. Dropping the shirt back into place, he finished with, "And then this..."

Lifting a hand, he motioned toward his face. The closest thing he could get to acknowledging the obvious, unable to form the words to say what was now etched into his skin.

A shock that he was still processing.

Likely would be for the foreseeable future.

Giving the man nearly a full minute to see if there was anything more he wanted to add, any additional details to be shared, Reed remained silent. Quiet that settled in the vast room, punctured only by the occasional crackle of the fire.

A scene that, under any other circumstances, could be construed as almost cozy.

"The Buckeye game," Reed repeated. "So this happened last night?"

"Must have," Morgan replied, "because that's the last thing I remember before waking up around noon today."

Chapter Eight

Less than an hour after first entering Cowan's home, Reed found himself back out in front of the structure. Billie by his side, he stood across from Cowan and Chief Brandt, neither having said a word since they left the library suite.

Wearing expressions on either end of the spectrum, Brandt's looked something close to what Reed was thinking. A mix of repulsion and anticipation, trying to put together next steps while still processing what was just shared.

The latter piece appearing to be what the governor was stuck on, a sickly pallor having settled on his features. A man clearly wishing not only that he had never heard the story told by Dean Morgan, but that his old friend had never called him.

Or that they had even met, for that matter.

"Based on the timeline he's giving us," Reed opened, "it's been nearly twenty hours since he was abducted. Eight since he woke up behind the wheel of his car.

"That puts us – best case – half a day behind on this already."

Leaving it there, Reed didn't bother pointing out that the way things had been handled had done him and Billie no favors. A circuitous route of everyone being more concerned with protecting reputations and mitigating potential damage than helping their investigation.

A process that included Morgan going home to shower and switch vehicles before calling Cowan. A talk that ended with Cowan inviting him over to speak before reaching out to Brandt, each successive step costing them precious hours.

Time when whoever did this could be targeting someone else, who that might be or what their ultimate goal were things Reed couldn't even begin to speculate on. For the moment, his focus had to be on what happened next.

A case going from non-existent to a headlong sprint in record time.

A pattern that seemed to be happening far too often whenever dealing with the governor.

"Is Morgan married?" Reed asked, putting his focus on Cowan. A question and stare the man barely seemed capable of digesting, clearly still trying to work through the story that had just been told.

One that was, admittedly, one of the more unusual Reed had encountered, though he couldn't pretend was anywhere near the most heinous.

By a considerable margin.

"What?" Cowan managed, folds of skin piling up around his eyes as he tried to compute what was just asked.

"Married," Reed shot back, nearly raising his hand and snapping his fingers in the governor's face. A move to try and draw the man from his revelry, pulling him into the moment. "He wasn't wearing a wedding band, but that doesn't mean anything. Is he married? Have a girlfriend? Live-in housekeeper? Anything?"

"Oh," Cowan said softly. "No. Divorced a few years ago. Why?"

"Billie and I are going to go over there right after we're done here," Reed replied. "I assume he'll be staying here with you for the night?"

Still in the throes of trying to make sense of the last hour or two, each question Reed asked seemed to take a moment of active thought. More time slipping away, again urging him to reach out and shake the governor awake.

"We haven't discussed it," Cowan said eventually, "but what does it matter? Why are you going to his home? You just heard him say he was abducted-"

"Don't think for a second that just because that's not where he was taken, they haven't been to his house too," Brandt inserted. "The only reason whoever did this did it in public was because they deemed the home unfit."

His jaw sagging, Cowan gasped audibly. A precursor to some other pithy response Reed had no time or energy for.

"And that's where his SUV is sitting, which is our crime scene," Reed added. "It's already probably been contaminated. We can't risk anything further by moving it again."

Acting as if what Reed was saying was a far greater shock than anything that had just taken place in the library, Cowan gaped. Running his focus between Reed and Brandt, his features crinkled, a host of objections about to be levied.

A litany of concerns that Brandt cut off before they could be aired, stating, "The detective is right. Whoever did this already has a pretty big jump and could be getting further away or setting up their next target as we speak."

Pausing there, she let the implication linger that if this one had such a close personal relationship to the governor, it wouldn't be a stretch to think any future target might as well.

A realization Cowan seemed to arrive at in real time, his eyes widening as Brandt turned away, speaking directly to Reed.

"I assume you're bringing in Earl on this?"

"First call once we finish with Morgan and get back to the car," Reed replied.

"Finish with..." Cowan gasped, the sudden insertion of his voice pulling both Reed and Brandt's attention that direction. Two looks that were nothing short of stone, each already firmly entrenched in working through how the rest of the night was about to go, not needing his ongoing objections.

Entreaties for them to be delicate that had been heard and noted, it now time for him to stand down and let them do what was necessary.

"What else could you possibly need to-"

"I'll need access to the house," Reed said. "A key or an electronic code for the doors, clearance into what I'm guessing is a gated community."

Flicking his gaze to Brandt and back, he added, "I'll also need to get a couple of photos of what was done to him."

Eyes widening, Cowan drew in a deep breath. His cheeks and chest both swelled as he stared at each of them in turn, the next thing out of his mouth already plainly evident.

More pushback about the need for secrecy that Reed cut off before it could be voiced, adding, "For evidentiary purposes. And to run it through our databases to look for other similar cases. Maybe run a handwriting analysis."

Forcing himself to stop there, so badly did Reed want to add that if they weren't allowed to begin doing what they needed to, there would be no point in looking into the matter. If all Cowan really wanted was to be able to tell his buddy that they tried, then that box had already been checked.

But if they were to have any chance at actually apprehending whoever committed such a massive violation, it would require doing a few things that might make Cowan and Morgan both a bit uncomfortable.

"I..." Cowan said, his distaste obvious as he tried to find the words. Some renewed form of protest that evaded him, ending with him simply saying, "Chief Brandt is the lone point of contact on this. Everything goes through her, and you keep me appraised every step of the way."

Chapter Nine

Earl Bautista sounded exactly like Reed expected him to. Much the same as Reed would have if the situation was reversed and he was the one receiving a call at such an hour on a Sunday night.

Voice graveled by far more than just the unfiltered cigarettes he was always working on, each word was emphasized for meaning, letting it be known he didn't care at all for the assignment or the rushed nature of it.

Two things Reed was sure to let him know originated with the governor, he nor his partner nor even Chief Brandt especially pleased to be getting put in this situation either. A case working largely in the dark, with only a couple of places they could seek assistance, every morsel uncovered along the way to be fed back through the chief and then on to Cowan's desk.

A return of the initial thought Reed had about him and his partner becoming concierge law enforcement, now heightened by the fact that they were forced to operate under such heavy strictures.

Unnecessary impediments to what he already imagined was going to be an ugly affair, Cowan's display out front managing to override the shock of seeing what was done to Morgan earlier.

"My team is spread pretty thin," Earl replied, barely getting through the line before clearing his throat and spitting away the resulting phlegm. Sounds that were especially pronounced inside the quiet of Reed's sedan, drawing Billie's ears upright in the rearview mirror. "If it has to be now, I can come over, but I'm going to have one criminalist with me at most."

"Hopefully, that'll be enough," Reed replied. "Based on the story we were given, everything the victim remembers took place inside the car. That's where he lost consciousness last night and woke up this morning."

"Just the car? That's it?"

"Far as I know," Reed said. Leaning forward, he peered out through the front windshield, inspecting the houses sliding by on his right, comparing them to the description given by the guard at the entrance to the gated community.

Directions that were done in terms of size and shape, each home corresponding to a hole on the golf course tucked in behind the monstrous structures.

Homes that made Cowan's look downright quaint by comparison, the farmhouse Reed shared with his partner hardly even qualifying as a garage in such a place.

"Victim drove himself home afterward," Reed added. "Billie and I are about to go inside the house now. We'll let you know if we find anything when you get there."

Offering nothing more than a grunt in reply, Earl ended the call, the screen on Reed's cellphone going dark in the middle console. A loss of light allowing for them to better see out, spotting their destination just moments later and pulling up along the front edge of the grass directly abutting the street.

A complete lack of curb, serving as a none-too-subtle reminder to residents that street parking was not allowed.

A community rule Reed dared somebody to challenge him on as he came to a stop and turned off the ignition, peering out through the passenger window at the house before him. A looming multi-story structure constructed entirely of brick, a raised entrance acting as the centerpiece before giving way to a four-car garage on one side and a wraparound wing extended wide in the opposite direction.

A home so massive it required more than two dozen windows to provide natural light, each and every one now backstopped by bulbs burning bright within. A total effect resulting in a harsh glow, making the place a veritable beacon along the street.

A classic defense mechanism, a recent victim both wanting the sanctity of being able to see everything inside while at the same time trying to appear defiant to anyone looking on from afar.

A move he doubted Dean Morgan meant to employ, likely heading to Cowan's before it was even dark enough to need lights. A reflexive reaction to waking up in his car and glancing into the mirror, seeing what had been done.

A response Reed couldn't begrudge the man for in the slightest, completely normal in the face of what happened, with the added benefit of making what was about to take place infinitely easier for him and his partner.

"You ready?" Reed whispered. Reaching across the passenger seat, he unlocked the glove box and drew out his service weapon before cracking open the door beside him. Twin actions that pulled Billie up out of the backseat, not needing to wait for him to open the rear door as well.

A coordinated sequence the two had done many times over the last couple of years, Reed saying not a word to stop her nor making any effort to reach for the pair of leads coiled in the back footwells. A long and short leash to be used when dealing with crowds or potentially sensitive scenes that were unnecessary in the face of a quiet house, Reed wanting her to have the ability to move freely.

An extension of what Brandt pointed out earlier, it almost certain that the perpetrators had been by before, meaning that there was a chance they had circled back, letting Morgan stew for a day in his humiliation before returning to finish things.

"This way," Reed said, slapping at the leg of his jeans.

Keeping his weapon gripped tight in hand, Reed followed the instructions given by Morgan earlier on the best way to approach. A bypass of the main entrance that Reed suspected was about more than just ease of access, instead following the concrete driveway as far as the garage before peeling off to the left.

Settling onto a sidewalk poured from the same material, they circled around the front corner of the structure, passing between manicured landscaping on either side. Fluffy beds of mulch interspersed with seasonal plants and hardy evergreens, the work looking to have been done by the same crew that covered Cowan's place.

One of many shared commonalities that Reed imagined existed between the two, his only hope that Brandt's earlier insinuation about any future targets also being connected to the governor was a scare tactic and nothing more.

Following the path for more than twenty yards, Reed and Billie made one last turn. A final right, swinging around the back corner and coming out on the rear of the home.

A space that was nestled into the curvature of the structure, the bulk of it occupied by a deck extending straight out. A sprawling expanse of wood stained dark, replete with an outdoor kitchen, a sunken hot tub, and enough seating for well over a dozen.

Chairs that had been stripped of their padded cushions for the season, their wrought iron frames resembling match sticks strewn across the deck. Prime positioning for enjoying spring and summer months, with a view to the eighteenth green of the golf course less than fifty yards away, separated only by a wrought iron fence.

A view that Reed gave little more than a glance, his focus settling on the pair of double doors providing entry from the deck into the main of the house. An entryway right into an open kitchen, with an elongated dining table to one side, and an island to the other.

Features plainly illuminated by the host of bulbs on the chandelier hanging down from above burning bright.

Pulling up just beyond the sightline of the door, Reed peered inside. A quick sweep for signs of movement, followed by doing the same of the backyard around them.

One last check that revealed nothing, allowing him to step forward and enter the security code into the pad affixed to the frame of the door. Nine digits, each evoking a small beeping sound, culminating with an elongated tone and the audible click of the lock on the door releasing.

"You ready?" Reed asked a second time.

A precursor to him reaching out and nudging the door open, letting it swing just wide enough for them both to enter.

One last chance to check for any hints of obvious presence before allowing his partner to go to work.

A pause lasting several seconds, revealing no signs of movement or sound of any kind, ending with Reed returning both hands to the base of his weapon.

"Clear!" he said, the word just barely out of his mouth before Billie took off, in search of anyone or anything that shouldn't be present inside the palatial house.

Chapter Ten

After scouring the house to make sure nobody was inside lying in wait for Dean Morgan to return and doing a quick check to ensure the SUV was still parked in the garage, Reed gave up on any notion of digging further. Knowing nothing more about the man than Cowan's very basic overview that he was a former CEO of some healthcare corporation, trying to sift through anything would be both an invasion of privacy and an exercise in futility.

Effort that would be better saved until after Morgan returned home and could go through things himself, letting them know what might be missing. At least, what had been disturbed or some heading on what an intruder may have been looking for.

A task that would be difficult enough on its own, let alone inside a sprawling residence such as Morgan's.

Satisfied that the home was free of anyone still lurking, Reed had led Billie back out through the rear entrance, the two of them immediately moving to a sweep of the grounds. A slow and painstaking effort with Billie left free to roam as she saw fit.

A meandering path with her nose lowered to the ground, searching for anything that might jump out at her.

Without knowing who they might be looking for – much less

having some sort of scent sample – there was no way for Reed to issue a command, asking her to latch onto something specific. Instead, he allowed her to move at will, trying to detect anything that her years of prior experience might have ingrained in her.

Time going back to her training in the Marines, where she was schooled not only in how to track a perpetrator, but also to detect chemical signatures. Explosives or gunpowder or anything else that might hint where someone may have been.

A hiding spot or a perch to sit and observe Morgan from afar.

A hunt she fell directly to as Reed moved behind her, a flashlight in hand, scouring the ground around the home. A pointed study of any patches of mud or piles of leaves. Places where the broad blade grass might be bent at an unnatural angle.

Anything to hint of someone beyond a possible golfer in search of a stray tee shot approaching Morgan's home, learning his schedule, searching for the opportune moment to nab him before ultimately deciding on his weekly football watch party.

Jobs that he and Billie were both still immersed in when a pair of twin strobes pierced the dark evening. Headlamps sitting up high, square in shape, attached to the van used by Earl Bautista and his crime scene crew. The standard ride of such teams across the country, the white vehicle appearing to almost float through the darkness.

A slow approach as it coasted to a stop behind Reed's sedan and the front headlamps blinked out, followed by both front doors swinging wide. On the passenger side, a thin guy with a shock of dark hair slicked back that Reed recognized from previous cases as Coby Zane exited, raising a hand to Reed and Billie as they gave up on their search and made a diagonal across the lawn.

A gesture Reed matched, lowering his hand just far enough so it was still extended before him as they met Earl out in front of his van.

One of the few people Reed encountered on a regular basis who was both significantly bigger and taller than himself, Earl stood at least three inches higher, weighing well over a hundred pounds more. Total dimensions that would put him close to six-six in height, and every bit of three-fifty in mass.

A man who was rock solid without being muscular, a fair bit of it hidden beneath the bib overalls he was wearing every single time Reed ever met the man. A fashion choice that always served as the exterior layer, the only change to ever occur being what rested underneath.

A long-sleeved thermal during the deepest of winter months, the rest of the year calling for a sleeveless t-shirt like the charcoal one he currently sported.

A color matching the grizzled scruff framing his face and jaw, offset by his head shaved clean above.

Grasping Reed's hand, he pumped it twice before releasing, his attention tracking to the house beside them.

"I knew it was a bunch of shit, us getting called out on a Sunday night like this. Now, I understand why."

Rotating at the waist, Reed glanced to the monstrosity he and Billie had just recently been inside. Excessive for a family of ten - let alone a single man - visible even from the street.

"Let me guess...major donor?" Earl asked.

Not once had the description of Morgan gotten that far, though Reed wouldn't be surprised.

Especially after seeing more than a couple framed photos of him and Cowan hanging on the walls inside.

"Let me put it this way – the guy is staying at Cowan's house tonight."

Repeating what Reed and Billie had been forced to endure on the phone earlier, Earl cleared his throat. Snapping his chin to the side, he spat out the resulting phlegm, a single tendril of spittle clinging to his scruff.

"Though I got to admit, rich asshole or not, he didn't deserve what happened to him," Reed added.

A comment that drew Earl's attention back, allowing Reed to give a brief overview of what had occurred and the state Morgan was now in. Details he hadn't shared over the phone earlier, the full rundown taking just a couple of minutes.

Time enough for Earl's features to have softened considerably, falling in line with a muttered "Damn" Reed heard from Coby eavesdropping as he unloaded supplies from the back of the van.

"Exactly," Reed said, reaching to his back pocket and extracting his cellphone. Pulling up the photos he took barely an hour before, he extended the screen toward Earl, allowing the big man to get a look at what happened.

A move Cowan probably wouldn't agree with, but Reed was beyond caring about, his chief concern now that he was far from the governor's residence on doing whatever was necessary to work the case.

"You've been doing this a long time," Reed said. "You ever seen something like this before?"

Saying nothing in immediate reply, Earl tilted his head. Peering down his nose, he studied the image for a moment, letting it resonate before replying, "Jesus. That's some crazy shit right there."

Taking that as all the response he needed, Reed nodded in agreement. "Yeah, me neither."

Clearing the image from the screen, he stowed the phone back into the rear pocket of his jeans and asked, "You want us to go through the house and open up the garage doors, or you want to follow us in?"

"You lead the way. No use inviting in more contamination than there probably already is."

Chapter Eleven

The spot was one The Angel had been in before.

Not the exact patch of ground hidden deep amidst pine and elm trees where he was standing, the air redolent with their scent, but one just like it in his mind. Years of staring at the ceiling above his bunk inside the state penitentiary, superimposing the stories he had heard and the characters involved into how he would handle things if he could.

If he hadn't been foolish enough to get behind the wheel after drinking that night.

Dumb enough to get himself sent away, unable to help when his family needed him the most.

Even worse, to have left it in the clumsy and incapable hands of The Tall Boy as the lone protector.

Throughout those many visions, there was always the inclusion of a vantage point just outside the home of the man they were here to visit. The one they had sat outside the school gymnasium because of, waiting for him to finish the unofficial workout that was not supposed to be going on inside.

Another in an unending list of violations, all of them much in line with everything The Angel knew about the man. Acts all directly indicative of the man's character.

Or complete lack thereof, his singular focus bordering on maniacal. An intense desire to win regardless of cost incurred, up to and including the reason they were here now.

In the preceding months, The Angel had paid the man several visits, crouching at the base of the elm tree. A towering hardwood on the edge of the copse of trees abutting the man's property, allowing The Angel to slip in undetected and sit for hours at a time.

A post that bordered on comfortable. A place he would much rather sit and watch from than being forced to hide in the rear of the SUV the night before.

Plenty of room for him to sit or stand, stretching as needed throughout his ongoing vigil, helping him get a feel for the man's habits. His schedule.

Plan out what he would do once the opportune moment arrived. A constant fight against his urges to go sprinting across the back lawn and into the house, knowing that no matter how gratifying such a thing would be, it would not accomplish anywhere near what they were about to.

Goals that were distinctly outside of The Angel's usual style, though he couldn't argue with their effectiveness. A concerted message that was being sent, far more powerful than anything he could mete out one person at a time.

Conscious restraint, knowing that if he was going to risk a parole violation or – more importantly – their mission, it had better be with good reason.

Two things he had been forced to make himself heed as he crouched and watched the man's home night after night. Twin reasons for going no closer, no matter how much he wanted to.

Desires fueled by envisioning what would happen if he merely stood to full height and marched across the backyard and knocked on the door. Scenarios of differing types and means, the only thing that remained the same being the outcome.

Possibilities that now The Angel couldn't help but allow to spool back across his mind. Actions that were just precious seconds away, unencumbered by either of the restrictions that were previously in place.

Sliding his gaze to the side, The Angel imagined his siblings still sitting somewhere in the van nearby, waiting for his call to tell them that it was done. They could start the engine and come closer to do their part.

Both resting in the front seats, they were probably staring out in silence or locked in conversation, discussing how he was the one to blame for the little dustup earlier.

The Tall Boy, constantly complaining about how rough he had it. The Artist, assuring him it was okay, running interference like she had always done, becoming even more pronounced in recent months.

Enabling that The Angel had no interest in, much preferring to be out here in the cold, doing what he does best. The role that was given to him specifically, with full knowledge that he was the only one with the stomach for it.

The mettle.

Dealing with the old man the night before was something requiring a bit more delicacy. Multiple factors to be considered, including the man's age, the public location of his abduction, and the fact that he had not had nearly as active a role in the past.

The financier who was a participant, for sure, but in more of a tangential manner.

A place in the pecking order that meant he went first as they worked their way in. Received less physical abuse in the process.

An appetizer on which The Angel had just started to release some of the angst that had been years building inside of him. A first attempt that was far from perfect, though was plenty sufficient to spark the fuse, leaving him practically aching with anticipation all day.

A constant watching of the clock, envisioning things, waiting to be in this exact position.

Just as he had for so many nights, staring up at the bare concrete, longing for a moment he long feared might never arrive.

Chapter Twelve

The initial examination of Dean Morgan's car turned up nothing readily identifiable. No scratches on any of the locks getting into the vehicle. No smudges of mud or other detritus in the backseat, where Reed guessed someone had hidden and waited.

There were no rips in the leather of the seats or scuffs on the steering wheel or dashboard. The clasp on the seatbelt hadn't been pulled from its casing. The metal rods holding the headrest in place weren't bent.

Certainly, no smudges of blood. Not a single sign to show that a struggle of any kind had taken place, consistent with Morgan's story of suspecting nothing until he felt a pinprick at the base of his neck.

A well-devised plan on the front end that was matched by their attention on the back. Care to scrub away any sign of passing, Earl and Coby able to pull a handful of prints from inside the vehicle but nothing more.

Identifying marks Reed was certain would all correspond to Morgan after waking, anything else either vacuumed up or stripped away with cleaning solvent.

A sum total that left everyone present at Morgan's less than optimistic about things moving forward as they departed.

A feeling Reed still carried as he pulled down the gravel drive along the side of the farmhouse he and Billie shared at just after midnight. An hour that felt like it should be much later, their day having started sixteen hours prior at the training facility on the east side of town.

Eight hours of intense physical exertion followed by the same on the opposite end of the spectrum. Concerted mental focus that left him feeling drained, even now as his mind raced, trying to put together all that had transpired throughout the evening.

Everything from the unusual summons to the non-existent crime scene, the case already setting itself up to be one of the more difficult he and Billie had encountered.

To say nothing of the unspoken pressure he knew would be applied throughout, Governor Cowan's personal connection to the victim meaning there would be no accepting anything shy of a fast and tidy closure.

Pulling up behind the dented pickup serving as Reed's personal vehicle, barely did he have time to climb out before Billie did the same, jumping through the front seats and hitting the ground at a jog. A recognition of where they were and the need to relieve herself after a long evening, the last stretch of it spent sitting in the backseat as they made their way home.

A path Reed made no effort to call her away from as she trotted for the backyard, her midnight hue shifting from a form to a silhouette to another of the long shadows covering the lawn. Pockets of darkness caused by the security light affixed to the back of the house, throwing a pale glow across the deck and out into the grass.

Intermittent stripes of illumination she passed in and out of, her nose lowered to the ground, oblivious to Reed's presence as he followed her down the drive before turning up the trio of stairs onto the deck. Slow, heavy steps with his feet thumping against the weathered wood, the full effects of the day and the resulting exhaustion gripping him.

Fatigue that he hoped only needed to be stemmed a little bit longer, a couple of small items to be checked off before he and Billie could turn in.

Rest that he knew would be much needed, the days ahead promising to be nothing short of a sprint.

Pushing through the back door into the kitchen, he started by unloading the accumulated gear of the day. His gun and badge that were never left in the car overnight – no matter the lock on the glove box – followed by the duffel bag carrying the gym clothes he'd worn throughout the training session.

A lightening of his load that ended with his wallet and, finally, his phone, extracting it from his back pocket and stepping back out onto the deck. Keeping it in hand, he tapped on the screen, calling it to life for the first time since leaving Morgan's to see a pair of missed messages.

The first was from Captain Wallace Grimes, his overseer at the 8th Precinct. A text sent a half hour earlier, prompted from having spoken to Chief Brandt. A quick check-in once she was finished at Cowan's residence to let him know what was going on and that she had gotten the governor to agree the two of them would be sharing point duties until the investigation was resolved.

Information that Grimes relayed, along with the instructions to reach out at any time if needed. The phone would be kept on and close by, just in case.

An offer that Reed appreciated, even if he already knew the captain made a point of always be accessible to those under his charge.

A fact he didn't bother to point out in his reply, instead relaying that they had just left the victim's home and promising to swing by the precinct in the morning for a full debrief.

Glancing up from his phone, he swept his gaze across the open meadow comprising the backyard to his home. Giving his eyes a moment to adjust from the bright glare of the screen, he focused on the deep shadows collected around the smattering of pine trees, picking up Billie near her favorite corner.

The urgency she displayed earlier gone, her body was bent forward, her nose just inches from the ground. An exploratory search that Reed watched, waiting for the incoming reply from Grimes he knew was imminent.

A response in the affirmative to meet in the morning that arrived in under a minute, no matter the hour or day of the week.

A text Reed glanced at briefly, seeing what he needed to and then returning to the other missed message. A couple sentences of text that he considered typing out a reply to before thinking better of it, instead opting for just two short words.

> You up?

A quick message that managed to prompt an even faster answer than that received from Grimes, the phone springing to life in his palm only a few seconds later. An incoming call that he accepted and immediately flipped to speaker, keeping the device extended before him.

"Hey there," he opened. "I didn't wake you, did I?"

"Close," Serena Gipson answered in reply. "But not quite yet. Chalk one up for the time zone playing in our favor."

Feeling the right corner of his mouth peel back in a smile, Reed replied, "Which brings the total to, what, one?"

"Eh, maybe two," Serena answered, adding in a small chuckle as well.

Mirth that was the only thing that could be expressed, given their current situation. Interaction that Reed wouldn't quite call long-distance dating, though he didn't have a better alternative title for it either.

Interaction that began when he and Billie were in tiny Warner, Oklahoma to help his parents move and just happened to stand witness to Serena being abducted by a serial kidnapper who had been working throughout the area. Asked to join in on her search by the local police force, they had dived straight in, flinging themselves into a hunt that lasted the better part of a week and ended by finding her chained up in a storm cellar, not far from expiration.

One of the more intense matters the two had handled, also having the double significance of being a rare instance of Reed keeping in touch after the fact.

A casual friendship that was starting to become more, in no small part through the insistence of Serena. Calls that began as updates from the cancer center where she was a nurse in training about how Reed's father was doing, later evolving into a standing Sunday morning phone date.

Weekly check-ins that had taken a step further since she came to visit around the time Reed was shot in the leg, the two now speaking multiple times a week, if not daily.

An arrangement Reed still wasn't entirely sure what to make of, only that he no longer felt any qualms of guilt over maintaining.

"What has you up so late tonight?" Serena asked. "I know you had training this morning, but I never guessed it would go until midnight."

"You guessed right," Reed replied. "Training went well, ended even earlier than it was scheduled to. It was everything else that came after that got ugly."

"How ugly?"

"Me if-forced-to-drink-coffee ugly."

Again, Serena laughed. A quick chuckle that could have been at finding his joke funny, or simply humoring the attempt at levity.

A sound there and gone in a moment, replaced by her asking, "Governor's office?"

"Always is."

"Well, like I said, it's not bedtime yet. I'm all ears."

Chapter Thirteen

Just shy of eight hours after sending the text message to Captain Wallace Grimes from the deck out behind his house, Reed and Billie strode through the door to the man's office to find him seated behind his desk. Despite the relatively early hour and the decided lack of foot traffic throughout the 8th Precinct, he was already in the standard position that Reed so often found him.

Full uniform minus only the jacket hanging neatly on the rack in the corner behind him. Cuffs and collar all buttoned down, his tie crisp and precise.

Fingers laced across his torso as he stared directly at them, he dipped the top of his head in greeting.

"Captain," Reed said, taking a few quick steps down the narrow entry into the office before it opened wide to his right. A corner spread with windows on two walls overlooking the parking lot and the side lawn providing plenty of natural light.

Illumination that was more than sufficient for the desk and pair of visitor chairs that comprised the bulk of the space, the office free of so much of the usual clutter that marked administrative suites. Expansive bookshelves and walls covered in mementos both personal and professional.

Unnecessary distractions Grimes had managed to distill down to a single narrow table along the wall, on it a framed picture of his wife and dog along with a matching photo of the day he was sworn in as captain of the 8th.

Nothing more.

A perfect summation of everything Reed knew about the man. One of many reasons why he had enjoyed working for him when he was a sergeant at the neighboring 19th Precinct and Reed was still a beat cop with his former partner, Riley Poole.

Also, a part of why he had accepted Grimes's invitation for him to move into the role of K-9 detective with the 8th in the wake of Riley's passing a few years prior.

"Detectives," Grimes said in reply, waiting until Reed was seated in the closest visitor chair and Billie lowered to her haunches by his side before continuing, "thanks for stopping by this morning. From what I gleaned from the chief, this one could be..."

"A pain in the ass," Reed finished, the thought out before he could even begin to stop himself. A continuation of the discussion he and Earl had the night before and the thoughts that had kept him awake most of the night.

A soft snort rocked back the captain's head. A preface of but a single sound before he added, "That would be almost word-for-word how the chief put it as well."

While Reed and Brandt hadn't had a chance to fully debrief after leaving the governor's home the night before - his need to be moving and Cowan's insistence on not going back inside until he did so making it impossible – there had been more than enough silent communication between them to relay they were of the same opinion.

Not just of the case they'd been handed, but everything surrounding it. The unusual circumstances. The truncated timeframe they would be under. The governor's personal connection to it.

The increasing difficulty level of each successive case they'd been handed since Reed and Billie started working with the BCI. Heightened hardship that was starting to almost feel as if it was by design.

As if the governor was hoping for them to commit a misstep so he could deconstruct the standing arrangement and bring them under his umbrella permanently.

An outcome Reed hoped the man was smart enough to know he did not want to push for too strongly, the ending not the one he likely intended.

"She also said - all other surrounding issues aside – that it was pretty grisly," Grimes added.

Having been to more crime scenes than he cared to remember, both as a beat cop and then later as a detective, Reed had seen grisly. A term that drew to mind images of dead bodies and blood spatter and a host of other mental snapshots he would just as soon rid himself of.

Give his head a good shake in either direction and forcibly fling them away, like Billie after exiting the bathtub.

What he saw the night before was not necessarily that, but it was certainly a first. A harrowing scene, both in what was done and in the effects it had had.

Devastation that would linger with Dean Morgan far longer than a gunshot or stab wound.

"It was..." Reed began, searching for the proper term a moment before giving up, settling on, "something. That's for sure."

Reclined slightly in his chair, Grimes dipped his chin half an inch in understanding. A slight movement that caused folds of skin to pile up the length of his jawline before unspooling as he returned to his usual position.

One of the few signs that he was now marching on into his early fifties, the couple of extra pounds and increasing bits of gray at the temples offset by his full hairline and smooth black skin.

"The chief relayed what Morgan said last night," Grimes said. "I take it his house didn't reveal anything?"

"Nothing," Reed said, shaking his head to either side. "Same for his vehicle, which is the closest we have to a crime scene."

Once more, Grimes tilted his head forward. A nod of understanding, without feeling the need to verbally follow up.

Another of the reasons Reed had been inclined to accept his invitation to move over a couple of years before.

"First stop this morning is to head upstairs," Reed said. "Going to beat the bushes on the databases, see if anything pops up. Something this unusual..."

Letting his voice trail away to clear the thought, he added, "I don't suppose you've ever seen something like that before?"

Turning his chin an inch in either direction, Grimes replied, "The only time I've even heard of such a thing was in a novel. *The Girl with the Dragon Tattoo.* And even that wasn't to the victim's face."

"That's kind of what I'm thinking," Reed said. "If it ever has happened, we should know pretty quick."

Pressing his hands down into the arms of the chair, he pushed himself to full height, matched by Billie doing the same beside him.

"Just the same, can I get you to go ahead and put a flag in the system in case anything else like this shows up?"

Chapter Fourteen

For all the signs of life the first floor of the 8th Precinct was beginning to show by the time Reed and Billie stepped out of Captain Grimes's office, the second story was the complete opposite. An open expanse to match the one below, the right side of the level was set aside for the dispatch desk, the dayshift operator barely glancing up as Reed said hello.

A response Reed trusted not to be anger or personal misgivings, the man he knew only as Lou putting his full focus on the task before him. Attentive staring at the radio, listening to the chatter on the CPD band, monitoring ongoing activity while waiting for the direct line to ring.

A job Reed left him to as he turned the opposite direction, slapping at the leg of his jeans and leading Billie through the loose tangle of desks set aside for the detectives who called the 8th home. Five or six mismatched pieces that sat at odd angles with an uneven number of chairs grouped around them.

Desk space that every precinct was required to have, providing a place for detectives to handle paperwork or conduct computer searches. Chores that every last one avoided if at all possible, Reed not surprised to find the place empty, the latter task the only reason he was here now.

Research he likely would have done from the kitchen table at his farmhouse if not for the fact that he needed to stop by to visit with Captain Grimes anyway.

Threading his way through the misshapen maze, Reed pulled up at the last desk on the floor. An aging piece with a scratched wooden top and dented metal frame supporting quite possibly the oldest working computer Reed had ever seen.

A workstation adequate for what he needed this morning but little more, even the chair he was allotted seeming to be of the same opinion, wheezing slightly as he dropped himself down into it.

An action Billie mirrored by his side, lowering herself flat to the tile floor as he booted the hard drive to life and waited for it to load. A process that took much longer than Reed would have preferred, having to wait several minutes before finally the home screen appeared before him.

Beginning with the Columbus Police Department database, Reed ran a few quick searches on everything he currently had available. Starting with the man he'd met for the first time the night before, Reed found Dean Morgan to be absolutely clean, not even a parking ticket marring his record.

A bit of low-hanging fruit he hadn't imagined would amount to much, though still needed to check on anyway.

A place to begin before turning to the thin list of facts he had to work with. A spotty narrative that led him to bypass trying to use the means of kidnapping altogether for the time being, trusting it was likely too broad to be of help. A rabbit hole that could include everything from car jackings to child abductions.

Same for the magic marker that was scrawled across Morgan's torso. A bit of extra insult to the man, but nothing more than a misdemeanor in and of itself.

Two items that could be used to winnow things down later perhaps, if he had a handful of possibilities to work with, but not on the front end, costing more time to sift through than they would be worth.

Transitioning instead to the more obscure part of what they were up against, Reed dove into the act itself. An unusual form of assault that neither he nor Earl had even heard of, much less seen, it coming as no surprise when his first few searches for anyone having been tattooed on their face turned up nothing.

Same for anybody having been sedated and tattooed.

Ten minutes of throwing every possible combination of search terms he could at the wall, the closest he managed to find was a matter of a girl going into a tattoo parlor and asking for a cluster of hearts framing her eyes. Twin groupings that were supposed to have consisted of three each, but ended up being twice as many.

A matter that had not ended up being pursued by prosecutors, the details of the matter highly contested, both parties telling radically different versions of the same story.

An issue Reed imagined ended up in front of a civil jury or settled out of court, either way of little value to what he needed.

Going straight to the corner of the screen, Reed closed out of the database. A complete exit that brought back up the plain blue background of the homepage, allowing him to click on the icon arranged at the bottom of the trio clustered together along the left edge.

The three prominent search engines for detectives such as himself looking for background on like-kind incidents or information about potential suspects.

CPD, whenever a common local link was a possibility, followed in order by the NCIC and N-Dex databases. Both run by the Criminal Justice Information Services Division of the FBI, the former – the National Crime Information Center – was more person specific. A central repository regarding fugitives, missing persons, even suspected terrorists.

Classifications that did not apply in the least, Morgan not even getting so much as a glimpse of his abductor.

Leaving that one alone for the time being, Reed instead went to the last option in order. The National Data Exchange, serving as an electronic warehouse for case files from local, state, federal, and tribal law enforcement agencies around the country. A veritable online dumping ground for all criminal information that could be mined for possible connections between individuals and incidents.

A tool that Reed had been able to strike a bit of gold with on the last case he and Billie worked for the governor, hoping that a similar fate could await this time as he began the process anew. A start with the same exact search terms used in the CPD database just moments before that revealed nothing, finding only nominally more success on his second attempt.

Matters from federal prisons in California and Washington, respectively, in which inmates awoke after violent incidents to find the markings of a rival gang etched into their skin.

Matters that sounded especially grim, folds of skin piling up around Reed's eyes as he skimmed through the details. Parts of escalation patterns that were almost certain to get worse, Reed reading through only the summaries of each before closing out of the program.

A return to the blue home screen that he stared at for several moments, his vision blurring as he thought of what striking out in all three databases meant. A crime with no predecessor that meant he and Billie were left with just the few random bits of data extracted from Morgan the night before.

Precious little with which to form a coherent plan.

Long odds made even worse by the prospect of a governor expecting results at any moment.

Chapter Fifteen

Reed could hear the sound of collective discussion as he and Billie reached the top of the stairwell and started to make their way down. A swell with two or three distinctive voices backstopped by a handful more providing underlying buzz.

A group that he would guess to be somewhere around a handful or so, the dayshift having arrived en masse while he and Billie were in with Captain Grimes and upstairs working the computers. A start to the week not unlike many other professions, people getting settled back in, talking over the events of the weekend.

Swapping stories about how they spent the time or the big games on Saturday or Sunday, depending on team affiliation.

Typical water cooler fare that Reed had missed out on after moving to the 8th and settling into a role on the nightshift.

Even more so once the liaison position with the state was instituted, he and Billie still housed in the 8th, but operating on a schedule that had rendered them little more than ghosts around the station, coming and going at odd hours.

A diminished state of presence that seemed to register on a couple of the faces as Reed and his partner descended into view, the crowd turning as one to regard the two of them making their way down. Visual examination paired with a slowing in the conversation.

"I'm sorry, are you two lost?" Derek Greene opened. A career officer who was a half-decade or more older than Reed, a broad grin split his features, bright teeth standing out against his black skin. Taking a step from the group, he extended a hand before him.

A gesture Reed matched, along with the smile, before replying, "We heard this is where all the cool kids were hanging out, thought we'd come take a look."

Releasing the handshake, he bent at the waist to peer past Greene and asked, "Are they not here yet? Should we come back in a little while?"

A joke met with a bit of exaggerated laughter from the group, Officer Wade McMichaels offering in reply, "Naw, it's the same old group around here, I think the problem is your definition of *cool* has just changed. You guys went off and got all High Society on us."

An opening his partner was not about to let slip past, Tommy Jacobs finishing with, "Yeah, you big state investigators probably think any gathering that doesn't have caviar and champagne just isn't good enough these days."

Pressing his lips tight in an attempt to keep from openly laughing, Reed felt his cheeks bunch. Muted chuckles that did nothing to keep his shoulders from quivering, mirth finally getting the best of him as his face creased into a grin.

"Hey, I don't seem to remember you two minding much whenever the state comes calling to offer overtime."

A quip earning a laugh from Greene and the young woman beside him as the smile fell away from McMichaels' lean face. Angular features to match his build, the man stretched nearly as tall as Reed, but weighing significantly less.

One hundred and seventy pounds of sinew, offset by his partner's shorter, rounder build. Soft features wrapped in olive skin and sporting various forms of facial hair, the choice of the moment being a circle beard around his mouth and chin, with the sides shaved clean.

"Hey now," McMichaels said in his best solemn voice. "There's no need to go there. We're all just having fun this morning."

"Yeah," Jacobs replied, bringing his hands together before him in a state of exaggerated apology. "Whenever you kind, hardworking state employees need help, we lowly local civil servants would be honored to lend a hand."

A routine Reed had seen the two use a number of times before, he raised his face toward the ceiling, audible laughter spilling out. Chuckles matched by Greene beside him, the pairing of McMichaels and Jacobs known for being voracious devourers of any overtime that might exist.

One of several reasons why Reed had requested they be available as on-call backup for any cases he and Billie worked with the BCI.

"Same old around here, I see," Reed said, glancing to Greene still smiling beside him.

"The more things change," Greene agreed, letting out another chuckle before sliding a step to the side. Motioning to the officer on his hip, he said, "Speaking of which, Reed, this is Julie Madsen, my newest assignee. Julie, these are Detectives Mattox and Billie, who – as you just heard – split their time between here and the BCI."

"*Split* being a very generous term," McMichaels added.

A quip that caused Reed's smile to expand as he extended his hand toward the young woman in uniform with sandy brown hair just barely long enough to pull back, loose strands tucked behind either ear.

"Officer Madsen, welcome aboard," Reed said. Releasing her grip, he motioned to McMichaels and Jacobs and added, "And congratulations on ending up with the only one of these guys worth a damn."

Prompting a renewed chorus of laughter from the group, Madsen gave it a moment to clear before replying, "Thank you, detective. It's nice to meet you."

"You as well, but please, just Reed."

"Julie."

Nodding his head in agreement, Reed took a step back, resuming his previous spot. A circle of a half dozen filling most of the front foyer, all six – including Billie – donning grins.

A rare bit of levity that Reed hated to see end, knowing that he would be the reason for it.

Or, more aptly, the answer he would have to give to the question he knew was coming. An ask he wanted nothing more than to avoid, hoping to make it through several more minutes of small talk before eventually exiting.

An innocuous question that Reed knew there would have no ill will behind it, just as surely as he knew it would invoke the same exact response from each of the officers that it had in him and Brandt the night before.

Earl at the crime scene a bit later.

Even Grimes barely thirty minutes ago.

"So really," Jacobs asked eventually, his arms folded in front of him. The start of a question that made Reed's core clench, bracing himself for it.

An ask he not only didn't want to broach, but knew he had no definitive answers for.

If he was even allowed to try, for that matter, after the display the governor put on the night before regarding secrecy.

"What brings you two out this morning?" Jacobs continued. "You weren't on the schedule last night, were you?"

"Weren't supposed to be," Reed said. "Had K-9 training yesterday and before we even made it home, got a call up to the governor's mansion."

"Oh man," McMichaels muttered. "Big time."

"No kidding," Jacobs said, glancing to his partner. "Did someone nab the fine China again?"

"Make off with a silver place setting?"

Once more, the partners managed to elicit chuckles from the group. More mirth that Reed allowed to linger as long as possible before finally answering, "Naw, this was legit. A case showed up on his doorstep, and, well..."

"As they say," Greene inserted, picking up on the insinuation, "it always rolls downhill."

"That it does," Reed agreed. A response that managed to peel away a bit of the jovial mood in the air, giving him the slightest hint of an opening.

Likely, the best he was going to do short of sidestepping the question entirely.

Something he would rather not do, the people around him friends and colleagues, possibly able to provide some bit of insight to a matter that was severely lacking it at the moment.

"Any of you," Reed began, sliding his gaze to the side to first check the frosted doors to the administrative suite in the back. Making sure they were closed, he moved on next to the small cluster of officers at the far end of the room, all clustered up with cups of coffee in hand, bantering about the same game Reed had started to watch before the call from Brandt pulled him. "Ever heard of a victim being tattooed?"

In unison, McMichaels and Jacobs both brought their brows together. Looks of confusion as they exchanged a glance, the latter the first of the two to speak.

"You mean, like they got one and regretted it?" Jacobs asked.

Contemplating his next move for but an instant, Reed very nearly reached to his back pocket. Sliding out his phone, he would go into the photo gallery, move past the picture of the inscription on Dean Morgan's ribs, and pull up the first shot he took.

The image of Morgan staring down into the fire with his eyes closed, the word **PRIDE** inscribed upon his brow.

A visual that would really drive home what had happened that Reed refrained from sharing just yet, knowing that word of it would be through the precinct – if not the greater CPD – within hours.

A problem Reed didn't want Grimes or Chief Brandt to have to deal with later.

"No, I mean they were knocked out and woke up to find it plastered across their forehead."

Chapter Sixteen

Reed hadn't meant to put a damper on the rare Monday morning good mood that was floating around the precinct, his final statement a legit inquiry that also managed to answer Jacobs's question without violating any standing directives from the governor. A simple ask letting them know what had befallen Dean Morgan without mentioning his name or even really getting into the full extent of the ink etched into the man's skin.

A physical maiming that would have evoked even more of a reaction than it did if the people gathered on the first floor had seen it.

Responses that were already laced with shock and repulsion, those two things sitting at the forefront of Reed's mind as he and Billie pulled into the parking lot of the Holman Brothers Steakhouse just north of the city. An old-school establishment with a brick exterior and a sign of faded black calligraphy letters against a gray backdrop.

A place that exuded posh not through the flashy manner employed by so many others today, but by trying so hard to do the exact opposite. A structure that looked like it would be better suited for an industrial complex somewhere, the untrained eye likely to drive right past without ever giving it a second glance.

Pulling in at exactly half past nine in the morning, the bulk of the parking lot was completely empty, only a delivery truck from a local bakery and a handful of vehicles parked down toward the rear entrance to be seen. Management and kitchen staff assigned to get the day started, even as the doors would not open for guests for another hour and a half.

A timeslot best suited for what Reed and Billie needed, the hope that they could speak with who they needed to and then get a look at any surveillance footage that may exist, there and gone before any hungry customers arrived.

An outcome he was fairly certain the Holman brothers – if such gentlemen even existed and were not merely used for naming purposes – would also appreciate, the sight of an obvious K-9 team there on an official matter not likely the best for business.

Pulling into the closest available spot, Reed left Billie in the back long enough to circle out and affix her short lead to her shoulder harness. Walking in tandem, they entered through the front door to find the hostess stand empty, same for the dining hall beyond.

An expansive space of dark wood and chandeliers, the general vibe matching that of the exterior décor. A utilitarian design meant to put the focus more on the menu and the service than whatever ambiance might exist.

Or so Reed suspected, having never heard of the place before, much less having eaten there.

"Can I help you?" a voice asked, the sound of it pulling Reed's focus in the opposite direction to find a man in his thirties with thick hair swept back from his forehead and gelled into place. Donning a chef's smock, he gripped a dish towel between his hands, drying them as he approached from somewhere in the back.

A process that slowed noticeably as his gaze tracked downward, landing on Billie by Reed's side.

An expected reaction, spurring the use of the short lead.

"Detectives Mattox and Billie," Reed said, omitting which organization they were there on behalf of as he reached to his rear pocket. Extracting his badge, he flashed it just long enough for the man to register it before asking, "Is the manager in yet?"

"Uh," the man said, his voice eluding him for a moment as he processed what he was seeing. Lingering surprise, coupled with open curiosity. A desire to ask if something was wrong, if anything had happened, that Reed had seen innumerable times before, this individual having the good sense to do what so many others often failed at and avoiding asking the obvious.

Social grace that probably suited him well in such an establishment.

"Not the *manager* manager," he said. "She doesn't come on until four. But the assistant is in." Lifting a hand, he motioned toward himself while turning back in the opposite direction. "Follow me."

Mumbling a thank you, Reed fell in behind the man. Billie matching his pace beside him, they passed by the hostess stand and along the front of an open kitchen, each peeking in at the activity well underway. Line cooks already putting in the work for the crowds that would be arriving, chopping vegetables and preparing stocks and deboning various cuts of meats.

Painstaking work there would be no time for later, assorted aromas already beginning to fill the air.

Heavenly scents that wafted across their nostrils, there and gone in an instant as the man led them on by the kitchen and down a narrow corridor running along the far side of it. A slow march that ended near the back corner of the building at a door standing open, bright light spilling out into the dim hallway.

A final destination the man made it clear he had no intention of escorting them all the way to, pulling up five yards short and motioning them onward before excusing himself with a nod.

A gesture Reed matched, allowing the man to head back to his tasks in the kitchen.

A far preferable way of spending the next few minutes than what was about to transpire in the manager's office at the end of the hall, for sure.

Keeping Billie's lead gripped tight in hand, Reed slapped at the leg of his jeans. An unspoken command for them to keep traversing the narrow hallway with wood rising to waist height before giving way to bands of aluminum and, ultimately, sheetrock painted white.

Bare surfaces that slid by on either side, ending at a doorway constructed of the same polished metal.

An optimal place for Reed to place his first two knuckles, tapping twice to draw up the attention of the sole person inside the room. A man that looked to be just a few years younger than Reed with long hair pulled back tight and thick-framed glasses pressed tight against his face.

Rising from his chair behind a desk the color of obsidian, he folded his hands before him, his brows rising high on his forehead.

"Help you, officers?" he asked, clearly pegging the two of them on sight.

Recognition that Reed still buttressed by flashing his badge, the same as he had with the chef before. "Detectives, actually. Reed Mattox, my K-9 partner Billie."

Returning the badge to his rear pocket, he added, "I'm told you're the acting manager this morning?"

"I am," the man said. Stepping around the side of the desk, he extended a hand before him. "Thomas Swanson. Nice to meet you both."

"You as well," Reed said, returning the gesture.

A quick shake that Swanson retreated from almost instantly, returning his hands back in front of him. "What can I do for you today?"

Cutting his gaze to the side, Reed took in the mass of electronics resting against the wall beside the desk Swanson was just seated behind. A bevy of monitors spitting out images in black and white, all affixed directly to the wall.

A mosaic of motion providing the backdrop for a handful of receivers and towers of various sorts.

Lights and cables Reed didn't pretend to fully comprehend, instead opening with, "How many cameras do you guys have monitoring the parking lot outside? And how far back do you store the footage?"

Chapter Seventeen

For the third time in as many days, the harsh scent of cleaning solvents found The Artist's nose as she laid out her tools on the counter. An acerbic chemical aroma that wafted up from the top of the bottle of rubbing alcohol beside her. Saturated the cotton balls she was clutching, sure to cling to fingers for hours after she was done.

A scent that bordered on repulsive the first time it crossed her nostrils, but after the last several months, she was more than used to.

Given the events of the last couple of nights, was even starting to find a bit of comfort in. An odor she would forever associate with this particular task and what it represented. Progress toward finally putting things right, each new time that she came in contact with it providing solace that they were that much closer.

Justice was being served in a way that the traditional channels would never provide, having fumbled the numerous opportunities they were given to do so.

Standing over the sink in the center of the kitchen, The Artist held the sopping cotton balls over the stainless-steel basin, letting the excess drip off. Fat droplets that pinged softly against the bottom, creating a misshapen pattern across the host of scratch marks cleaved into the metal.

Decades of being scrubbed clean, their mother attacking any stray bits of food residue or detritus as if it had personally wronged her. Effort that The Artist herself had taken part in on numerous occasions, having stood in this very spot many times throughout her childhood, and again upon returning months before.

A clean break from her previous life. One she had run away to at the first available moment when she was just eighteen, having traveled across state lines without any intention of returning.

The self-righteous rebelliousness of the late teen years that eventually began to wane, first seven years ago with the event that precipitated her eventual return, and then again just two years prior.

Occurrences that very nearly brought her back, any resolve she had to stay away completely obliterated six months prior.

A third thunderous blow to the family, paired with direct marching orders. The removal of any lingering impediments, those alone being the reasons why The Artist had stayed away.

A desire for retribution she knew she'd be unable to withstand, at last granted to her and her siblings.

Transferring the wad of sodden cotton to her left hand, The Artist reached for the closest of the items resting on a towel beside the sink with her right. An itemized order arranged from most important to least, the assembly needed for what she was doing these days much smaller than what she was used to.

No brushes or knives of varying sizes and shapes. No odorless paint thinner for cleaning them or paper towels to wipe them dry. Not an easel or a lamp or any of the other things she'd grown so fond of working with.

Hell, not even a full color palate, only a single vat of plain black ink required. A harsh, distinctive hue in line with the message she was asked to impart.

A delivery method that was unlike anything she had heard of before, matched in its uniqueness only by its effectiveness.

Taking up the closest item, The Artist held the thick needle up to the light streaming through the window before her. A quick inspection of the stainless steel to insure it was still in pristine condition, with only a couple of uses on its tally.

A check to ensure it was as she remembered when packing it and the tattoo gun it was attached to up the night before. A slow and careful stowing away of items in the garage of the house while her brothers carried their second target back inside.

The ultimate insult, letting it be known that they could get to him whenever and wherever they wanted.

A reminder each time he went to bed at night that someone had been there. Had violated him in the most profane way possible, just as he had helped do to others years before.

One last insertion of shame that would mark him, making him feel uncomfortable even in his own home.

The better part of two years now, The Artist had known this was coming. Not this exact thing - that much there was no way she or her siblings could have ever envisioned – but some form of retribution.

Retaliation that would be handed out for what was done to them. The massive loss that was inflicted upon the entire family, impossible to ever be made right.

Not after all they had been through. The years of struggle both physical and emotional. The nights of wrestling with the anger and the desires, held at bay out of respect for their mother's wishes.

Time enough for The Artist to have moved beyond any uncertainty that might exist. Any questions as to what they were doing.

Any qualms whatsoever as she lowered the needle back before her and attacked it with the wad of cotton balls, scrubbing away the last victim.

Preparing for the next.

Chapter Eighteen

In the fifteen hours since Reed had last seen Dean Morgan, the man had had the chance to shower and change his clothes. Gone was the drink in his hand and the resulting red tendrils threaded through the sclera of his eyes. He'd even managed to leave the safe confines of the governor's personal residence and make his way back to his own home.

Still, there was no mistaking the feeling of disgrace that enveloped him. The sense of shame that seemed to seep from his pores as he first met Reed and Billie at the front door, and lingered even now as they sat in his office deep within the recesses of his home.

A room Reed and Billie had been through the night before, clearing it for intruders and checking for signs of entry, that looked markedly different under the full light of day. A space that was set up to resemble a workroom, when in reality it was something more of a shrine.

An altar to all Morgan had accomplished in a long and storied career, with plaques and framed photographs – including a few with Cowan himself - hanging in even rows and awards of various kinds covering the bookshelves lining the back wall. Everything from marble obelisks to crystal bowls, all engraved with Morgan's name and the presenting organization, their dates going back decades.

A total haul easily outnumbering the volumes displayed by size between them. The expected titles on leadership and business acumen, serving as little more than spacers between the next set of accolades.

A safe space for Morgan to retreat to, exulting in his past successes. Accomplishments Reed had spent a decent chunk of time sitting at his kitchen table and reading up on the night before. A quick check to assuage his curiosity after speaking with Serena Gipson that had turned into a rabbit hole, giving him a crash course on Morgan and the company he oversaw for two decades known as Buckeye Care.

A corporation that started out as a local healthcare supply and logistic provider before expanding into one of the largest such suppliers in the world.

A robust expansion that was largely spearheaded by Morgan.

A massive achievement responsible for the home they were now sitting in and, Reed had to believe, was in some way the root cause behind the tattoo emblazoned upon Morgan's skin.

A single term that now seemed to be completely lost, Reed again getting the impression he was speaking to a broken man as he sat in the leather armchair beside Morgan. Billie on the floor between them, all three were turned toward the flatscreen monitor mounted to the wall above his glass-top desk.

A video image frozen in the center of it, Reed regarded Morgan's profile as he stared at the screen. The letters P and R plainly visible across his forehead, the rest of it disappeared out of sight with the curvature of his skull.

"The Holman Brothers Steakhouse has cameras watching the front entrance, but not the entire parking lot," Reed explained. "Given where you were parked, we were able to get a partial view of your vehicle. Not enough to clearly identify a suspect, but at least enough to see what happened."

Leaving any further explanation until after they watched the video, Reed extended a hand, jabbing the remote control at the scene of the parking lot frozen on screen. A shot that was taken at an angle, providing a full view of the driver's side of Morgan's SUV, the rest of the vehicle – and the parking lot beyond – all past the scope of view.

Far from an ideal vantage, but definitely better than it could have been had he parked even a single space further from the door.

Already cued by Thomas Swanson earlier to the moment just after arrival, the image sprang to life in time to see the driver's side door of the SUV swing wide and Morgan himself emerge. Wearing slacks and a quarter-zip pullover with an Ohio State logo embroidered on the chest, he had a phone pressed to his left cheek. Deep in conversation, a broad smile was splashed across his features.

His right hand gripped the keys, which he raised and extended toward the SUV as he walked away.

"Best guess, whoever did this was either waiting in the parking lot or followed you in, staying close enough to use a fob jammer," Reed said, speaking as the video continued to roll. "It's kind of like a scrambler, intercepting the signal from your keys to the vehicle."

Pausing a beat, Reed added, "See, after you hit the button here, the vehicle doesn't lock."

A conclusion drawn from the fact that even without sound, there was no visible flash of lights. No outward display of the lock command being received and acted upon.

Something that Morgan likely would have noticed, if not for the fact that he was lost in conversation.

A point Reed didn't dare mention, knowing how such information would likely only heighten the intense self-flagellation already going on beside him.

"After that, they were smart," Reed said. Extending the same hand, he pushed the video forward, moving it in triple speed. Pace fast enough to send people and cars rushing by as nothing more than blurs, moving in and out view.

Considerable foot traffic for a Saturday game night that Reed had gone through twice at Holman's, seeing nothing unusual. Nobody who appeared out of place or paid special attention to Morgan's SUV. No one following too closely as he entered or exited.

A long gap in the middle that allowed him to jump ahead, bringing it back to the normal speed less than fifteen minutes before Morgan's departure.

"I also figure they knew why you were there, kept tabs on the game so that they didn't have to climb in too early."

Slowing the video by a factor of four, Reed let it run at half of normal speed. A pace that seemed especially exaggerated after what they were watching just moments before, with people and vehicles moving in slow motion.

Viewing that would be painful if engaged in for very long, though Reed needed only to let a minute or so unspool.

Less than that of real time, ending with him pausing the view, freezing it onscreen again.

"This is where they entered," he said. Extending a finger, he added, "If you focus on the rear driver's side window, you can see the opposite door open up."

Nudging the video ahead again, he continued, "And here, a shadow appears along the bottom, which it looks like is whoever was waiting for you getting into position."

In his periphery, Reed saw Morgan raise a hand to his mouth. Drawing a sharp inhalation, he stared at the screen, his eyes wide.

A pose maintained even as Reed returned the video to playing, pushing it back to triple speed. A quickened pace, bringing them up to the point when Morgan exited from the restaurant and went straight to the driver's door.

Using his fob, he aimed it at the vehicle, the device acting as it was designed and flashing the lights, even though it was already unlocked.

Expected behavior that gave Morgan no indication anything was wrong as he climbed in, started the engine, and drove away.

A finale Reed let run to completion before stopping the playback, the screen across from them going completely black. A reflective surface putting the three of them on full display, Reed and Billie both staring straight ahead while Morgan hung his head, intent on looking anywhere but at the device mounted on the wall.

"Mr. Morgan," Reed said, his voice barely more than a whisper as he kept his gaze on the screen, using it to track any movement from the man beside him. "Can you think of anyone who might want to do this to you? Any personal enemies? Your ex-wife?"

Lifting his hands, he motioned to the room around them. "Maybe somebody from work?"

Chapter Nineteen

Six years, Reed had been a detective. Time that was fast approaching an equal split between Riley Poole – his best friend and partner since the moment they finished their training rotations out of the academy – before her tragic death during a routine traffic stop, and now Billie.

Years of speaking with witnesses and victims both, clear patterns having emerged. Methods of obfuscation that weren't necessarily aimed at trying to impede an investigation, but were rather steeped in self-preservation.

A lens for viewing the world that made true introspection almost impossible.

A stance meaning that while he could ask individuals if they had any obvious personal enemies and expect an accurate answer, anything beyond that was risky at best. Questions imploring them to delve into the other aspects of their life or to consider stuff below the surface that many were simply incapable of, unable to see the ripple effects of prior actions.

Others they may have harmed, even without intent.

Human nature, Reed able to admit that he would probably react the same way.

Basic psychology, meaning that despite Dean Morgan claiming he had no enemies, could think of no reason why someone would come for him, Reed could not just leave it at that. Not when they were seated in a temple to his past life, the excess of praise heaped upon him no doubt coming at the expense of at least a few over the years.

Especially given the very specific term that was chosen to be inscribed across his forehead. A word that could be ascribed to an infinite number of things, be it companies forced to fold or opposing leaders made to resign or even his own personnel let go in the course of corporate machinations.

A host of reasons that might not register with Morgan in any meaningful way, but quite obviously had with someone else.

Things far more likely to cause someone to track him down and brand him forever than a disgruntled former spouse two years after the fact. Or a waiter he might have stiffed after sitting at his table watching the game for hours.

Or any of a host of other common interactions that might have gone sour.

A fine line that Reed had to be careful didn't lead him into fixating on the man's work, though for the time being, it did seem like the obvious frontrunner. The basis for Morgan's relationship with Cowan, and the very reason Reed and Billie had been called in the first place.

Upon sharing with the man that no matter how certain he might be that the attack on him could in no way be attributed to his work they still needed to follow up, the humiliation that had only just begun to wane came rushing back. A visible wave that swept over Morgan, his fears magnified many times over by the concern that his successor would become privy to what took place.

A reaction that seemed extreme in the moment, though now that Reed and Billie sat across from the current Chief Executive Officer of Buckeye Care, made infinitely more sense. A woman who had had her secretary do everything she could upon their arrival to brush them aside, letting it be known that she had a company to run and no time to afford employees of the past.

A term she had gone out of her way to use again upon finally giving Reed and Billie a few minutes, the disdain she felt for Morgan quite palpable.

Distaste that seemed to extend now to Reed and Billie by proxy, the woman unable to maintain eye contact for more than a moment before forcing herself to look away.

"Do I even want to know what that old bastard has his nuts in a twist about this time?" Susan Cartwright asked, showing the least bit of concern for professionalism, despite her title. A dismissive question matching her body language as she sat in a reclining leather captain's chair across the conference room table from them.

A seating arrangement – and meeting location – that was not lost on Reed, very much getting the impression that she did not want Billie anywhere near her or her office.

An extension of whatever trepidation there might have been at Holman Brothers earlier or a fear of dogs or something else entirely Reed wasn't sure, knowing only that they were on the clock, to be granted not a nanosecond more than was absolutely necessary.

"This time?" Reed asked, seizing on her question and parroting back the last two words.

A question that caused Cartwright to look his way, fixing her gaze on him for a moment, before exhaling slowly. "I take it you don't really know Dean, do you?"

"Met him for the first time last night," Reed replied.

"Lucky you," Cartwright replied, leveling green eyes on him. Matching emeralds that were framed by red curls and burgundy lips, only a few smile lines to be seen, despite appearing to be every bit of fifty.

Creases that would get no deeper during the course of the meeting, her demeanor making it clear that the chances of her cracking a grin in their presence were nonexistent.

Folding her right leg over her left without once looking away, Cartwright continued, "I'm sure to the stockholders or his friends around town – fellow titans of business, politicians he could trade favors with, which is probably why you're here now – he's a hell of a guy. The stuff of legend even, making a lot of money for a lot of people, and giving even more away to others."

Twisting her chin an inch to the side, she added, "Son of a bitch knew how to play the game, I'll give him that."

Even while keeping his features neutral, Reed couldn't help but think back to the other office he and Billie were in just a couple of hours before. A veritable mecca to all things Morgan, erected without hesitation or bashfulness in the slightest.

Hubris that had no doubt been cultivated throughout his career, it not hard to imagine at least some of what Cartwright was alluding to being true.

Fact, mixed with more than a healthy dollop of personal acrimony.

"But you saw a different side of him?" Reed asked.

Snorting derisively, Cartwright looked away for the first time since sitting down. Glancing to the bank of windows lining the far wall, the penetrating glow of midday reflecting from the tabletop between them, she said, "You could say that."

Not wanting to press again, Reed instead went to the interrogator's best friend. A tactic that worked exceedingly well during interviews with most people, achieving almost a perfect score with individuals such as Cartwright.

Those with an obvious story they wanted to tell, suffering from the need to drag things out in getting there.

Performative measures that Reed afforded the woman, watching her stare at some indeterminate point in the distance for the better part of a minute before eventually pulling her focus back his way.

"Sexist pig didn't want me in this seat," Cartwright eventually spat out. "Always claimed it wasn't about my gender, that he just didn't think I was the best candidate, but we both knew that was bullshit.

"He was pissed the board didn't take his recommendation for successor, and he did everything in his power to submarine my appointment."

If Reed didn't know better, he could almost be talked into believing that the simmering hostility across from him could be responsible for what happened to Morgan. Vitriol there was no attempt to hide, her eyes blazing as she stared back at him.

"Why didn't the board take his recommendation?" Reed asked.

"Some of the members didn't like how he had handled things during his last couple of years on the job," Cartwright replied. "Thought it best to take things in a different direction, bring in some new blood."

Once more, Reed chose to remain silent.

Quiet that lasted but a few moments before Cartwright sniffed, either nostril drawing up slightly before settling back into place.

"And since we both know what your next question is going to be, the most obvious example would be his decision to lay off nearly a thousand employees right before announcing that the upcoming year would be his last."

Chapter Twenty

Barely ten minutes after leaving them outside of the Buckeye Care conference room, Susan Cartwright made good on her word, a ping on Reed's phone letting him know that an email had arrived. A message that matched her demeanor throughout their entire encounter, only a single line of text preceding an attached Excel worksheet.

The requested information, per our conversation.

A total of six words, all dripping with disdain, not so much as a closing or even a standard email signature at the end. Palpable hatred for being drawn into something simply because of her position on behalf of the man who fought so hard to keep her from it.

An acrimony for the entire affair Reed could not pretend he wouldn't harbor as well if in her spot, his limited interaction with Morgan and the edifice he had constructed unto himself more than enough to prove how difficult he probably was to work with, even if all he had as yet encountered was a fractured facsimile of the man.

A concession that still didn't mean Reed wasn't resentful of the fact that he and Billie were the ones receiving Cartwright's ire instead of the person it was actually meant for.

Having pulled over into a neighborhood park not far from the Buckeye Care office to give Billie water and allow her time to relieve herself, Reed drew the spreadsheet up on his phone. Leaning against the side of his sedan, he swiped sideways through the information, riffling through the various columns that were included. Everything from job title to future contact information that he glanced through briefly before going back to the start and scrolling the same list vertically.

A check that revealed more than seven hundred and eighty names, not quite as high as Cartwright had intimated, but still plenty who might be harboring a grudge at the man responsible for terminating their employment.

Flicking his gaze up from the screen, Reed watched as Billie finished what she needed to and began to work her way across the grounds. Assuming her usual stance, her body was bent forward, her nose just a few inches above the grass.

Optimal positioning for her to inspect the assorted smells of whatever or whoever might have been through in the past, chronicling each one in her mind. A task honed through centuries of evolution, the animal resembling a black wolf falling to it without glancing to him or the small handful of people openly ogling her from the far side of the park.

A thin early afternoon crowd comprised mostly of mothers and small children either just picked up from school or not yet old enough to start. Young ones who rose no higher than Reed's stomach, festooned in puffy jackets and hats of bright colors.

Winter gear that was probably pulled from shelves and closets just weeks prior, meant to serve as an integral part of their wardrobe for the next several months.

Outward chill that Billie was oblivious to as she paced across the open swath of grass.

Another of her inherited traits, the thick fur enshrouding her far better protection from the elements than any parka could ever be.

One corner of his mouth curling upward in a grin, Reed left his partner to her task. Lowering his attention back to the phone, he cleared away the spreadsheet, replacing it with his address book. Finding what he was looking for, he hit send, barely getting the phone to his ear before a familiar voice answered in the same way as nearly every time they spoke.

A colloquial greeting employed on all but those moments when they were deep in the throes of a case, neither wanting to expend the time for greetings.

A status Reed couldn't help but think would soon apply here as well, though hadn't quite come to pass just yet.

"Dude," Derek Chamberlain – or Deke, as he preferred to be known by all but his most hated adversaries – answered. "How's the wheel?"

Feeling the other corner of his mouth crease back, Reed raised his gaze again, tracking his partner as she made her way across the lawn. A silhouette immersed in some invisible hunt, even as a few of the children on the far side ventured a few steps closer.

Initial fears pushed aside in the name of curiosity as to what she might be in search of.

"You sound like Serena."

To those who put too much stock in the plain white t-shirts or calf-length socks Deke wore, took in the plume of hair extended from his head like palm fronds, or even heard that after graduating from college he returned back to the basement of his grandmother's house where he grew up, they would think he was a classic case of arrested development.

The proverbial millennial who refused to grow up or move out.

Easy barbs that they might grab and fling his way, just as Reed had on occasion during their first few years of knowing each other. Stilted interaction that Reed was still not proud of, wishing only that he had come to see the truth while Riley – Deke's friend and neighbor going back to their freshman year at Ohio State, and the reason Reed ever met him at all – was still with them.

That truth being that the basement where Deke spent most of his time wasn't a child's playhouse, but a subterranean office that served as the epicenter for one of the top cyber security experts alive. A site that conducted work all over the globe and generated more money than a fair chunk of the suburb where it was located combined.

A place chosen not for fear of moving on, but out of loyalty to the woman who raised him, wanting to keep her safe and comfortable as she slipped further into the throes of dementia.

A host of realizations Reed had arrived at during the course of their continued work together after Riley's passing, none of them surprising him more than the fact that once he had gotten out of his own way, he and Deke had actually been able to become friends themselves as well.

"I'm taking that as a compliment," Deke answered.

"Not sure it was one," Reed said, the faint smile growing a bit larger, "but the leg's getting there. Thanks for asking."

"Of course," Deke replied. "And the lovely Miss Gipson?"

"Also, good," Reed answered, eschewing for the time being something that Serena had brought up the night before. An off-handed mention of her finishing her schooling at the end of the semester, with her time at the cancer center ending soon thereafter.

A topic that she pushed no further, but Reed had the distinct impression was being set up to be discussed again in the near future.

"And your grandma?" Reed asked.

"Great!" Deke said, practically yelling the word in reply. "As you know, there were a few rough spots over the summer, but she's really settled into a groove this fall. Keeps going on and on about how much she loves the new oven, can't believe you came over here on an injured leg to help us get it in."

"Happy to help," Reed said, "though I would appreciate it if you don't mention the part about doing it on an injured leg to Serena next time you see her."

"Done and done," Deke replied. "Speaking of which, I'm guessing this unexpected contact is in the name of needing something done?"

"It is," Reed said, launching right into a quick overview of the case that they had been handed barely eighteen hours earlier. A truncated stretch that felt like it should be so much longer, a handful of things already done, the reward but a small bit of tangible information to work with.

Beginning with the summons to the governor's home, Reed ran Deke through everything up to that point. An overview that was punctuated with multiple sharp inhalations, though Deke refrained from commenting in any way until complete.

And even then, only after taking a few extra moments to stew on what Reed had just shared. Time that Reed guessed was spent trying to form a mental image of Morgan's mangled features, even if he would never ask to see an actual photo.

Sensibilities that were much more attuned to facing tough cases through a computer screen, as opposed to actual hands-on interaction.

"Damn," Deke eventually muttered, the sound just barely audible. "That man must have pissed somebody off to do something like that."

Recalling the man sitting in front of the fire the night before and the myriad injuries sustained, Reed couldn't help but nod.

"You have no idea."

"You think it might be one of the people on that list?" Deke asked. "A former employee with a major ax to grind?"

"Not sure," Reed said. "I want to say no, that the chasm between what he did and what they did is too big, but you never know."

"Ain't that the truth," Deke replied.

"Do you think you could take a look, just the same?" Reed asked. A question interrupted in the middle by the sound of an incoming call. An audible click that caused him to pull the phone away and glance to the screen, the name of the man they'd started the day with splashed across it.

Contact that could not be good, the reasons Captain Grimes would be reaching out again already all decidedly negative in nature.

"Will do," Deke replied. "And I heard that, so I'll let you get it. When I know something, you will too."

"Appreciate it," Reed said, cutting the call with Deke and accepting the incoming line. A quick transition that opened with him saying, simply, "Captain."

"Detective," Grimes replied, his tone confirming what Reed suspected just moments before.

"Please tell me this is just a perfunctory call to let me know that the governor is already pressing us for time."

Snorting softly, Grimes replied, "If only."

"There's been another one?"

"There has been another one."

Chapter Twenty-One

The Tall Boy awoke in pain, both physically and mentally.

The former, he was used to. Aches and pains going back to when he was still a pre-teen, starting the growth spurts that would mark his teenage years. Jumps of three-to-five inches at a time that took him from standing the exact same height as his twin brother to towering over him.

A height discrepancy that would end up being greater than a foot, exacerbating the growing tension that was already starting to become obvious. Underlying animosity that The Angel rarely tried to hide, taking their differences in demeanor as a personal slight.

In his eyes, The Tall Boy was soft. An affront far worse than any other, that could eventually be overcome if The Angel pushed hard enough. Was mean enough.

Demanded more at all times.

A second paternal figure that was never asked for nor wanted, taking up a callous approach that bordered on abuse, no matter how many times he tried to call it tough love. Brutal treatment that became even worse after The Tall Boy stretched to such a stature, The Angel often commenting that his size was wasted on him.

A gift he was not deserving of, no matter how hard The Tall Boy tried to put it to good use.

Endless nights on the driveway clanging basketballs off the old iron hoop nailed directly into the side of the garage. Even more inside dusty gyms once he got old enough, beating his body into submission trying to prove his worth.

Pounding that left him with the joints of a man decades older, each morning an effort to make it out of bed and directly into the shower. Stumbling steps using furniture arranged in a very specific manner as supports, allowing him to fall sideways beneath the hot water.

Absorbed impact from jumps too many to count, added to by the other assorted problems that so many of lesser heights always failed to consider. Everyday actions like trying to get into cars or ducking through stairwells or even folding himself into a basic airplane seat.

Issues that left their mark, that part of things The Tall Boy was used to. A daily rite that would only get worse with age he knew, having long since made peace with it.

The part he didn't wake up anticipating was the mental strain that he felt. Tension that began with the reappearance of The Angel in their lives the better part of a year before. A slow reintegration that The Tall Boy had tried to bring about in doses, fully aware that his brother blamed him for what had happened and wanting no part of being completely immersed in the man's presence.

Arm's length interaction that had worked well enough for a while, until extenuating circumstances no longer allowed. A sudden thrusting together of them and their sister all three, brought back into the same home where they had spent the better part of their lives together.

A house rife with existing roles and lingering wounds, left for years to fester. Strained relations that soon rose back to the fore, kept at bay only by the task they had been given six months before.

A goal to focus on rather than each other, now serving as the source of the remaining mental anguish The Tall Boy was under. Concern not for what they were doing – that much being the only part that felt right, especially after so long – but for the manner in which it was being conducted.

The speed with which the attacks were being carried out.

The varied approaches and assorted locations where they were occurring.

Opportunities aplenty for things to become unraveled. Possibilities for mistakes to be made. For one of them to be nabbed before what they hoped to accomplish could be completed.

Stretched out on the same mattress that he had slept on throughout his teenage years, the extra-long dimensions still no match for his length, The Tall Boy rested with his heels hanging just over the edge. Blankets drawn up to mid-shin, he left his feet bare, the cool air from the window cracked open beside him nipping at his exposed toes and ankles.

A trick he picked up during college, using the elements as overnight ice bags.

His fingers laced behind his head, The Tall Boy stared up at the pale glow of late morning striping the ceiling above him. A pattern of light and shadow that he let blur into a mosaic, his thoughts entrenched in the events of the night before.

The feel of the door beneath his knuckles as he knocked. The echo of it reverberating through the quiet house. The pounding of the man's footsteps as he ran toward it, summoned from his sleep.

The start of a sequence that The Tall Boy had been through a dozen times already, scrutinizing each aspect of it. Constant questioning as to whether or not they were right to do things in the man's garage.

If the desire of his siblings to violate the man's home was the smartest of decisions.

Questions he was still in the midst of, interrupted by the faint sound of tapping against the wooden frame of his door. A sound just loud enough to invade his thoughts, causing him to blink himself back into the moment before sliding his gaze from the ceiling to the far side of the room.

A relocation of focus, ending on his sister standing in the doorway. Her light brown hair swept up into a bandana, she stood in a pair of boxers and one of his old oversized t-shirts, the caustic smell of rubbing alcohol engulfing her.

"You up?" The Artist asked, taking a single step inside the room, but coming no closer.

"Getting there," The Tall Boy answered. "What's wrong?"

"It's almost time to start getting ready. We've got another big night ahead."

Chapter Twenty-Two

When Reed asked Captain Grimes to put a flag in the system that morning, it was supposed to be more of a preventative measure. A way to ensure nothing slipped by undetected while he was working the Morgan case, the odds of something so rare that Earl nor any of the officers in the 8th had even heard of such a thing happening twice in consecutive days almost unfathomable.

An occurrence that now meant they were not just dealing with a random event, but a serial attacker. Someone with a point to make, unlikely to stop unless forced to.

A viewpoint he shared with Chief Brandt as he tore west across I-70 toward the town of Springfield, site of the most recent attack. Not wanting to attract the extra attention of running with lights or siren, he nudged the gas a full fifteen miles above the posted speed limit, taking advantage of the fact that the flow of afternoon traffic out of the city had not yet gotten too thick.

Clasping the steering wheel in both hands, he fought back the host of random thoughts and notions that flashed through his mind, forcing himself to wait until he got to Springfield and got more information before drawing any sorts of conclusions.

An internal debate Billie seemed to pick up, monitoring his physiological cues as she paced in the backseat, a dark shadow moving across the rearview mirror.

"When you say serial, I take it the tattoo was similar?" Brandt asked.

"GREED," Reed said, relaying the only concrete piece of information he had. Not a victim name or race or even gender, all he knew being that someone had been attacked with a tattoo gun.

Again.

A second word it was impossible not to now identify as part of the fabled seven deadly sins. Motivations so strong there was even once a movie made with the same title, seven different victims each suffering particularly gruesome outcomes, all attributed to one of the sins.

"Definitely seems connected," Brandt agreed. "Would also seem-"

"That they're planning five more of these," Reed finished, knowing exactly where she was going with it.

Accepting the information in silence, she took the better part of a full minute to stew on it. A thought process that ultimately ended with her muttering, "Shit."

Bobbing his head in agreement, even without her there to see it, Reed said, "That was my thought, too. Why I'm calling you now. I know Cowan wanted this thing wrapped up within the hour..."

"But this just got a hell of a lot bigger."

"In every way," Reed agreed.

Again, Brandt fell silent. Another minute to consider what was just said and the full meaning behind it.

An expansion not just in the number of cases they now had, but the geographic spread as well, Springfield a full forty-five miles from the greater Columbus area. Likely myriad other factors too that would have to be considered moving forward, altering things tremendously.

"He's going to love that," Brandt muttered, not specifying who the *he* she was referring to was, even as Reed fully understood it to be Cowan.

What had started as a simple favor for a donor, an attempt to run interference, have an investigation conducted without media attention, was already growing to a point that far exceeded what any of them foresaw the night before.

Threatened to grow much larger in the days ahead if Reed and Billie couldn't connect the dots between Morgan and Springfield quickly.

"And since he was already so good about giving us the time we need anyway," Reed added.

"Right," Brandt muttered, palpable disdain dripping from the single word.

A sentiment Reed let linger for a moment, flicking his gaze to the green signage posted along the side of the road. A standard rectangle with the next three cities listed in order of distance, Springfield sitting at the top, just under ten miles out from where they were.

"Normally, I'd say just let him stew," Reed said, "but I'm guessing that won't work this time."

"Definitely not."

Exhaling slowly, letting it push his shoulders back into the seat, Reed let a handful of different retorts roll through his mind. Sharp jabs about how things had been handled thus far. Barbs as to how much harder what they were trying to do was when working under Cowan's onerous strictures.

Points that he knew he didn't need to say aloud, the chief making it clear she was in total agreement.

"Any time you can buy us on this would be greatly appreciated."

"I'll do what I can," Brandt replied. "Some good news wouldn't hurt, though."

Dropping the turn signal, Reed nudged the sedan from the center lane over to the right. A preemptive move, done in anticipation of their exit fast approaching.

"Captain Grimes has already had Springfield PD pull down the report," Reed said. "They know we're on our way and have agreed to sit on it until we have a chance to look at things."

"That's a start," Brandt said. "Anything on Morgan?"

"We got a video from Holman Brothers which lays out pretty well how it all went down, though it doesn't provide a clean look at our attacker or even how they got there. Seems they knew where the cameras were and how to avoid them."

Letting that sit for a moment, Reed continued, "Sat down with Morgan himself again earlier. Man swears he doesn't have an enemy in the world, has never hurt a fly, but his successor at Buckeye Care painted a pretty different picture."

"How different?" Brandt asked.

"One of his last acts as CEO was to lay off close to eight hundred people. Deke is combing the list now to see if anything jumps out."

Snorting in reply, Brandt said, "Guess that must have slipped his mind when you talked to him earlier, huh?"

"Must have," Reed said, flipping his turn signal up while lifting his foot from the gas, preparing to exit from the freeway. "Shocking, huh?"

"Stunning."

Chapter Twenty-Three

Reed didn't need the automaton serving as announcer on his GPS to direct him over the last half mile or so. A stretch of flat ground with mostly farmland on either side, only a thicket of woods breaking up the sightline, abutting a string of houses sitting just off the road along the right.

A handful in total of similar size and shape, all made of brick, a single story in height.

Structures that were virtually indistinguishable from one another, with the obvious exception of the half dozen cruisers clustered in front of the last house in the row. Vehicles filling the driveway and scattered across the front lawn, whatever little bit of aid they might have offered by pulling down the case file from the online system completely mitigated by the display they were putting on now.

A visual show of force that would be impossible to ignore by the neighbors or anybody driving past, word of mouth no doubt having sent news of something happening across much of the area.

Stories thin on facts but rife with speculation, bound to draw in more curiosity. Another obstacle for them to contend with, to say nothing of the animosity it would likely draw down from the governor's office.

"Shit," Reed muttered, the single expletive enough to pull Billie's muzzle up through the front seats. A vantage allowing her to see out of the front windshield, her breath warm on the back of his wrist as they coasted the last fifty yards and turned into the driveway.

Making it no further than a couple of feet before running out of space, Reed angled the sedan to the side, easing onto the soft grass of the lawn. An entry that managed to draw over the interest of the quartet of uniformed officers huddled together by the front stoop, all four turning and openly staring as Reed turned off the engine and stepped out, allowing Billie to spill down after him.

Looks that were anything but inviting, the reception reminding Reed of something similar they'd endured down in Waverly on their last case working on behalf of the BCI.

Always the outsiders, guilty until found innocent. A team made to prove their worth at each new stop.

A feeling that had just managed to subside within the walls of the 8th Precinct after transferring over from the 19th when they were plucked away, forced into this new position with the state.

Under the watchful gaze of the group by the front door, Reed circled around to the backseat and drew out the short lead from the rear footwell. Clipping it to the ring nestled between Billie's shoulder blades on the harness she wore, he paused just long enough to pull his own badge from his back pocket, looping it up over his head.

The official uniform whenever approaching officers from a new department, hoping to stymie any initial distrust.

An effect with a middling success rate, this time going down as a win in that it spurred one of the officers to step up the couple of stairs to the front of the house and pop his head inside. A few moments with his top half out of view before he reemerged, followed in order by a man in slacks and a tie.

Sleeves rolled to mid-forearm and sandy brown hair slightly askew, he looked like someone who had just been slapped in the face with something similar to what Reed and Billie were hit with the night before.

A poor omen, causing Reed's stomach to clench as he and his

partner crossed from the grass onto the concrete walk stretched across the front of the house.

"Detective Mattox?" the man asked, passing between the four officers positioned to either side of the front steps. Men in their twenties and thirties who were split evenly between uniformed and street clothes, every spare body likely called in, regardless if they were on duty or not.

A detail Reed would be sure to omit the next time he spoke to Chief Brandt and she asked for a bit of good news to relay on to the governor.

"Yes, sir," Reed said, meeting the man's outstretched hand. "Reed Mattox, my partner Billie."

Pumping Reed's hand twice, the man went the extra step of glancing to Billie and dipping his chin.

A muted greeting that was likely more habit than anything, though was still more than was received at some other places.

"Tanner Moss," the man said, "Springfield PD. Thanks for getting here so fast."

"Thanks for bringing us in," Reed replied.

"Gladly," Moss said, releasing Reed's hand and taking a step back.

The man hadn't used his rank when introducing himself, though if Reed had to guess based on his age and attire, he would guess him to either be a captain in civilian clothes or a senior detective. Having at least a decade on Reed, his light brown hair had receded multiple inches at either temple and been combed to the side, leaving it hanging at an angle across a trio of forehead wrinkles.

Lines that were matched by creases around his mouth and underscoring his eyes, telltale features of a career spent in law enforcement.

"Captain Grimes said on the phone that this could be part of a string?"

"Normally I would say too soon to tell," Reed replied, "but if this is like what we saw last night, be hard to call it otherwise."

Hooking either end of his mouth down in a frown, Moss nodded. Flicking his gaze to the side, he stared out for a moment, contemplating the response, before turning back to Reed.

Lifting a hand, he motioned to his brow.

A muted question that Reed answered with, "Yeah."

The downturn of Moss's mouth grew more pronounced as he turned toward the door, lifting his right foot onto the first step. "I guess at least this way I don't need to warn you about what you're about to see."

"Nope," Reed agreed, following the man on toward the entrance.

Taking another step, Moss tilted his head to the side, motioning through the open door, and added, "GREED."

Dipping his chin in understanding, Reed said, "We met PRIDE just last night."

Chapter Twenty-Four

The man seated in the living room was fifteen years younger, thirty pounds lighter, and had significantly more pepper than salt in his hair as compared to Dean Morgan. His olive complexion was darker and based on the amount of leg he had bent up beneath him, he was likely six inches or more taller.

Differences that were all superficial, the two things that immediately jumped out making him all but the same as the older man that Reed and Billie first met at the governor's home the previous evening.

The dark ink scrawled across his forehead.

And the look of shock and sorrow gripping his entire being.

Perched on the front edge of an armchair, the man looked like he had just been pulled from bed. Barefooted, he wore only a pair of sweatpants and a white ribbed tank top, a red and black plaid blanket draped across his shoulders.

Elbows braced atop either knee, he flicked his dark eyes up at Reed, the pupils appearing misshapen under the puffy skin marring his brow.

"Matt, these are the detectives from the state we told you about," Tanner Moss said, his tone much softer than when speaking with Reed outside a moment before. "Detectives, this is Matt Seesel."

His mouth open, as if there was more he wanted to say, explanations as to who Seesel was or what they had found already, he pulled up short. Extending a hand before him, he motioned toward the victim, implying that the floor was Reed's.

A gesture that could have been borne of either deference to Reed's position or not wanting to engage with the matter anymore than necessary, the answer likely resting somewhere in the middle.

Circumstances that, at the very least, managed to push aside the usual wariness Reed and Billie were forced to deal with.

Taking a step forward, Reed swept his gaze around the interior of the room. A space that looked like it had been sold or rented furnished, the offerings clean though older, not a single item that wasn't necessary present. A basic sofa-armchair-coffee table configuration, all pointed toward a flatscreen television resting on a simple wooden stand.

Fixtures that were free of personal touches in any way, whether they be candles or books or basic knickknacks.

The sole photographs of any kind resided on a shelf on the inset bookcases framing either side of the TV stand. Framed images of high school basketball teams in red jerseys with the name Redskins emblazoned across them in white.

A mascot Reed imagined no longer existed, given the recent political climate.

At the very least, the jerseys so proudly displaying it.

Resting between the two images was a basketball balanced on a small stand. The words STATE CHAMPS were stamped across it in all capitals, a series of signatures scribbled around it using the same black marker.

Imagery that Reed couldn't help but equate to the block letters now inscribed in Seesel's forehead nearby.

"Mr. Seesel," Reed began, stepping up onto the edge of the loop rug in the center of the room. "My name is Detective Reed Mattox, and this is my K-9 partner Billie. Like he just said, we're from the state, came right over when we got word of what happened."

Flicking his focus up from the spot on the floor where he had previously been staring, Seesel fixed his gaze on Reed. A stare that made the disbelief he harbored obvious. Same for the sweat lining his brow and the twitch of the single muscle in his cheek.

"Yeah?" he asked. "Had to come and see for yourself?"

"Yes," Reed replied. An answer that was clearly not expected, causing Seesel's eyes to widen, even if the puffy skin marring his forehead would allow no other movement. "But not for the reason you think."

Taking another step forward, Reed said, "Last night, my partner and I were called in about another incident involving the same M.O. As part of our investigation, we put out an alert for anything similar in the area, which is why SPD called and asked us over."

The last sentence wasn't an exact telling of how things had gone, though Reed didn't mind fudging the details. Non-essential facts that could be contorted a bit out of appreciation for how Moss and his men had received him and Billie.

A jurisdictional pissing match that hadn't come to pass, enough to constitute a win for local-state relations.

"We needed to come and see if it was connected to our other case, and if so, start processing it as such immediately."

His red eyes still fixed on Reed, Seesel dipped his chin just slightly. A silent bit of acknowledgment, followed by asking, "Is it?"

"Yes."

Remaining completely still, Seesel accepted the information in silence, letting it process before asking, "Somebody else woke up like this? Who?"

"Yes," Reed repeated. An answer to Seesel's first question that would be the only one he provided for a while, not wanting the conversation to focus on what had already happened.

Curiosity about a shared victim that could taint any additional information the man might have to share.

"But before we get to that, let's start with what happened here last night."

Matching Reed's gaze long enough to let it be known that he recognized what had just happened, that he had more questions that they would soon be getting to, he eventually slid his focus to the side. Just as Morgan had the night before, he fixed it on the ground in front of him, resuming the pose he was in when they arrived just moments before.

A point of detachment, wanting to separate himself from what was about to be shared.

Shame, manifesting in the only way it could, given the circumstances.

"Not a lot to tell," Seesel said, his previous tone having receding to little more than a whisper. "I teach phys ed over at Plainfield High and coach the basketball team. Official practice starts next week, so every night from now until then we're holding open gyms.

"Unofficial workouts to get the kids who've been playing football the past three months back into it."

Rotating his gaze over as far as Billie seated on the floor at Reed's side, Seesel continued, "Last night, open gym ran until a little after nine. On the way home, I stopped and got some food, ate it in front of the TV, went to bed around eleven.

"Had barely turned the lights off when I heard a clatter coming from the garage. Stuff banging around. Sounded like one of the shelves I have out there had fallen over or something.

"I was going to leave it until morning, but then I heard someone start knocking."

Moving his stare back to face forward, he said, "Got up to see what the hell was going on, barely stepped foot in the garage when something hit me hard in the ribs. Knocked all my wind out, doubled me over."

The deeper he got into the story, the more his features distorted. Extra helpings of shame, mixed with self-loathing. Ire.

Untold more things all splayed across his features, only nominally less obvious than the letters now imprinted on his skin.

"Felt something stick me in the neck. Next thing I knew, I woke up back in my bed, this shit all across my forehead."

Even after he pulled up there, Reed gave him another few

moments. Time both to add anything extra, and to steady himself after going through the tale for a second or third time.

Retellings that were having a palpable effect on him, just as they likely always would.

A low point in life he would be forced to relive with every new person that looked at him for at least the foreseeable future.

"Outside of that initial punch, was there anything additional done to your torso?" Reed asked.

Without even looking over, Seesel rocked himself back from his knees to sit upright. Grasping the tail of his tank top in either hand, he lifted it to his chest, revealing a ribcage that was already mottled with purple and black splotches.

Early bruises that were significantly worse than what Morgan had sustained, serving as a canvas for the words **COCKY PRICK** scrawled across it in the same magic marker.

A sight that clearly came as a surprise to Moss, the man drawing in a sharp breath by Reed's side. A sound hinting of shock that caused Seesel to snap the shirt back down and resume his previous posture.

Moves laced with resentment, making it clear that whatever else Reed was going to get for the time being had to be quick. A shrinking window, after which they would have to wait until the next day just as they had with Morgan.

Raising his stare, Reed again took in the spread around them. A visual schematic, allowing him to add some context to the narrative just shared.

"Did you see anybody in the garage?"

"No," Seesel muttered. "The light switches are outside the door. I never made it that far."

"What time did you wake up today?"

Again, Seesel's features crinkled. "I don't know, maybe two hours ago? Does it matter?"

Turning his neck so he could peer up at Reed, he continued, "Look, I answered your questions. It's your turn to answer mine.

"Who the hell was the other victim?"

Chapter Twenty-Five

While The Artist and The Tall Boy had both returned back to their rooms on the second story of the old farmhouse where they all grew up, The Angel wasn't about to do such a thing. Of the various reasons why, none were bigger than the fact that as children, he and his brother had been forced to share.

A family that was too large for just three bedrooms even after their father passed, meaning that somebody needed to double up. A pairing that was only natural, he and The Tall Boy having shared space since they were in the womb.

A living arrangement that grew increasingly tedious with each passing day, The Angel asked their mother repeatedly throughout his teenage years to allow him to move into the basement. A quick renovation project that would have been easy enough, shoving everything to one side, leaving him with plenty of space for his meager requirements.

Space for a bed, a television in the corner, a bare rafter above to hang his punching bag.

Requests that were all summarily denied, his mother refusing to touch a single thing on the lower level of the house. An original forebear of what modern society liked to call a man cave, where their father had kept his workbench and an assortment of every known tool on the planet.

A site he would retire to each evening, always tinkering with some small engine or broken electronic. A side job that he took on, putting back together whatever pieces of junk their friends and neighbors would bring by.

A form of supplemental income that the old man always acted like was so important to keeping them afloat, though The Angel always suspected was more about hiding out. An assumption proven at least partially correct years later when finally he was able to venture down and really look into things, finding the mini fridge hidden away in the corner, still stocked with Coors Light that had expired years before.

Refreshments that The Angel himself could have made good use of as a reprieve from having to share a room with The Tall Boy, if only he'd known about it sooner.

Claiming that the basement was the only place where she still felt connected to her late husband, it wasn't until their mother's passing six months prior that The Angel was finally able to move below ground. The very first thing he did after returning home from the hospital, not trusting himself to go anywhere else.

Brimming with sorrow and anger and a host of other things, he knew if he went to a bar, or a public gym, or anywhere that someone might say the wrong thing, it would be a repeat of that night so long before. The instant when he did something stupid and got himself sent away, this time likely to be for good.

An eventuality he could not and would not allow ever again, preferring to see his life end than to ever spend another moment in a cell.

Leaving his siblings to their tears and their prayers and all the other shit that The Angel had given up on years ago despite their mother's nickname for him, he had driven straight home. Popping the lock on the latch to the basement door, he'd gone straight down and rearranged the place in short order.

As good a place as any to direct everything that was hurtling through him, he'd started small, piling items up and moving them to the far side. A process that soon grew into a frenzy, snatching up one item after another and launching them across the room.

With no regard for where things landed or what condition they were in after doing so, he worked until his arms and back burned with lactic acid. His shirt clung to him, shrink wrapped to his skin with sweat. His shoulders and lungs both burned from exertion.

A frenzied burst that left one half of the subterranean space littered with wood and metal carnage. Fractured pieces from long ago, their last bit of usefulness being in allowing him to burn off some of the animosity flowing through him.

The other half of the available space became the bedroom The Angel had always requested. A private sanctum that was more than sufficient for that same small list of items, feeling downright palatial after what he was forced to exist in for the preceding eight years.

Ample floor space for him, and for what would become the epicenter of the charge that the siblings were given at the hospital just days before. A task that they had all longed for for years, always kept from doing so by their mother and her pious nature.

Or so they thought, not realizing until shortly before her passing the truth of it.

That she too harbored the same anger, the same ill will, that they did, her own reluctance spurred only by her desires to one day be welcomed into Heaven.

A final destination she felt was finally within reach, leaving the task of vengeance to the children she knew didn't carry the same compunction. The three of them were much better suited for such a thing, the proof of which was stretched the entire length of the wall in front of The Angel. A collection of every bit of data and research compiled going back since that very day six months before.

Effort that started small, scouring social media and online searches, before quickly expanding outward. Physical reconnaissance and even a few staged in-person encounters.

A total accumulation of information that far surpassed even what The Angel knew about his own siblings these days. Data he had long since committed to memory, though still he found solace in standing before the spread.

Long hours of staring at the faces of their impending targets. Imagining the ways in which they would be taken down.

The looks on their faces when they woke up the next day and peered into the mirror for the first time.

Doing that very thing, his bare arms folded over his torso, The Angel heard the door at the top of the wooden staircase open. Rusted hinges that squealed loudly, followed by the creaking of nails and lumber that were even older rubbing together as someone descended.

An unceremonious soundtrack announcing the arrival of the only person who ever dared venture down while The Angel was home.

"Is it time?" The Angel asked, launching the question before his sister had even come fully into view.

A descent The Artist continued until completely visible before stopping three steps from the bottom, one hand resting on the rail, the other on the exposed beam framing the top of the staircase. "It is."

Flicking his gaze upward, The Angel asked, "He ready?"

"Almost."

"That's not what I meant."

Tapping at the beam overhead twice, The Artist turned and began to head back in the opposite direction. "I know."

Chapter Twenty-Six

Reed and Billie left Matt Seesel in the armchair in the front room, a look of confusion splayed across his features. Genuine befuddlement as he tried to work his way through the series of questions just thrown at him, attempting to place any connection he might have to Dean Morgan or Buckeye Care or even the north side of Columbus.

An expression that was notably better than the shocked repulsion in place when they first arrived, letting it be known that he was awake and coherent, even if his effort did only nominally more to help their investigation.

Added questions atop the pile they already had an hour before, none from either case having a single obvious answer. No clear connection beyond the tattoos and magic marker now splashed across the skin of two people and the pattern they were meant to display.

A worst-case scenario for an investigator, an additional crime scene supposed to make things easier. A basis of comparison, providing for clear contrast from which to draw conclusions.

Not become another seemingly indecipherable case unto itself.

"Down," Reed said, pausing on the edge of the kitchen directly connecting to the back end of the living room. Easily identifiable by the open doorway between them and the transition from carpeting to linoleum, police tape was stretched across at chest height, impeding anybody but law enforcement from entering.

The official entry into the crime scene, being as far as Billie could go for the time being. One of the rare places she wasn't able to join Reed on an investigation, the risk of contamination too high.

Making not a sound in protest, Billie lowered herself to the carpet, the front of her paws mere inches from the metal stripping separating it from the kitchen. Standing by her side, Reed snapped on a pair of latex gloves, waiting as Moss appeared in his periphery.

Positioned perpendicular to Reed, he glanced over to Seesel behind them before muttering, "We found signs of forced entry on the outside door into the garage."

Returning his gaze to Reed, he flicked it over to the wall beside them, a plain wooden door set in the center of a stretch of bare drywall. Access to the garage beyond, made obvious by the wooden key rack hanging beside it, only a single hook currently in use.

Jutting his chin that direction, Moss said, "Best we can tell, once the attacker drew Seesel into the garage, they did most of what they came for out there. After it was done, they carried him right through here and down the back hall to the bedroom.

"Likely left the same way."

Even spoken in a low voice, Moss made sure to use vague terms, omitting words such as *attack* or *tattoo*. Coded speak that Reed understood well, grunting softly in reply as he ran his gaze from the door across the kitchen. A direct path that would certainly be the fastest, there no reason to come into the living room at all.

If what Moss was saying was how it really played out.

"What makes you think it was done out there?" Reed asked.

"Two things," Moss answered. "One, the smell. Two, the place has been swept completely clean."

Again, the answer was far from a full explanation, though Reed grasped what was being relayed. The application of a tattoo – especially one as large and bold as the one now adorning Seesel's face – would require certain things. The ink, at bare minimum, along with some rubbing alcohol for the skin or cleaning solution for the gun used to apply it.

Things that would all have a distinct chemical scent, noticeable even in a garage.

"Is there a broom?" Reed asked.

"There is," Moss said. "We cordoned it off, left it leaning against the wall out there until the crime scene techs could get here."

Bobbing his head twice, Reed slid his focus back to the kitchen before them. "Can I snag a pair of shoe covers from you?"

Seeming to have anticipated the question, Moss fished out a set of paper booties from his pocket. Handing them over, he waited as Reed slipped them on over his running shoes, the massive coverings enveloping his entire feet, held in place by thin bands of elastic.

Once they were in position, Reed crouched under the string of police tape and moved into the kitchen. An open rectangular space paralleling the living room, the entry to the garage on one end, counter space with a refrigerator and oven on the other.

Bisecting the two was a dining room table, the furnishings just as thin as where Reed had started. Spartan décor that hinted Seesel spent very little time there, the faint scents of pizza and takeout Chinese just barely present.

Quick meals to match whatever he picked up the night before.

Young bachelor living, even at an age when such a thing should have started to wane.

Standing just inside the tape, Reed was able to see the full length of the house. A central corridor that stretched from the garage door, through the kitchen and down a hallway ending at the master bedroom on the far end.

A view that was obscured by the wall enclosing the back of the living room earlier, now giving him an even better idea of how things played out.

And, again, bringing along more questions as well.

"How cold is it in the garage?" Reed asked, letting his gaze linger on the hallway before sliding it over to Moss.

Not expecting the question, the man's jaw moved up and down

twice. False starts before finding his voice, replying, "Pretty standard. Not as cold as outside, but much worse than in here. Why?"

Shifting his focus once more, Reed moved on to the garage door standing closed nearby. "Wondering not only why they would bother to bring him inside, but take him all the way back to the bedroom."

The night before, they had scrubbed Dean Morgan's SUV clean. According to Moss, they had swept the garage once they were done with Seesel.

Attention to evidence removal that seemed at odds with tromping the length of the home and back.

A risk that Reed could only surmise meant they were afraid of him freezing out in the garage, but even then, didn't explain carrying him so much further than necessary, tromping through the entire house.

Unless that in itself was the point.

"I don't know," Moss admitted. "The officers who first arrived said they went through the whole house, didn't see any sign of their passing."

Nodding in agreement, Reed said, "No, they wouldn't be that foolish, but from the looks of things, they didn't go the extra step of vacuuming on their way out. Maybe the crime scene crew will be able to pull something. Shoe indents in the carpet or a stray print somewhere."

Positive outcomes that Reed didn't mention were unlikely, though still needed to be examined.

Possible evidence that had already been contaminated by the arriving officers and Seesel himself, sure to raise Earl's ire when he arrived.

"I'll be sure to get with the first on the scene, have them give impressions for comparison," Moss said.

"Appreciate it," Reed replied. "Also, if you could, get someone here to take a blood sample from Seesel. Our first case waited too long to call, had already metabolized whatever they used to sedate him."

"Will do," Moss said. Reaching for his phone, he began to retreat. "You going on back to the bedroom?"

"No," Reed replied. "We'll wait and let our crime scene guys have a first crack at the house and garage."

Not wanting to insult the man who had brought them in and honored their request to pull down the file, Reed left the comment there, omitting any part of pointing out that the last thing the house and garage needed was another set of footprints, his own trip under the tape meant to get a better view, but nothing more.

"Billie and I will see what we can find outside first."

Chapter Twenty-Seven

The last time Reed called Earl Bautista, the man was annoyed. Irritated not about being called on a Sunday night, but about the way in which it had gone down. A direct contact on behalf of the governor with the expectation that he was to drop everything and run directly over because the victim was a personal friend.

A situation in which nobody had perished and there was no known active threat.

More than sufficient grounds for the agitation he was feeling, making no attempt to hide it. A stance Reed was certain in the moment he would share if in the man's position, running the best crime scene crew in the city supposed to be one of the few roles in law enforcement that was beyond bureaucratic intrusion.

This time around, though, Earl was just flat pissed.

Not about being called, but because some enterprising young officers had committed a textbook error, making his job that much harder.

"Please tell me you're shitting me," Earl spat, the words coming out as little more than gravel. Scratchy sounds from deep in his throat, flung out at a volume that was loud enough even for Billie to hear, her ears rising as she moved closer, pressing herself against Reed's leg. "This is you just messing with me after last night?"

Standing out alongside his sedan parked just off the edge of the road, Reed turned back toward the house. A scene that at least appeared a bit more subdued under the cover of darkness, helped considerably by the crowd of vehicles out front having thinned.

Reed's first request from Moss after making a preliminary trip around the house and finding out how many officers had tracked through the crime scene, letting his own frustration surface before walking it back slightly. A suggestion that perhaps there didn't need to be so many people onsite now that any immediate threat was gone and their attention turned to containment and analysis.

"Nope," Reed muttered, his own tone letting it be known that he was right there with Earl. Another party who had been foisted onto a case he wanted no part of, each additional moment seeming to make it worse.

"Good God Almighty," Earl muttered, altering his preferred exclamation of choice slightly, moving from the son directly to the father. An escalation pattern that was expected, if a little more subdued than Reed anticipated, knowing that at any moment a string of expletives could be unleashed.

A tirade that would be lurking for the foreseeable future, Moss and his men well served to stay hidden from sight once the large crime scene crew leader arrived.

"We have signs of forced entry on the door into the garage, which is where they tattooed the victim," Reed said. "We also have a broom they may or may not have used to sweep up when they were done.

"First real evidence of their presence aside from the victims themselves. I'm going to let Billie take a crack at it, see if we can't see where else they went.

"Take your time."

Still muttering from the initial information Reed imparted, Earl eventually managed, "I can't promise how soon it'll be. Coby and Janice are out on a B&E, I'm finishing up some testing for Homicide in Worthington.

"Could be a few hours before I'm over there, and who knows what the scene will look like by then."

Turning his gaze to the side, Reed studied the pair of officers still posted out front. Onsite guards Moss had assigned until further notice, each doing their best to hide the furtive glances they were tossing his way.

"We'll stick around until you get here. Do what we can to keep it clear."

Mumbling something too low to make out, Earl ended the call. Words that likely weren't meant for Reed anyway, merely letting out more of the bottled hostility before getting back to his testing.

Acrimony for the officers, and the governor, and probably even Reed for continuing to call and give him extra assignments.

"Come on, girl," Reed said, stowing the phone back into his rear pocket with one hand while slapping at the leg of his jeans with the other. A non-verbal command that drew Billie up from her haunches, falling in beside Reed as they tracked parallel to the road before turning and following the driveway up to the garage.

Not bothering with the lone wide door stretched across the width of it, they worked their way on around to the side, headed for the same entrance the attackers used the night before. A plain metal door painted white, easily visible against the dark brick of the house.

Resting above a small square of concrete, it seemed to float in the waning light of late afternoon, the lone sign of life on the entire end of the house.

Snapping on a pair of gloves from the evidence kit in the trunk of his sedan, Reed approached the door from the side. Careful to avoid any spots of mud or especially thick grass that might be housing a foot-print, he stopped just short of the concrete square.

Twisting the knob on the door, he cracked it open a couple of inches and snaked a hand inside. A blind search that ended with his fingertips grazing the handle of the broom that was propped against the wall beside it.

Placement Moss had mentioned earlier, adding to the working theory that the attackers had swept on their way out, leaving it at the last possible location before making their exit.

"Alright, girl," Reed said, clasping the top of the broom and drawing it through the small opening. A standard wooden shaft with a plume of straw encased in a steel band, held tight by canvas stitching.

The type of thing that still hung in his parents' garage but was becoming more of a rarity, replaced by plastic and synthetic fibers.

Organic matter that would far better hold a scent.

One of just a few tiny things to go in their favor over the last day.

"I know this won't be easy, but just do your best," Reed said, offering the broom out to his partner. A sample that was much larger than she was used to, taking her a few extra moments to assess.

Deep, probing inhalations along the full length of it. Repeated breaths, drawing in the various scents, imprinting it in her mind.

Chapter Twenty-Eight

The officer looked barely old enough to have enrolled in the police academy. A recruit so young Reed was reminded of a favorite expression of his late partner, who used to refer to those just months on the job as still having spots.

An allusion to baby deer she had picked up in a James Bond movie somewhere, always delivering the line with a faux British accent. Effort that was woefully off the mark, though did manage without fail to elicit a smile from Reed.

An expression that he had to beat back now as he heard the line in his head, staring at the young man across from him. One of the pair that Moss had left behind to guard the entrance to Seesel's house, even younger up close than he appeared when Reed was inspecting them from the road.

The first to volunteer when Reed had popped around the side of the garage and asked for someone to come help him, he stood shifting his weight slowly from one foot to the other. Anticipatory energy leaving him nearly unable to stand still as he waited for instructions.

"Looks like this spot here was used for surveillance," Reed said, swinging his flashlight to the base of an elm tree a few feet away. A towering specimen was the better part of a century in age, with a trunk well over a foot in diameter.

The centerpiece of the thicket Reed had inspected while letting Billie assess the offered broom from the garage. The one tree that stood out even from afar, providing an optimal vantage for someone to lean against, almost completely hidden behind the saplings and pine boughs pushing up on either side. A spot that was largely void of dying leaves, the ground underfoot instead padded with a thick layer of needles.

Soundproofing for footsteps coming and going.

Marked out with a trio of crime scene indicators, Reed didn't go the extra step of telling the officer not to tromp through it. Information he hoped he didn't need to share, the young recruit having more sense than his cohorts inside the house earlier.

Swinging the flashlight back over before him, Reed held up a plastic bag. Pinched between his thumb and forefinger, the small Ziploc was largely empty, only a single item tucked deep in the recesses of it.

A small tangle of thread and lint, likely dropped when whoever was doing surveillance pulled a hand from a coat or jeans pocket.

A nominal find, but more than enough for Billie to catch a clean scent. A better sample for her to work from, rather than trying to unravel the competing smells on the broom. The attacker and Seesel and whoever else, whether they be a property owner or prior tenant or even a friend or family member who might have used it to sweep at some point.

The rare instance when Billie's heightened abilities were actually a detriment, making it difficult for her to pick out exactly which scent she was supposed to focus on.

A slow and meandering process that had still landed them in the grove of trees, the hope being that with the newest find, they would be able to pick up a clear heading. A way to determine how the attacker approached, as well as potentially some footprints or tires tracks from wherever they parked.

Anything more than that would be welcomed but was unlikely, the level of care used at the two scenes thus far nothing short of meticulous.

"I found this on the ground near the base," Reed continued. "It had to have come from our attacker, so we're going to let Billie track them out, see what we can find."

Aiming the flashlight at the ground between them, the device gave off enough glow for Reed to see the young man nod. A guy in full black uniform and coat, with blonde hair buzzed short and splashes of red on his cheeks from the chilly early evening air who had introduced himself as Clint Bryan.

"Now, I can do it alone, but with it getting dark, it's easier with two of us. I watch her, you keep an eye on everything around us. Got it?"

"Got it," Bryan replied. "Lights?"

"Whatever you need," Reed answered, not bothering to add that once Billie got locked on, there was very little in the world that could distract her.

A working dog, performing what thousands of years of evolution had honed her to do.

Leaving it at that, Reed lowered himself into a crouch. Grasping the top of the evidence bag in both hands, he pulled apart the press seal across the top. Holding the flaps open wide, he extended them before him, waiting as his partner leaned forward and pushed her nose deep inside.

Putting nearly her entire muzzle into the bag, she drew in more than a dozen breaths in order. Unlike the long, probing sniffs from earlier, she used short, choppy inhalations that Reed had likened to hyperventilating the first time he heard it.

Repeated breaths meant to really drive home the scent, each successive one cementing it deeper in her mind, locking it there for as long as necessary.

A process that took but a few moments before she stepped back and looked up at it him expectantly, ready to be on the move again.

"Alright," Reed said. "Get ready to run."

Sealing the top of the bag closed, he tucked it into the front pocket of his zip-up hoodie, stowing it away in case it was needed again in the near future.

"Search!"

Already warmed up from the first hunt, Billie took off at a trot. Able to snatch the fresh scent up from the bed of pine needles as plainly as if it was floating in the air, she cut a path right through the back of the thicket.

A winding route that wrapped around a handful of pine trees, lasting for more than fifteen yards before she was able to burst out the other side. An emergence into the grassy meadow surrounding it, allowing her to increase her pace again.

A rise that pushed her up to a full jog, causing Reed and Bryan to do the same at her back. Two grown men moving at a clip just shy of running, fighting to keep up with Billie's darkened silhouette.

For more than half a mile, the three moved in a misshapen triangle. An arrowhead led by Billie and the sound of her inhalations, followed by Reed and Bryan both fighting to catch their breath behind her.

Deep rasps of the icy air that burned their throats and lungs.

Pain that extended down into Reed's leg, felt in the scars on either side of his calf with each step over the uneven ground. Repeated jabs that caused his teeth to clench as he kept pace with his partner, watching her every move.

Continuous oversight that lasted the better part of ten minutes before finally, mercifully, coming to a halt. An impromptu jaunt through the wintry countryside, ending along a faint two-track access lane carved through the thick grass.

Twin paths that had been recently used, the backsides of bent blades showing up plainly under the glow of Reed's flashlight.

Chapter Twenty-Nine

Any hint of the sun was long since departed. A total absence of light, rendering the entire sky nothing more than a dark drop cloth. A solid black background, only a few flecks of stars and the bright orbs of oncoming traffic breaking up the visual beyond the immediate scope of the front headlamps of Reed's sedan.

Weeknight traffic well beyond any towns or cities and hours past what would be considered rush hour anyway.

A stretch of highway that was nearly desolate, leaving Reed alone with his partner and his thoughts, working his way through all that the last few hours had presented. An unexpected detour that he had taken in the hope of it providing guidance to the case he was already working, only to have it be an entirely new thing unto itself.

A second instance that wasn't quite as perfect as the first, though still Reed held little hope that their efforts there tonight would render much.

A shoe size or tire tread, perhaps, though nothing concrete. Likely no fingerprints or stray fibers or anything that might render a suspect.

Nothing from Seesel as to who might do such a thing or why. No connection to Dean Morgan, or even the greater Columbus area.

Not a clue how a high school teacher and coach could ever be connected to something warranting GREED tattooed across his forehead.

His left wrist draped across the top of the steering wheel, Reed slid his gaze from the road before him. A straight stretch of highway headed east back toward Columbus, without even the occasional hill to break up the sight lines.

As good a spot as any for him to reach into the middle console, grabbing up his cellphone. Thumbing it to life, he scrolled through his recent call log, found the most recent unsaved number, and hit send.

Flipping it to speaker, he dropped it down atop his thigh, the sound of the ringtone pulsating through the car. The first noise of any kind since they left Seesel's house earlier, the sudden intrusion drawing Billie upright in the backseat.

An interruption to a well-earned bit of rest after two long days. A stretch that began with training on the east side, and had just culminated with two different searches across the land surrounding Seesel's home.

Appearing as dark spires extended above the scope of the rearview mirror, a pair of moist discs were framed perfectly therein.

A sight Reed was still taking in when after three rings the call was picked up, Dean Morgan on the other end.

"Hello?"

"Mr. Morgan, this is Reed Mattox. My partner and I are on the road now and were hoping to ask you a few questions, if you don't mind."

After what had taken place a couple of nights before, Reed would be surprised if the man had left the sanctuary of his house, the only possible relocation being to return to Governor Cowan's place.

A move he couldn't picture someone with an entire room erected as a personal monument making, doing so the first night acceptable in the face of overwhelming shock, but a return on the second night being a sign of weakness.

The kind of thing anyone who fashioned themselves as a titan of business would never allow.

"By all means," Morgan replied. "Have there been any new developments?"

"There have," Reed replied, "though likely not of the kind you are thinking or wanting to hear."

Pushing straight forward before Morgan could pose any more questions, Reed launched into a quick overview of the call they'd received earlier and how they had spent the afternoon. A quick telling of things that elicited a handful of noises – sharp inhalations, small groans – in all the appropriate places, but prompted no actual words of any kind.

Nothing at all until Reed was finished and asked, "First and foremost, does the name Matt Seesel mean anything to you?"

"Seesel?"

"Yes. S-E-E-S-E-L," Reed added, spelling out the unusual last name in hopes that it might trigger something.

A moniker Reed had heard in other forms, but never that particular formation. An odd spelling that might resonate as Morgan tried to place it.

"No," Morgan replied after several moments. Exhaling slowly, he added, "But I'll go back through my contacts and files this evening. Maybe he was attached to a project or something without our paths crossing."

The same thought had already occurred to Reed, one of the first things he did after speaking with Seesel being to check the list sent over by Susan Cartwright earlier. A quick scan that didn't reveal Matt's name, nor any other Seesels.

Information Reed didn't attempt to share just yet, not wanting to dissuade anything Morgan might delve into later.

"Please do," Reed said. Flicking his gaze to a semi truck speeding past him on the left, he continued, "How about Springfield? Do you have any connection to the town? Maybe own property or do business there?"

"Springfield?" Morgan asked. Doing just as he had with Seesel's name, he began by repeating it, this time the single word threaded with confusion. Perhaps, even a bit of surprise. "You mean, like over near Dayton?"

"I do," Reed replied. "Ring any bells?"

Muttering softly to himself, Morgan rolled around the question.

Semi-internal dialogue that lasted several moments, ending with him replying, "No. Not at all. Best I can recall, I don't think I've been to Springfield, except to drive through it on my way to Indianapolis for Buckeye games a few times."

Having expected as much, Reed considered shifting topics. A renewed approach, coming back to the matter of his prior work history that they had discussed earlier.

Questions regarding the massive layoff he had been responsible for that had somehow failed to register with him when they spoke before.

Inquiries he decided to let wait. Asks that would be better served after he had had more time to sit and work through everything new that the day had presented, and Morgan had been given a bit more time and space since the incident.

Needed distance to ensure when they did speak, he didn't resort to feigned ignorance or righteous indignation, both much easier to conjure over the phone than when sitting across from one another.

"If you don't mind, my partner and I would like to stop by again tomorrow after we've had a chance to look at everything from today," Reed said instead. "In the meantime-"

"If the name Seesel is written anywhere in this house, I will find it," Morgan replied, cutting Reed off before he could even fully form the question. "You have my word."

Chapter Thirty

Despite it still making him supremely uncomfortable, The Tall Boy understood the timeframe they were on.

For the last six months, since finally being told why they had been asked to wait and given the go ahead to seek the retribution they all craved, he and his siblings had done nothing else. He had given up his coaching clients and taken the summer off from the AAU circuit. The Artist had taken a leave of absence from teaching and returned to Ohio after a decade away. The Angel had worked only what was absolutely necessary to maintain his parole.

All three had taken out credit cards. Debt that none of them could afford that would be dealt with in the future, once this was done and they were all far away, the requisite purchases and flexibility both far outweighing any threat of bankruptcy.

Measures that had made it possible for them to spend the last six months habitually pouring themselves over every single aspect of what was happening. Endless details, all sketched out and affixed to the basement wall, out of sight from any stray visitor who might arrive.

A concern in the immediate aftermath of their mother's passing, there seeming to always be some fellow church member stopping by with a casserole, that had mercifully slowed over time, eventually stopping a few months before.

People finally getting the hint, letting the siblings put their full focus into what they were doing. Scrupulous planning for every possible eventuality, meaning that not one thing that had happened came as a surprise.

Not the restaurant where Dean Morgan chose to watch the Ohio State game or what time Matt Seesel went to bed. Months of oversight and recording, all of it plastered to that damn wall. A personal scratchpad for The Angel to stand in front of, overseeing it as if he was the only one to put in the work, all others required to go through him to be granted access.

Information that The Tall Boy had hammered into his brain in whatever stray moment existed when his brother was away, meaning he was intimately aware of the decisions that were being made. He knew each of the names of the people that had been hit. Those who still remained.

The roles they played in what took place years before and the retribution that would be dealt them for it. Punishment heightened by the amount of time they let pass without even attempting to make good on their transgressions. Turn themselves into the authorities. Confess to their prior acts.

Hell, even offer an apology.

Options that not one had taken, seduced by time and distance into thinking that they had gotten away with it. A belief that had been allowed to linger to the point it had taken root, manifesting into something much worse.

A steadfast conviction that they had done nothing wrong.

That being why the Tall Boy and his siblings were doing this now.

All of that, he understood perfectly well, without question.

What he still couldn't get past was the feeling that things were moving a bit too fast. Their need to go quickly, to strike before anyone was able to put together the overarching driver behind all of this, meant they were careening ahead at a pace that wasn't sustainable.

In their own haste to operate freely while they still could, he couldn't shake the feeling that they were missing something. They had failed to fully understand how much extra heft the stress of the situation would weigh on them.

The added hours it would demand. The load of accumulated nerves and adrenaline and everything else, making them start to cut small corners. Take risks that were going to eventually catch up to them.

A pattern that he foresaw ending badly.

A thought he had made the mistake of sharing with his siblings on the drive out to the home of their third target, his brother rewarding the notion with a swat across the back of The Tall Boy's head. The same sort of slap he'd been delivering since they were kids, given hard enough to sting before being massaged away with a smile.

Pretending that it was nothing more than playful.

A little fun between brothers.

A shot that tonight was definitely harder than The Tall Boy remembered them previously being, the crown of his head still stinging as he stepped out of the van. Pulled into the tall weeds lining the side of the road near the driveway of their third target, it sat at an angle, the dark color just barely visible in the heavy shadows provided by the trees clumped around the entrance to the property.

Far and away the most remote of the spots on their list, matching with the person they were here to see. A retiree with no set schedule that they were forced to draw out another way.

A scheme The Tall Boy also wasn't entirely comfortable with, adding to the roiling in his stomach.

A constant churn of nerves and adrenaline that drove him on as he stepped up out of the thick grass and joined his brother at the mouth of the drive. A straight path of mud and stone extended out before them, visible for barely more than ten yards before being swallowed up by the forest encroaching from either side.

An apt metaphor for what was about to occur if there ever was one.

"Quit it," The Angel snapped, his first words since they turned off the highway earlier, their bite sounding especially pronounced in the quiet night air.

"What?" The Tall Boy asked.

"That worrywart bullshit of yours," The Angel replied. "I'm doing the hard part here. All you've got to do is knock on the door and try not to do anything stupid."

Chapter Thirty-One

For damn near thirty years, The Angel had been trying to tell The Tall Boy he was going to get himself killed. His soft-spoken demeanor and insistence that people were generally good was going to put him in a situation where somebody was going to take advantage of him.

If not physically, then mentally or emotionally, someone inevitably bound to see past the man's imposing stature to what was essentially a child tucked away inside. Somebody who had spent his life playing a game and had never been made to realize that that's not how things really worked.

A lesson that The Angel would have thought the events of the last couple of years, the reason they were doing what they were, would have driven home.

And now that it was clear that it hadn't, he had to question whether it would ever really take hold.

One more disappointment on a list as long as his twin brother's mutated legs.

If the diverging paths the two had taken in the last decade had instilled anything in The Angel, it was that not everything happened for a reason. There was no such thing as a greater good. People were not generally kind or decent.

Quite the opposite, in fact, The Angel's experiences in prison proving that there was no greater animal on the planet than mankind. Nothing more savage or instinctual, constantly in a predatory state, seeking out a future target.

A thought that had first risen to the fore with The Tall Boy's admission on the drive over, still resting at the front of The Angel's mind as he crouched on the edge of their third target's porch. Hidden just out of sight, he was forced to listen to his brother prattle on. Some concocted tale about a flat tire and needing assistance and a whole lot of crap that the old man was clearly not buying.

More bullshit to draw him out, meant to sidestep the more obvious approach.

Kick in the damn door and whack the old man across the head, a little bump for The Artist to have to deal with no big deal. A minor inconvenience compared to everything else they'd been through.

And still a pittance to the bastard for what he had done.

Or, rather, in his case, had refused to do.

One line after another, The Angel listened to his brother spew out. A tale that was already veering off the track, each successive sentence making things worse.

A decreasing chance of success that The Angel could feel, almost as palpable as the anger rising from the man hidden behind the front door standing open and the desperation that seemed to seep from The Tall Boy. Pleading that permeated his voice, The Angel having heard it enough times to pick up on it instantly.

More of the same damned pathetic whining he'd been listening to for years.

Always the victim, somehow forgetting that it was his failures that made this all necessary to begin with. His insistence on going away to ride the bench in college, not there when it mattered most.

Acts that The Angel never would have let come to pass if he was a free man when it all went down.

"Please, sir," The Tall Boy said, "I know it's late, but I'm parked just off the end of your lane here. If you could just give me a quick hand, I would be appreciative."

Taking a step, he put his heels along the edge of the front planks, the top of his scalp almost grazing the crosspiece holding up the roof of the cabin's porch above him.

A spot on his head The Angel couldn't help but wish he could take another shot at, this time bypassing the open-handed swat for a proper punch. A hard right that would put his brother down, allowing him to handle things as they should be.

"Or even if I could just borrow a shovel from your barn there," The Tall Boy said. Shifting his body to the side, he lowered his left foot, dropping down onto the top step.

A retreat from the porch that The Angel saw instantly was the end of any chance they had.

The Tall Boy had taken things too far, blowing any chance at believability the thin ruse might have.

Raising a hand, The Tall Boy motioned for the man to follow him, turning his back to the door. "Really, I'm just right out here. Won't take a minute."

His second mistake in as many moments, resulting in a sound The Angel hadn't heard in years, but recognized in an instant. A metallic click that dumped adrenaline into his system as his eyes widened, his focus on the door standing half open a few feet away.

A straight line silhouetted by the light spilling out from within, making it easy to see the elongated barrel of the rifle that he just heard cock come into view.

His legs already folded up as he crouched just beyond the pair of windows along the front of the cabin, The Angel rocked his weight forward. Putting his hands down on either side of his knees, he raised his backside into the air.

A modified sprinter's stance that he held for but a moment before exploding across the short distance between them. Three quick, choppy steps over the uneven floorboards, his feet thumping against the uneven surface.

A hard charge, unleashing a guttural yell from deep in his diaphragm as he hurled himself off the ball of his right foot and twisted his shoulders to the side, slamming his entire right side into the door. A full-body launch that mashed the plank of wood into the man on the other side, tossing his slight form sideways.

Unexpected contact that caused him to jerk back on the trigger of the rifle he was carrying, unleashing an explosion of light and sound. A bright flash and a deafening roar, the sound reverberating through the woods bunched tight around the cabin.

A sensory onslaught joined by the smell of gunpowder and the acrid taste of smoke in the air.

The results of a single blast at short distance, propelled from the front tip of the barrel into the wood just above where The Tall Boy's head was seconds before. A metal projectile that chewed through the soft pine as the weapon it was fired from hit the floor with a clatter.

A stumbling block that The Angel very nearly tripped over as his momentum carried him forward, his toe smacking into it, whipping it back against the front of the cabin.

Extending his hands to either side, The Angel elongated his strides. Clumsy, awkward steps as he fought to slow himself, clawing at anything within reach.

A stumbling slowdown that took nearly the full length of the porch before he was able to come to a stop, turning and throwing himself back in the opposite direction. A quick dash that nearly matched his initial charge, needing to neutralize the man whose feet were still extended beyond the threshold of the door, keeping it open at an angle.

A man who had clearly been underestimated, ready for a moment just such as this.

An error The Angel did not intend to let happen again as he snatched up the rifle from the floorboards. Not bothering to expel the spent shell casing or to even hold it in the proper position, he wrapped both hands around the hot barrel, intent to use it like a club.

A bludgeon to do what he wanted to all along anyway.

Measures that were proven unnecessary as he lashed out a foot and kicked open a door to see the man lying flat on his back. Eyes wide, his mouth gaped, fighting to draw in air.

A battle there would be no winning as he clutched his chest with both hands, a few final convulsions wracking his withered body.

Chapter Thirty-Two

To say The Artist was surprised would be dishonest. It would mean she had to stand on the front porch of the dilapidated cabin and take in the full scene around her and pretend that she hadn't seen something like this coming.

A statement that was too far to make, even for someone like her.

An envisioned scenario that was one of the first to enter her mind after being handed marching orders while perched beside the bed of their failing mother. A series of snapshots that had, thus far, almost all come to pass.

The good ones, such as the sights of Dean Morgan and Matt Seesel lying motionless, fresh ink shining from their foreheads, and the bad.

The nauseating tension of watching The Angel stow away in the rear floorboards of Morgan's SUV. The crumbling interaction between her siblings.

The inevitable moment of hesitance from The Tall Boy, starting with his comment on the ride over, manifesting with the gunshot sounding out into the night air.

Despite all that, what The Artist could easily admit, though, was that never did she see it being quite this bad. A head-on collision with

Hell itself, instantly elevating what they'd been doing into a different stratosphere.

A precipice they'd all been pulled over, with no chance of ever getting back to the top.

Twice through, she had heard the story of what happened. A narrative that dovetailed perfectly with the flash of light and gunshot she'd seen from the foot of the driveway a couple hundred yards away. Curiosity getting the best of her after too much time had passed, she'd wandered out of the van, her entire body seizing tight at the combined sight and sound.

Involuntary reactions that lasted but a moment. Shock that was quick to pass, letting her tear straight ahead, pounding down the gravel lane.

A tale she'd arrived just in time to witness the end of, a perfect capstone for what her brothers described as leading up to that moment. A confluence of both of their own worst tendencies, The Tall Boy leaving himself exposed and The Angel overreacting in a major way.

Their respective personalities both shining through, causing her now to fall back into her assigned role. The same position she'd been in since they were just kids.

The reason why she had left the minute she turned eighteen, wriggling out from under the cumbersome weight of it.

The exact same one still as to why their mother had first told her about this project, making sure she had a firm grasp on the enormity of it, before making her brothers privy as well. A weight that had been dropped like an anvil, knowing that such a final request would not be denied.

For all her children might disagree with her devout religiousness, not one would dare object.

Not when what she was asking was something they had all wanted for so long, this the only possible way she could devise it without putting herself in direct violation of a commandment.

Hands balanced on her hips, The Artist stood in the center of the front porch, framed by the light spilling out through the open doorway.

A spot where she could feel the faint warmth of the home on one cheek, the growing chill of night on the other.

Rotating her gaze in a full arc, she took in the trio of men before her, The Tall Boy sitting on the front steps, no doubt a pose meant to diminish his enormous physical presence. A weak attempt at becoming invisible, his go-to move whenever facing strife of any kind.

A default that was endearing when they were children, but now only managed to well a bit of disgust within The Artist.

Self-pity that there was no time and place for right now.

A few feet away, The Angel stood with his arms folded, drawing each breath in loudly. A powder keg about to explode, vitriol lingering even after the short fracas minutes before.

Adrenaline that looked to be waging a battle inside of him, the reason for the rifle still leaning against one of the porch posts, within easy arm's reach.

Between them, half in and half out of the cabin, lay the man they were there to see. The oldest of the marks on their list, special measures having been taken to accommodate.

A rebalancing of the drugs that were to be administered. An acknowledgement of the hour at which they approached.

Considerations that had been rendered moot, his mouth and eyes all three open wide, gasping for air that would never fill his lungs, staring at something that would never register in his brain.

"We'll just have to go on without him," The Artist said.

"What? No," The Angel spat, pushing back even faster than she had anticipated. A response that was emitted before he could have even really had time to consider what she was saying.

A contrarian nature, rising to the fore in the face of adversity.

"We'll take him inside, prop him up in bed or in a chair or something," The Artist continued. "The man did have a heart attack. We'll just change the location a bit."

"Why?" The Angel snapped. "We're not done yet."

"No," The Artist conceded. Extending a hand beside her, she continued, "But in case you haven't noticed, the man is *dead*. I wouldn't think I have to explain to a man on parole how that changes things."

"Like how, exactly?" The Angel asked, his eyes narrowing as he took a step forward.

Dropping her hand to her side, The Artist let it slap against her thigh. Glancing sideways to The Tall Boy, she was not surprised in the least to see him looking anywhere but at her.

Support that she had always offered him, lost when she needed it most.

"Oh, I don't know," The Artist shot back. "Like maybe it escalates things to *murder*? Kind of defeats what mom asked us to do in the first place?"

Taking another step forward, closing the gap so they were separated only by the pair of lifeless feet on the floor between them, The Angel said, "Mom told us to send a message."

"Yeah! A message! Not-"

"What the hell do you think sends a better message than this?" The Angel inserted, cutting her off. "How the hell is the fact that we didn't set out to kill him but he ended up dead just the same *any* different from what all of them did?"

Chapter Thirty-Three

Captain Grimes listened to what Reed had to share in silence. His standard way of accepting and processing new information, Reed was able to easily visualize the man sitting in a chair in his home, having assumed his usual stance.

Fingers laced over the slight protrusion of his midsection, his chin was likely pulled back into his throat, folds of skin stacked up beneath it.

Though well after the end of the workday and no doubt out of his uniform and into whatever the man wore at home, Reed always envisioned him still in his formal attire, everything buttoned up and pulled tight.

"Have you spoken to Dean Morgan yet?" Grimes eventually asked, his first words since Reed finished speaking nearly two full minutes prior, giving an overview of everything that transpired in Springfield.

Standing barefoot in the kitchen of his farmhouse, Reed crossed one arm over his torso, his opposite elbow propped atop it, keeping the phone up against his face. Leaning against the counter with the remains of dinner still on a plate behind him, he met his partner's gaze as she sat on the floor nearby, her chest upraised as she balanced her weight on her front paws, her unblinking eyes on him.

"Briefly, from the road," Reed said. "Said he doesn't know Matt Seesel, can't remember if he's ever even been to Springfield."

On the other end, Grimes gave a glottal click in response. Another of his trademarks when intaking information, the sound somewhere between a grunt and a sigh.

A noise that seemed to perfectly match what Reed was thinking, nothing thus far coming as easily as it should.

"I told him to take the night to think about it," Reed said. "Dig through his records, whatever. I'll circle back with him tomorrow."

Again, Grimes made the sound, this time before asking, "What else are you thinking?"

His turn to sigh, Reed glanced over to the dining table nearby. An elongated rectangle with a pair of cushioned wooden chairs on each side, the closest pulled out a couple of feet, the tabletop surrounding it covered in paper.

Handwritten notations and a quartet of photos. Blown up images he had taken with his cellphone over the last twenty-six hours and printed from his home printer earlier. Two each from both of the victims, one displaying the new tattoos across their forehead, the other the hand-written slurs across their torsos.

Six total words, equally split by meaning and victim.

"I heard back from Moss over at SPD a little while ago. There were traces of ketamine in Seesel's system, which must be what was used to sedate him.

"In addition to that, we had signs of forced entry, along with the broom and the lint ball found in the woods out back. Tire tracks from where the perpetrator parked and possibly some fingerprints or shoe impressions," Reed said, rattling off the full list.

A litany of things that sounded more impressive when all piled up, though – with the exception of the ketamine and the fingerprints, neither of which he was holding out much hope for – were the kinds of things to buttress a case, not necessarily break it.

"I have a call in with Deke about the employee layoffs from Buckeye Care, though after the attack on Seesel, that seems far less urgent. We're supposed to meet up with Earl in the morning to get a full rundown on everything he was able to pull from the house."

Pausing there, Reed considered a third option he'd been tossing around the last hour or so. Something he'd mentioned to Governor Cowan initially to make a point, arising again after staring at the photos.

"Also, I'm thinking about contacting Dr. Mehdi and seeing if she'll take a quick look at the tattoos and the markings on the torsos."

Again, Grimes made the sound. "Handwriting analysis? You think there might be something there?"

"Might be," Reed said. "The longer I stare at these pictures, the more I get the impression they were done by more than one person.

"Hoping she might have some insight to add."

"More than one victim, attacked by more than one perpetrator..." Grimes replied, voicing a thought Reed had had just a short time earlier. A statement he let drift away, neither of them needing to hear it to completion.

A summation of a difficult case that was growing exponentially before their eyes.

A macabre twist on the classic Ponzi scheme.

"Have you spoken to the chief?" Reed asked. "Any word from the governor's office?"

"Not since earlier today," Grimes replied. "We talked briefly after she said she spoke to you on the drive to Springfield. Said she was planning to call and try to spin the second case as a reason to give a little more space, not squeeze tighter."

Snorting softly, Reed added nothing more.

A point he trusted the captain fully understood about how obvious what Brandt was planning should be, though that didn't necessarily mean a lot when dealing with Cowan. Likely, even less when one of his buddies possessing equal hubris was involved.

"I'm taking her silence since to mean it must have worked," Grimes finished.

"Let us hope," Reed agreed. Using his hips, he leveraged himself forward from the edge of the counter, allowing his momentum to carry him back toward the table. "Thanks a lot, captain. Speak soon."

Ending the call there, Reed lowered the phone before him. Grasping it in both hands, he cleared away the phone feature and went into his address book, scrolling down several times until finding what he was looking for.

Tapping on the icon of a miniature note card, he waited as a blank text message came up before typing,

> Dr. Mehdi, I apologize for reaching out so late, but was hoping you might have ten minutes to meet with me and Billie tomorrow. Time of day doesn't matter. We'll gladly come to you. Thanks ~ Reed Mattox.

Setting the phone down atop the photos by his side, Reed remained standing. Pressing either palm into the front edge of the table, he put his focus on the notepad resting where his dinner plate was barely an hour before.

A small spiral bound booklet used for jotting down thoughts and ideas in the midst of cases, flipped open to a page with seven entries already scrawled out in his own hand. Each of the fabled sins, separated by a couple of lines.

The top two already with victim names attached and the secondary titles that were affixed to their stomachs in Sharpie.

A running list that he hoped didn't get further fleshed out in the hours ahead, though at this point saw no reason to believe the attackers had any intention of slowing.

Fixed in that position, Reed stared at the small slip of paper until his vision began to blur. A slip deeper into his thoughts that lingered until the phone beside him chirped once, coordinating with the screen of it flashing bright.

A combination strong enough to penetrate the haze, pulling his attention to the side.

> Sure thing, detective! Usual time and place?

Needing no further explanation to know exactly what she was referring to, Reed left the phone where it rested, tapping out a quick reply.

That would be great. See you then.

Chapter Thirty-Four

At twenty minutes before midnight, Reed forced himself to look away from the images strewn across the kitchen table. Shuffling them into a pile, he turned his notepad upside down and dropped it upon them, nothing more to be gleaned from continuing to stare down at the pictures or the list of sins.

Visuals that were more than seared into his psyche, no doubt sure to linger through the hours of attempted rest ahead.

Rising from his preferred corner chair, he let Billie out to use the bathroom one final time and washed his dinner dishes, leaving them to dry in the rack by the sink. Last preparations in hopes of getting a half dozen hours of sleep, his first appointment scheduled for early the next morning.

The next step in his ongoing battle to be better about self-care while in the middle of a case, his default setting to push all else aside and fling himself headlong toward it. Total immersion that in the past left him often forgoing rest or even food for long stretches.

Habits that were nowhere near sustainable, Reed only getting through under the watchful eye of Riley insisting that he take the occasional break. A role he was now forced into after partnering with Billie, his concerted effort to make sure her needs were always met reminding him to occasionally do the same for himself.

Something he had a feeling was going to be of extra importance on this particular case, any hope of a quick resolution unlikely, no matter the desires of Governor Cowan.

Leaving Billie to her bed under the same kitchen table he'd spent most of the night working from, Reed had made his way to the bedroom, tossing and turning for twenty minutes before eventually resigning himself to laying flat on his back. Unable to turn off his mind and the scads of questions riffling through it, he laced his fingers behind his head, his eyes glazing as he stared at the ceiling.

A low-energy state he remained in for an unknown amount of time before eventually being drawn back into the moment by a flash of light from the nightstand beside him.

The bright glow of his cellphone screen letting him know he had received an incoming text message that he snatched up. Getting as far as typing out a couple of words in response, he thought better of it, deciding to tap on the phone icon instead.

A moment later, the familiar voice of Deke was on the line, answering with a simple, "Dude. Late night."

"Eh, you know I don't sleep when we're in the middle of a big one," Reed said. "Since I was up, figured it would just be easier to give a call."

"True that," Deke replied. "Good timing, too. Was just about to head upstairs and grab dinner before starting in on some stuff for my other job."

Feeling either corner of his mouth curl back in a smile – both at the mention of the middle of the night being time for dinner, and at the veiled mention of Deke's own work waiting for him – his attention was pulled away before he could comment by the sound of a small whine escaping from the side of the bed.

Billie having heard his voice and made her way in from the kitchen, padding silently throughout the house.

A stealth entrance made even easier by her midnight hue, nothing save the flash of her eyes and the shape of her ears to give away her position.

Extending a hand beside him, Reed waited as his partner stepped forward, dropping her chin into his palm. Flexing his fingers and thumb, he began to massage either side of her muzzle as he asked, "You were able to scour through the list Buckeye Care sent over?"

"I was," Deke said. "And I found some stuff, but I doubt it's anything that's going to really move the needle for you."

Sliding his hand up and over Billie's face, Reed settled his fingers into the thick hair between her ears. Flexing them forward and back, he matched the pressure of her pushing into him.

A canine scalp massage that had fast become one of her favorite things in the world.

A stress reliever for them both, performed at least once a day, often without thought.

"How so?" Reed asked.

"Well, for one thing, it looks like the layoff was more about creative bookkeeping than anything else," Deke replied. "More than half of the people who quote-unquote *lost their jobs* never actually missed a day of work. They were just shuffled off the Buckeye Care payroll and moved into one of the subsidiary consultants they were contracted with."

Since joining the CPD over a decade before, Reed's work had been of a decidedly criminal nature. Infractions against people and property that had always put him well beyond the scope of white-collar crime, though he was aware that it existed.

A burgeoning sector that had been given its own division not long after Reed started, growing quickly in the time since.

Investigators who were as much accountants as anything, tasked with looking into matters that were more evasive than evil in nature.

Much like it sounded this instance fell under.

"What about the other half?" Reed asked.

"Same old stuff," Deke said. "A Facebook group where people could go and talk trash about the company or Morgan himself. Couple of stray comments in various other places.

"Mostly empty threats that died down within a few months."

Running the math in his head, Reed knew that Morgan had been retired for more than two years. Even extending the definition of a couple months to six, that still put things at over a year and a half in the past.

A long time for someone to go silent before unleashing something like what was done to Morgan.

"Nothing since?"

"Nada," Deke replied.

"Hm," Reed said, letting the new information resonate as he continued working at Billie's scalp. Muscle memory completed while processing what Deke just said.

Information that fit with what he had been suspecting since leaving Springfield, the inclusion of Matt Seesel widening the scope tremendously.

"I know you've got your own things you need to get to," Reed said, "but can I ask you to run one more thing for me when you get the chance?"

"Sure thing," Deke answered. "What's up?"

"Well, since we last spoke, we've had another incident arise."

Chapter Thirty-Five

Stripped bare to the waist, The Angel's entire upper body was bathed in sweat. Perspiration that accentuated every ridge and angle of his shoulders and torso, running along the carved outline of his abdominals and along his ribs jutting out beneath the skin.

Beads that gleamed atop the swaths of dark ink etched into his skin, the work done and the place it was received both a far cry from what he and his siblings were now imparting to others.

Identifiers of a much different sort, hinting at a life far more difficult than anybody they'd encountered in the last several days could possibly fathom.

Same for his siblings as well, if The Angel really wanted to admit it.

In the wake of leaving the old man's house earlier, The Angel had been brimming with rage. A crest of the lingering angst he had been feeling all week, it being impossible to do what they were and not tap back into what had originally put all this into motion.

Two distinct incidents, neither having receded in severity, no matter the number of years that passed.

The initial, serving as a source of unending anger. An intrusion so heinous that his family had feared even mentioning it to him, the full reveal not coming until months after the fact.

An attempt to shield him that had done nothing but spike the vitriol he felt, immediately going back to his cell and destroying everything in sight. A full assault that encompassed not just the pillows and blankets and mattress on his bed, but the stainless-steel sink affixed to the wall and even the young cellmate who had the misfortune of coming in on the tail end of it.

Total destruction that earned him an extra eighteen months on top of what he was already there for.

Added time that meant he was still there when the second incident occurred. An event of tremendous shock and sorrow, multiplied a dozen times over by knowing that his own mistakes had caused him to be away both times.

The start of nights of self-flagellation that still continued. Hour after hour of wondering how it might have gone differently if he'd been around.

The effects his particular brand of intervention might have had.

A guilt he had carried for years as a result, at last getting the chance to make good. A stab at retribution, unfettered by his physical circumstances or promises to their mother or anything else.

A chance for him to repay a debt.

Something that couldn't happen if he was going to continue to be saddled with bullshit like tonight. His brother's second guessing and his sister's unheeded worries, threatening to shut things down before even reaching the halfway point.

An outcome The Angel would not allow, content to cast aside their mother's wishes and go at it alone, leaving every last one of the remaining targets looking exactly like the old man if he had to.

Practically bursting with angst by the time they left the shithole the guy pretended was a cabin, it had been all The Angel could do to make it home. An interminable drive with him tucked into the far back, his arms folded, his legs bobbing up and down in short order.

Adrenaline that first appeared with the sound of the rifle cocking, thrumming through his system, refusing to subside without proper release.

More or less sprinting into the house, he'd gone straight to the basement, attacking the old heavy bag that he'd finally been able to hang from the exposed beams of the ceiling above. Not even taking the time to wrap his hands, he'd gone right to work.

Slow, heavy punches that had grown into a frenzied beating, bobbing and moving through the long shadows created by the pile of their father's old stuff and the bare bulbs extended down from the ceiling.

His own personal sanctuary, where he spent an hour flinging his fists at the bag as hard as he could. A bludgeoning of the vinyl that had taken such abuse over the years that the entire middle third was encased in duct tape.

A protective wrap that was no match for him this evening, the seams of it cracking as he threw one body blow after another. Hard shots that he felt all the way to his shoulders, his knuckles bright pink and stinging as he envisioned each of their targets, pausing only occasionally to strip away clothes.

Garments that were either too hot or were slowing his punches, The Angel going until everything except his jeans and his boots were wadded into a pile on the floor.

A bundle that now rested under his arm as he emerged through the door on the main level to find The Artist curled up in a rocking chair in the living room. Feet pulled under her haunches, a quilt was wrapped around her shoulders, a mug with a white tag hanging over the side clutched between her hands.

Staring listlessly into the crackling fire before her, she remained oblivious to The Angel's presence for several moments, finishing whatever thought she was in the midst of before eventually shifting her focus his way.

"Did you win?"

"I always win," The Angel replied. Dropping the wad of clothing onto the end of the sofa, he stepped forward to the fire, letting the warmth touch the sweat lining his torso. A contrast that sent pinpricks of sensation the length of his body.

"I'm not sure I would call tonight a win," The Artist countered.

His back to his sister, The Angel extended both hands. Putting his palms against the front edge of the mantel, he rested his weight against it, feeling the grain of the wood digging into his skin.

A forward lean, allowing the heat and the smoke of the flames to wash over him, filling his senses.

"The old bastard got what was coming to him, and we did what we came for," The Angel countered. "That is the very definition of a win as far as I'm concerned."

Snorting softly, his sister said nothing in immediate reply.

Quiet that lasted the better part of a minute, ended by her stating, "You can't end up back in jail over all this. And he can never go. You know that."

Maintaining his pose, The Angel stared into the fire. Flickering tendrils of red and orange and yellow that he let blur into a miasma of color, his head bobbing in agreement with her statement.

One of the few things they had been in total agreement about since their return to cohabitation, there was no possible way The Tall Boy would survive a day on the inside. Not with his look, or his demeanor, or any of a dozen other reasons that would make him a prime target.

Essentially, the same exact list that filled The Angel with repulsion each time he was forced to deal with him.

"I take it you don't think he can handle what needs to happen tomorrow?"

Chapter Thirty-Six

The first light of dawn wasn't the golden streaks of a new sun rising over the horizon. It wasn't the piercing glow of a summer morn, dangling the promise of a warm and bright day ahead.

An offer Reed probably wouldn't have believed anyway, trusting the previous two days as a harbinger of what he could expect.

Another cold and trying day, perfectly encapsulated by the first gray smudge of light appearing through the windshield before him. A faint glow resting just past the buildings of Columbus in the distance, not yet strong enough to even preclude the use of headlights as he and Billie made their way into the city.

An early morning coupled with it being one of the last few days before daylight savings ended, the clocks shifting things back to start the day an hour earlier.

A world still enveloped in darkness, making it all the more notice-able when his cellphone came to life beside him, the screen illumi-nating the interior of the sedan. An unexpected flare much like Deke's the night before, the sight of it drawing Reed's attention over.

Another incoming message that he decided to handle the same way as the last, opting against sending a reply in favor of simply hitting the phone icon in the corner of the screen.

A call that was picked up after less than a single ring, complete silence following for a moment before eventually Serena Gipson managed to say, "Mph. Morning."

Threaded heavily with grog, the words were just barely decipherable. A sound that peeled one corner of Reed's mouth back even as he said, "I'm sorry, I saw your message and thought you were up. Go back to sleep."

"No, no, I am," Serena said, the words and her tone decidedly at odds. "Awake, at least."

Reed's smile grew a bit larger as he said, "So go back to sleep. Billie and I were in the car and thought-"

"Already?" Serena asked, cutting off his attempt to end the call short. "Or should I say, still?"

Opening his mouth to attempt a third time to insist she return to slumber, Reed let it go. An effort that would merely be brushed aside much like the last two, only consuming a bit more of the short time they both had.

He, before they arrived at their destination.

She, before she was forced to rise and begin her day.

"Already," Reed said. "Going to meet with Pia, and this is the only time she had."

"Pia," Serena replied, the name escaping with an audible exhalation. A sound hinting that despite her protestation, she was still not quite ready for the day, morning having arrived even earlier in the central time zone. "Remind me who that is again?"

"The psychologist who occasionally consults with the department. I met with her-"

"Oh, right right right," Serena inserted, cutting him off, the veil of grog beginning to lift. "After the thing, a couple years ago."

A statement meant to relay understanding without directly mentioning that Reed had first met the doctor in the wake of Riley's passing. Department-mandated sessions after losing a partner, the efforts of her and Captain Grimes the leading reasons why he had decided to stay on with CPD.

A cop at all, for that matter.

"Is everything okay?" Serena asked.

"Yeah," Reed answered, "I asked her for a couple of minutes to look at the handwriting on our two victims. I'm getting the impression we might be looking at multiple attackers, but wanted a professional eye on it."

"There are two now?" Serena asked. "When did that happen?"

A crease formed between Reed's brows as he glanced over to the screen. A quick look before returning his focus to the world outside, the outer belt encircling the greater Columbus area fast approaching.

A six-lane expressway going in both directions with scads of lights already dotting it. Everything from semi trucks to electric sedans, all filled with people who hadn't gotten the message that it was still far too early for the day to be starting.

"Yesterday," Reed said. "I texted you about it last night. Billie and the broom and all that? You don't remember...?"

"No, I do," Serena answered. "I just didn't realize that was a whole new case."

Starting to reply that it wasn't a new case, but just another victim, Reed let it go. The girl he first met more than six months before was many things.

A student.

A waitress at the local diner.

A pseudo-parent to her two younger siblings.

A nurse-in-training who was helping care for Reed's father during his battle with cancer.

What she was not was fully functional so early in the morning. Especially before inhaling a couple of cups of liquid caffeine.

"How are things over there?" Reed asked.

A weak attempt at gently nudging the conversation in a different direction that Serena either didn't notice or didn't bother to comment on.

"Good," she replied instead.

Ignoring the on-ramps to send them either direction around the outside of the city, Reed pushed the sedan straight on past.

"Your dad came by the center yesterday. Said to say hi to you for him."

"Did you tell him it would probably be easier to just pick up the phone and say it himself?" Reed asked, a faint grin creasing his features.

"I did," Serena replied. "He said he'll be sure to do that on Saturday, after the Oklahoma game."

The smile grew larger on Reed's features as he hooked a right, moving them off the larger road and onto a smaller neighborhood street. Lined with multi-story homes made of brick and white siding on either side, many of the stoops still contained remnants from Halloween.

Sagging pumpkins and orange bags filled with leaves, jack-o-lantern faces emblazoned along the side.

Bucolic suburbia, having not yet started to awaken and face the day.

"I have no doubt that is exactly what he said."

Easing down a pair of blocks, Reed could see the place where they were headed come into view. A patch of grass that was roughly a hundred yards in length and half as much across, the far edge lined with aging playground equipment.

A space that during the afternoon Reed imagined was filled with dogs and children all with energy to burn, though this morning contained just a single car. A lone vehicle in the small lot meant to hold half a dozen, the running engine sending out a small plume of steam from the tailpipe.

"Damn," Reed whispered.

"What?"

"She's already here," he replied. "I hate to cut this short-"

"Go," Serena replied. "We can talk some more about what I mentioned the other night next time."

Chapter Thirty-Seven

Reed didn't bother handing the stack of images to Dr. Pia Mehdi, instead fanning them out across the roof of his trunk. Coupling them up by victim, he placed the images of Dean Morgan to the left and those of Matt Seesel on the right, only a small gap separating them. Room enough for them to be seen as different incidents, while at the same time making it easy for the doctor to take them all in at once.

Micro and macro level views she could rearrange as she so chose.

Taking advantage of the lack of wind, he put all four in place before backing away. Not wanting to appear like he was rushing her analysis – or even forcing her to think out loud – he circled around the side of the vehicle to find Billie having resumed the same path that was once her morning routine.

An elongated oval still faintly visible in the thick grass comprising the center of the public park on the edge of Hilliard, not far from The Bottoms where Reed and Billie worked.

A force of habit ingrained through their first year together, when they would frequently stop on their way home after the overnight shift. A period of time in the wake of Riley's passing in which Reed was actively trying to avoid human interaction, asking Captain Grimes for the timeslot.

A daily shift that saw him and Billie begin between eight and nine each evening, often finishing at this exact time at this exact place.

A way for Billie to relieve herself and to burn through any remaining energy before they headed home to sleep.

A location Mehdi was kind enough to meet them at before her day started, helping him get through the assorted emotional responses to the death of his partner. An interaction he could readily admit he had resented the hell out of at first, only later coming around on the progress they made.

A difficult slog forward that eventually saw them move from patient-doctor to working colleagues, the doctor having consulted on a couple of different incidents in the time since.

Matters such as this, when her unique training could be beneficial for a case that was especially slow in gaining traction.

"I assume you've already put together that you're looking at different people here," Mehdi said after the better part of five minutes.

The first she had spoken since Reed placed the photos before her after their initial greeting, he turned at the sound of her voice to find her standing at the corner of his sedan.

Just approaching her mid-forties, there was not a line or blemish to be seen marring her light brown skin. Glossy black hair was void of any grays, pinned back to accentuate a round face with dark eyes.

A look that always gave Reed the impression he had seen her on the big screen in a movie somewhere, even if he could never quite nail down which one.

Dressed in black slacks and a charcoal turtleneck, she stood with hands thrust into the pockets of her overcoat. Staring at him expectantly, she had one leg cocked to the side, hinting that her initial assessment was complete.

Signal enough for him to join her, following the unspoken instruction and retracing his steps from a couple of moments before.

"I did have that impression, which is why I wanted you to take a look," Reed said. "I wanted to make sure I wasn't just jumping at shadows, taking the differences between the tattoos and the markers to mean more than was actually there."

Drifting to the side, Mehdi retook her previous post behind the lid of the trunk, waiting until Reed made his way to her side before saying, "Definitely not."

Extending a hand, she started with the images of Morgan.

"In all four pictures, the writer uses block letters, which actually makes it a bit easier. On this side alone, both PRIDE and **RICH BASTARD** share three letters. R, I, and D."

Tracing her finger along those three letters of the tattoo, she said, "As you can see here, the letters are all oriented upright. The edges are rounded, almost artistic in nature."

Moving down to the shot of the magic marker on Morgan's abdomen, she continued, "Whereas here, they are slanted forward. The connections are uneven, almost like the lettering is stick figures, jotted down in a hurry."

Keeping the same finger extended like a pointer, she slid it to the opposite side and said, "Over here, they only share the letter R, but you can see the same thing."

Pointing to the shot of Matt Seesel's forehead, she said, "Form," before lowering it to his ribs and adding, "versus function."

Sliding his gaze to match her movement, Reed took in the assessment.

"Form versus function," he echoed. "Meaning?"

"Meaning, whoever did the facial work fashions themselves something of an artist," Mehdi said. "They want what they're doing to look good. They don't want people to get hung up on trying to figure out what it says instead of fixating on the fact that it's there."

Continuing to flick his gaze between the handful of images, Reed nodded.

"What do you make of using both tattoos and markers?" he asked.

"More of the same," Mehdi said. "Both individuals have something to say, but whoever is using the marker is just venting. They're pissed off and want to make sure their targets know it."

"Hence, the bruising," Reed added.

"Exactly," Mehdi replied, shooting a finger his direction before returning it to the images before them. "They can't be trusted with tattooing the face, so they do what they can. They throw some punches, scrawl out a few insults, while the other one has the patience to actually say what they want heard."

Returning her hand to her coat pocket, she added, "Basically, your classic male-female dichotomy. No offense."

Feeling his brow come together, Reed glanced over to see Billie jogging over to join them. Her tongue wagging after her morning run, it served as a splash of pink against her inky silhouette.

A visual that he saw long before he could hear her panting as she crossed from the grass onto the asphalt, slowing her pace to a walk.

"None taken," Reed replied, "mainly because I'm not sure what you mean."

Dropping his right hand by his side, he waited for Billie to slide under it, feeling the ebb and flow of her musculature as she panted, fighting to catch her breath.

"Are you saying the tattooist-"

"Is a female?" Mehdi finished. "Yes, I believe so. Based on penmanship, letter formation, etc., I'm almost certain of it."

Feeling his brows rise, Reed kept his gaze on the images before him. Renewed focus, in the wake of the bombshell that was just lobbed his way.

A point of reference that would radically shift things, nothing about the case thus far – from the handling of the victims to the nature of the violation – fitting traditional patterns of female perpetrators.

"I'm also pretty certain they're new to this," Mehdi offered.

Still fighting to process what was just shared, Reed blinked several times in order. Habitual behavior, meant to push aside the revelation of a moment before, allowing him to focus on what else was being proffered.

"What makes you say that?"

"Eh," Mehdi replied, drawing the sound out for a few seconds. "Call this one more of a hunch. Just kind of something I'm seeing here, though you might want to talk to a professional about it."

"I thought I was?" Reed asked.

A final question that elicited a faint smile from Mehdi as she replied, "Funny, but you know what I meant."

Chapter Thirty-Eight

Earl Bautista was sitting on the picnic table on the lawn behind the crime scene crew's workshop when Reed and Billie arrived. A small chunk of ground no more than a dozen yards square, it was framed between the shop and the parking lot on two sides, a security fence and a sidewalk on the others.

Sitting in the middle of it was a mature oak tree, most of its lingering leaves long since turned, the remainder forming a thick layer on the ground. A crinkling carpet that allowed Earl to track Reed and Billie's progress as they approached, the man not once turning back as he sat atop the table, his feet resting on the bench seat below.

An unfiltered cigarette in hand, he stared straight out, waiting until Reed and Billie drew even before saying, "Remind me to never take a job in Springfield again."

Folds of skin appeared around Reed's eyes as he winced, drawing in a sharp breath. "That bad?"

"Worse," Earl commented. "Spent half the night pulling finger-prints and shoe indents from the carpet inside the house and the ground outside it, then the rest of the night eliminating most of them on account of overzealous jackasses tromping all over everything."

Exhaling twin plumes of smoke through his nostrils, he began to speak again, only a single sound making it out before he shook his head in disgust. Lifting the butt end of his cigarette, he got it nearly to his mouth before stopping and lowering it, crushing it against the wooden plank he was perched upon.

One more for the small pile beside him, to be taken in and deposited in the trash once they were done.

A grouping large enough to hint he had been out here for some time, the quiet and the cool air having done nothing to tamp down the hostility emanating from him in waves.

"I was thinking on the way back last night," Reed said, "it really isn't fair that you get stuck covering all these cases for Cowan's little pet project. We appreciate like hell your help, but-"

"No," Earl said, picking up on what Reed was about to say. The suggestion that they could contract with other teams as well to help lessen some of the load.

Especially at times like this, when Earl's crew was already spread thin and the workload on the BCI side was heavier than usual.

"That's not what I meant. Just a shitty night, that's all," Earl said, extending a foot to the side and sliding his considerable bulk over to make room for Reed. "I know you guys have shit to do too, so you want the verbal overview or the official writeup?"

"Verbal's fine for now," Reed replied, taking up Earl on his silent offer and planting his left haunch on the tabletop. Keeping his right foot on the ground, he stuffed his hands into the pockets of his hoodie, Billie remaining on all fours by his side.

"Starting off big," Earl said, "looks like you're going after multiple perps. No prints anywhere, but we found shoe indents in the carpet and the mud outside that we couldn't match to anybody else.

"Your vic swears nobody has been by since his parents visited for Labor Day – and that they went nowhere near the side of the house - so assuming that's true, they have to be from a couple nights ago."

Despite being braced for it by the observation from Dr. Mehdi earlier, Reed still couldn't keep his stomach from clenching. A tightening in his core at the thought that with each new layer to the case, their job kept getting more difficult.

More victims. More geographic spread.

Now confirmation of more attackers as well.

"One of the people you're looking for is massive," Earl said. "At least, his feet are anyway."

Extending the same foot he'd just used to slide across the top of the picnic table, he said, "I wear fifteens, and this guy has at least two shoe sizes on me."

Fixing his gaze on the offered boot, a plain tan canvas work shoe with rubber soles and rawhide laces, Reed studied it for a moment, trying first to imagine what two additional sizes would look like. From there, he tried to envision the person needed to fill it, Earl already one of the largest human beings he'd ever interacted with.

A mental conjuring that was nothing short of monstrous, easily capable of inflicting the injuries seen marring Dean Morgan and Matt Seesel's torsos. Same for applying the words in magic marker that Dr. Mehdi had said were clearly the work of a man.

More difficult to imagine was that same person doing any of the other more delicate matters that had been uncovered thus far. Things like slipping into the back of Morgan's SUV undetected or getting Seesel back into bed without leaving behind more than a shoe impression.

Tasks that would be left to the other half of the team.

The female wielding the tattoo gun, no matter how fledgling she may be at it.

"And the other one?"

"Much smaller," Earl said. "We only got the outer edge of it, but I'd say a seven at most."

Dropping his gaze to Billie beside him, Reed watched as she tilted her focus up to meet it. Dark eyes with just the slightest bits of white around them, framing them against her black fur.

"We just came from meeting with Dr. Mehdi. Based on handwriting, she thinks one of our attackers is a female."

Letting out a short grunt in reply, Earl bobbed his head. A slight movement that Reed could still feel through the plank he was seated on.

"Size seven in men's would be a nine in women's," Earl said, "which still fits within the average range. I could definitely see that."

Since the initial surprise of hearing it, Reed had been wrestling with the notion. An idea he at first balked at due to the violent nature of tattooing someone's forehead that he eventually began to walk back, small details coming to mind.

The things that a large male could not perform, or even the fact that Seesel had been brought back inside and returned to bed.

A notion he found far more likely to be the work of a female wanting to ensure survival, even in the wake of such a heinous violation.

"The house?" Reed asked.

"Not much," Earl replied. "No usable prints in the house or on the broom or even the garage as a whole. Closest we got were the scratches on the side door, which were consistent with a pick gun, and some tire indents from the spot where they parked."

Again, the thought Reed had had the night before while speaking to Captain Grimes returned. While the list of evidentiary pieces pulled from Seesel's house sounded lengthy, it was decidedly lacking in anything damning.

Supportive bits of data, at best.

"Anything else?" Reed asked.

"Naw," Earl spat. "I've put all this in a report and will send it over later, but that's about the long and short of it."

Glancing over, he added, "You?"

"Actually, yeah," Reed replied, turning to meet his stare. "I don't suppose you know any good tattoo artists in the area, do you?"

Chapter Thirty-Nine

Posted up at the front window of the tiny local coffee shop, The Tall Boy had a perfect view of the sidewalk leading to the establishment's lone point of entry. A small business nestled into a strip mall not far from Otterbein University in the suburb of Westerville, similar shops abutting it on either side.

A dry cleaner to the left and a boutique women's clothier on the right, neither of which were open, making at least the first part of his job easier. The task of sitting and watching everybody who approached the place, whether they be on foot or by car.

A flow of people that was steady but not overwhelming. Certainly, nothing compared to if he had been forced to sit outside of a Starbucks or Dunkin Donuts.

A constant vigil, waiting for the fourth target on their list. The transition point from which things needed to move even faster than they had before. The exact instant at which the threads connecting each of those already hit would become more obvious, laying out a clear path for those that remained.

Speed that became all the more paramount after what took place at the cabin the night before.

"Marilee!" the barista behind the counter shouted, her shrill voice much too loud for the small interior. A sound that reverberated as if she was afraid Marilee might have retreated to her vehicle or even gone for a stroll down the street, wanting the girl to know that her beverage was prepared.

Announcements arriving every few minutes like clockwork, each one making The Tall Boy flinch slightly.

Movements triggered by both the auditory assaults and by the sheer volume of adrenaline coursing through him. Anticipatory energy that had spiked the instant the old man had shot the gun the night before, every physiological response in The Tall Boy's body firing reflexively.

Natural reactions that had made sleeping impossible. Same for any attempt at slowing the tremors causing his right thumb and pinky to twitch opposite each other.

The reason why he had ordered a decaffeinated coffee upon arrival, but outside of occasionally lifting it and pretending to take a swallow, had not actually imbibed a bit, afraid of what even the thought of caffeine might do to his system.

For months now, The Tall Boy had been staring at pictures taped to the basement wall of the young woman he was there to spot. Images taken from Facebook and Instagram accounts. Official headshots from the graduate department at Otterbein where she worked and studied.

Hosts of static pictures and videos alike, the young woman a fixture of the new generation. One that was weaned on social media culture, believing that every single thing they ever did was for an audience, needing to be documented.

Hundreds of shots that The Tall Boy had studied enough to imprint her appearance in his mind, even if this was the first time he himself had ever been inside the coffee shop. A reversal of roles from previous scouting missions in the past, when The Artist or The Angel would be sent in.

Two people who blend well enough to not be noticed if they were around on a handful of occasions.

The ability to hide in plain sight that The Tall Boy did not share, instead coming at things from the opposite direction. Assurance that never before had anybody on the premises seen him, his unique dimensions sure to be remembered.

An ideal lookout for when it really mattered, meaning the girl would not think twice about his being there, even as he texted the others waiting nearby that she was close and would soon be headed their way.

His phone resting on the table in front of him, The Tall Boy went through the charade of tapping at the screen every few seconds. Random online searches rife with scrolling and even the occasional facial expression, going through the expected rigmarole when staring transfixed at one's device.

Performative measures while continuing to play back the events of the night before. What happened at the cabin, but also the conversation on the first floor he overhead between his siblings. A talk that took place after The Angel got done beating the bag in the basement into submission, the sounds of his punches and his accompanying grunting finally dying away.

Silence that had lasted but a moment before he ascended the stairs and they both started talking, spending just a few minutes discussing what took place earlier before turning the discourse to him.

Shared doubts as to if he could handle this most basic of tasks, both believing him asleep, forgetting how well sound carried in the old farmhouse.

Or perhaps not caring, wanting him to hear every word. An open challenge that they laid out, making it clear there could be no room for errors like the one that took place at the cabin.

If such a thing could even be construed as an error, the situation unfolding a bit slower than The Tall Boy would have liked but still going to plan, up until The Angel decided to insert himself. A release that they all knew he was aching to unleash, able to reign himself in until the third victim before finally taking a life.

Sitting with his body folded into the uncomfortable metal chair, his right elbow braced atop the table, The Tall Boy continued to stare down at his phone until long after the screen had gone dark. A swirl of thoughts and recollections that demanded his attention, blocking all else from mind.

Complete concentration, interrupted not by the sound of the barista unleashing another name, but by the bell affixed to the top of the door. A penetrating jangle that jerked his gaze upward, sending a torrent of palpitations through his chest.

Sensation that brought a surge of heat to his features as he slid his phone from the table and drew up the untouched cup of decaf, keeping both in hand as he climbed to his feet. Circling wide, he fell in behind the young woman in spandex pants and a scoop-neck sweater, dark hair pulled into a ponytail at the nape of her neck.

A favorite look of their fourth target, seen in no less than a handful of photos The Tall Boy had spent so much time staring at in recent days.

Images matching both the outfit and the smile she flashed as she passed him on her way to the counter.

"Good morning."

Chapter Forty

The name of the tattoo artist Earl Bautista suggested Reed and Billie go to meet with went simply by the name Wolf Man. A guy Earl said he had known for over fifteen years, the bib overalls he was so fond of hiding more than a little ink, Wolf Man the only one he trusted to go near him with a needle.

Even if he didn't have the slightest clue what his actual name was.

Upon hearing the suggestion, Reed's first question was to ask how early the man's shop opened. An inquiry Earl had scoffed at, saying the man more or less lived there, the place serving as his base of operations back in his younger days when the Wolf Man was still a partier, and continuing on now, when the spot was more of a local hangout.

A place where the old timers would get together in the morning and shoot the breeze, the same as a lounge for aging bikers or a strip of sand for guys too long in the tooth to actually climb on a board and paddle out into the surf.

A description Reed had chuckled at in the moment, foolishly believing Earl had been leading him on, but as he and Billie pulled up in front of the freestanding establishment just south of Dublin in the northwest corner of the city, came to realize just how wrong he had been.

Standing a single story in height, the frame of the building was made of concrete block painted black, the entire front façade done in vertical sheets of glass tinted dark. A canvas on which a street artist had painted an image of a wolf staring straight ahead, its jowls pulled back exposing even rows of white teeth.

Arched above it was the name **WOLF MAN'S**, the title finished with **TATTOOS AND PIERCINGS** below it, all of it done in white bubble letters with gray trim.

Signage that was anything but subtle, the little remaining window space filled with neon displays announcing various offerings within. Types of tattoos and body piercings that could be had, in some instances even going the additional step of listing prices.

Just as Earl had intimated, despite the hour more than a handful of vehicles lined the parking lot. A collection ranging from a pickup with sprays of mud down the side to a chopper motorcycle with custom paint, orange flames against a purple backdrop.

An assortment that filled most of the front row, Reed going instead for the rear, facing out toward the street. Pulling in, he killed the engine and circled around to the back, grabbing up Billie's short lead and affixing it to her harness before leading her across the lot and through the front door.

An entrance that brought whatever conversation had previously been ongoing to a halt, every person in the shop turning in unison. A collection as disparate as the automobiles they had driven there, people were strewn across padded tattoo chairs and seats with metal frames usually reserved for waiting customers.

A crowd that included men in their sixties with sleeveless shirts and long, graying hair. Ladies in jeans and tank tops. Even a young woman, with a plume of dark hair, laying on her stomach atop one of the tables, a female artist with purple and green braids and a nose ring standing behind her, a buzzing tattoo gun in hand.

A group that had but one thing in common – aside from their open stares - that being the presence of copious amounts of visible ink.

"Jesus," one of the men muttered, "I know he joked about getting a wolf for the shop one day, but I thought he was just bullshitting."

To his right, a lone man chuckled, leathered skin peeling back over a row of teeth that was equal parts natural and silver.

A quip Reed couldn't help but smile at as well, sweeping his gaze across the group for which one might be the person he was looking for.

A search that presented no obvious choices, prompting him to say, "Good morning. Looking for Wolf Man?"

Any faint bit of mirth that might have existed from the earlier comment vanished. Gone too was any of the open curiosity that had crossed their faces earlier, features pulling taut as they stared back, none making any attempt to answer the question.

A shift in demeanor that was palpable, Billie moving a step to the side, pressing her ribcage against the outside of his calf.

"Earl Bautista sent us over," Reed added. "Said he might be able to help."

"Help with what?" the same man who cracked the joke earlier asked, his tone laced with accusation, decidedly at odds with his previous tenor.

A question that was still in the air, Reed not even given the chance to answer, before a voice called from the back, "Big Earl Bautista?"

To the person, every individual inside the shop turned toward the back. Synchronized movement that told Reed he had found the man he was looking for as the crowd parted, revealing a man in his early sixties with a lengthy goatee and longer hair that had just started to recede at the temples. Loss that was offset by most of the original dark color remaining, spilling down across broad shoulders and thick arms that were etched from deltoid to wrist with colorful designs.

Roughly the same height as Reed, he outweighed him by a good thirty pounds, all of it solid, despite his age.

"That's right," Reed replied.

Dressed in black jeans and a sleeveless Led Zeppelin t-shirt, a matching belt, vest, and set of boots of the same black leather completed the look.

Boots that sounded out as he took a step forward, glancing between Reed and Billie.

"That must make you cops."

"Right again," Reed said. Reaching to his back pocket, he drew out his badge, fanning it across himself for everybody to see. "Detective Reed Mattox, and this is my K-9 partner, Billie."

Taking another step forward, Wolf Man drew even with the woman applying the tattoo and the young girl on the table receiving it. Sliding his focus from the badge down to Billie, he asked, "Belgian?"

"Yes, sir," Reed replied, tucking the badge back into place.

"Thought so," Wolf Man said. "Served with a few Malinois in my unit. Army. First Iraq."

Tilting his head to the side, Reed answered, "Billie was Marines. Afghanistan."

Off to the side, someone let out a whistle. A sound that drew a thin smile to Wolf Man's features, his gaze never leaving Billie, even as he twisted his head to the side and said, "Donna, go get this girl some water. Bottled, from the fridge, not tap."

Responded to in much the same way Reed imagined most orders were around the shop, a woman in too-tight jeans and a red halter top peeled herself away from the group. Heels clicking against the tile floor, she scurried toward the back, hurrying to do as told.

An exit that Wolf Man waited until was complete, the sound of her shoes dying away, before asking, "What can we do for you, detectives?"

"Actually, this morning we're just here to consult your expertise," Reed replied.

A response that wasn't meant to be a joke, but still managed to evoke a round of laughter. Hearty chuckles that filled the air, lasting several seconds before Wolf Man said, "Well, I don't know how much of that we might have, but we'll be glad to do what we can."

Chapter Forty-One

Reed couldn't help but get a sense of déjà vu as he stood in the center of Wolf Man's tattoo parlor. A throwback to just twenty-four hours prior when he and Billie had descended the stairs from the second floor of the 8th precinct to find the group of officers all gathered up, laughing and in good spirits.

A mood completely dashed the moment one of them asked Reed what he was working on and he shared even a few oblique details of the case.

A feeling that was now heightened by the inclusion of a second victim and – more importantly - images, every last person down to the girl getting the new tattoo gathered up behind Wolf Man, staring at the two photos he held wide to either side.

All conversation having died away and the tattoo gun turned off, the only sounds were the faint call of classic rock music somewhere in the back and the groaning of the ancient fans rotating overhead.

A state of quiet that remained for nearly three full minutes - long enough for Billie to have finished with her water and rejoined Reed's side – before Wolf Man looked up. A fair bit of the flush that colored his cheeks from laughter gone, he stared at Reed.

"You say these were done without their consent?" he asked.

"Both were done without the victims even being conscious," Reed said.

Over Wolf Man's left shoulder, one of the men let out a low whistle. A sound that carved through the quiet air, lasting several seconds, before dying away.

A sentiment a few of the others seemed to agree with, bobbing their heads in unison.

Drawing both pictures back directly in front of him, Wolf Man lowered his gaze. A pose he held as the woman who had been applying the tattoo just moments before leaned in from the side and asked, "You don't think somebody here...?"

"No," Reed assured her. "Like I said earlier, my questions this morning are strictly information gathering. Our staff psychologist had some insights after looking at these that I wanted to flesh out a little further.

"After I spoke to her, I had to swing by and meet with Earl, who suggested you guys as the place to start."

Extending a hand beside him, he splayed his fingers wide. Scratching at the air, he tried three times before touching Billie's ears and settling his hand between them.

Force of habit, their standard pose whenever thinking through something.

This time, doing so aloud.

"Obviously," the same man who spoke twice already began. A deputy of sorts, Reed imagined, serving as a second-in-command to Wolf Man himself.

Based on semblance, Reed would also surmise a family tie, whether it be a brother or cousin.

"This is a crowd that likes its ink," the man continued. "But something like this here? That ain't right."

Evoking several nods of agreement from the crowd around him, Wolf Man was the last to join in. A nod that was really more raising his focus from the pictures, fixing it on Reed and Billie.

"What can we do for you, detectives?" he said, a repeat of his prior question, without any of the accompanying mirth.

"Well, if you don't mind, I'd kind of just like your general opinion first," Reed replied. "Blank slate, just to see if anything jumps out at you."

Grunting softly, Wolf Man nodded. A movement of no more than an inch or two, but enough to cause his goatee to brush against his chest.

"I got you," he said. "No preconceived notions."

"Exactly."

Again, Wolf Man nodded, pulling the pictures up to within just a few inches of his face. Aligning their edges side by side, he tilted his head to the left, his eyes narrowed, studying them intently for a moment.

For the first time, seeing past the salacious images, winnowing his focus to the tattoo work itself.

A study that took just an instant before he declared, "Well, it's pretty much shit."

"Amateur hour," one of the older men behind him added.

"Total rook," his deputy chimed in.

Comments that brought a few of the others from the periphery in tighter, circling around behind or craning their necks to get a better view.

"Yeah," said the woman with multi-colored braids. Extending a hand, she motioned to the closest image and said, "See the lines here?"

"Yut," Wolf Man said, the word little more than a grunt.

"And the shading on that middle E there?" Donna, who had grabbed water for Billie, added.

"Jesus Christ," the deputy added. "They even had their hairlines to use as a guide and still got the heights all wrong."

Despite having seen the pictures enough times to have the overall images seared into his mind, the subtle details that were being mentioned evaded Reed. Specifics he couldn't get an exact feel for without viewing them himself.

Drawing his phone out from his back pocket, he pulled up the original images he had taken of both Morgan and Seesel. Using his middle and index fingers to enlarge the size, he brought the screen to within a few inches of his nose, his brows knitted as he stared down.

A winnowed view through the lens of everything being mentioned, each aspect critiqued jumping out at him.

The types of errors that would have a paying customer standing in the middle of the shop screaming, or going online to leave scathing reviews, or – if done to the wrong person – even aiming the grille of their vehicle through the glass windows lining the front.

"You have them there?" Wolf Man asked, drawing Reed's attention up from the screen.

"Yeah."

"See what we're talking about?"

Sliding his focus back down, Reed nodded. "I do. It was a little tougher to see when just looking at them as a whole..."

"But once you know what to look for, kind of hard to miss," Wolf Man finished.

"Yeah," Reed said, bringing the images closer one last time. Starting with Morgan, he slid it to the side and peered in closer at Seesel, seeing every last thing that was just mentioned pop up in order.

Inconsistencies that hinted at an unpracticed hand. Nerves. A lack of time.

Or, most likely, a combination of all three.

For a moment, Reed considered asking about Mehdi's mention that the artist was a female. A question that was steeped in her assessment of the handwriting, backed by the footprints found by Earl.

A combination that made it as close to fact as he could get for now, anything the crew before him had to add basically conjecture.

Speculation he chose to sidestep, instead asking, "Where would someone get the supplies needed to do this?"

Though not intended as a joke, it still managed to pull out a few chuckles. Sounds matched by Wolf Man snorting loudly, his head rocking back an inch.

"Supplies?" he asked. "Shoot, these here are almost prison ink, done with broken pens and a needle.

"About the closest thing we can give you to a lead on whatever did these is to try and find the shittiest tattoo gun in the state and then arrest whoever is holding it."

Chapter Forty-Two

The Artist couldn't help but feel like she was ten years old again. The lone female in the trio, she was forced to ride on the hump in the backseat of the family station wagon, no matter that she was the oldest.

A seating arrangement made even worse by the fact that not once did her brothers ever seem to notice she was even there. Little more than an impediment, she would sit with The Angel to her left and The Tall Boy to her right, the two of them constantly sniping at one another.

A constant barrage of attacks both physical and verbal, the pair of them usually leaning forward or back, though occasionally going directly through her in search of their target.

An ongoing battle that didn't truly relent until the passing of their father when The Artist was fourteen, allowing her to graduate up into the front seat.

A position she couldn't help but find herself recalling with envy as she sat perched in the center of the small apartment that served as the second floor of a two-story garage behind a home in Westerville. A space that was barely large enough for its single occupant and the beta fighting fish on the table who resided there, a lone wall directly through the center separating a joint living room and kitchen from a combined bed and bath.

Total floor space that checked in at barely five hundred square feet, a minuscule amount even for a graduate student like The Artist knew their latest target to be.

An area made even smaller by the fact that already the place was festooned to an absurd degree in Christmas décor, despite the fact that Halloween was just barely a week past.

Her knees buried into the same white drop cloth they'd been using for each of the previous stops, The Artist laid out her implements on the floor beside her. To her left, The Angel leaned against the windowsill along the front wall. A self-appointed post allowing him to keep an eye on the driveway below, making sure that the owner of the property didn't make an unforeseen midday stop at home.

An outcome they all knew had no chance of occurring, each of them quite aware that the young girl between them was here alone until noon on weekdays, tucked away doing whatever it was people who preferred to hide in school rather than get actual jobs did.

A nice, leisurely start to her day that included a trip to the yoga studio each morning and a stop by the local coffee shop before returning home.

A site that was left vacant for more than an hour, making it simple for The Angel to slip inside and wait for her. Posted up just behind the door on the foyer inside the door after getting the text from The Tall Boy, he'd moved in and jabbed her with the needle loaded with the sedative siphoned off from their mother's late-stage care, catching her before she made it up even a single stair.

A climb he went ahead and finished for her, hefting her onto a shoulder and carrying her up the steps. Dropping her onto one end of the sofa, he'd posted up on the other, sitting there waiting with his legs crossed and his arms outstretched by the time The Artist and The Tall Boy arrived, supplies in hands.

The start of an ongoing verbal barrage that was as yet unending, repeatedly pointing out to his siblings that that was how it was supposed to go.

No making up stupid stories on the fly. No attempting to coax anybody outside.

An onslaught that The Tall Boy was content to let go for a while, until The Angel's comments became more pointed. Barbs that caused him to snap to his feet from his spot in the papasan chair in the corner, his finger extended before him.

The start of a tirade that would quickly escalate, the two of them continuing on a collision course that could be ill afforded.

Especially not at the moment, with all of them standing inside the home of their fourth victim. A space that would likely soon be scoured by a crime scene crew, once the girl woke up and discovered what was done to her.

What she had earned so many years before.

"Don't you two have work to do?" The Artist snapped, interrupting The Tall Boy before he could get so much as a word out. An insertion she had to keep from being overhead by anyone who might be in the area, letting her tone do the heavy lifting for her.

A razored edge that drew over both of her brothers' attention, neither saying a word.

"Some scrubbing to do here, since you both insisted on making the trip up?" she said. Cutting a glance between the two of them, she added, "Or, I don't know, maybe some final prep work on the visits that got moved up to tonight?"

Waving a hand before her, she tried to find another productive use of time to fling at them. Anything to show them how ridiculous their little pissing match was, here and now, of all times and places.

Distractions she didn't need, this still an entirely new thing for her. A task she didn't particularly care for and wasn't entirely effective at, requiring concentration they were making impossible.

Words that evaded her, the best she could do being to let them see the disgust on her features as she lowered her attention back to the young woman sprawled on the floor by her knees.

"Hell, I don't care what you do, just shut the hell up while you do it so I can work."

Chapter Forty-Three

"I was just about to call you," Reed said, accepting the incoming call as he gave a wave to the same security guard he had encountered outside the gated community Dean Morgan lived in on their previous visits. A fleshy man with a mustache Thomas Magnum would be envious of who had stood and made a show at first of asking Reed who he was and why he was visiting, but as this was their third trip in as many days, he let them go with merely an upward nod.

"Or, I was going to call around noon, when I figured you were up and about."

"Ha!" Deke shot back in response. "Usually, you'd be right, but today you caught me working a job for a company out of Japan. Time zones, man."

Even after more than a decade of knowing the man, much of that time spent with him assisting in myriad ways on the cases Reed worked with both Riley and now Billie, he still had only a loose knowledge of exactly what it was Deke did. An ethereal job title Reed had essentially created in his own mind, assigning the title *cybersecurity expert* and letting that suffice as an umbrella for the various things he was capable of.

Assorted skills and abilities that, at some point, Reed wouldn't mind delving into further. Professional and personal courtesy extended to the man he had come to rely on, and someone he now considered a friend.

Even if he was likely to only understand a fraction of it.

"What's going on?" Reed asked.

"Oh, the usual," Deke replied, letting the words slide out with a sigh. "Everybody thinks their data is the most important thing on the planet, everyone else wants to steal it, same old stuff.

"The reason I was calling you though, was to let you know I ran down that stuff you were asking about last night. From what I can tell, there is no direct connection with Matt Seesel going back to either Dean Morgan or Buckeye Care."

Pausing there, he let the information resonate a moment before adding, "Sorry, man."

Reed had known when he first asked Deke to look into things it would be a long shot. A chance connection that was tenuous enough to have slipped both Morgan's and Seesel's mind – perhaps even to the point that neither was aware of it – but would still be sufficient to provide a lead moving forward.

A commonality Reed and Billie could start with, working outward from there.

Another thing on the list of items that had been more difficult than they needed to be since they took the case. A slog that was presenting plenty of extraneous data, and scads of accompanying questions, but nothing in the form of an actionable heading.

A pattern that was fast becoming old, both for Reed and for a governor he knew would soon be demanding answers.

"Don't be," Reed replied. "I knew it was a shot in the dark."

"You want me to keep digging?" Deke asked. "Give it the six-degrees treatment?"

"Naw, that's okay," Reed replied. "Something that tenuous likely wouldn't be enough to get them both branded across the forehead. Appreciate you looking into it."

"You got it," Deke answered. "Anything else right now?"

Opening his mouth to reply in the negative, Reed caught himself, pulling up short. Glancing to the street outside, he rolled past the same handful of homes that were fast becoming familiar before easing into the driveway of the last one on the street.

Easily the largest of the bunch, both in size and scope.

Something Reed, having been around Morgan a couple of times now, could not imagine was by accident.

"Maybe," Reed said. "I don't suppose there's any way to look into tattoo supplies, is there? See what private citizens might have been buying ink or a gun recently?

"I just talked to a few experts, they were pretty certain that we're not dealing with a pro here."

Deke's initial response was a sharp intake of air. A more pronounced version of his reaction when Reed first explained the case, detailing how exactly Morgan had been attacked.

A sound that was made worse now, thinking that it had been done by someone who had no idea what they were doing, just wanting to inflict the most glaring violation possible.

"I mean, maybe in theory," Deke said, "but not really. This wouldn't be like tracking bomb components or something. We're talking things that could be purchased over the counter or on Amazon."

Matching the response against what Wolf Man had said earlier, Reed nodded. Putting the sedan into park, he took up the phone and held it out before him, saying, "Yeah, that's what I figured, just thought I'd ask. Probably the same with something like ketamine too, right?"

"Pretty much," Deke replied. "A controlled substance like that could come from any vet or doctor's office in the country. Heck, they've even given it to grandma a few times when things have gotten especially rough.

"If we had a name to match with either thing it would be easy, but just to try and throw a blanket search out there would probably do more harm than good."

Nodding once more, Reed said, "Thanks, again. Say hi to Japan for us."

Chapter Forty-Four

Dean Morgan met Reed at the door wearing the latest in chic workout attire. Running shoes, wind pants, and a quarter-zip pullover with the collar flipped up, all of it prominently bearing the universally identifiable Nike Swoosh.

Same for the ball cap that rested atop his graying locks, sitting up high so as to avoid the still tender skin on his forehead. A move that Reed understood was supposed to distract from the fresh tattoo emblazoned on his skin, when in reality it merely framed it, making it even harder to miss.

An eyesore made worse after Reed's crash course in basic tattooing, courtesy of Wolf Man and his crew.

To the item, every single piece of clothing looked brand new, Reed willing to bet if he were to check Morgan's trash can, he'd see the recently removed tags resting right on top. A change in look, or a determined stance to start working out, making sure nothing like this ever happened again.

The next step in the progression, especially for a man like Morgan.

People who had been victims for the first time in their lives and had no idea how to react.

"Detectives," he said, peering past Reed and Billie and out into the street. A furtive glance, as if he were under constant surveillance and needed to keep an eye out for interlopers.

A move Reed imagined would last for months or even years, an invasion like the one Morgan endured not likely to go away soon, no matter how much logic might inform him otherwise. Reasoned thinking telling the man that if his attackers wanted anything else, it would have happened while he was unconscious a few nights before.

Not now, after they had already moved on to at least one more victim, Reed only hoping that he wasn't going to get a call later in the day informing him of a third.

"Come on in, I was just in the basement working out."

Saying nothing to the greeting or the comment that followed it, Reed stepped inside, his partner doing the same beside him. Taking only a few paces, they allowed Morgan to shut the door in their wake, grunting softly as he led them past the staircase to the second floor and the office they had been in the day before.

Stiff steps from lingering soreness that this time took the trio past the steps and deep into the home, emerging from a narrow hallway into a kitchen that Reed imagined rivaled something found in most bed-and-breakfast establishments. A spread that was done in the same modern style as the rest of the home, with polished marble countertops and stainless-steel appliances.

Kitchenware that, like the clothing Morgan was wearing, looked so new it practically gleamed. High-end furnishings that had probably come with the house or been put there by an interior designer, not touched since.

A supposition enhanced by the sight of Morgan pulling open one side of the largest home refrigerator Reed had ever seen to reveal stacks of pre-made containers on the shelves.

A food delivery service, including everything from condiments in packets to beverages in sealed plastic bottles, the latter of which Morgan grabbed from the shelf. A dark green concoction of some sort he reached for without thought, nearly turned all the way back before pausing and asking if they would like anything.

A half-hearted offering Reed turned down on behalf of them both, launching right into his reason for being there. A continuation of the conversation that began the night before, Reed having even less hope for what it might produce after the discussion with Deke on the ride in.

"Wanted to stop by, see if you might have had a chance to think about what we discussed last night."

Peeling away the ring around the top of the container, Morgan popped the top off and took a long pull. A drink that elicited a small wince from him as he finished and pulled it away, examining the writing on the label.

A quick check done out of habit, no matter the infinitely more important topic being discussed.

"I did," Morgan replied. "Went back through my old emails, searched every document on my computer, even Googled Matt Seesel and pulled up his picture to see if it would trigger anything."

Setting the bottle down beside him, Morgan pulled out a drawer by his side. From it he extracted a stack of photos, tossing them down on the island between them.

"Hell, I even dug up every photograph my ex-wife didn't take in the divorce to see if I might spot him somewhere. Nothing."

While Reed couldn't help but appreciate the man's thoroughness, he wasn't surprised it had ended without result. Between the conversation they had in the car the night before, Seesel also saying he didn't know Morgan, and Deke not being able to find any direct contact, Reed had not expected Morgan to be able to find anything.

A perfunctory question he needed to ask just to be certain before drilling down on more pressing matters.

Topics that might actually help him and Billie make some sense as to what was happening.

Taking a step forward, Reed slid the offered photos over in front of himself. More than two dozen in total, he fanned them across the marble, giving himself somewhere to stare that wasn't directly at Morgan.

A means of lowering any defensiveness that might arise with the next topic.

"We also spoke to Susan Cartwright yesterday," Reed said, "and she mentioned the mass layoff that took place not long before your retirement."

Twice in as many seconds, Morgan scoffed. First at the mention of his successor, and then again regarding the layoffs. Sounds that confirmed what Reed had anticipated, his focus remaining on the images before him.

Photos that were mostly of children in their elementary and high school years. Shots that were almost all staged, whether they be annual school photos or baseball and football team picture days, the lone outliers being a few with the same cluster of kids and their parents all grouped together

The next two generations of Morgans, Reed would guess.

The man's children and grandchildren, none of which featured him.

Depersonalized images speaking either to how small a role Morgan had played in their lives, or a curated collection serving as a middle finger from his ex-wife.

"Layoff, my ass," Morgan spat. "That was just some headline the papers put together to try and attract readers. And I didn't hear any shareholders complaining after we bumped their stock six points overnight from that, either."

Shuffling the pictures back into a stack, Reed slid them back across the counter.

"You ever get any pushback from anybody else about it? Employees or their families who were angry? Any online threats?"

Lifting his right shoulder in a shrug, Morgan said, "Sure, we had the usual number of trolls online making their comments, but it wasn't anything real."

Falling in line with what Deke had mentioned from the internet forums, Reed pressed, "Nothing in person?"

Snorting in derision, more of what Reed suspected was his real personality peeking through with each successive interaction, Morgan said, "Never. Bunch of keyboard warriors who like to talk tough from their basements but would never act on it."

Raising a hand, he motioned to his forehead and added, "Damned sure, never something like this."

How true such a statement might be, Reed didn't particularly want to get into. A tangent that would likely take them far afield and chew up precious time, he left it there, instead switching directions once more.

A final topic that had come up a couple of times on the day already, needing to be discussed.

"The crime scene crews at Seesel's house found signs that this was a team approach. At least two people, with one of them likely being a female. That ring any bells for you? Anybody you might have seen that night at Holman Brothers? Maybe a jogger or someone you may have crossed paths with around here?"

Eyes widening, Morgan pulled his chin back an inch. A look of surprise that he let linger, processing what was just shared.

Contemplation that ended not with him answering Reed's question, but posing one of his own in return.

"You think a woman did this to me?"

Chapter Forty-Five

Under a pale gray Autumn sky, Reed and Billie walked the same path outside Matt Seesel's house as they had the night before. A slow amble using the various tracks through the tall grasses and patches of mud to lead the way, examining things again. A second pass, this time armed with what little information Earl had been able to provide and with the benefit of it still being full daylight.

Starting at the side entrance into the garage, they walked across the backyard and on to the thicket of trees nearby. A site that looked even better as a hiding place in the afternoon, Reed examining things in both directions and determining that Seesel would have had to be looking directly at it to notice someone, and even then only if there were bright colors or a flash of movement to draw his attention.

Something that was unlikely enough, made even more so by the fact that the person doing the watching was the smaller of the two, likely the female in charge of applying the tattoos.

From there, they had followed the path Billie had been able to unravel the night before. A meandering trail through the trees that ended nearly a half mile away along the rutted two-lane cutting between two fields.

A walk that took nearly twenty minutes roundtrip, Seesel himself opting to remain in the garage. Dressed in jeans and a sweatshirt with the hood raised as far as possible without touching his face, he stood completely rigid from some combination of shame and soreness, his gaze fixed on the concrete floor before him.

Day one of the sequence Dean Morgan was also working through, the older man having moved into anger while Seesel still dealt with shock and denial.

Stages Reed suspected the younger man would have a much tougher time getting through, not armed with nearly the same hubris as his forbearer.

Barely moving the entire time, it wasn't until Reed and Billie crossed back from the side yard into the garage that Seesel even seemed aware of their presence, blinking himself alert before leading them both inside. A return to the living room where they had all met for the first time the day before, Seesel resuming his stance on the edge of the armchair, Reed taking up the closest end of the sofa, Billie by his side.

Across from them, the police tape was no longer stretched across the opening into the kitchen, though smudges of fingerprint dust were still visible on the table and counters.

A space it seemed Seesel had avoided entirely, venturing out of his perch on the armchair only when absolutely necessary.

His version of being able to hide at the governor's mansion the first night after the attack.

"Mr. Seesel," Reed began, "my partner and I wanted to swing back by today, both to examine everything under full light of day, and also to continue the conversation we had yesterday."

Pausing there, he waited for Seesel to pry his gaze away from the looped rug on the floor before him. A flicker of movement indicating that he was listening, the words were registering, before continuing.

"Having had a day to think about things, did you happen to recall anything at all about Dean Morgan? A chance encounter? A shared acquaintance? Anything of the sort?"

In the last twenty or so hours, it appeared that Seesel had not ate or drank anything. A lack of sustenance and hydration that left his features appearing even more drawn, the look enhanced by his expression being pulled taut.

A stare he turned and leveled on Reed, seeming to be deep in contemplation of the question, before slowly shaking his head.

"No."

"No to which part?" Reed asked.

"No, to all of it," Seesel answered. A flat statement that contained no emotion of any kind, his gaze remaining neutral. "I couldn't think of anybody by that name, so I looked him up online.

"Didn't recognize him at all. Never lived anywhere near there. Heck, I've never even been a member of Buckeye Care. Always got my coverage through the state school system."

The answer was almost word for word what Morgan said earlier. An inversion of exact details, but a similar sentiment that Reed had also expected.

A box to be checked, having now asked them both twice and getting the same answer all four times.

Leaving it there, Reed moved on to ask, "What about enemies of any kind? Someone who might have had a personal slight with you?"

"Enemies?" Seesel asked. "I've never thrown a single punch in my life. The last two girls I dated are both happily married. The last wager I made was for a pizza during March Madness. I'm probably the most non-political person you'll ever meet in your life."

Almost to the person - a lone outlier the only one who came to mind - never had Reed conducted an interview and had someone answer that question in the affirmative. A tendency for people to believe they were universally beloved, incapable of ever incurring wrath, even from afar.

Predilections he would say Morgan was guilty of, though given the bland state of the home Reed was now sitting in, he was inclined to believe about Seesel.

"How about at work?" Reed pressed. "Anything there?"

Displaying quite possibly the most personality since Reed first met the man, Seesel snorted. A derisive inhalation that rocked his head back an inch.

"Work?" he asked, his focus back to pointing at the rug in front of him. "I'm a physical education teacher, detective. The worst grade I've ever given a student is a C, and that's because he only showed up once a week."

Flicking his gaze to the side, he added, "And believe me, that kid was way too stoned to ever even conceive something like this, let alone pull it off."

Meeting his gaze, Reed nodded in understanding. Without looking away, he motioned to the photos on the far side of the room and asked, "What about with coaching?"

Any mirth of a moment before fading away, Seesel brought his mouth back into a tight line. Shaking his head, he said, "Naw. By the time kids get to high school, you've pretty much already weeded out the problem parents who don't understand why little-Johnny-who-can't-dribble isn't playing more."

"Opposing teams?" Reed pressed.

Tilting his head to the side, Seesel said, "You might get the occa-sional person who is mad you're beating their ass, but it never goes past a stray comment or two. People get fired up in the moment, but by the time they hit the parking lot, they've cooled down.

"I mean, let's be real, this isn't the NBA or D-1 college. We're talking small high schools here."

"No problems with boosters or anything like that, either?" Reed asked.

Again, Seesel made a sound, this one hinting of bemusement. "I've been here one full season thus far, so we're still in the honeymoon phase."

Flicking a hand out before him, he gestured to the photos and basketball still resting on the shelf across the room, "And after we won a state title at my last stop, I could have never won another game and they wouldn't have cared."

Following the man's gesture, Reed let his focus settle on the pair of images. Photos that he peered at from across the room, passing his gaze across each of them.

A cursory study that made it halfway through before pausing, drawing him to his feet.

"Your last stop," Reed said, echoing Seesel's words. "Where was that?"

Taking a step forward, Reed saw Seesel raise his head, following him across the room.

"Uh, Coshocton, a couple hours east of here."

Saying nothing in reply, Reed closed the gap between himself and the photos, his attention poised on the thing that had caught his eye a moment before. A sight he had not been looking for nor expected, jumping out at him just the same.

One of a handful of players that were present in both, prominently filling a spot in the back row.

A young man in his late teenage years who Reed had just seen not two hours earlier while standing in Dean Morgan's kitchen.

"Who is this?"

Chapter Forty-Six

No part of The Angel liked how things were playing out. Starting with the shitshow on the front porch of the old man's cabin the night before, things had been on a spiral. A downward trend that continued even at the home of their fourth target, the interaction between him and his brother deteriorating to a point that The Artist basically kicked them both out.

A fraying of nerves and relations that was threatening to unravel things at the most inopportune moment.

For the last six months, their entire lives had been about planning and surveillance. Whatever time wasn't allocated to absolute essentials like the job he was forced to show up at or meeting with the fat ass parole officer he was assigned to, spent in service of this one goal.

Mountains of work, enough to cover an entire basement wall, all on a precise countdown, aimed at a moment coming ever closer. An anniversary to serve as a final bit of poignancy, so that each time their victims looked in the mirrors and saw the reminders plastered to their skin, they knew why.

Exactly what had happened and the role they played in it.

If given his preference, this would have all already been completed long before. Performative exercises in pageantry including dates and tattoos and all the rest.

Skirtings of the true retribution that The Angel would rather focus on. Outcomes not just to shame them, but to make them truly pay for what was done.

Put them on an equal playing field as he and his family, the acts of grieving done not by those attacked, but to those left behind.

A course of action that was not possible, stymied by their mother insisting that things not go that way. A strict adherence to her faith that demanded that none of them do anything that would be in direct violation of the commandments.

Ironclad rules that precluded equal justice, requiring The Angel and his siblings to get more creative. Scheme up something that was a bit more bold. Would make an unmistakable statement.

Handfuls of options that were debated at length before finally their mother agreed to what was now taking place, under the caveat that they wait until she was gone. Until after her soul was departed and safely in heaven, not to be judged for what might transpire.

A bunch of crap The Angel – nor his siblings, he suspected – really bought into, though forced himself to wait out. A daily watch as she wilted away that doubled as a countdown to when they could get started.

A human hourglass that finally ran out in the spring, allowing them to get to it. The beginning of a headlong sprint that had included endless hours spent tucked inside sweltering trucks or choking down cups of coffee from some boutique shop. Long nights of scouring through social media accounts. Endless visits to Google Earth.

Damn near every waking hour, spent in preparation for right now.

So many times throughout those trips, The Angel had sat and imagined how it would all go. Visualizations that began rooted in fact, soon careening into the stuff of fantasy. Mental imagery that went from action flicks to snuff films, envisioning what would happen to the people.

The signs that would mark them for life. The shame they would carry, forever keeping themselves hidden from view, forced to hang their heads for fear of what others might say or think.

Endless wanting that had at last arrived, only to be derailed by The Tall Boy's affable demeanor and the crazy old bastard with a shotgun and a bum ticker. Two things that had both gone off simultaneously, throwing everything they had been planning into disarray.

An entirely new trajectory that none of them had ever imagined, let alone planned for. A change in timeframe that meant after leaving the apartment of the graduate student in Westerville, he and his brother were forced to part ways.

A worst-case scenario that The Angel could already sense was going to end badly.

As much as the night before, if not worse.

Seated behind the wheel of his mother's aging Buick, The Angel stared diagonally through the front windshield at the two-story home just off the opposite corner of the intersection from where he was parked. A location that was close enough to provide a clear view to the driveway running up the side of the place, while still being far enough removed that no one had ever so much as glanced his direction.

A different street entirely that nobody ever really looked at, let alone noticed the late-eighties vehicle with north of two hundred thousand under the hood and pockets of rust lining both bumpers.

A vehicle The Angel had spent an inordinate amount of time in over the last six months, to the point that the smell of his own sweat had finally overtaken the musty smell that had infused the vehicle. The automotive equivalent of mothballs, settling in after years of barely being used.

Reaching to the passenger seat beside him, The Angel took up the remaining half of a king-sized Snickers bar. Sugar and protein to fuel him through the next several hours, the number of things remaining to be done much longer than originally anticipated.

A shortened window based on what happened at the cabin the night before and the increased visibility of their targets as they worked their way through the list.

The need to finish up and get far away, any concern for the last couple of months of his parole be damned.

Tearing off half of what remained of the candy bar, The Angel chewed slowly, watching as the front door to the house across the street opened right on cue. Through it passed a man in jeans and a canvas coat, a small cooler in hand.

A blue-collar stiff, on his way to the evening shift at the local mill. A second job picked up in anticipation of the arrival of the child still growing inside the woman who exited behind him.

A figure The Angel had been watching for months now, seeing her transition from a lithe brunette to a waddling balloon easily into her third trimester.

A woman's whose name and background he knew intimately well, though in his mind went by just a single word.

ENVY.

Chapter Forty-Seven

The player in the back row of both team photos on the shelf in Matt Seesel's living room was named Chance Murphy. A six-foot-three swingman who was a classic late bloomer, bursting onto the scene his junior year and helping to lead the team to a state quarterfinal berth.

A tie for fifth place that made it all the way to the top the next season, Murphy and a trio of other seniors helping the school to its first state title and Seesel to a bright spot on his resume.

An apex that he rode for a while at Coshocton before deciding to transfer over to Plainfield High School. The last peak before the start of a slow decline, this latest incident a couple of nights before threatening to be a valley from which he might not escape.

As Reed asked about the team photos, Seesel had momentarily managed to shed the despondence that was draped over him like the blanket a day before. Rising from his spot in the armchair, he'd walked over and stood on the opposite side of the pictures, a look of fondness on his face as he explained the significance of the two images.

An expression lost in past glories, lingering for several moments before receding. Back to the original state of despair as he pulled his gaze away, focusing on Reed beside him.

"One of the many things about high school sports is they aren't like the pros, or even college. You can't just go out and recruit. Sure as hell can't go to a draft and pick the best players available.

"All you have to work with is whoever lives within your school district."

Extending a hand beside him, he waved to the pair of photos without looking over.

"Sometimes, you strike gold, end up with a bunch of kids who've been playing together since they could walk. You couple that with total community buy-in, and you have something special."

Shaking his head, he continued, "Most of the time – especially at these smaller schools – you get a mishmash of sizes and styles and try to make the best of it."

Turning away from the wall, he pushed out a long breath through his nose. An audible sigh, before adding, "Which is why you probably won't see any of the teams I coach here at Plainfield up on this shelf anytime soon."

Moving back across the middle of the living room, Seesel found his way to the same armchair. Bypassing the front edge of it, he dropped down heavily, the padded seat wheezing beneath his weight.

An unceremonious deposit that Reed listened to without looking back, his focus instead still locked on the pair of team photos. Two groups of kids in their teenage years, virtually the same assemblage gathered in both images. Faces that he largely disregarded, his attention alternating between the two shots of Chance Murphy.

A young man who apparently was a multi-sport athlete, donning a tank top and shorts in these photos, as opposed to the shoulder pads and cleats he wore in the shot resting on Dean Morgan's island.

Uniforms of the same color scheme, the latter not bearing the same questionable team name across the front that would have caught Reed's eye sooner.

The sole thing connecting the two men recently attacked with sedatives and a tattoo gun, despite neither having mentioned the other.

A connection so tenuous, even Deke hadn't been able to find mention of it on his first attempt.

"Tell me about him," Reed said. A question that went without reply for a moment, causing him to turn back to face Seesel. "Chance Murphy."

Hands draped along the armrests of the chair, Seesel lifted his palms toward the ceiling. An expression of resignation, even without voicing as much.

"Not a lot to tell beyond what I already said," Seesel replied. "He played football and ran track as well. The kind of kid who was always on the team, often a starter, but definitely never a star, up until the summer between his sophomore and junior years.

"That's when a growth spurt gave him six inches, took him from being a very average shooting guard to a damn good small forward."

Taking a step forward, Reed extended his right hand beside him. A silent call that drew Billie to his side, his fingers finding the thick fur between her ears.

"Did you know his family?"

"I knew his parents," Seesel said. "Sylvia was a team mom, came around a lot to decorate and pass out treats. His dad was a little more removed, but still showed up at all the games.

"Derron, or Derrick. Something like that."

Once more, he shrugged with his hands, twisting his palms upward.

"Like I said before, never met Dean Morgan."

After seeing the collection of sterile images at Morgan's house, the statement didn't come as a surprise to Reed. Any connection Morgan likely had to his grandson was peripheral, at best.

Not the sort of person to be on a first-name basis with his high school basketball coach.

"That's all there was?" Reed asked. "Just, nature running its course?"

"And a lot of hard work," Seesel replied, the faintest hint of defensiveness creeping in. "It's not like there was some steroid scandal or anything, if that's what you're asking."

Continuing to knead the tuft of black hair atop Billie's head, his fingers leaving furrows through the thick fur, Reed said, "Were there any other kinds of scandals? Anything at all that someone might draw a connection to?"

"Definitely not," Seesel replied, the underlying tone growing stronger. "Not those kids, or any of the teams I coached for that matter."

Stated with absolute certainty, Reed half expected the man to leap up from his chair and start stamping his feet. Demand respect in his home. Start proselytizing about morals and values that he worked to instill.

An outburst Reed anticipated, even while turning to regard the photos one last time. A final mental image to use while taking a new path moving forward.

A tirade that never came, Seesel instead surprising him with the words, "But now that I think about it, there was one sort-of-something that happened back around that time."

Chapter Forty-Eight

The matter Matt Seesel alluded to was now just shy of seven years ago. From the sound of it, a small incident at a party outside of town, the senior class celebrating a football victory over their rivals to close the season.

The type of thing that could easily be nothing. Kids getting together and experimenting with drugs or alcohol. A fight breaking out over something that to the teenage mind seemed like a mortal affront.

Something so benign that the local sheriff went through the required paces, spoke with Seesel, the football coach, the parent who owned the cabin, but ultimately decided it wasn't worth pursuing.

A minor issue that didn't need to taint a whole lot of kids before they even graduated high school.

As Seesel put it, a sort-of-something, but nothing more.

Hearing the story out loud, it wasn't unlike a fair number of stories Reed had heard over the years. Young people making mistakes, given a second chance before it became a cloud that hung over them moving forward.

At the same time, it didn't take a great deal of imagination to conjure a scenario in which it was much, much worse. The sort of thing that might escalate further, getting to a point that connected people, even without them knowing.

A horrific night so bad it left lingering scars all these years later, to the point that someone felt the need to now do the same to others.

The very last question Reed asked Seesel was if he ever took any kind of bribe in connection to that incident. A question he could tell offended the man, causing a shift in demeanor for the second time since their arrival.

A transition from an engaged state to a quick flash of rage, making it unequivocally clear that he had never taken a dime beyond the pittance he was paid for teaching and coaching. The start of some heavy-handed tirade Reed cut off by explaining to him that the only thing he had in common with Dean Morgan was Chance Murphy.

Or, in simpler terms, the sole connection between a high school gym teacher and a retired CEO was the young man who may or may not have been involved in an incident.

A macro level view that it was clear Seesel still didn't appreciate, though he did at least understand, stating as much before again relaying his innocence.

A response Reed wanted to believe at face value, the events of the last day stripping Seesel of any ability to lie, though still needed to check out.

"Dude," Deke answered on just the second ring. Despite having still been awake when they spoke earlier in the day, there wasn't the slightest hint of grog present.

In the background, Reed could hear the ongoing clatter of fingers hitting a keyboard, whatever was happening in Japan still demanding his attention.

Something that, hopefully, he could stand to be away from for just a couple of minutes.

"Hey, sorry to keep bothering you, but I'm on the road and was hoping you could run a name for me. If you're tied up, I could call and ask Captain Grimes to do it."

Stopping there, he didn't add that while he knew Grimes would be glad to do it, saving them the trip all the way back to the precinct, he knew that Deke could give a much more comprehensive overview.

In a fraction of the time.

"Shoot," Deke replied, firing it back without pause.

An opening Reed seized, saying, "Chance Murphy. Spelled just like it sounds. Dean Morgan's grandson, played on basketball teams coached by Matt Seesel seven and eight years ago in Coshocton."

In lieu of an answer, he heard the telltale sound of Deke's keyboard coming alive again. Indicators that he was already on it, even as Reed added, "May or may not have been involved in some sort of incident that went down during that time."

Saying nothing in immediate reply, Deke continued to peck away. Background noise over the speakerphone that blended with the sound of the highway passing beneath the tires of Reed's sedan.

He and Billie's fourth such trip across the interior of the state in less than a day, each successive one starting to feel a little longer. Miles that were beginning to wear on them both, coupled with the first tiny inkling of things coming together.

A connection, no matter how small, that was allowing anticipation to begin to build.

"Okay," Deke said after barely a minute of searching, "got him here. Chance Murphy, age 25. Currently residing in New Albany after attending Xavier for college and then spending two years living in the Short North."

Matching the information with what Seesel shared earlier, Reed nodded, remaining silent.

"As for the incident that may or may not have happened," Deke added, "there is no mention of it anywhere."

"He could have been seventeen at the time," Reed added. "Maybe a sealed juvie file?"

"Nope," Deke replied. "Record is clean."

Chapter Forty-Nine

"Good afternoon!"

Reed's first thought after getting off the phone with Deke was to contact Chance Murphy directly. Either give him a call or go and visit him at home, asking him what transpired in the fall of his senior year.

An incident that he would no doubt recall, though what form the story may take after so much time, Reed couldn't be certain. Years during which it may have morphed into something new, shaped by the misremembering of youth and the forces of self-preservation.

A less-than-reliable witness Reed decided to put off for the time being, beginning instead with the sheriff who had gone to speak with Matt Seesel. An account from the man who looked into things and deemed there was not enough to warrant further investigation, much less charges.

Someone who, with luck, might have notes or even a file some-where Reed could consult. A list of names he spoke to or even the motivation behind all of it.

Something more than the thin connection between the two victims Reed currently had, not yet even enough to be confirmed as the cause behind what was happening, let alone to start alerting others or putting them under protection.

Right now, it was nothing more than a heading. A line of pursuit for the hours and days ahead as he and Billie tried to piece things together before anybody else was attacked.

The fact that there would be more being the only thing Reed knew with certainty, it not by mistake that the people he was hunting had chosen to use items from the famed list of seven deadly sins as their tattoos of choice.

"Hi, Sheriff Broderick?" Reed said. Seated behind the steering wheel of his sedan, the door beside him was standing wide, his left foot planted on the asphalt below.

One of a handful of parking spots lining the side of a small park outside Grove City, located on the southwest corner of the greater Columbus area. A spot he was familiar with from having worked a case in the area more than a year before, he and Billie crisscrossing the entire western half of the city in search of a young girl buried alive.

An incident that still made his stomach clench, even now as he sat watching his partner work her way around the grassy expanse nearby, looking to relieve herself from an early dinner a few minutes before.

Fuel for whatever lay in the hours ahead, Reed having done the same, the remains of his sandwich still resting in his lap after being interrupted by the incoming call.

A return from the sheriff of Coshocton County, getting back to Reed barely fifteen minutes after he first phoned.

"Yes, sir," the man replied in a voice that was nothing short of booming. A cadence that gave Reed the immediate mental image of a large, jovial man wearing a uniform and a perpetual smile. "This Detective Mattox?"

"It is," Reed replied. "Thanks for getting back to me so fast."

Pausing for only an instant, long enough to let the initial greeting pass, he continued, "Sheriff, this is going to sound like an unusual request, but I was hoping to speak with you about an incident that took place almost seven years ago to the day. Would have involved some kids – possibly ball players – from the local high school, and was eventually dropped without charges."

Even with the preface that it was an odd ask, Reed could tell how far afield it must have sounded, hearing it out loud for himself.

A request that must have been confusing as hell, causing him to quickly jump in with a bit more information. An explanation of the case he and Billie were working and the possible connection they had made between the first two victims.

Additional data that seemed to break through some of the bewilderment, prompting Broderick to reply, "Ah, I got you. And it sounds like something I would remember, though I didn't come on until a couple of years after.

"Wasn't elected sheriff until a few more beyond that."

Curling the fingers of his left hand resting atop his thigh into a ball, Reed squeezed tight. A clench that traveled the length of his arm and into his shoulder, matching his molars coming together tight.

Not one single thing had gone right since he and Billie were summoned from the bar on Sunday afternoon. Multiple cases featuring even more trips across central Ohio, with very little to show for it.

A slog that had just revealed the tiniest bit of light, only to again be curtailed.

"Is there anybody there who might remember it?" Reed asked. "Anybody else we could speak to?"

"Here?" Broderick said. "Most of the staff has turned over since then, but we do have one old boy who's been around since the nineties. He's away for hunting season right now, but let me give him a call when he comes down out of the tree stand, see if he remembers anything."

Again, Reed clenched his fist tight enough to feel his fingernails digging into his palms.

"I'd appreciate that, sheriff."

"Of course," Broderick said. "In the meantime, do you want the contact information for the guy who was the sheriff here before me? Old Bert isn't much for the phone, but he's still plenty sharp. If you stop by, he might be able to help you."

Chapter Fifty

Sheriff Broderick turned out to be something of a clairvoyant, four consecutive attempts by Reed to contact his predecessor - a man named Bertran Alexander - coming up empty. Calls equally spaced while Reed decided to forego shooting directly across the city at a time that was fast approaching rush hour, instead opting to take the outer belt.

A choice that added an additional ten miles or so in distance, but managed to shave the better part of half an hour in terms of time.

A savings he hoped to put to good use by being able to sit down and speak to the former sheriff, wanting to hear what happened before circling back with Chance Murphy or his grandfather. A plan he was resigned would have to include showing up at the man's residence unannounced, his hope being that Broderick's inclusion of a home address meant it was something that was expected.

Welcomed, even.

Fixed in the left-most lane of traffic, Reed put the cruise control at sixty-five, allowing his thoughts to swirl as he worked his way around the outer belt. A continuation of all that the day had uncovered, trying to put together what he had learned into some form of a coherent framework.

A means of linking the two incidents that had already occurred and the fear that many more were on the horizon. Further still, of connecting them back to what appeared to be a team of perpetrators with no signs of slowing.

A task Reed was still in the middle of, trying to formulate a cogent story to present to Alexander when his phone erupted from the middle console. An unexpected sound in the quiet of the sedan, Billie's head poking up through the front seats at the same time Reed shot out a hand, snatching up the device.

Giving the screen nothing more than a glance, he accepted the call, flipping it to speaker and dropping it down into his lap.

"Captain."

"Detective," Grimes said, his voice drawn even tighter than usual. A single word relaying that something new had occurred, Reed's pulse picking up slightly.

A cue Billie seized on, the side of her face coming to rest against his arm.

"What happened?"

"There's been another one."

On cue, Reed felt his entire upper body draw tight. A clamp much stronger than when speaking with Sheriff Broderick earlier, causing his molars to come down hard, his lips peeling back to expose his teeth. A loud sigh shot through his nostrils, paired with his left hand tightening around the steering wheel.

Reflexive actions that he held for several seconds, waiting until he could feel the burn of lactic acid before slowly starting to release.

"What happened?" he repeated.

"Carly Mayes," Grimes replied. "Graduate student at Otterbein. Missed her own class around noon, when she didn't show up for the one she was supposed to be teaching later in the afternoon, a friend went to check on her.

"Found her unconscious in the living room of her apartment."

Delivered without inflection, Reed waited for him to continue. The inclusion of the part he didn't want to hear, but knew was the most relevant.

The aspect that had precipitated him calling Reed, certain it was another of theirs.

"GLUTTONY."

Flicking his gaze up to the signage passing overhead, checking their position, Reed asked, "Where?"

"Westerville, just off campus," Grimes replied. "I'll send you the address as soon as we're off."

Grunting softly in reply, Reed asked, "Do I even want to know how we got word of this one?"

"Chief Brandt called me," Grimes said. "She put out an order to all the local captains telling them that anything like this was supposed to go straight to her.

"The goal was to keep the governor from getting wind of anything, though based on my conversation with her a few minutes ago, I don't think it worked."

As much as Reed wanted to believe that nobody in CPD would go running to Cowan, he knew better. While his relationship with Chief Brandt had improved tremendously in the last couple of years, there were many who weren't of the same mind about her.

People who didn't like how she was doing the job or thought she had overstayed her welcome or who simply didn't like seeing a diminutive female as the face of the organization.

To say nothing of those who might just be looking to curry favor with the highest-ranking official in the state.

"How much heat we talking?" Reed asked, leaving the question deliberately vague, knowing that his captain would understand.

"You know Cowan," Grimes responded.

A statement that was all the answer Reed needed.

He did know Cowan. And he knew that the man always wanted everything done yesterday.

"Tell the chief we're on our way."

Chapter Fifty-One

The Artist didn't like this one bit.

Far less, even, than what took place at the old man's cabin the night before. The argument she lost with The Angel, the scales eventually tipped by him browbeating The Tall Boy into taking his side.

A deciding vote that was anything but neutral.

An outcome that would not repeat itself, The Artist this time having an equal share in the decision-making process, their trio whittled down to just two for the time being.

A splitting of the forces, hoping to get a second and third attack done in short order. A new approach after the events of the previous evening. A way to get through things quicker, leaving them all to descend on the last target on their list together.

A final blow of summation that would simultaneously reveal exactly what they had been doing and why, while letting them also disappear. Leave the area and even the damn state forevermore, any ties they might have had to it finally severed.

The death of their mother and the justice they'd all been wanting to hand out for so long both accomplished, letting them fade from view.

Lofty goals that with each passing moment started to feel a bit less likely. Plans they had spent months perfecting, had even managed to execute flawlessly through the first couple runs, that were now becoming shaky at best.

The first wobbles, threatening to send them careening sideways.

An impending fiery crash that started with the old man, threatening to become a pattern with what was now sitting between The Artist and her brother.

"How the hell did this happen?" she demanded, snapping her attention up from the drop cloth in the center of the garage floor. A location chosen because it connected directly to the house and provided an easy escape into the alley out behind it.

An enclosed space with no windows or clear lines of sight, allowing them to do what they needed to without being seen, the real heavy lifting of the project already done by The Angel earlier in getting their target to this point before exiting to go and pick up The Artist from where she was parked a few miles away.

Effort that, unlike most of their previous victims, The Artist hoped was a bit more gentle. Less of the pounding body blows that her brother loved to throw, adding a little extra to what was already a tremendous amount of pain and humiliation. A few bruises and cracked ribs that normally she looked the other way on, but not on this.

Not with them already having one life on their hands, not needing to add another in what was clearly a growing fetus inside their fifth intended target.

"How?" The Angel repeated, his eyebrows rising slightly. "I wasn't there, so I can't say exactly, but I have a pretty good idea how these things usually go."

Folding her arms across her torso, The Artist merely stared straight back. Fighting the urge to raise a middle finger, to potentially set off another of her brother's famous outbursts, she instead arched an eyebrow.

"I mean, I know it's been a long time for you," he continued. Words that only made the look of disdain on The Artist's features grow more pronounced. "But hell, I was in jail for eight years, and even I didn't forget how it works."

"Are you done yet?"

"For this poor woman's sake, I hope she didn't have to say that," The Angel replied. One last attempt to keep up what he probably viewed as witty banter. Innuendos it was obvious he was enjoying, as few things outside of beating on that damned punching bag in the basement or tormenting The Tall Boy seemed to. "If she's going to be stuck like this for nine months after, she should at least enjoy herself."

"How long have you known about this?" The Artist pressed, getting past her brother's macabre sense of humor.

An effort that was thwarted again as one side of his mouth curled upward. Extending a hand to the girl between them, he said, "Well, based on when mom died and this all started, and the size of that belly there..."

Turning to the side, The Artist began to pace. A short path covering the length of the garage, the space half filled by the mid-sized SUV occupying one of two spots. In the front of the other sat a pile of boxes and assorted Christmas decorations.

Items that would soon be up, for the moment relegated to reflecting the glow of the pair of lightbulbs on overhead.

"So you've known about this all along?" The Artist snapped. "All that time doing research. All those visits you insisted on handling yourself. This was why?"

Leaning against the exposed studs of the wall across from her, The Angel crossed his arms. Raising his left foot, he balanced the toe of it on the row of concrete block forming the base of the garage.

His best approximation of looking bored, the mirth he'd been carrying finally starting to fade.

"Of course, it was. Our brother is petrified of his own shadow, so I knew he'd crap down his leg. I knew you would be a tougher sell, but after last night, I figure we're good."

Ceasing her pacing, The Artist turned and openly glared at her brother. "After last...? What the hell is that supposed to mean?"

The left side of The Angel's face scrunched as he replied, "Oh, come off it. You tattooed a dead man not twenty hours ago. You really mean to tell me *this* is where you draw the line?"

Beginning deep in her core, The Artist could feel indignation rise.

Warmth flushed her skin. The taste of bile climbed along the back of her throat.

"That was different, you sick bastard," she spat, having to force herself not to scream. "That old man was already dead. We couldn't do any more damage to him."

Stabbing a finger at the motionless figure between them, she added, "Not only is this one alive, but she has another life growing inside of her!"

Rolling his eyes to the side, The Angel shook his head, brushing aside her concerns.

"Which is why I used some of mom's old diazepam instead of the ketamine," he said. "The baby will be fine. Besides, this is perfect. The whole idea was to make people face up to what they did.

"Now this one will have to explain to her child every damn day what is written across her face."

Each additional word The Angel said spiked the growing animosity The Artist felt for him. A man who already had questionable views and decision making, taken to an entirely different level by his time in prison.

The perfect greenhouse, allowing a budding sociopath to bloom.

"No. Absolutely not. I'm not doing it."

"Fine," The Angel said, unfolding his arms to raise his palms to either side. "Don't do it. *I* will. But believe me when I tell you, I won't be nearly as gentle, or as careful."

Chapter Fifty-Two

In spite of the standing order from Governor Cowan two nights before to be as invisible as possible, Reed chose to run with the flashers on, using the lights to push vehicles to the side as he tore north up I-270. A trade he was willing to make, reasoning that he would douse them once they got off the freeway, whatever looks of curiosity he got from the motorists he passed by a fair price for the time saved in getting there.

Precious minutes that would enable him to tamp down whatever scene he was about to arrive to find, his only hope that the CPD in Westerville was better equipped than the folks in Springfield had been. Likely to be in a neighborhood much more dense than where Matt Seesel lived, should a similar show of force be present, there would be no keeping away the media.

Reporters with cameramen in tow, their vans lining the street, to say nothing of the throngs of nosy neighbors, all with devices practically affixed to their hands. Video recording and internet posting capabilities that continued to evolve by the day, annihilating Cowan's request in a matter of minutes.

Another problem Reed would like to avoid if possible, both for the sake of their investigation, and for Chief Brandt still attempting to keep the governor at arm's length.

A bullet he didn't want her to have to take in the name of buying him and Billie some more time.

Having typed the address Captain Grimes gave him into the GPS on his phone, Reed alternated his gaze between the screen and the road ahead. A gray corridor four lanes across, illuminated by a mix of orange sodium lights lining the median and the front headlamps of vehicles such as his own.

More than sufficient glow to allow him to run well above eighty, tearing north around the outer belt, his earlier decision to avoid fighting crosstown traffic not looking nearly as sage as it had earlier.

Seated upright behind the wheel, he could feel Billie's hot breath on his arm, the both of them practically willing the sedan forward. A conscious wish that they could already be at the site of the red dot on the phone's screen, each passing second bringing with it more possible outcomes.

Drawing more attention.

Raising the chances of changing the perpetrator's process, now as Reed and Billie were starting to make their first bits of real headway since being handed the case a couple of nights before.

A series of eventualities that riffled through Reed's mind, taking up a fair bit of active thought as he hurtled north. A drive of just over ten minutes before he was able to exit, hitting a wide thoroughfare lined with the requisite gas stations and fast-food restaurants. Chain businesses of every kind with signage and storefronts aglow, their combined effect making it feel much earlier in the day.

A street Reed chose to navigate by keeping his flashing lights on, letting them push commuters to the side.

A tact he continued for more than two miles off the freeway, waiting until he made another turn, this one onto a much smaller avenue, before killing them. A shift away from the bright bustle of before, moving them into a residential neighborhood.

A winding two-lane with small apartment complexes and duplexes standing tight to one another on either side, Reed following the directions on his screen for another half mile before making one last turn.

A right onto a street that was much smaller than even the one before it. A road that was barely wide enough for his sedan and the rows of vehicles parked on either side.

Framed by private single-family dwellings butted up close to one another, tall trees filled most of the yards. Void of most of their leaves, they provided a clear line of sight into front windows with televisions blazing and families sitting down to dinner.

People oblivious to what was occurring just a couple of blocks ahead, Reed's pulse increasing as they drew closer to the destination flashing across the screen of his phone.

An end point that they arrived at barely a minute later, demarcated by a cruiser sitting silent along the curb. Beyond it, a second one was pulled into the driveway of a two-story home with brown clapboard siding and a waist-high hedge lining the front, resting with its tail end just in from the edge of the sidewalk.

Two vehicles without wigwag lights or front headlamps blazing, as unobtrusive as possible given the circumstances.

And light years beyond what they had arrived to find at Matt Seesel's the day before.

Sidling up to the curb along the right side, Reed pulled in directly behind the first cruiser, using the sedan to block the second one from view. A makeshift shield for the vehicle pulled into the driveway, halving what all but any foot traffic would be able to see as they made their way past.

Killing his own lights and ignition, Reed left Billie in the backseat and hopped out. Jogging around to the backseat, he took up the same short lead used a few times in the last couple days already and clipped it to her harness.

A process they were able to finish in just a few seconds, both of them barely across the sidewalk and sliding between the cruiser and the side of the building before they were met by a young officer in uniform.

"Detective Mattox?" the officer said, a young man in his late twenties with coal black hair buzzed short on the sides and left long on top, combed straight back and held in place with copious amounts of gel.

Standing several inches shorter than Reed, he was wiry without being skinny.

His features pulled taut, he stopped just far enough back from the front of the cruiser to give Reed and Billie room to come around.

"That's right," Reed answered. Motioning to Billie beside him, he added, "My K-9 partner, Billie."

"Dillon Wyght," the officer answered. Hooking a thumb over a shoulder, he added, "Officers Yang and Bintner are on the door. My partner, Melanie Christ, is upstairs with the victim and her friend now."

Following the path of Wyght's motion, Reed looked down the length of the driveway. A stretch of concrete that opened into a wide roundabout behind the main house, providing access to both it and a freestanding garage on the backend.

A structure with the bottom hollowed out for parking or storage, individual bays separated by support beams holding up a closed space on the second floor.

An area that Reed guessed doubled as living quarters for their newest victim, with lights blazing bright behind blinds pulled low.

Rotating back around, Wyght jabbed the same thumb toward the side of the house. "The owner is a guy named Ted Christianson. He just got home from work downtown about twenty minutes ago, pulled up and saw our cruisers, got all worked up.

"We were able to talk to him for a few minutes, but the more questions we asked, the more frantic he became."

Tracking his gaze to follow Wyght's motion, Reed peered in through a side window. A small opening into what looked to be the kitchen, with no signs of movement visible.

"What's the relationship between him and the victim?" Reed asked.

"Strictly landlord-tenant," Wyght answered. "They'd never met before August, when she answered an ad and moved in."

"Any problems?" Reed asked.

"None," Wyght replied. "Friendly, but not friends, Christianson said she largely keeps to herself. Busy with school, has a couple of classmates who will stop by once or twice a week.

"Never any confrontations. Nothing after hours."

In line with everything else they'd experienced for the last few days, Reed nodded. A series of cases that looked to have all been planned for months and executed as such, taking care to snip away anything obvious.

"Any cameras on the place?" Reed asked.

Giving his head a shake, Wyght replied, "No."

"Anybody see anything?"

"Nobody's come forward," Wyght answered, "and we were told to secure the place and wait for you before starting any kind of canvas."

Grasping the unstated part of what Wyght was hinting at, Reed nodded again. A quick sign of understanding while moving his focus back up to the pair of windows with blinds lit up from within.

A scene sure to be both similar, and vastly different, from what they'd encountered with Morgan and Seesel.

"Let me go up and try to talk to her first," Reed replied. "After that, if we need to start knocking on doors, we will."

"You got it," Wyght agreed.

Slapping at the leg of his jeans to call Billie along, Reed took just a single step before pausing. Glancing sideways to Wyght, he asked, "Just so we know, how bad is it up there?"

"Unlike anything the four of us have ever seen."

Chapter Fifty-Three

Officers Yang and Bintner standing on either side of the entrance to the apartment seemed to be of the same opinion as Officer Wyght about the scene upstairs. Both straddling the crack separating the driveway from the open garage, they were each visibly uneasy, making no attempt to go any further than where they stood.

A move that was warned off by the sound of sobbing echoing out from above, plainly audible even with the door standing closed behind them.

Both just a couple years younger than Reed, they each nodded as he and Billie approached, neither saying a word as they passed between them and through the plain wooden door. An entry into a small landing with tile flooring and a staged area for coats and shoes, the main point of the space being to funnel entrants up the staircase aimed toward the back of the building.

Wooden steps that squeaked under Reed's and Billie's combined weight, each successive rise causing the sound of crying to grow more pronounced. Wailing interspersed with heavy breathing on the verge of panting, a few stray whispers mixed throughout.

The soft assurances of the friend who had called it in, Reed guessed, climbing a dozen steps or so before turning on a mezzanine and heading back toward the front. A new angle giving him his first glimpse of the interior of the repurposed space, clearly meant originally to be storage, later made into an apartment.

A spot that was probably put together on the front end of the Airbnb and VRBO boons before the owners got sick of the constant cleaning and advertising involved and made it a permanent domicile.

One that Carly Mayes had done her best to convert into a home, the area aglow with Christmas lights. Bulbs of various colors giving off a soft glow, extending all the way to the stairs.

In the air, Reed could detect the smells of peppermint and cinnamon. Some combination of holiday candles and efforts by the friend to make something that would be soothing to Carly.

Or to mask the faint undertones of the same chemical scent that Tanner Moss mentioned detecting in Matt Seesel's garage the day before.

A sensory deluge that under most circumstances might be somewhat comforting for the young woman, though this evening was having absolutely no effect. A fact that grew more apparent as Reed and Billie climbed the last couple of stairs, the source of the assorted sounds that had been leading them upward finally coming into view.

Curled into the corner of the sofa resting against the far wall was Carly Mayes. A young woman in her mid-twenties who Reed had never seen before in his life, though had no doubt as to her identity based on the sobs pouring from her and the new tattoo across her forehead.

Ink that was so fresh it hadn't yet had time to even dry, the combination of the Christmas lights and the bulbs attached to the ceiling fan overhead reflecting from it.

Block letters that were probably the same size as those adorning Dean Morgan and Matt Seesel, though looked so much more pronounced given the length of the word and her diminished stature. Two factors that meant dark ink took up nearly all of the available space, the G and Y in GLUTTONY touching her hairline above either temple.

Twisted into a ball on her left side, her knees were curled toward her chest, a wad of tissue clutched in both hands. A fleece blanket was threaded across her waist and between her arms, fuzzy socks and thick sweats peeking out in between.

Beside her on a papasan chair in the corner sat who Reed presumed was the friend who called it in. A young black woman of approximately the same age with mocha skin and straightened hair pulled back behind her. Wearing an Ohio State sweatshirt and a pair of black running pants, it looked just as Grimes described, like she had stopped by after class, never imagining this was what she would be pulled into.

In either hand was a mug and a bottle of water. Attempts at being helpful that looked to have thus far gone unused.

On her face was an expression that hinted of feeling supremely helpless. Sorrow for her friend and pleading that she aimed at Reed as he and Billie trudged up the last couple of steps, stopping on the edge of the room.

A look he matched by pressing his lips together and tilting his head forward in silent greeting before sliding his gaze to the side to take in the last person present.

Melanie Christ, the partner Officer Wyght alluded to earlier, standing beside the sink in the small kitchen carved out in the corner. Every bit as young as Wyght, Reed was again reminded of his old partner and her line about the newbies having spots.

A memory that was there and gone in an instant, even his departed friend's faux British accent not enough to penetrate the cloud of sorrow enshrouding the tiny space. A suffocating presence that had brought a flush to the officer's pale features, her shoulders visibly rising and falling as she drew in deep breaths.

Starting there, Reed made a hard right turn at the top of the stairs. Needing no more than a handful of steps, he and Billie came to a stop just shy of Christ.

Keeping his back to the room, he leaned in close and whispered, "What have we got so far?"

Flicking her gaze to the side, Christ replied, "Absolutely nothing. I've tried to engage her in conversation a couple of times, ask her some questions, but it's just been this – or worse – since I got here."

Resisting the urge to do the same, turn over a shoulder and reexamine Mayes again for himself, the sound of her ongoing sobbing telling him plenty, Reed asked, "How long ago was that?"

"Call came in about an hour ago," Christ said. "We were on patrol in the area, got here shortly after."

Grunting softly, Reed asked, "The friend?"

"She answered what she could, but didn't know much."

Gesturing toward the open doorway leading to the rear of the makeshift apartment, Reed asked, "What's back there?"

"Bedroom, bathroom," Christ responded.

Lifting his chin just barely in a nod of understanding, Reed turned back to face the opposite direction. A scene that was exactly as he left it just moments before, with Mayes curled on her side, seemingly unaware of anyone else even being present, and her friend staring directly at Reed.

A look he matched, tilting his head back a second time before dipping it to the side.

An unspoken message that she matched with a nod of her own, carefully placing the mug and the bottle of water onto the floor by Mayes's side and rising to her feet. Straightening her sweatshirt as she went, she cut a diagonal across the small living room and passed through the open doorway, Reed and Billie both following her into a bedroom even smaller than the front half of the apartment.

A space barely large enough for a twin bed, a dresser, and an end table, everything already festooned in the same early Christmas décor.

"How you holding up?" Reed asked, again putting his back to the scene in the living room.

With the benefit of an extra wall separating them from Mayes, the sound of her crying was significantly lower. An underlying presence that still allowed them to speak at normal volume and be heard.

Bobbing her head several times in order, the young woman said, "I, uh..." A few short syllables before exhaling loudly and saying, "Yeah, it's a lot. I never..."

"Us either," Reed admitted. "It is a lot, and believe me, all of us – Carly included - appreciates you being here."

Looking as if she might respond, the girl let it go by again sighing loudly. Pressing her lips together, she bobbed her head once more, the tail of her ponytail swinging behind her.

A combination of nervous energy and uncertainty and more of that same helpless feeling Reed witnessed when they entered.

"My name is Detective Reed Mattox, and this is my K-9 partner, Billie. We are from the state Bureau of Criminal Investigations. Do you mind if we ask you a few questions?"

Again, she nodded, though remained silent.

"Good, let's start with your name."

"Marissa," she replied, leaving it at that before adding, "Lange. I'm a friend of Carly's from school."

"And I understand you were the one who found her?"

"I was," Marissa said. "We were supposed to have a class together at noon today, but she never showed, which is odd. Carly *never* misses class.

"I texted her to see if everything was okay, but never heard back. Later, when she didn't show for her teaching assignment, and hadn't called to let anybody know or make arrangements, I got a bad feeling something was wrong.

"I live not far from here, so I decided to leave early, swing by and check on her."

Noting how she had stopped short of mentioning exactly what she found when she arrived, Reed opted to avoid making her state the obvious, instead asking, "Was there anybody else here when you showed up? Notice anybody leaving the house? Cars driving away?"

Shaking her head to either side, Marissa replied, "No."

"Anything out of place?"

It was clear that previous mental images were returning by the increased pace of her breathing. Prior shock that was still fresh, bringing a veneer of sweat to her features.

"Uh, no. Just Carly laying on the couch with the, um..."

Like both Morgan and Seesel before her, she motioned toward her forehead, refraining from saying the word.

Avoidance that Reed could not fault one of them for in the slightest.

"I know it's hard," Reed said. "Believe me, we hate doing this as much as you do. We just have a few more questions right now, and then we'll let you go back and be with your friend."

Almost as if on cue, Mayes let off another outburst. A wail of emotion that reverberated through the apartment, causing all three of them to turn in unison toward the doorway.

A fixed pose held for several seconds, ended by Reed asking, "Did you wake her, or did she wake on her own?"

"I did," Marissa whispered.

"How long ago was that?"

"Right before the police got here," Marissa said. "Maybe an hour?"

"Last one," Reed replied, "has Carly said a word since then?"

Chapter Fifty-Four

As seemed to so often be how it went when Reed and Billie were in the middle of a case, late afternoon had become early evening, which had then somehow slipped into late evening. A loss of hours that he had barely noticed, each stop throughout the day taking more time than he could have anticipated.

Moments such as Matt Seesel recalling his state championship team in Coshocton or Carly Mayes fighting against the inconsolable sorrow of waking up to find what had happened to her.

Things there were simply no way of rushing along, Reed's drive for expediency surpassed only by the need to be thorough.

Time on the job that he knew would be matched by his captain, no chance existing that Grimes would abandon his post at the 8th until he heard back from Reed about what he found at the newest scene. A certainty that meant it came as no surprise when the man picked up after only a single sound, barely letting it finish ringing before snatching up the phone.

"Grimes."

"I need a favor," Reed opened, not bothering with his own introduction as he worked his way back through the same streets he and Billie had just driven less than two hours before. A route that was decidedly thinner than on their previous pass through, much of the traffic in the area already having made it home or well on their way to getting there. "Two of them, actually."

"I'm listening," Grimes replied.

If he had any hesitation, any need to temper expectations of what he could provide, he didn't show it in the slightest.

"First, we need to send someone over to check on Carly Mayes," Reed said. "As you can imagine, the poor girl is an absolute wreck. We waited well over an hour, and still couldn't even talk to her.

"I was able to get a little bit out of her friend, but not much. I'm afraid if we don't get her calmed down, she could end up having a full-on nervous breakdown."

On the other end, Grimes made his usual clicking noise. A sound that others would deem akin to a grunt, the captain adding nothing more.

"Again, I know this is supposed to all be quiet as hell, so I'm calling you instead of the EMTs directly."

"I'm on it as soon as we hang up," the captain said. "I know of some private physicians that the department sometimes contracts with for matters that need to keep a low profile.

"I'll need to call and update the chief anyway. I'm sure she'll know the best person to send over."

Much like his own standing arrangement with Dr. Mehdi, Reed had figured there would be a similar situation with medical professionals. People on call for times just like Grimes had mentioned, when discretion was absolutely paramount.

The reasons behind them being anything from needing to protect witnesses to not wanting to alert the media.

A topic he hadn't phoned with the intention of hitting on, but now that it had been breached, felt the need to at least mention.

"You might also want to tell her when you speak that I don't know how much longer we can keep a lid on this. I didn't see anybody outside the house just now, but it would be impossible to think the neighbors didn't notice two sets of officers and a K-9 team rolling up this evening.

"And at some point once she gets calmed down, we're going to need to get Earl and his team in there too."

Again, Grimes made the same sound. "I will. I'm pretty sure she is already aware of that, but I'll be sure to relay it again."

"Just like I'm sure you're already aware of what the answer will be, which she'll have to relay again as well."

Already pointed out to Reed the last time they spoke, it had played on loop through his mind for the last couple of hours. A silent mantra not out of wanting to do as the governor asked, but from being inside the home of Mayes.

A small space made to feel downright suffocating by the sheer devastation of what had happened. Shock and sadness and a host of other things pouring out of her, matched in varying amounts by the other two ladies present.

Palpable emotion that was impossible to ignore, silently beseeching Reed and Billie to go faster. Work harder.

Do more to make sure it didn't happen to anybody else.

"That's what we're doing now," Reed said. "I know it's getting late, but Billie and I are driving toward Coshocton now."

Despite what Reed told Marissa Lange before they left the bedroom, he ended up having two additional questions for her. Add-ons that he called her down to the mezzanine to ask while he and Billie were about to exit, the three of them huddled together, the ongoing sound of crying still audible around them.

The first question was how long she had known Mayes. A baseline ask to determine if there was any point in posing the second.

That being what he was really after, to know if Marissa knew where Mayes was from. If ever she had mentioned the town of Coshocton.

An actual last inquiry she had answered in the affirmative, solidifying Reed and Billie's next stop.

The place they were headed when Grimes last called them, hours before.

"The former sheriff?" Grimes asked.

"Yep," Reed said, flicking his gaze to the rearview mirror for a moment. A quick look past the outline of Billie's ears toward the smattering of headlights visible. A check to make sure he could veer into the middle, moving around the car going exactly the speed limit in the far left lane, and then leaning hard on the gas again.

Additional fuel that sent them hurtling forward, leaving the slow-moving vehicle in their wake, letting them shift back to the outside.

"I've tried him twice more," Reed said, "and haven't gotten anything. Starting to get worried something might have happened to him, too."

And if not, the plan was to stand outside his front door and bang on the damn thing until he opened up and told them what happened years before.

What Seesel had alluded to as a small incident, fast becoming the frontrunner for what was tying together the various victims. People from different age and socioeconomic brackets, all connected to a specific time and place, and nothing more.

"What's the second favor?"

"Can we go ahead and get McMichaels and Jacobs up on standby? If what the sheriff shares is what all this ties back to, we're looking at four more targets before this thing is over."

Chapter Fifty-Five

The engine had been off for more than an hour, though still The Tall Boy couldn't help but feel like the interior of the van was getting warmer. Heat that was slowly raising his body temperature, the point of fogging the windows around him not far off.

An eventuality that would be bad enough on its own, noticeable to anyone who might happen past. A couple out taking a stroll after dinner or, in a couple of hours, needing to take their pets out one last time before bedding down for the night.

Making it worse would be the fact that it would obscure The Tall Boy's view. Completely nullify his point in being there, leaving him only with the options of either turning on the engine and running the exhaust, or reaching out with his hand or a rag of some sort and stripping the condensation away.

Choices that were anything but valid, causing the trepidation he felt to climb. Internal worry that only managed to heighten the warmth he felt.

All of it a cycle feeding onto itself, like one of those images of a snake swallowing its own tail.

For the better part of the last twenty-four hours, The Tall Boy had been able to feel the assorted emotions surging around him. The return of the sorrow about the topic as a whole. Grief that he couldn't help but feel mixed with a bit of guilt, there at least a touch of validity to the barbs The Angel was always making.

Acrimony about those very comments, and the reemergence of The Angel into his life at all. A presence that he never would claim to have missed, now back and trying to make up for lost time.

Uncertainty regarding his own inclusion. Misgivings that didn't just stem from his brother, present even before things between them deteriorated further, but from whether he had the mettle for this.

Questions that had been running through his head for months now, spiking with each new aspect of the plan that was laid out. Silent doubts that ratcheted up as they identified each successive target and began to work through the research on them, putting together exactly how it would play out.

Scenarios The Tall Boy had let unspool in his mind, trying to imagine himself doing everything that was required. Being the hero now that he couldn't be back then.

Fantasies that he could never quite get to mesh in his own head, coming to fruition the night before on the porch at the old man's cabin. A catastrophe that very nearly got him and The Angel killed, and almost ended what they were trying to do before they were even halfway finished.

A worst-case scenario that he had carried with him to the coffee shop that morning, using the comfort of finally being away from his siblings and around other people to help massage it away. A needed bit of calm that was short lived, dissipating with each passing moment back in his brother's presence.

Constant banter, refusing to acknowledge where they were or what The Tall Boy had done to assist, instead focusing on the night before.

A single error that he would hold against The Tall Boy forever, just as he blamed him for what took place a couple years before, as if the decision to accept a scholarship and go play basketball was somehow directly linked to what happened.

For seven years now, The Tall Boy had been carrying greater guilt than his brother could ever begin to realize. Questions that had kept him up for months on end in the immediate aftermath, still circling back to the fore with far more regularity than he would ever admit.

Inquiries there was no way to know the answer to, just as there would never be a way to fully alleviate the regret he carried over it.

The sorrow that still emanated from the mere thought of it.

For years, he had been telling himself that the best he could do was wait for an opportunity at justice. A chance for retribution that might finally put something right.

A bit of absolution that he was beginning to fear wasn't coming.

At least, not on its own.

Chapter Fifty-Six

Never before had Reed been all the way into Coshocton County, his furthest jaunt east being to Newark six months prior. A trip that was also in service of a case, he and Billie spending a couple of days in the area before finally identifying their suspect and moving back into Columbus for the arrest.

An incident that Reed hoped wasn't about to become a pattern, the better outcome for this matter being that he and Billie were able to get it wrapped as soon as possible. A way of finding what they needed and who was behind targeting various people across central Ohio before they were able to get to the four remaining items on their list.

The seven deadly sins, no doubt chosen because of their connection to something in particular, even if Reed as yet had only a vague idea what it was.

A story he hoped former Sheriff Bertran Alexander was about to share with them.

The man's address programmed into the GPS on his phone, Reed had blown past Newark more than fifteen minutes prior. Resisting the urge to run with his lights and flashers on – a desire that had grown with each additional unsuccessful attempt to get the man on the phone – he had instead driven with the speedometer fixed at eight-five.

A pace that managed to slice a good bit of time off the expected transit, Reed pulling north off the highway forty minutes after leaving Westerville. Still a good ways from the town of Coshocton itself, he followed the directions of the automaton as they pushed him into the countryside comprising the outskirts of the county.

Thickets of woods liberally splashed between fields of corn and wheat, the former sheered clean and plowed under for the winter, the latter already sprouted yet too short to be seen at such an hour.

"In one-half mile, turn right," the digitized voice instructed Reed, his gaze instinctively swinging in that direction. A quick scan that revealed only a couple of lights in the distance, none looking particularly close or promising.

A sight that made his stomach clench, Billie picking up on the reaction instantly and appearing from the backseat. Heavy, warm breaths into the front as she stared out beside him.

A sense of impending action, feeding directly off the emotions rolling from Reed.

Intuition that he couldn't shake, even while having absolutely no data that something was wrong aside from the repeated missed calls to the former sheriff.

"Get ready," Reed whispered, releasing his right hand from the wheel and curling it back. Wrapping it around Billie's neck, he furrowed his fingers through her thick hair, flexing them twice.

A nod of affirmation that she returned, pressing back into his grasp.

"Turn right. You have reached your destination."

Releasing his grip on Billie, Reed shot a hand down toward the phone. Depressing the power button on the side, he killed the GPS system and the accompanying light of the screen, plunging them back into darkness.

A way to better see out as they turned from the road onto a lane that was probably gravel at one point in time, most of it washed away, replaced by mud and dead weeds. Carved between tall grasses on either side, it was framed by a stainless-steel mailbox resting at an angle atop a wooden stump on the left, with a rusted corner post for a wire fence on the right.

The sole two signs of life that could be seen as Reed tapped on the gas, nudging them forward into woods beginning just a dozen yards or so from the road. Tree cover that started thin, with just a few stray hardwoods and saplings, before becoming thicker.

Forestation that grew dense fast, mixing in low-growing brush and evergreen trees. A thick screen on either side rising above the top of the sedan, blocking any view to the outside.

Overhead, bare limbs extended at odd angles. Arms reaching into the heavens, trying to pluck down one of the handfuls of stars that were just barely visible.

The lone bits of light aside from the front headlamps for more than a hundred yards, the tunnel continued to move inward, pine boughs brushing against the sides of the vehicle near the midpoint of their journey, before finally starting to recede again. A slow retreat on either side that nearly matched the front end in length, culminating at a clearing that had been carved from deep in the center of the forest.

A circle barely thirty yards across, with room enough for a small freestanding garage and a cabin that looked to have been made by hand. Two structures that were connected by a concrete path, an older model Ford pulled up to within inches of it.

Items that were all aglow in a faint pale light being emitted from a lone security lamp attached to the back of the cabin.

The sole illumination on the grounds, not a single bulb or flickering fireplace could be seen behind the windows along the front of the home. A lack of activity matched by the frost clinging to the windows of the Ford.

"What do you think the odds are the sheriff is just out of town?" Reed whispered as he pulled into the center of the circle.

A question that got a twitch of Billie's ears in reply as he killed the engine but left the headlights on, aimed at the rear of the truck to cover as much of the grounds as possible.

"Yeah, me neither," Reed agreed, reaching straight past his partner for the glove box. Drawing out his service weapon, he went directly back in the opposite direction, the sound of loose gravel crunching beneath his feet there to greet him as he exited.

Chilled air touched the warmth on his brow as he gripped the gun in both hands, assuming a combat stance as he waited for his partner to join him.

An exit that was just barely complete, her momentum carrying her a step beyond Reed, before she pulled up abruptly. Body drawn taut, she stared at the front of the cabin, everything from muzzle to tail assuming a straight line.

A full-body alert, letting him know that she had picked up a scent that definitely wasn't supposed to be there.

Chapter Fifty-Seven

The first person on the scene was Sheriff Broderick, who Reed had spoken to on the phone earlier. A man whose appearance matched what Reed initially thought, thick throughout with tufts of red hair high atop his head and rosy cheeks to match.

A look that made it easy for Reed to see the cheery demeanor he had conveyed on the phone earlier being his default setting.

A man who was just a beard and red jacket away from being Santa Claus, spreading cheer as often as possible.

Joy that was nowhere to be seen as he stood on the front porch across from Reed and Billie. His chin drawn back toward his throat, most of the color was drained from his face. In his hands was gripped a Coshocton County Sheriff's Office ball cap, the brim of it moving in circles as he rotated it with both hands.

Standing on the muddy gravel of the driveway nearby was a pair of deputies who reminded Reed of the team at Carly Mayes's apartment earlier. A male and a female who in any other setting he would take to be a couple, both fit and attractive, in their late twenties at most.

Not yet trusting what they'd arrived to find enough to venture closer, they stood a few feet back from the steps leading up onto the porch as Reed explained what had happened. Speaking in a voice loud enough to be heard by all, he outlined how he and Billie had been pulled to a different scene after speaking to Broderick earlier, deciding to make the trip to the cabin thereafter, once a bevy of calls had gone unanswered.

How Billie had picked up the scent of the deceased upon arrival, sending them crashing inside to find Bertran Alexander's body. Not just cold, but also stiff, Reed posited that he had been dead a day or so at least, though he would leave exact time of death to the medical examiner.

Several times throughout the narrative, Broderick sucked in sharp breaths of air. Sounds that were matched by the young man wincing frequently, especially at the use of words such as *deceased* or *stiff*.

A narrative that took several minutes for Reed to complete, the young woman the first to speak in the aftermath, asking, "Is it one of yours?"

Asked without inflection or accusation, it was still difficult for Reed to take the question any other way. A case that had initially been entrusted to him and his partner that was continuing to accelerate, spanning multiple counties and as many victims.

A collection of people that, at a glance, had no obvious connections, pulled into the sick retribution scheme of whoever was behind all this.

Revenge almost certainly stemming back to some unknown incident that he had hoped Alexander might be able to shed light on, the man's inclusion – and death – all but confirming that as the connective piece.

Even if Reed still had no idea what it might have been, beyond a vague explanation from Matt Seesel about a post-game celebration years ago.

"It is," Reed confirmed. "Each of the previous victims have been tattooed across their foreheads. A single word in block letters, ascribed to one of the seven deadly sins.

"Thus far we've had PRIDE, GREED, GLUTTONY. Sheriff Alexander is now SLOTH."

Beside him, Broderick lifted his face toward the roof of the porch. Spinning in place, he put his back to Reed, exhaling loudly.

A visceral reaction not entirely unlike the way Reed had reacted upon first seeing Alexander's body.

A response he allowed the man to carry out, his focus staying on the two deputies below.

"I'm not sure you can pick it up from down there, but when we arrived, there was also the smell of gunpowder in the air." Depressing the rubber plunger on the end of his flashlight, he raised the beam to the far side of the porch, settling it on the wooden crosspiece connecting each of the four supports holding the roof in place.

Tilting his head toward it, he waited as each of the younger deputies stepped forward. Remaining on the ground, they twisted their bodies around to peer upward, staring at the shard of blonde wood sticking out at an angle, displaced by the impact of a bullet at short range.

"Just inside the door, we found a rifle that was fired recently," Reed added. "Based on that and the complete lack of puffiness or bruising around the tattoo, best guess is that Alexander tried to fight them off and perished during the struggle. No visible cause of death makes me think he suffered a heart attack, though again, I'll leave that to the medical examiner."

A few feet to his left, Broderick slowly turned back. Any hint of color having drained from his features save the undersides of his eyes, it looked as if he was on the verge of vomiting and crying simultaneously.

"I remember Ol' Bert told me before he stepped down that it wasn't exactly his idea," Broderick said. "I knew he'd had some heart troubles in the past, but I never guessed..."

Adding nothing more, he let his voice fall away. A moment of silence during which the deputies both retreated to their previous positions, their gazes fixed on Reed.

"So the tattoo, and all that..." the young man began. Extending a hand before him, he waved at the door to the cabin at Reed's back.

A search for words that went no further, though Reed understood what he was getting at.

"Staged," Reed finished for him. "What these guys are doing, it's all about sending a message. Alexander was clearly a part of that, and they weren't about to let his unexpected death derail their plans."

"What message?" the young man asked.

Pushing a breath out through his nose, Reed glanced over to Broderick. A quick look to check and see how much had already been shared.

A silent question to determine if he should divulge whatever remained. An ask that the sheriff met with the same sober expression he'd been wearing for the last several minutes, void of instruction either way, still working through the host of things thrown at him in short order.

A response that wasn't exactly in the affirmative, but didn't tell Reed not to either.

"Seven years ago, there was an incident that took place near here involving some high school students at a party," Reed said. "We don't know any more of the details at this point, aside from the fact that Sheriff Alexander looked into it, but never elevated it to an official case."

"And now someone is going after all the people involved?" the female deputy asked.

"It looks that way," Reed said, "but again, without knowing exactly what happened, we can't be a hundred percent."

"No," Broderick inserted, his detached tone ending the back-and-forth, drawing over the attention of the other three, "but you can be pretty darn close."

Blinking twice to remove the glazed look, pulling himself back into the moment, he fixed his stare on Reed.

"Right before you called, I was able to get Don Sweeney on the phone from Montana. The guy I told you about who has been here for decades, but is away on a hunting trip right now."

Reed didn't know the man was on the other side of the country, effectively precluding any chance of speaking with him in person, but the rest he recalled from their prior discussion, relaying as much with a nod.

"Anyway, he knew exactly what I was talking about, but not for the reason you think. Said he didn't know a thing about the case." Jutting a thumb toward the outer wall of the cabin beside him, he continued, "Old Bert handled it himself, said there wasn't much to it."

Lowering his hand, he continued, "But what he did recall was a couple of days later some woman came tearing into the station, ranting and raving. All sort of crazy stuff about immoral high schoolers and the devil and anything else you can imagine.

"Guess it got to be something of a joke," Broderick finished. "Kind of thing where whenever someone would cuss or something, one of the others would tell them to be careful, that was a sin."

Chapter Fifty-Eight

After completing so many projects in such a narrow window of time, The Artist felt like her entire right arm was asleep. A tingling feeling that resembled the micro vibrations of the tattoo gun, all touch sensors in her fingers dulled beyond recognition, no matter how many times she flexed them.

An ongoing task she took to by individually curling one after another back toward her palm as she sat in the passenger seat, staring out through the side window.

Something she did without even conscious thought, barely aware it was happening until The Angel asked, "You okay over there?"

Snapping her head toward the sound of his voice, The Artist's eyebrows rose. A silent question unseen in the dark of the car, prompting her to ask, "Hmm?"

"Your hand," The Angel said, flicking his focus toward the road ahead before glancing back her way. A quick look with neon lights from the various fast-food joints and store signs passing by outside coloring his features.

A sight that was vastly different from the one she was used to seeing in the driver's seat. The Tall Boy, with his long frame filling the entire space and his solemn expression hinting of constant worry.

Ongoing analysis of everything they were doing, trying to foresee any potential problems.

Any errors that could be avoided.

Any sources of blame that could be tossed his way.

Replacing him in the seat was The Angel. A man much smaller in stature, allowing The Artist to see most of the driver's side window behind him. Light that passed inside, fully silhouetting his features.

A face that might have been cherubic by birth, but was often marred by his omnipresent glower. A resting state that vacillated between irked and enraged.

A default setting that started when they were kids, having grown far more pronounced during his years away.

And then, somehow, even more so in the last six months, the lone exception being standing in someone's garage and finding the entire thing amusing.

Behind the wheel of their mother's car since they left the home of their fifth target just a little while before, the last twenty minutes had resembled something from a bad crime caper. Evasive driving that was nowhere near necessary, more likely to get them caught than to let them slip away unnoticed.

Constant lane changes and redirections that did nothing for the unsettled feeling resting in The Artist's stomach. Her earlier apprehension made worse by the circuitous route taken to eventually get back to the highway.

A path that The Angel claimed was to keep a constant lookout for anyone who might be tailing them. An ongoing search for an enemy The Artist did not believe existed, the town of Coshocton never quite rising to the level of being a bustling hub.

Damned sure not on a Tuesday night in November, the thermometer dipping down into the thirties.

"You gonna be alright?"

Realizing for the first time what her brother was referring to, The Artist glanced down to the balled fist of her right hand. Fingers all curled around her thumb, she was squeezing so tight the knuckles flashed white beneath the skin.

A clench she let slowly unfurl, splaying her fingers wide before dropping both hands down atop her thighs with a slap.

"Yeah, just a little numbness is all. Been a busy couple of days."

"Yeah, well, it's going to be a busy night, too," The Angel replied, rolling his gaze up to meet hers before turning his focus back to the road outside.

A look that evoked handfuls of retorts within The Artist. Comments about how he didn't need to be enjoying things quite as much as he was. Questions as to whether he even still had a soul, seemingly unfazed by events of the last day.

A dozen others all lined up in order, cut short by her phone coming to life between them. A burst not of light, but of sound. Vibrations of the device rattling against the cupholder it was resting in, the burner phone an ancient flip model, void of a screen.

An interruption they both recognized instantly, evoking a scowl from the driver's seat as The Artist reached for it.

"What does his ass want now?" The Angel muttered. "More second thoughts to share with us?"

Questions The Artist took as rhetorical, not worth answering as she flipped the phone opened and accepted the incoming call. Trying for a moment to figure out how to put the damned thing on speakerphone, she gave up after several seconds, instead thrusting it up against her ear.

"Hello? Hello? You there?" The Tall Boy asked, rattling off the questions in short order. Asks with increasing speed, his tone laced with concern.

Worry that The Artist took as a poor omen, her hand tightening on the cold plastic.

"I'm here. What's going on?"

Exhaling slowly, he replied, "Sorry. Had me worried for a minute there."

Making a point of keeping her gaze turned outward, The Artist asked, "Everything alright?"

"Yes and no," her brother answered. "Nothing is wrong, but I haven't seen anything of Murphy yet."

Rotating her neck a couple of inches, The Artist glanced to the glowing digits of the clock in the center of the dash. One of the few things that still worked in the derelict old rig.

"This late? And he's still not home yet?"

"I guarantee that's because The Tall Boy got made," The Angel muttered, looking up to the rearview mirror before drifting from the left lane to the center. Another unnecessary maneuver, with no sign of stopping.

"Nope," The Tall Boy answered, having either not heard his twin's comment, or choosing to ignore it instead. "Every single time before, he was back by seven, eight at the latest."

One of the most important targets on the entire list, Murphy was one The Artist had assisted in scouting for months. A constant rotation between the three, taking into account every possible variable.

Days of the week. Direction of approach. Even placement of where to park and keep a lookout.

The only answers The Artist could come up with for why there would be a difference tonight, of all nights, being that they had messed up at a previous stop and Murphy had been alerted, or what The Angel just suggested.

The Tall Boy had been made.

"Are you absolutely sure-"

"Yes, I'm sure," The Tall Boy snapped. "I'm even parked on the neighboring cul-de-sac and peering across the ravine at his place. Trust me, there are no cops anywhere, and not a single light on in his place."

In the driver's seat, The Angel alternated his focus between the road ahead and the side of her face. Back and forth, one time after another, his features growing increasingly taut.

"What?" he asked. "What the hell happened now?"

"Nothing," The Artist said, lifting her opposite hand and using it to cover the mouthpiece. "No sign of Murphy."

Again, The Angel took to muttering. More of the same remarks he'd been lobbing a moment ago. The same sort he'd been tossing at their brother for months on end, no matter the visible effect they were having on him.

Words The Artist was beyond trying to reply to, instead pulling her hand away from the receiver and dropping it back into her lap.

A return to the previous conversation just in time to hear The Tall Boy say, "I'm thinking I'm going to go in on foot. Get a closer look, maybe wait for him there."

Chapter Fifty-Nine

The better part of three hours removed from the last time they spoke, Reed knew there was no way Captain Grimes was still behind his desk. Evening having given way to night, the man had probably hustled home at some point, sprinting through greeting his wife and changing his clothes before posting up somewhere.

A favorite recliner or a back-porch rocker or even an upright chair at the kitchen table like Reed preferred to use.

A spot where he could throw down dinner while keeping a constant vigil on his phone, meaning that when Reed did call back, he was again able to answer within the first ring.

A single word greeting per usual, simply, "Grimes."

"What a mess," Reed replied. Tucked up behind the wheel of his sedan, he sat with his weight leaning forward. His left hand steered while his right held his phone just a few inches from his chin.

A place it would stay for just the short duration of this conversation, Reed having the better part of twenty minutes before he needed to consult the GPS again.

"How bad?" Grimes asked.

"Former Sheriff Alexander is dead," Reed replied. Bypassing

compassion in the name of brevity, he added, "SLOTH on the fore-head, Lazy Sack of Shit on the torso."

Two more entries on the notepad in the passenger seat, joining Carly Mayes's name, though he hadn't got the chance to check for anything on her stomach.

Exhaling slowly in reply, Grimes repeated, "SLOTH. That makes four."

"That we know of," Reed replied.

"And it seems like things are escalating. This is the first victim that was also killed."

"It is," Reed said, "though if I had to guess, it was an accident. No visible signs of causation beyond a few red welts on the torso and a cut on his cheek.

"Looked to me like Alexander was ready for them, or at least put up a fight. Ended up giving himself a damn heart attack."

Skipping over a lot of the details, Reed stuck only to the high points. The essentials to let Grimes know what had happened before launching into what came next.

Things there would be plenty of time to relay later in the course of a full debrief, but for now would have to wait.

"Is Earl there now?" Grimes asked.

"En route," Reed said. "He was finishing up something in the city, was about to head to Mayes' apartment when I called and told him to go to Alexander's first. Scene was older, and had a casualty.

"He agreed, said he was okay with us leaving so long as the Coshocton Sheriff's crew didn't make a mess of things like Springfield PD did."

A condition Reed had assured the man they would not, all three solemnly pledging to guard the place until Earl and his team arrived and to stay there until everything was completely processed.

A vow that Reed got the impression was a mix of wanting to look out for one of their own – retired or not – and the fact that none of them were that inclined to go inside anyway, Broderick's noticeably different demeanor enough to warn the deputies off.

"Where are you headed now?" Grimes asked.

"New Albany, current home of Chance Murphy. Grandson of Dean Morgan and star player on the first team Matt Seesel ever coached. Involved in that same incident that Sheriff Alexander looked into and eventually dropped."

He didn't bother mentioning Carly Mayes, her role in things as yet still unclear. Her friend had said she was from Coshocton, and if forced to guess Reed would say she was also around twenty-five, though until he had a chance to speak with her, anything else would be pure conjecture.

Guesswork that Alexander was supposed to have put an end to, cut down before ever having the chance.

A fact that could have been as Reed guessed and simply unfortunate timing, or could have been a deliberate means of keeping him quiet. An overdose of whatever the attackers were using to subdue their victims, ensuring that when he went under to receive his tattoo, he never came back up.

Like Reed told the deputies earlier, there was just no way to know until the medical examiner on her way out with Earl arrived to take a look.

"The only active number Deke could find was a landline, which keeps coming up empty."

"I'll call the chief and let her know," Grimes replied.

"Appreciate it," Reed said, trusting that Brandt would sit on it entirely for the time being, there being no way of telling how the governor would react to the death of a retired sheriff in the area. "Where we at on McMichaels and Jacobs?"

"Up and ready," Grimes replied. "You want me to go ahead and have them start rolling your way?"

"Yes," Reed replied. "Plan is to get there, make sure he's secure, and then drill down on whatever the hell happened seven years ago.

"After that, we're going to need to get him away and keep him safe, along with any other names he gives us."

"Two more, anyway," Grimes finished.

"Exactly," Reed replied, flicking his gaze up to check the mileage sign slipping by along the right side of the highway. A number that seemed to be replenishing itself instead of dwindling, their destination still feeling too far away.

"Thanks, captain. Talk soon."

Chapter Sixty

The town of New Albany sat just far enough off the outer belt encircling Columbus that it could be considered either a freestanding city of its own or a suburb of the state capitol, depending on how one wanted to look at it. A trick pulled off by the unique curvature of the freeway in the northeast corner of Columbus and the gap of open space resting between it and the outskirts of New Albany.

An open swath of ground not found in most other bergs dotted around the outer belt, meaning that it was one of the rare few to contain the full spectrum of housing options. Everything from urban apartments to gated communities to small suburban cul-de-sacs like the one Chance Murphy lived on.

A street that would pass as the nicest in a place like The Bottoms, but in a town that was home to the corporate headquarters of multiple national brands, was decidedly on the lower end of the spectrum.

A neighborhood with single-story brick homes and two-levels with painted siding and shutters, Chance Murphy's house falling under the former. A squat, rectangular structure with brick painted white and mulch beds lining the front, juniper bushes nearly buried beneath leaves from mature oak and elm trees in the yard.

A place that was quaint if not modest, Reed guessing that in a town like New Albany it still brought in north of three hundred grand.

A house Chance Murphy likely didn't own – at least by himself – at twenty-five, regardless what he did for a living.

Easing just past the driveway extended down from the side of the house, Reed sidled to a stop along the curb and killed the ignition. Pulling the keys, he checked the front of the house, seeing not a single light on within, nothing but a lone security lamp attached to the side of the garage to provide illumination.

Glow strong enough to provide detail on one end, the rest of the home was shrouded in shadows.

Darkness that wasn't helped by the neighbors on either side, security fencing lining one edge of the property, the house on the other end just as dark as Murphy's.

"Shit," Reed said, scanning the front for any signs of life before cracking open his door. Leaving it wide behind him, he allowed Billie to climb out as well, bypassing the use of a lead as they circled around the front of the sedan and up onto the concrete walk. A straight path bisecting the lawn, extended down from a porch of the same material stretched across much of the front of the house.

An elevated platform with a couple of Adirondack chairs and a fall spread of mums and pumpkins all looking a week or more past their expiration date.

A setting Reed took in upon approach, casting it aside as he hopped up the couple of steps onto the porch and went straight for the door. Starting with the doorbell, he pressed it twice, hearing it chime within, before raising his fist and pounding the side of it against the door a handful of times.

Combined noises that would be unmistakable if Murphy was anywhere inside the home, up to and including a basement. Loud enough to wake him in the event the lights were off because he was already asleep.

Taking a step back, Reed cocked his head to the side, listening for any sounds of movement from within. Any creaking of floorboards or voices calling out that they were on their way.

Noises that eluded him, nothing save the sound of a few dried leaves rattling in the trees nearby finding his ears.

Complete quiet that lasted several moments, ultimately punctured not by anything or anybody within the house, but by his partner beside him.

A single sound that rolled from deep within her diaphragm, snapping Reed's attention to the side. Right hand instinctively reaching to his hip, he twisted in the same direction, his focus landing on Billie standing two windows down from him.

A pane of glass providing a clear view into the darkened living room, something inside having caught her attention, putting her on alert. A stance with her weight balanced between all four limbs, her neck extended as she stared inside.

One of a handful of poses she could strike when alerting on something, not consistent with the smell of gunpowder at Bertran Alexander's cabin, or even the scent of death that had seeped through his front door.

Meant to maximize balance, Reed recognized it as his partner's stance whenever she was preparing to run. A sure sign she had spotted movement, anticipating an imminent chase.

A signal for him to come closer, swinging wide toward the front edge of the deck, before settling in behind her. A vantage to let him see whatever she just had, without impeding her own view.

Drawing his weapon, Reed could feel hits of adrenaline begin to seep into his system. Chemicals that brought warmth to his skin, his pulse climbing as he crept into position, peering through the glass.

Aided by the darkness inside leaving no reflections across the windowpane to obscure his view, Reed swept his gaze across the length of the space. Knees flexed to match his partner, he held his weapon before him in a combat stance, both hands around the base.

"What'd you see, girl?" he whispered, his pulse thrumming as he inventoried the scene before him. Every silhouetted item of furniture big enough to hide someone.

A set piece that was completely still as he flicked his gaze in either direction, silently willing whatever Billie had spotted to show itself.

A hope he let linger for nearly a minute before deciding to help things along.

"Chance Murphy!" he called, making sure his voice was loud enough to be heard within. "CPD! Open up!"

Chapter Sixty-One

The Tall Boy's mistake wasn't that he went inside. After nearly three hours of sitting out on the curb, he knew that it was only a matter of time before somebody noticed him.

Even at such an hour, there was still plenty of vehicle and foot traffic. People getting home late from work or trying to get through their evening chores before calling it quits for the day. Quick workouts or chances to let their dog relieve themselves or whatever else.

On a cul-de-sac such as the one Chance Murphy lived on and the one paralleling it opposite the ravine behind his house, there were only so many places to hide. So many relocations that could be performed before he started to draw unwanted attention to himself.

Notice that he could already sense starting to mount as one time after another, headlights washed over him. Penetrating glare that rendered him a silhouette.

Same for dogs letting out small whines as they circled his van. People glancing over as they walked past. Looks that were starting to feel more pointed, practically burning as they rested on his skin.

Close encounters that were beginning to feel too numerous to continue slipping by. The start of an internal countdown that kept going faster and faster, his pulse rising in direct correlation with the windows fogging around him.

An endpoint getting ever closer, inevitably going to end badly.

A complete certainty that meant The Tall Boy had no choice but to act, no matter how many times The Artist told him to stay put. A view that was shaped by spending most of the evening with The Angel, the two of them no doubt spending the time while she worked to compare notes on recent events.

A blow-by-blow assessment of all that had happened, ascribing every last error or shortcoming to him.

The Angel's despisal of The Tall Boy having finally taken hold, infecting their sister as well. Mistrust that now permeated both of them, soon to encompass what happened long ago as well.

Blame for years of heartache and strife, written off as a mistake that he alone should have been able to thwart.

As if he wasn't the one who had suffered the most from it, both then, and every single day since. Loss that was so much more profound than either of them could ever imagine.

The very reason why he was here at all, willing to take part in all this, impart so much torment on others, and then completely disappear.

Actions he would have thought would grant him some latitude with his siblings, though it was apparent the events at the coffee shop that morning had meant nothing. A perfect setup without either of their help, him alone sitting there all morning and delivering Carly Mayes to them on a platter. Making it so easy that all they had to do was walk down the driveway and up to her apartment, the pair of them then having the nerve to act as if he couldn't do the same a second time with Chance Murphy.

An assumption he had proven wrong just moments before, climbing out of his van and marching toward the corner. The first of a couple right turns and a short walk past a row of houses, just another person out for an evening stroll like so many who went by him earlier.

A regular along the quiet street who didn't so much as garner a glance, even as he made one last turn into Murphy's driveway and circled around to the backdoor.

An entry that was every bit as easy as he'd seen The Angel do a couple of times already, putting him inside the darkened home less than ten minutes after leaving his vehicle. A nice, warm spot for him to sit, even helping himself to a soda from Murphy's refrigerator as he waited.

The waiting being where he actually made his mistake.

Two of them, in fact, the first being in that he sat and waited too long. When Murphy didn't show up within the first half hour, he should have reasoned that he wasn't coming home.

Never before in all their canvassing of the place had he made it back later than eight. A strict adherence to coming home and either going for a run or hitting the gym in town.

Routine that was like clockwork, this the first time The Tall Boy – or his sister – could remember a deviation.

A sure sign that something was amiss. He'd been tipped off by his old coach or his grandfather or even the cops starting to put things together.

All reasons for The Tall Boy to vacate.

The second, and more profound, error he made was that he didn't wait long enough. Sitting inside the darkened house, his entire body had tensed at the sound of the pounding on the front door. A full clench that was accompanied by ribbons of sensation hurtling through him as a man called out for Murphy, identifying himself as the police.

An exploratory search that likely would have gone no further, had the officer been on his own. A lone beat cop working the pavement, checking to see if Murphy was home and everything was okay.

A basic sweep that The Tall Boy would have been content to let pass, if not for the K-9 companion that was present as well. An animal that looked directly through the front window and seemed to peer straight into the shadows where The Tall Boy was posted, its entire body pointed at him like an arrow.

An indicator there would be no avoiding, forcing him into movement long before he was ready.

A mad dash through the kitchen and out the back door, hitting the spongy grass of the backyard at a full sprint. Elongated strides with his pulse thumping, his entire focus on getting to the ravine behind the house.

A deep trench more than thirty yards on either side, the goal to get down and back up again before the cop or his dog could reach him. Return to his van and get away, or at the very least warn his siblings what had happened.

A singular purpose resting at the front of his mind as he chewed up the swath of open ground behind Murphy's house.

Long strides with his pulse racing, the cold air clawing at his windpipe as he gulped it down, running as fast as he could.

Chapter Sixty-Two

It took a full moment for what Reed was seeing to register with him. A flash of movement on the other side of the glass. A dark shadow that became a full silhouette as it burst from behind the sofa and through an open doorway leading into what Reed guessed was the kitchen beyond.

A tall figure in full flight, Reed's eyes widening as palpitations passed through his chest.

Seeing Billie alert after he knocked and called out initially, his first thought was what happened at Bertran Alexander's cabin earlier. They had arrived too late for the second time on the night, the scent of Murphy's deceased body not yet strong enough for Billie to detect until that instant.

A thought he should have known was foolish, two-plus years of working with his partner making him fully cognizant of her capabilities. The two-hundred-and-forty-five million scent receptors she possessed and the mind that was largely predicated on processing whatever they picked up.

An infallible sense that was far beyond anything he did or would ever possess.

Having that earlier experience seated at the front of his mind, though, it had taken just a little extra time for things to click. For his mind to transition from standing outside, fearing Murphy might have perished, to seeing him sprinting for the back door.

A connection that, once it was made and the neurons began firing anew, sent him tearing straight across the remainder of the front porch. A conscious choice not to bother bursting through the door and trying to get through the house, but to go after the only logical place the young man could be heading.

An all-out sprint across the raised concrete and around the side of the house with Billie moving in lockstep beside him, hoping to cut him off at the garage.

An effort that turned out to be his second mistake in under a minute, Reed arriving by the rolltop door on the end of the structure not to find it starting its slow ascent, but instead Murphy's darkened form crossing the backyard on a dead run. A long-legged stride across the lawn sloping away toward the rear of the property, going like hell for the ravine beyond.

A deep trench separating the cul-de-sac from the next one over, his options for escape from there growing tremendously.

Standing at a complete stop in front of the garage door, Reed lowered himself into a semi-crouch. A drop of a few inches allowing his legs to flex and then push off, feeling a slight twinge in his calf as he drove himself across the concrete before hitting the spongy grass of the back yard.

A move Billie easily matched beside him, her form a dark shadow pulling ahead. Long, easy strides that Reed followed, putting his focus on her instead of Murphy fleeing as they crossed the open lawn, heading for the taller grass signaling the start of the descent into the ravine.

A close watch, waiting for the moment when he was certain she had picked up their target. The exact instant when he saw recognition set in, the distance chewed up with each step growing wider.

A sure signal, allowing him to call out, "Hold!"

Letting the word out as nothing short of a bellow, the sound rolled down into the ravine. A starting gun propelling Billie after the young man fleeing from them, her pace nearly doubling as she shot forward.

A switch from four individual legs working beneath her to two pairs, each touching down only long enough to fling herself forward. Momentum aided by the downward slope, gravity allowing her to cover four or five yards at a time, her body hanging suspended above the ground.

A pace that no man – no matter how young, no matter the lead they possessed – could hope to outrun. Speed and athletic grace that Reed most recently witnessed on the training ground just a couple of days before.

Exercises that all ended exactly the same as this one, Billie needing no more than a handful of bounds at full velocity to reach the edge of the yard. An optimal launching point, allowing her to leap forward, covering whatever gap still remained between her and Murphy.

An incoming collision the man never saw coming, the full force of her weight slamming into him, impact hitting just between his shoulder blades. A blast much harder than even what Reed had taken from Kona, sending Murphy's hands out to either side as his top half folded forward at the waist.

A collision he was woefully unprepared for, letting out a thunderous grunt as he toppled headlong to the ground. The start of a roll he was unable to stop, even as Billie leapt free, following him toward the bottom of the ravine.

Three consecutive revolutions he performed, crashing through the dead grass and leaves, each contact with the ground eliciting another sound. Grunts and curses that rolled up and over the edge of the ravine as Reed pounded ahead, his weapon still in hand as his arms were fixed at ninety-degrees, fighting to catch up.

A frantic run to ensure that Billie was okay.

And that there would be no further attempt to flee by Murphy.

Turning his body sideways to avoid a similar fate as the young man just moments before, Reed bounded forward. Assuming a skipping motion, he bounced his way down the side of the ravine, touching down with both feet before pushing himself up and to the side, letting the lay of the land and his own momentum carry him forward.

A descent that was far from graceful and not free from pain, but allowed him to remain upright, covering the ground in just a matter of seconds.

A few frantic moments with uneven ground under foot and stray sticks and grasses pulling at him, ending with him reaching the crumpled form laying at the bottom of the ravine. An elongated heap of twisted limbs and accumulated leaves overseen by Billie just a few feet away, her entire body rigid as she called out one time after another.

Deep braying warning the figure not to even consider moving further.

Caution that was heeded as the man remained on his side, arms curled up over his head to protect himself.

"Chance Murphy!" Reed said, sliding to a stop beside his partner. Extending his weapon before him, he opened his mouth to begin anew, continuing the statement of arrest he was about to make.

Words that never reached his lips, pulled away as the young man before them lowered his arms, revealing his face for the first time.

Features belonging to a man who was decidedly not Chance Murphy.

Chapter Sixty-Three

"Watch your head," Officer Tommy Jacobs said. Perfunctory words that didn't quite coincide with the effort employed as he shoved along the elongated form of whoever the hell Billie had just tracked down and Reed pulled up out of the ravine behind Chance Murphy's house.

A process that perfectly reflected the frustration all three men were feeling, Reed watched as the overgrown man was stuffed into the rear of the cruiser McMichaels and Jacobs shared. Someone tall enough he was forced to sit sideways to fit, Reed staring at the man's silhouette a moment before looking back to Wade McMichaels beside him.

A form tall enough that he would have noticed it couldn't be Murphy's 6'3", had he not been preoccupied with the man trying to flee the scene.

"Thanks for getting here so fast. Our sedan isn't equipped for transport."

Grunting softly, McMichaels looked away just long enough to see his partner join them. The three and Billie standing in a diamond formation, red and blue lights passing over them in even sweeps.

Bright glow from the pair of arriving New Albany police squad cars. Standard blue and whites Reed had requested before even dragging the man up out of the ravine.

Additional manpower to help sit on the house and to keep watch for Murphy.

"That your guy?" McMichaels asked, motioning with the top of his head toward the cruiser sitting behind Reed's sedan.

"One of them, hopefully," Reed said. "Earl and the doc both pegged this as being a two-man operation. One male, one female."

"Any sign of the female?" Jacobs asked, stating the same question Reed had been rolling around since forcing the man onto his stomach and securing his hands behind his back.

The very first thought he'd had upon seeing McMichaels and Jacobs arrive, handing the man off to Jacobs before breaching the house with Billie and McMichaels. A three-person team searching for Murphy or the accomplice that had turned up nothing.

"None," Reed muttered. "None of Murphy either. Based on him running like hell out the back, I'm thinking he was in charge of securing the targets. Maybe parked on a neighboring street and walked in, would call in the girl to go to work once everything was set."

Tilting his head toward the cruisers nearby, Reed added, "NAPD is setting up a canvas as we speak."

In unison, both officers turned to stare past the house, peering into the darkness.

"Any idea who he is?" Jacobs asked, the first to rotate back.

"None," Reed said. "No ID of any kind on him. No wallet. Not even a set of keys."

Muttering something indecipherable, McMichaels turned back as well. "Guessing he didn't say anything either?"

"Not a word," Reed confirmed, sliding his focus to the side at an oversized SUV rolling into view. A vehicle much larger and newer than any of the cruisers along the street or even Reed's sedan.

A monstrous ride with the emblem of the NAPD stamped on the door, a pair of silhouettes visible behind the front windshield.

The ranking officer for the local police if Reed was to guess. A potential jurisdictional squabble he did not have the time or the energy for, flicking his gaze to the men beside him before moving it back to the approaching SUV.

A mental sequence that seemed to play out beside him as well, McMichaels returning to his previous muttering as a low groan escaped from Jacobs.

"Yep," Reed agreed, dropping his tone to just loud enough for the two of them to hear. "Billie and I will deal with this. You two get this guy back to the 8th and processed as fast as you can. Prints, facial rec, whatever it takes."

"Get us a name. We'll be there as soon as we can."

"You got it," McMichaels replied.

"Roger that," Jacobs added.

Confirmation given while already drifting toward their cruiser, both intent to get inside and away before the arriving men could exit their vehicle.

Desires Reed could not begrudge them in the slightest, his main focus on ensuring that nothing impeded drilling down on their newest suspect for everything they could, even while knowing there was still more to be done here.

"Thanks, guys. We'll see you soon."

Receiving a wave in farewell from both, Reed remained centered at the foot of the driveway. Billie on all fours beside him, they stood and waited, watching as McMichaels reversed their cruiser out and headed the opposite direction.

An exit creating a hole for the SUV to slide into, the driver leaving the lights and engine both running as the passenger door opened. From it stepped a lean and angular man with a head and face that looked to have both just been shaved, the shiny surface reflecting the glow of the nearby wigwag lights.

Older than Reed by at a least a decade, his sharp features were made even more pronounced by a complete lack of body fat. Hard ridges that were no doubt matched by a body hidden beneath jeans and a fleece pullover, the collar left unzipped and gapping at the throat.

Striding straight ahead into the glare of the SUV's headlights, he extended a hand before him on approach.

"Detective Mattox?"

"Yes, sir," Reed replied, meeting the man's grip. "My K-9 partner, Billie. Chief Duncan?"

"Rex," Duncan said, releasing the shake and taking a step to the side. A better vantage to swing his gaze across the front of the house, surveying the assorted movements nearby.

"Reed. Appreciate your team getting here so fast."

"Appreciate you calling us in," Duncan replied. "Some of the stories we've heard about working with the state haven't exactly been flattering."

"Not us, and definitely not on this," Reed replied.

Rotating his focus back from the house, Duncan fixed his gaze on Reed. "And what is this, exactly?"

"The short answer?" Reed replied. "We've got one intended target and one additional attacker, both of which are still missing."

Chapter Sixty-Four

The Artist was within sight of the turn, about to drop the blinker and start down the cul-de-sac, when she saw the flickering lights. Thin bits of red and blue rotating in equal measure, just barely visible against the night sky.

Telltale indicators she had been watching for for three days and counting. A light even stronger than the Bat Signal, relaying a story without saying a word.

Small shifts in color that caused her entire core to seize. All saliva to leave her mouth. Even the air to flee her lungs as she sat clutching the steering wheel in both hands.

The last thing she had said to The Tall Boy was not to go inside. Seeing for days now – months, really, if she was being honest – what the situation was doing to him, how being back in such close proximity to his twin brother, being forced to relive what happened, was pulling him down, she had feared something like this might occur.

He might try too hard, press too much, and end up doing something foolish. An eventuality she had hoped was dodged the night before during the fiasco at the cabin in the woods. A wakeup call to them all just how thin the margin they were working with really was.

A near miss from which they could progress forward, deftly

maneuvering the last couple targets before disappearing. All three of them, the last vestiges of the family, headed somewhere warm, never to be seen in Ohio again.

A future she could practically see evaporating as she kept the tires on her car pointed straight ahead, barely lifting her foot from the gas to slow its speed.

Otherwise, she gave no indication she even saw the lights. No glance over. Not even a hand extended to turn down the radio.

Nothing to hint she was anything other than a local resident returning home from a long day in the city, regardless of the license plates on her vehicle. Another of thousands doing that very same thing, the cul-de-sac just one of many in a row riffling by on either side.

Cheap housing thrown up when the town first started to become an entity unto itself, having escalated in value in the years since not through any improvement themselves, but by the market around them skyrocketing.

Information that she hated like hell that she even knew rising to the fore of her mind. A defense mechanism, putting her focus on anything else in the world besides the obvious for a few moments.

A topic to ponder while feeling as if a weight was balanced upon her sternum. Pressure that meant The Artist had to actively work just to pull air in and out. Concerted effort that caused her shoulders to rise and fall, her chest to distend and retract, as she tried to breathe.

Releasing her grip on either side of the steering wheel, The Artist spread her fingers out wide. Using only her palms to keep it pointed straight ahead, she consciously fought to keep her entire body from seizing tight.

A clench she could ill afford right now, her attention winnowed to the two-lane in front of her. A ribbon of gray asphalt with a pair of yellow lines striped through the center.

A metaphor of sorts she was certain, unable to grasp exactly what it was relaying as she followed the route for more than a mile, letting it deposit her on the main thoroughfare of New Albany. A town she had spent the first eighteen years of her life living less than an hour away from, but never even entered until just a few months before.

Reconnaissance for this very night, never once considering that this was how it would go.

The penultimate target on their list, supposed to be part of a rising crescendo. A final middle finger to everyone involved, instead of being the place where it all unraveled.

Not now, as they were so close.

Especially not with those remaining being the ones most responsible for what happened long ago.

Remaining frozen in the same position, The Artist rolled through the center of the small downtown. A street packed tight with shops and eateries that during the summer were bustling with people, tons of customers filling chairs lining the sidewalks, though tonight was noticeably quiet.

A subdued midweek late night, with just the stray patron visible through the glass along the fronts of various businesses. Lights and signage and people that The Artist just barely noticed, continuing her pattern of controlled breathing until reaching the far end of the small strip.

A location sufficiently removed from the cul-de-sac to put fear of suspicion in her wake, allowing her to slide into the parking lot of a Tim Horton's. An establishment known mostly for coffee and donuts, the sole person visible inside a cashier staring at her phone, no doubt counting off the last few minutes until closing time.

A bored teenager who barely glanced up before returning to her device, signaling for The Artist to do the same.

Snatching up the burn phone from the middle console, she bypassed the last unsaved number in the call log and went immediately for the next in order.

The second of the only two people in the world to have called in or out since taking the damned thing out of plastic a week before.

"How bad?" The Angel answered, eschewing any sort of greeting.

"They got him," The Artist whispered in return.

A spark to the fuse that was her brother, the response set him off on another outburst she knew he'd been rehearsing since she left him a half hour earlier. A profanity-laden tirade about The Tall Boy's stupidity, and his inability to be trusted, and everything being his fault.

All of the high points The Artist had heard more times than she cared to remember, letting it blend into white noise as she stared straight ahead. A cacophony of sound without anything in particular standing out that she let run unabated.

A few extra moments for her to try and catch her breath. Make sense of what she saw.

Decipher what this meant for them all moving forward.

"You still there?" The Angel asked a full ninety seconds after he started.

The first words actually directed at The Artist, pulling her back to the conversation, her mind swirling. Handfuls of questions about how to proceed that she best summarized by asking, simply, "What do we do now?"

An inquiry her brother answered just as simply, replying, "We finish it."

Chapter Sixty-Five

This time, Reed didn't feign trying to comport with whatever heavy-handed strictures the governor had placed on them. Whatever requests or mandates or however else one wanted to term the directive that was given to him to maintain as low a profile as possible.

Asks that Reed was never quite comfortable with, but willing to try and accommodate when this was a case of one of Cowan's old buddies and a possible donor having been humiliated in a most abhorrent way.

Now that it was a case of serial attackers – at least one target of which was dead, another missing – any such efforts were cast aside. A conscious shedding of all that wasn't absolutely vital, Reed's greatest interest in getting across town to the man they had just pulled out of the ravine behind Chance Murphy's house.

From there, in discovering who he was working with and why.

The damned story that Reed and Billie had been all across the interior of the state trying to uncover, thus far coming up with nothing more than it had something to do with a state championship basketball team in a small town seven years before.

Or a party after a football game.

Or a sheriff's department investigation that may or may not have happened.

Hardly the sorts of plots that bestselling novels and Emmy-winning television were based on, though he had seen more done for less.

The latest in the sole universal truth his career had imparted on him, that being that there were no limits to humans. Not the heinousness they are capable of or the slights they could contort in their minds or the amount of time they could let something fester.

A collision of all three fast starting to appear like what they were now dealing with.

Driving with the siren blaring and flashing lights flickering from one headlight to the other, clearing a path before them, Reed and Billie made it from New Albany back to the 8th Precinct in just shy of twenty minutes. Time that was spent with Billie pacing in the backseat, the arch of her spine passing along the bottom of the rearview mirror, Reed wanting nothing more than to be doing the same in the front seat.

Coiled energy that had him practically bobbing in his chair, barely making it into the visitor stall in front of the precinct before jumping out, he and his partner both hitting the door at a jog.

Two flights of stairs later, they were on the third floor, finding Officers McMichaels and Jacobs waiting outside of the interrogation room. Beside them was Captain Grimes in a pair of jeans and a pullover sweater, a stack of papers in hand.

Items all three were clustered around, looking up in unison at the sudden arrival of Reed and Billie.

"Please tell me that's an ID on our guy."

Extending the pages before him, Grimes waited until Reed accepted them, still breathing hard from the sprint up from the sedan, before replying, "Joseph Hendricks. Twenty-eight-years-old, from-"

"Coshocton," Reed said, knowing the last part of the sentence before even finding it on the top sheet. A screenshot of a driver's license made out to the name Grimes had just rattled off, along with all the other accompanying information.

A date of birth and an address that Reed skipped over, checking to make sure everything else fit with the man he and Billie apprehended earlier.

A check that made it as far as seeing Hendricks' picture and his stated height at 6'8" before moving to the next page in order.

Another image of a driver's license, this one from the state of Indiana, made out to a woman three years older named Mary Hendricks. A sight that immediately drew to mind the elusive female he'd been hearing about for a couple days, his gaze going to the bottom corner to see that she stood more than a foot shorter than her brother.

Ample difference to account for the differing shoes sizes found at Matt Seesel's.

"Nothing more on Joseph?" Reed asked, flicking his gaze up for a moment. A quick glance to see all three men staring back, offset by Billie pressed tight to his leg.

Feeding on the concentrated energy in the room, her entire body was coiled tight, striated muscle felt plainly against Reed's thigh.

"Not on him," Grimes replied.

A reply with just enough inflection that Reed got the hint that he was supposed to keep going. The stack of papers he'd just been handed had more vital information to be seen.

Lowering his focus back to the thin pile clutched tight in both hands, Reed shuffled the top two pages aside. A pair of driver's license printouts that gave way to an identification of a very different type.

"James Hendricks," Reed said, reading the top line for the booking sheet in front of him. Standard paperwork for an inmate serving time at any state or federal facility in the country, this one originating from the Mansfield Correctional Institute an hour north of Columbus.

"Joseph and Mary were both clean," Grimes said. "No prints in the system, nothing more than a speeding ticket between them.

"The third sibling, James there, went down for vehicular manslaughter that was bumped up for being under the influence and under twenty-one. Got ten at sentencing, was later extended for an incident in his cell. Served eight total before being paroled less than a year ago."

His gaze dancing down the length of the booking sheet, Reed took in each of the details of what was just mentioned. Facts that jumped out at him in order, registering for just an instant before he moved on again.

A quick pass, getting the general gist of things before returning to the top to take in the attached photograph of the man who was said to also be twenty-eight-years-old, though to look at, barely resembled a teenager.

Round features, with full lips and curly hair that looked distinctly out of place with the sneer he wore.

A pairing that gave the impression of a child trying to play tough, putting on his best mean look for the camera.

"Five-foot-six," Reed read. "That's more than a foot shorter than his brother. Shorter than his sister even."

Glancing up, he asked, "Are we sure they're related by blood? Were there any adoption records in the system?"

"Oh, yeah," Grimes said. Jutting his chin out, he added, "Check the dates of birth on the two males."

The booking sheet still clutched in one hand, Reed glanced down to it, taking in the numbers listed. A date he muttered to himself, committing it to memory, while flipping back to the top sheet in the pile.

"Joseph and James are *twins*?" he asked.

Asked as a purely rhetorical question, Reed wasn't looking for an answer. Had one been offered, he likely wouldn't have even heard it, his mind already racing to process the new information. Unexpected data that now threatened to turn their working assumptions sideways.

There was obviously no way to know exactly who Joseph Hendricks had been working with. Not without knowing his motivation, the story behind it proving especially elusive.

At the same time, the combined evidence did provide a compelling case for a familial connection. Association that had seemed strong enough to the captain on first pass to warrant inclusion.

"Dr. Mehdi said she was certain that the tattoo work was done by a female and the bruising and markers by a male," Reed said. Audible thinking with his head still tilted down as he riffled through the pile of papers. "Earl said they had differing shoe sizes consistent with that."

Shuffling the pages back together, Reed snapped his attention up to see all three men staring back at him, Billie still pressed firm to his side.

"We've been assuming all along this was a two-person team, but what if this was a family job, and all three are involved? What if the smaller footprints Earl found actually belonged to James, meaning-"

"Meaning we've got two people still unaccounted for out there somewhere," Grimes finished.

Chapter Sixty-Six

Reed had been inside enough interrogation rooms during his years as a detective to know that suspects almost always played things one of a few different ways. There were of course the outliers who thought they were smarter than everyone else or the individuals with morbid desires or even those with some wires that weren't quite connected internally, but by and large they tended to go one of three ways.

The first of those were the ones who were just angry. A tact that had two forms, the most prevalent being for them to start spouting off the instant anybody entered, saying they had the wrong person or making threats or whatever else came to mind.

Classic posturing done at a decibel that reverberated from the concrete block walls. People – almost without fail men – who were used to bullying their way to whatever they wanted and had no reason to think this would be any different.

The other half of those who chose to go the vitriolic path were those who said absolutely nothing. They made a point of either staring directly at the interrogator or putting their focus on the table before them, sometimes even the one-way glass on the far wall.

A pointed look as they drew in loud breaths, nostrils flaring and veins bulging along their necks and forearms. A human time bomb, about to explode if they weren't released with an apology immediately.

Two branches from the same tree that Reed had yet to see be successful even a single time.

The second group of people to sit in the stiff wooden chair on the far side of the metal table secured directly to the floor were the self-preservationists. The people who started talking the instant the door opened, pleading with the interviewer and the universe and any associated deities they could think of for mercy.

A verbal deluge of anything they knew or had ever heard. Anything to save themselves, even if it meant turning on every friend or family member they'd ever known.

A font of bullshit that investigators were forced to sift through, trying to decipher what little bits of truth might exist.

Of those first two types, there was no clear favorite. Both came with their own pitfalls, forcing the investigator to trudge through, trying to glean out some little bit of usable information. A task that could include attempting to make them talk or getting them to shut up, Reed having done both more times than he cared to remember.

Exercises in insanity that still, without fail, he would take over the third group. The one where an apprehended person turtled up, slipping into a state that bordered on catatonia.

System overload causing all else to shut down, rendering them incapable of processing basic questions, let alone formulating responses.

A category Joseph Hendricks looked to fast be headed toward, the man having not moved an inch in the time Reed and the others spent watching from the observation room on the far side of the one-way glass. Fifteen minutes that matched what Officers McMichaels and Jacobs said he'd been doing since they left Chance Murphy's house earlier.

A full hour that continued as Reed and Billie entered, his too-tall body remaining folded onto the chair that looked child-sized beneath him. His wide eyes fixed on the plain metal top of the table before him, he gave absolutely no acknowledgement of their presence.

Not a flick of the eyes toward the door. Not a flinch as it swung shut behind them.

Not even a reaction to the solid black wolf that had slammed into him earlier, now back to within just a few feet, sharing a confined space.

Poor omens all for what was about to happen and the information Reed was in search of.

"Joseph Hendricks," Reed said, starting with just the name and nothing more. An exploratory opening to see if he could evoke any reaction.

An initial step he let linger as he slid out the chair directly across from Hendricks and lowered himself into it, forcing his way into the man's point of focus.

"Age twenty-eight, of Coshocton. Formerly a pretty good basketball player, catching on with Akron and even scoring sixteen points in an NCAA tournament game for the Zips. An upset bid that fell just short against a pretty weak Duke team."

The last lines were a bit of trivia Reed had been able to pull off Google. Very basic information to try and get the man talking after a very perfunctory dive before stepping inside to speak with him.

Baseline information that Deke was working to add to in that very moment. Just enough initial data to show the man that they were onto him. They knew who he was and where he lived. Even what he had done in the past.

Anything to get him to open up.

Divulge something useful.

"Bounced around after that, tried playing a bit of ball overseas, eventually ended up back home, coaching basketball and working part-time at the local grain mill until quitting six months ago."

Pausing a second time, Reed rolled his gaze upward to stare at the young man. An individual that looked radically different from the one first handcuffed at the bottom of that ravine, any bit of defiance, or urgency, or even fear, having dissipated from his features.

In their place was nothing more than the same gaze, wide eyes fixed on the tabletop between them.

An expression hinting at age well beyond twenty-eight, markedly different from the youthful features of his twin brother.

"What happened six months ago?" Reed continued. "Decided that lugging bags of feed wasn't for you?"

More prodding that elicited absolutely nothing, the man merely sitting with his shoulders rolled inward, as if trying to make himself appear as small as possible.

Without knowing exactly what that incident at the cabin years before included, there were only so many options available. So many buttons Reed could push.

A preciously short list he had no choice but to keep working through, hoping to evoke a response, before they were forced to be off again, hoping to locate Chance Murphy or figure out some other way to determine who else might be targets.

"Was there an issue with a customer? Chance Murphy stop by with a problem one day? Matt Seesel lodge a complaint?"

For a third time, Reed paused, his gaze scrutinizing Hendricks on the opposite side of the table. A probing stare, hoping to see any sign that what he was saying was registering.

Any kind of reply to the names being alluded to.

Anything more than the same stony visage that had been in place since Reed and Billie first arrived back at the 8th.

"Or was it something closer to home?" Reed pressed. "Maybe something to do with one of your siblings?"

Chapter Sixty-Seven

The last of The Artist's tears left her body six months prior. The conclusion of an eighteen month stretch that saw her spend more time sobbing than she had in the rest of her life combined.

Twin tragedies that together served as a classic cautionary tale she had used to harden herself in the time since.

A self-imposed mandate to thicken her skin and sharpen her psyche, meaning that as she sat in the Kroger's parking lot gripping the steering wheel in both hands and leaning forward over it, drawing in deep breaths, her body's inclination might have been to cry, though she would not allow it.

No physical manifestation of the sorrow she felt about what must have certainly happened to The Tall Boy.

No tears to be released over something that could not be changed, the only remaining option now to try and move ahead from it. React in the best possible way.

A path forward that she could not quite wrap her head around, those damn flickering red and blue lights dominating her thoughts. Flashing strobes against a night sky that might not have been enough to evoke tears, but were certainly strong enough to cloud coherent thought.

An ongoing battle lasting more than an hour, still waging when the passenger door to her car swung open. A quick burst of movement without warning, followed by a gust of chilled night air.

Sensory assault followed by a form dressed in all black swinging down into the seat beside her. A move so quick and smooth it seemed almost practiced, depositing the small frame in the passenger seat.

A sudden entry that ended with the vehicle still rocking under the addition of weight as he pulled the door back shut, extinguishing the sounds and cold air that had flooded in just seconds before.

"Hey," The Artist whispered, not even bothering to have relinquished her grip on the steering wheel with either hand.

"Hey," The Angel replied, glancing her way before turning his focus forward and peering out. A quick check that was followed by each side and finally the back, as if expecting a SWAT team to have been sitting on her vehicle.

A full assault in a suburban grocery store parking lot, waiting only on his arrival before beginning.

"You okay?"

Of the adjectives The Artist could ascribe to the last couple of hours, days, months, even years, okay was nowhere near the top. Or even on the damned thing.

A list that could easily fill sheets of lined notebook paper, many of which The Artist had passed through her mind while looping her way out of New Albany earlier, her car pointed east toward Newark and the fallback location she and The Angel had discussed in their previous conversation.

Time alone on the road to let her try and make sense of things, putting apt titles to the various events that had transpired. Everything from the shock of that initial incident years ago to the sorrow of their mother passing to now the horror of whatever happened to The Tall Boy.

Three overarching terms, with dozens of others mixed in. Every possible evoked human response, along with some others The Artist never thought she would be capable of.

The emotional equivalents of turning on a damned tattoo gun and touching it to the brows of complete strangers.

More things from the last couple years she wished she could strike from her memory, never to return.

"No," The Artist whispered.

Grunting softly in reply, The Angel continued on a second pass around the perimeter of the car. One more sweep around a vehicle sitting on the edge of a smattering of cars parked outside of a twenty-four-hour grocery store late on a weeknight.

Force of habit or something more performative, trying to give the impression he was in control, everything could be salvaged.

A toss up The Artist did not have it in her to even try to decipher.

"You get rid of the phone?" he asked.

Dipping her chin, The Artist said, "Pulled the battery, tossed it in a dumpster before leaving New Albany. You?"

"Crushed the damn thing under my boot and then kicked it in a sewer drain," The Angel answered. "Nobody coming after me, regardless of what they find in that idiot's van."

A spike of ire rose within The Artist, her features contorting as she rolled her gaze to the seat beside her. A hardened stare she left long enough to make him glance her way and acknowledge before turning back straight ahead.

It was no secret that the twin brothers she grew up down the hall from had been on differing trajectories since they were all still in elementary school. Diverging tendencies she had been privy to on all those car rides in the backseat, her mother coming to realize the same a few years later.

Small differences that grew more pronounced, multiplying over time into the two radical extremes she'd been back to living with the last six months.

Still, they were all on the same team.

They were family, brought together in the name of quite possibly the last common thread they all shared.

"Enough," she said. A single word letting it be known that there was enough shit on their plate at the moment.

Taking cheap shots at their brother didn't need to be one more thing.

Twisting his features into a scowl, The Angel looked as if he was about to fire back. Another snide remark about The Tall Boy or more complaining about The Artist taking up for him.

Words that, to her surprise, didn't pass his lips, his hands rising in front of him instead.

A sign of surrender that he held for a moment before lowering them back into place and saying, "I spent most of the ride over here thinking about things, and it looks like LUST is probably off the table for now."

A comment as unexpected as his first question as to whether or not she was okay, The Artist felt her eyes widen. Her jaw sagged.

Three congruent circles as she again turned to stare at her brother.

"But that's okay," he continued, unfazed, "he isn't the most important one remaining right now anyway."

Filled with shock at the words spilling forth, The Artist couldn't begin to mount a response. Releasing her grasp on the wheel, she turned her entire upper body to the side, openly staring.

A more pointed position that he was oblivious to for the better part of a minute, only coming to even notice her after a quick glance over. A passing look in the middle of explaining his plan, needing a double take to see her gawking at him.

"What the hell's wrong with you?" he snapped.

"Seriously? You're telling me that in the hour since our brother was *arrested*, you've been trying to figure out how the hell to finish this thing?"

"Are you seriously telling me you *haven't* been thinking that all this time?"

Chapter Sixty-Eight

Joseph Hendricks might not have said a single word, though that didn't mean he didn't give up anything. A slight flicker of his eyes at the mention of his siblings didn't tell Reed everything he wanted to know, but it gave him a place to start.

A bit of confirmation, providing direction to aim the next steps.

And a story that was slowly coming into focus for him and Billie to keep chipping away at.

Barely was he outside of the interrogation room, the door slamming shut behind him, before Reed had his cellphone out. Diving into his recent call log, he scrolled down a couple of entries and hit send, Deke appearing on the other end of the line at the same time as Captain Grimes and Officers McMichaels and Jacobs filing out of the adjacent observation room.

All three with faces drawn taut, they said nothing, circling up around the phone held in Reed's outstretched hand.

"Still working, man," Deke answered, bypassing his traditional greeting.

"Need you to expand your search to the entire Hendricks family," Reed replied. "Start with Joseph, include his brother James and his sister Mary."

"You got it," Deke replied. "What am I looking for?"

"Anything you can find," Reed said. "Namely, most recent addresses, cellphone numbers, anything we can use to get a location on them."

"No sweat. You'll know something when I do."

"Appreciate it," Reed said, thumbing the phone off and stowing it back into his rear pocket. Looking up to the assembled trio before him, he said, "I assume you all noticed what happened when I mentioned his family?"

"Hard to miss," McMichaels replied.

"Especially when it was the only sign of life he gave in there," Jacobs added.

"Exactly," Reed said. "Dr. Mehdi and Earl both told me there was a male and a female involved. Based on what I saw just now-"

"Could be any combination of the three," Jacobs finished.

"Exactly," Reed said, "or all three. With James being that much shorter, the jobs of tracking and disabling could fall to the brothers while the tattooing is the sister."

Stopping there, Reed added the new information to what he'd been working with for the last couple of days. A two-person team that could now be expanded by fifty percent, tremendously opening up the possibilities.

Especially when one of those three already had a record and had spent time in prison. Years in what was essentially a criminal finishing school, making him privy to all sorts of people and information.

Cutting his gaze to the side, Reed pushed aside the mental image of the man on the opposite side of the table in the interrogation room. In its place, he pulled back the printouts that Grimes had handed him when he and Billie showed up a short time before.

Three pages, each with identifying information.

"The oldest is Mary," Reed said, his focus fixed on Billie beside him as he thought out loud. A stare she matched, even while shifting close enough for him to extend a hand, threading his fingers through her thick fur. "Followed by the twins, Joseph and James."

Hearing the names aloud, he slid his attention upward and asked, "What do those sound like to you?"

Holding his right hand up before him, Jacobs extended his index finger. "Mary."

Next up was the middle finger. "Joseph."

His ring finger went last. "James."

"Those are Biblical names," McMichaels added.

"And the tattoos being applied are the seven deadly sins," Grimes inserted.

"Exactly," Reed said. "When I asked Sheriff Broderick about the incident that his predecessor chose not to pursue seven years ago, he called the only person on their staff who was still around then. Guy said he didn't know what happened, but he remembered a woman came into the station one day ranting about sinners and immorality and all the rest.

"Said she was a borderline fanatic, to the point it became something of a running joke around the office afterwards."

Grunting softly, Jacobs said, "So you think this was maybe the mother? She came in to file a report, or even showed up after it didn't go anywhere?"

"Maybe," Reed conceded. "Can't automatically assume yet, but the connection seems too strong to ignore."

"It does," Grimes agreed, "but the ages of these three don't match with a high school party seven years ago. Thirty-one and twenty-eight are way too old to have still been attending something like that."

Nodding his head in agreement, Reed took in a deep breath. Holding it for several seconds, he slowly pushed it out through his nostrils, forcing his mind to slow down. Process what was coming in new, adding it to the framework he and Billie had been able to put together the last couple of days.

A task offset by the sense of urgency flooding through him. Desires to find Chance Murphy, as well as Mary and James Hendricks.

Opposing emotions that had him practically thrumming, needing to be moving again soon.

"You're right," Reed said. "There's still too much we don't know to put together a full narrative. And until we hear what exactly happened that night, there are still too many holes to know why the Hendricks family is doing this or who they might target next."

"Okay," Grimes said, "but where do we go to get the rest of the story? The sheriff was put down before he could share, and none of the victims have known what happened."

"Actually," Reed replied, slapping at the leg of his jeans as he began to drift toward the stairwell nearby. The first steps in what he imagined was going to be a sprint through much of the rest of the night.

Provided their next stop was able to accomplish what he suspected it might.

"That may not be entirely true."

Chapter Sixty-Nine

"Duuuuude."

Ten years, Reed had known Deke. Six of those, he had actively worked with him directly, encompassing his entire career as a detective. Before that was the occasional one-off project that Riley handled, slowly evolving into its current manifestation with Deke as an official consultant for both the CPD and BCI.

An employee with his own ID number and place on the payroll, collecting handsome fees for his invaluable services.

During all of that time, Reed had heard his colloquial greeting more times than he could count. A personality quirk that Reed originally attributed to him being a west coast transplant before eventually coming to realize that was just his nature.

Affability, likely as a coping mechanism in the face of the stresses associated with his work and home.

An explanation Riley had given many times, though it wasn't until being more fully exposed to what Deke did that Reed came to understand.

Forced to guess, Reed would ballpark the total number of interactions that started with that single word in the triple digits. Ample opportunity for him to decipher the meaning behind any inflection there might be, this particular greeting a far cry from his usual opening.

Extended to several syllables in length, it was threaded with both shock and urgency.

Something found that had caused him to call back just minutes after hanging up, wanting to relay it on before there was any chance he could have finished with all Reed asked him to look into.

"What's going on?" Reed asked, reaching out and flicking off the siren on his sedan. A sudden absence of sound that made the interior seem especially quiet, leaving the job of pushing any vehicles out of their way to the headlamps flashing from one side to the other.

Flickering halogens alternating a distinct pattern across the asphalt before them.

"I don't have everything," Deke replied, "but this was something I thought you'd want to know."

"What's that?"

"You guys missed one."

As Reed had just conceded to Grimes and the others, he was aware there were holes. An incomplete story that was just starting to come together, pieced out of disparate crime scenes and snippets of information.

A tale with deficiencies so glaring that outside of Chance Murphy, they still didn't know who the remaining two targets might be.

"One what?"

"One of the Hendricks," Deke replied. "There were four of them, not three."

As fast as any initial confusion about Deke's opening might have arose, it vanished. Complete understanding that caused Reed's eyes to widen and his jaw to sag, his left hand tightening around the steering wheel as they hurtled their way around the northern end of the Columbus outer belt.

When he and Billie had gotten to the precinct just a short time earlier, the captain was waiting with the trio of printouts in hand. An initial identification of Joseph Hendricks, along with additional family members in the area.

A list Reed had taken as exhaustive, not once considering that there may have been more that the search didn't catch.

"Were?" Reed asked, seizing on one of the last words mentioned.

"Exactly. Past tense," Deke replied. "The fourth family member was a female named Anna. Four years younger than the twins, she would be twenty-four now."

"Which would have put her at seventeen seven years ago," Reed muttered. "Average age for a high school senior."

"Exactly," Deke repeated, "which she was, at Coshocton High, up until dropping out in November and finishing by GED."

Reed's right foot moved a little further toward the floorboard. A nudging of the accelerator, pushing them faster to their destination.

One of only two places he could think of to find out exactly what happened that night in the cabin, the other still having not turned up in the form of Chance Murphy.

"What happened to her?" Reed asked.

"Suicide, not quite two-and-a-half years ago," Deke replied. "By that time, she had moved clear across the country and was attending Boise State University in Idaho. Not sure about the details. Haven't gotten that far yet."

Nodding in understanding, Reed stared straight ahead. Eyes wide, his head spun, trying to force aside the adrenaline in his system so he might think clearer.

Begin to make sense of the enormous volume of information just handed to him.

Despite admitting barely twenty minutes earlier that the story had deficiencies, there was no longer any doubt that whatever had sent Anna Hendricks into hiding – and maybe even eventually contributed to her taking her own life – was the connective thread tying the assorted victims together.

A lone commonality in both time and place that there was no other explanation for.

"Which is why she didn't show up in the system when Captain Grimes ran her brother," Reed whispered.

"Yep," Deke agreed.

Pulse thrumming, raising the temperature inside the car and pulling Billie up through the two front seats, Reed glanced to the spiral-bound notepad sitting beside him. A quick glance to the white paper with blue ink scrawled across it, not needing to be able to make out the words to know exactly what was written.

A list he had been through a hundred times, running it once more through his mind.

A quick trip, ending with the most recent victim. A sheriff who had looked into the incident before opting not to pursue it.

"Deke, can you dig into the mother as well? I'm not sure if the captain looked her up, so she may be alive or dead," Reed said.

A question that was replied to with the keyboard on the opposite end of the line erupting. Plastic chatter that lasted several moments, continuing as Reed saw his intended exit appear on the signs positioned overhead.

A destination he had been to once already, coming in from the opposite direction.

A change in approach he hoped was indicative of a better result on this return visit.

"Sarah Hendricks," Deke said, his voice appearing to replace the sound of him banging on the keyboard. "Born 1961, deceased six months ago, both in Coshocton, Ohio."

It didn't take a lot to imagine the woman's passing serving as the precipitating event for what was happening now. An impediment removed, followed by months of meticulous planning before getting started.

Maybe even a dying wish that her extreme devoutness didn't want to be associated with in life.

"What was the cause of death?" Reed asked.

Another couple of keystrokes. "Cancer. Doesn't specify which kind."

Bobbing his head, Reed recalled the conversation he and Deke had earlier in the day.

"I bet anything that's where they got the ketamine they're using now," he muttered. A statement that was more of a thought, half whispered before raising his voice and asking, "Where was she living at the time of her death?"

"Looks like she owned a homestead outside of town," Deke said.

"And what happened to it?"

"Husband is long deceased; everything went to the kids."

Tapping the brakes to slow their momentum enough to exit, Reed drifted into the right lane, taking it off the freeway and down into the suburb of Westerville.

"Can I get you to do me one more favor?" Reed asked, working the steering wheel hand over hand as he turned west, his flashing headlights still clearing the road.

"Shoot."

"Can you call Captain Grimes, give him the address, and have him send McMichaels and Jacobs that way?"

Chapter Seventy

Reed didn't know who the doctor Captain Grimes and Chief Brandt had called and asked to check on Carly Mayes was. The first time he had ever made such a request, he didn't know if the CPD kept someone on staff for just such a situation or if they had called the closest local hospital and asked them to arrange something.

Long gone by the time Reed and Billie arrived back to the second-floor apartment out behind the house in Westerville, all he knew was that whatever they gave Mayes had worked.

A sedative of some sort that had not completely removed the devastation – or even the signs of its recent passing – from her features, though had pulled things back so she was no longer struggling for air, fighting for breaths between sobs.

It had also made it so she was able to sit in the papasan chair in the corner, her narrow frame enveloped in a fuzzy Christmas blanket splashed liberally with polar bears wearing Santa caps. A matching mug clasped between her hands, the smell of cinnamon engulfed her, likely taken from the same brew that Reed had noticed perfuming the air on their first visit.

A scent so strong it was almost overpowering to him, no doubt bordering on torturous to his partner seated on the floor by his side.

Having pulled over a chair from the small folding set in the adjacent kitchen, Reed rested with his back to the Christmas lights, their multi-colored glow splashed on the floor to either side. A third point in a triangle with Mayes to his immediate left and Marissa Lange filling the third spot on the end of the couch.

Sitting with one elbow propped on the arm of the sofa, Marissa's entire lower body was buried beneath the fleece blanket Mayes was previously using. On her face was an expression stating she had no desire to be a part of the impending conversation.

Continued presence Reed had tried to alleviate by offering for her to step outside, kept close only by Mayes requesting she stay.

A fear of being left alone, and worry about whatever was about to be discussed that Reed couldn't help but agree with, knowing that nothing good was likely to come from what was about to be shared.

No matter how necessary it might be.

A swap of positions that was the only visible difference between this trip and the last, with the obvious exception of Officer Melanie Christ having relocated downstairs with her partner. A post Reed had told them both to maintain until hearing back from either him or their captain on the way up, it unlikely that the Hendricks family would circle back, but not entirely impossible.

Not after what they had done to Bertran Alexander.

And the fact that their brother was now in custody, possibly forcing them into a state of worry, needing to wipe away anyone who might know the full story of why they were doing what they were doing.

A tale Reed now knew likely caused Anna Hendricks to drop out of high school and eventually take her own life, though needed to be careful not to force on Mayes, not wanting to sway anything she might share.

"Let me start by saying how sorry my partner and I both are to be here like this," Reed began. "I cannot even imagine what you must be going through. Wouldn't dare insult you by trying to insinuate I did."

Pausing there, he waited for some sort of a response to the opening. Words in reply, or a greeting, or anything to acknowledge what had just been said. Anything at all to signal it was okay for him to continue, the overwhelming emotion of earlier pushed aside by whatever pharmaceuticals were passing through her system.

The closest he got was her lips thinning as she pressed them together, not a single sound escaping.

Likely, the best there was going to be.

"I assure you, we would not be here right now, putting you through this, if it wasn't absolutely necessary," he continued. Glancing down to his lap, he peeked at the small notepad now balanced atop his thigh. A means of keeping everything and everybody straight in his mind, matching it against whatever was about to be shared.

And a way of recording any additional names that arose.

"But there have been others. And we're afraid there will be even more if we don't get to the bottom of this."

For a moment, Mayes looked as if she had turned to stone. Any slight twitches of her facial muscles ceased. Even her chest stopped rising and falling as she took in air.

Everything went completely still, her eyes glazing as she stared down at the mug in her hands.

A pause that lasted several seconds before she snapped her eyes upward and asked, "There were more?"

"Yes."

"How many?"

Meeting her gaze, Reed allowed a moment to pass, not wanting to let the conversation descend into a rapid back-and-forth, before replying, "Three."

A silent tear slid down Mayes's left cheek as her eyelids fluttered shut. Her nostrils flared as she pulled in air, the emotion of the moment threatening to do again what it had for most of the day.

A wave that Reed let crest, watching as her features began to quiver, before ultimately being able to beat it back.

Peeling her eyes back open, red threaded the sclera as she stared back at him.

"Who?"

"I will tell you," Reed replied. "I promise. But first I have to ask you about something, and I want to do it before telling you who else because I don't want it to affect what you might say. That fair?"

Cutting her focus to the side, Mayes fixed a look on Marissa. A quick check to see if the deal was acceptable, or if Reed could be trusted, or whatever other internal debate she might have been waging.

A silent question that was answered in the affirmative, allowing her to return her attention and nod.

"Okay," Reed said. "Let me begin by asking, how old are you?"

Of the assorted questions she might have anticipated, it was clear that did not make the list. Pulling her chin back a quarter inch, she stared at him a moment.

"Twenty-five."

One of a couple of different acceptable answers, Reed didn't press it any further, instead moving to, "And where did you go to high school?"

The look of confusion on her face grew more pronounced. "Coshocton High School."

Both answers lining up with what he was hoping for, Reed launched straight forth, saying, "This is going to sound a little bit odd, but I want to ask about something that happened seven years ago. This would have been in November of your senior year."

For an instant, the same look remained. A lingering bit of confusion demonstrated by faint lines around her eyes, just barely visible amidst the swelling encasing the top half of her features.

Uncertainty that soon faded as her eyes widened, recognition clicking into place.

A new expression that told Reed that she already knew where this was going.

"You know what I'm referring to, don't you?" Reed whispered.

Another tear dove over Mayes's cheek, cleaving a path across the smooth skin. A glistening streak that was soon matched by one on the opposite side as she nodded.

Setting her mug to the side, she pushed the blanket covering her away and grasped the bottom of her fleece pullover. Raising it no more than a few inches, she fixed her gaze on the wall beside her, letting

Reed lean forward and take a look at the letters scrawled across pale skin.

Writing that was backstopped by bruising that wasn't as bad as the others, but was still plenty vicious.

DRUNK BITCH

"This is about Anna, isn't it?" Mayes whispered, her eyes still pinned to the wall beside them. "That's why someone did this to me?"

Retreating back into his seat, Reed glanced down just long enough to add the newest entry to the top sheet on his notepad. A quick addendum to make sure nothing was omitted, another slot filled, leaving just three rows remaining.

Spaces he hoped weren't actively being completed at that moment somewhere close by.

"It is," Reed replied.

Lowering her shirt back to its original spot, Mayes reached across her body, pulling the blanket back into place. A final layer of protection, wrapping herself in a cocoon, before she slid her attention up to face him.

"I didn't even know it was there until after the doctor came," she said. "Didn't exactly get that far on the first go-round."

Sliding a hand to the side, Reed rested it atop Billie's neck, his fingers threaded through the thick hair.

"What happened at the party that night?"

"They set her up," Mayes replied. "Set *us* up."

Falling back on the same tactic used with Susan Cartwright just a day before, Reed remained silent. Forced quiet with his focus meeting hers, no matter how much he wanted to urge her along. Spur her forward, in the name of finally getting the complete story.

And, hopefully, getting out ahead of the Hendricks siblings while there was still time.

Action that would have to wait just a bit longer, the story to be told and the fragile state of the young woman telling it both demanding as much.

"You know how every school has what they call the ugly duckling? The one person who was always kind of chubby, or nerdy, or whatever, until one day they weren't?" Mayes opened. A start Reed wasn't expecting, though nodded as if in total understanding just the same.

"Well, that was Anna. It was honestly both of us, which was why we were friends going clear back to elementary school, but it was really pronounced for her.

"Her father had passed when she was young, leaving her with her three older siblings and her mother. Four very different people with very different personalities, meaning she just kind of adapted by being a wallflower.

"Something that was easy when she was younger and had thick glasses or a few pimples, but by the time we were in high school, wasn't so easy."

Raising one shoulder in a semi-shrug, she continued, "I mean, you can't hide that kind of pretty. She tried, but it didn't matter. The ugly duckling had become a swan, and people noticed. *Boys* noticed."

Not one word had been said yet about the night in question, and already Reed had a faint idea where things were going. Not the particulars, but the sentiments underlying them.

Thoughts that made his stomach clench as he said, "Boys like Chance Murphy."

"Yes," Mayes answered, "which was weird, because he was a late bloomer, too. Wasn't until that big growth spurt that he really became that popular or such a good athlete, but..."

Letting her voice trail off, she flicked her gaze to the side.

For a moment, Reed thought she might ask if they got him too. A question he would have no idea how to answer, repeated attempts at contact going unanswered.

A question that, luckily, she didn't pose, her thoughts entrenched in the story she was telling.

"Anyway, at the time, Chance had been dating a girl named Nadine Hart. She was a good athlete, popular, all the stuff you'd expect for the star basketball player and quarterback of the football team.

"They were together through most of junior year and into summer, but then broke up. He didn't really go with anybody after that, except to take Ava Kirkwood, a senior cheerleader, to Homecoming.

"Word was, she wanted it to be more, but he said no. Gave her the same story he told Nadine, that he didn't want to have distractions during his senior year."

Not one bit of Reed had any idea where the story was going. His initial thoughts faded in the face of a tale that sounded like a plot to a teenage-aimed drama on Netflix that he'd seen advertised a few times, but had never deigned to watch.

How any of it fit with what he was looking for he didn't know, trusting just that eventually it would get where it needed to.

After days of stumbling forward, trying to piece things together, it was better to have too much information than not enough.

"Anyway," Mayes continued, "around that same time, Chance started talking to Anna some. Nothing serious – it's not like they ever went out or anything – but more than in the past. Enough that Nadine and Ava both noticed, thought that Anna was the real reason why he turned them down."

Back to clutching the mug in both hands, Mayes lifted it as if she might take a drink, making it no higher than halfway before thinking better of it. A look bordering on repulsion crossed her features as she stared down into it, slowly lowering it to her lap again.

"We should have known something was up when they invited us to that postgame party," Mayes said. "We'd been hearing about them all through high school, these big bashes they'd have at this cabin out in the woods, but we were never invited.

"We were teenagers, though. Just happy to be included. When somebody asked if we wanted to ride out, we went. Just like when someone offered us a drink, we took it."

Pausing there, Mayes fell silent for several moments. Long enough that renewed moisture appeared on her checks, running the length of her face and dripping to the blanket below.

Enough that when she finally looked up, her eyes were even more bloodshot, shimmering with tears.

"I don't know what it was they gave us. I know I don't remember a damn thing that happened that night. Neither of us did.

"Not until the tape showed up online a few days later."

Feeling the tightness in his core become even more pronounced, Reed asked, "Tape?"

"Yeah," Mayes whispered. "It wasn't a sex tape, there wasn't enough there to call it that, but it was definitely suggestive. Somebody put them together in a room, let them start fooling around, and filmed the whole thing."

"Her and Chance?" Reed asked.

"Yeah," Mayes repeated, "though you really couldn't tell. It had been pretty heavily edited, so all you ever saw was his back."

Sniffing loudly, she added, "They weren't nearly so kind to Anna."

In his periphery, Reed saw a flash of movement from Marissa. Her first of any kind since they started talking, he looked over to see her running a hand beneath each eye, wiping away tears of her own.

One of many acceptable responses to the story being shared, ranging from that all the way to balling up a fist and pounding it into the couch cushion she was sitting on.

Reactions he himself would be having if in any other situation.

"What happened after that?" Reed asked.

"After that was mostly rumors and conjecture," Mayes said. "Her mother had always been religious, but after her brother went to jail and the other two moved away, she became fanatical about it.

"She didn't even want Anna going to public school, so when she found out what happened..."

Pulling her right hand away from the mug, she held it wide a moment. A motion paired with a sigh, before bringing them back together and continuing, "First thing she did was pull Anna out. After that, she went on the warpath. Tried to get everyone involved arrested.

"When that didn't work..."

Again, she let her voice trail away. A bit of quiet preceding her continuing, "For a while, that was all anybody talked about. Some people said she was going after the sheriff for taking bribes to look the other way. The basketball coach for cutting a deal to keep his star player out of trouble.

"Even me, for blacking out that night and letting it happen."

One by one, Reed could feel the pieces falling into place. The people involved, and the careful selection of the words affixed to them, both in ink and marker.

"Like most things, though, it eventually passed," Mayes said. "The team won a state championship. A few months later, we all graduated. A few years after that, I even heard Anna moved away and started going to college too, though if that's true I don't know.

"We never spoke again after she left school, and it's not like she's on social media or anything."

Lifting her chin just an inch, she flicked her gaze from Marissa to Reed. A quick pass before settling her attention back on the mug still clutched between either hand.

"To be honest, I hadn't even thought about all that in quite a while," she added, her voice just barely audible. "Now, I guess it's something I'll never forget."

Chapter Seventy-One

With each word Carly Mayes had shared, two competing emotions had welled inside of Reed. Twin spires that kept climbing higher with each additional question he asked, and every resulting answer she gave.

On the front end was extreme guilt. Pure self-loathing at what he was putting the young woman through, able to watch in real time as it slowly ebbed away at whatever tiny bit of resolve she had.

Someone who was only awake and upright through the power of pharmaceutical intervention, forced not just to relive what had happened to her, but to delve into the motivating forces behind it. A story that she had clearly agonized over for years, now brought back to the fore in a most horrific way.

Revelations that Reed wished nothing more than that he could spare her from - much like omitting telling her that Anna had taken her own life years before - but was forced to keep going. A drive that must have seemed sadistic to her and Marissa both, no matter how many times he tried assuring her he had no choice.

Others like her were still being targeted, the only way to protect them being to completely flesh out the tale. A story it had taken him and Billie days to find, this quite possibly their only chance at getting all of it in time.

The back half of the evoked responses Reed had been forced to hide as he sat perched on the edge of the kitchen chair was acrimony. Anger and frustration at the story that Mayes shared and the way it was handled so long ago, to say nothing of the tact the Hendricks family was taking now.

Deep rooted hostility it had taken an extreme measure of will to keep hidden, even as it eventually propelled him down the stairs and out the door, Billie close on his heels. Barely slowing to remind Officers Wyght and Christ to stay put as they hit the concrete below, they'd jogged down the driveway and past the main house, every light burning bright inside.

A beacon shining out over the mostly darkened street, warning away anyone who might dare come near again.

A needless gesture that Reed wasn't about to tell them to stop. A bit of assurance to them and Carly and Marissa all, even with the officers posted up out back.

Passing through the bright glow spilling out from the windows, Reed and Billie jogged down the driveway and along the sidewalk. Jumping into the sedan, he made no effort to take off just yet or to even put the keys in the ignition, instead going for his cellphone.

Pulling the door shut behind him to make sure the series of calls he was about to make weren't overheard by anyone who might happen past, he brought the device to life, diving into the recent call log. A quick scan that pulled up what he was looking for, the list of people he needed to speak to quite lengthy.

Individuals spread across the interior of the state, their roles varied, their connections to the case even more so.

A hierarchy Reed had tried to put together in his mind while listening to Mayes upstairs, jumping straight to this one as the most logical place to start. A progression that had to begin with protecting whoever might be remaining as targets, ensuring they didn't suffer a similar fate to the young woman upstairs.

"Broderick," the sheriff answered after a pair of rings. An opening that was still mired in the shock and sorrow of the last time Reed had seen the man, a far cry from the buoyant person he first spoke to earlier in the day.

Another casualty of a scheme that Reed was only just now fully grasping.

"Sheriff Broderick, this is Reed Mattox."

"Detective," Broderick said, letting the word slide out with a sigh. "I was going to call you in a bit, but your man just got here about an hour ago and is still going over the place."

So much having transpired over the course of the evening, Reed had momentarily forgotten that Earl was still out at Bertran Alexander's cabin. A crime scene Reed and Billie had been at just hours before, despite it feeling like so much longer.

An event preceding both his encounter with Joseph Hendricks in New Albany and his meeting with Mayes in Westerville, to say nothing of everything in between.

A progression from a blind hunt, hoping to garner the story motivating all of it from Alexander, to now knowing exactly who was perpetrating such acts and their reason for doing so.

His hope now for Earl to get enough concrete evidence to pin on them while he and Billie were able to block them from getting to anybody else.

"That's not why I'm calling," Reed said, pushing right past Broderick's opening. "Sheriff, do you happen to know or can locate a young woman named Ava Kirkwood? Approximately twenty-five years of age, I believe she resides right there in Coshocton."

The woman's exact address, Reed was not sure of. Mayes had told him she was pretty sure she still lived in their hometown, while the last name on their list had moved closer to the capitol city.

Geographic placement feeding into the order of things that needed to be done now.

"Uh," Broderick replied, needing a moment to get by the surprise of the question before saying, "yeah, I know Ava, but it's not Kirkwood anymore. Heck, I was at her wedding to my old neigh-"

Finally understanding why the question was posed, the significance behind it, Broderick stopped.

"You don't think...?"

"Yes, I do," Reed replied. "I don't have time for the full backstory right now, but please believe me when I say she is in danger. You guys need to get over there right now."

In the background, he could hear movement. Clothing and papers rustling. Footsteps hitting against a solid floor.

Signs that the sheriff understood the urgency of the situation.

Immediacy that Reed added to by saying, "Sheriff, you saw what happened to Bertran Alexander. Please, get over there, kick in the damn door if you have to, but find that girl and stay with her.

"Or even better, get her out of there and get her someplace safe until you hear back from us."

Trusting that his message had been imparted, the sounds of ongoing motion all the response he needed, Reed ended the call there. Swiping the active phone screen away, he backed out a single step to the recent log, scrolling down a couple of entries.

Another unsaved number that he recognized on sight, having first called it just hours before.

Hitting send, he worked his way through a couple of ringtones and a bored dispatcher at the New Albany Police Department, finally getting where he needed to ninety seconds after hitting send.

A minute and a half of sitting folded in the front seat of his sedan, his left leg bobbing up and down. Active agitation matched by Billie in the backseat feeding from his anticipation, pacing from one side of the vehicle to the other.

"Duncan."

"Chief Duncan, this is Reed Mattox," Reed opened, bypassing any additional greeting and cutting right to it.

A tact he trusted the man he met earlier would understand entirely.

"Two things. First, we have now identified two additional accomplices working with Joseph Hendricks, who we apprehended earlier. I'll have my captain send over full details shortly so you can alert your team."

Grunting his understanding, Duncan offered nothing more, letting him continue.

"Second, have you been able to locate Chance Murphy?"

"No sign yet," Duncan replied, "though we have been able to locate the vehicle that was driven by the suspect to his house. Parked on the neighboring street, it looks like he had left the vehicle there and walked in on foot.

"In the vehicle, we also found a burner phone with two outgoing numbers in it, both of which have been turned off.

"Our crime scene crews are currently going through the van and the phone as we speak."

Chapter Seventy-Two

Reed was perfectly aware of the time. An hour that would generally be considered much too late to be calling someone that he barely knew, trusting that the intrusion would be brushed off by the person he was calling having spoken to Captain Grimes earlier.

Especially when the alternative was making the drive over to the gated community the man lived in and banging on his front door until he answered, adding to the pair of officers Reed hoped were already sitting outside his home.

Still parked along the street in front of Carly Mayes's apartment, Reed had cracked open the driver's side door. Just far enough to extend his left foot out, the sole of his running shoe rested atop the asphalt.

A choice to risk a spare word being overheard in the name of letting in some cooler air, both to lower the body temperatures of him and Billie, and to keep them from fogging the windows. Condensation he would be forced to wait for the defrost to clear or to reach out and wipe away, neither particularly appealing.

Another thing for him to deal with, more than enough already on his plate at the moment. What seemed like dozens of different items all in flux, the previous two calls just the start of what he needed to get done in short order.

A proverbial air traffic controller, trying to direct things with nothing more than a cellphone to work from.

"Hello?" Dean Morgan answered, the word coming out in a grumble.

A combination of grog and annoyance Reed pushed past without comment.

"Mr. Morgan, this is Reed Mattox. Do you have a cellphone number for your grandson?"

Unlike upstairs with Mayes a few minutes earlier, Reed made no effort to blunt down his request. Same as he felt no guilt in making it.

Things that, like calling so late, he had to figure Morgan would get by on his own.

Or he wouldn't, the man's feelings far from Reed's biggest concern.

"What?" Morgan responded. Another one-word answer, this one infused with just enough confusion that Reed could almost envision his tattooed forehead crinkling as he asked. "At this hour?"

"Yes," Reed replied. "Earlier this evening, my partner and I stopped by his home and apprehended one of the men responsible for what happened to you and the others."

Using that as a lead-in, a way to get past whatever lingering slumber, any residual irritation there might be, Reed paused just long enough to ensure it registered before continuing with, "Since then, we still haven't been able to locate Chance. The only phone numbers we have are a landline he clearly isn't there to answer and a cellphone that has been disconnected."

Resisting the urge to keep going, to begin yelling at the man, telling him to get his ass out of bed and find them a working number that they could use, Reed stopped. Having said enough, he waited for things to connect in Morgan's mind, his gaze tracking to the second floor of the home before him.

A shadow moving behind a curtain, the owner attempting to be stealthy as he peeled back a corner and peeked out.

Another move that was completely unnecessary, though Reed couldn't pretend he was sorry to see it.

If only such vigilance had been employed earlier in the day.

"Okay," Morgan said, the single word followed by the sound of footsteps. "I remember his mom giving me a new number for him a while back. Something about work providing him with a cellphone and just to use that from now on.

"Hold on."

Saying nothing in reply, Reed waited as the sound of a bed creaking could be heard. Precursors for lights flipping on and bare feet shuffling across hardwood floors.

Sounds of movement that Reed could track against the mental images in his mind, having stood in that home multiple times in recent days. Progress that he wanted so badly to hurry along, yelling out for Morgan to get his ass moving.

His grandson could be in trouble.

Urgings he let pass in silence, waiting as the sound of more light switches flipping on sounded out. The clear din of papers shuffling was heard.

"Okay, here it is," Morgan said, the fact that he had to go and track down the damn thing instead of merely pulling it up on his phone not lost on Reed. Signs of a relationship that was distant at best, making Morgan's inclusion in the scheme that much more random.

A weak connection that it was no surprise hadn't registered with him or Seesel when asked about it earlier in the week.

Validation of at least some of the accusations made by Morgan's ex-wife in the wake of their divorce.

Using the same notepad that he'd been carrying for a couple of days, Reed flipped over the top sheet with the list of sins and assigned people scrawled out in blue ink. Going to the next page in order, he took down the offered digits and was about to end the call there, stopping just short of doing so.

A couple of extra seconds taken in the name of asking about something Mayes alluded to just a short time prior.

One more piece that Reed would have to track down eventually, it better to just get now, amassing as much information as possible in the name of finding his grandson and going after the remaining Hendricks family members.

"Last thing," Reed said. "Seven years ago, did you offer up a large sum of money to help your grandson out of a jam? This would have been around this time of year, when he was a senior in high school?"

Much as he had at Reed's first request, Morgan sputtered in reply. Confusion that was likely laced with incredulity.

"Are you asking me if I bribed someone?"

"Yes," Reed said. "Did you pay off the sheriff of Coshocton County to keep him from looking into an incident that took place at a party?"

"No!" Morgan said, flinging the word across the line. "And I resent the hell out of-"

"Did you give your grandson money?" Reed yelled back, cutting him off, not giving a damn what Morgan resented. "Your daughter? Anybody who might have used it for that, even if you didn't know it?"

Again, Morgan answered in the negative. The start of another tirade that made it but a single word before he stopped.

Falling complete silent, he drew in a long breath, taking several moments before eventually saying, "Actually, that isn't true. I did give my daughter some money. Several thousand dollars that she said was for Chance's future."

Whatever bit of self-righteousness, indignation, that was present initially faded. In their place was realization as he continued, "I always assumed that meant it was a deposit to hold his college acceptance, but that wouldn't make any sense. He hadn't even committed to Xavier yet, and when he did, it was on a full-ride."

Never in his interaction with Morgan had Reed thought he was a particularly likable man. Everything about him, from his home to his showing up at Cowan's to even how mention of him was received by his successor at Buckeye Care, hinted that he was a ruthless businessman who had put that above all else.

Greed that had fed the rumors Mayes alluded to.

False accusations that had gotten him pulled into something that Reed couldn't help but admit the man didn't deserve.

A permanent marring for an action he wasn't even aware of, the need for vengeance overriding a complete and accurate vetting of all that took place.

If only the care the Hendricks family took in planning the attacks was matched by their efforts in researching the motivations behind them.

"Stay by the phone," Reed said. "Somebody will be in touch."

Saying nothing more, this not the time for offering apologies or condolences, Reed signed off the call. A repeat process of what he went through just minutes prior, this time leapfrogging down the call log to a saved entry.

A number he last spoke to earlier, picked up after just a couple of rings.

"What's going on?" Deke asked.

"I have the work cellphone number for Chance Murphy," Reed said. "Any chance I can get you to run a trace for me?"

"Hit me," Deke replied.

A prompt Reed followed, reading the number from the notepad still resting on his thigh. The start of a sequence of keystrokes and clicks, ending with Deke saying, "Okay, looks like he's got it turned off for now, so I can't give you an exact location, but I can tell you where it was the last time it pinged against the closest tower."

Chapter Seventy-Three

Unlike Dean Morgan a moment before, there was no waiting through a half dozen ringtones with Matt Seesel. There was also no grog or irritation in his voice.

If anything, it was something closer to relief, the man answering by blurting out, "I swear I was just about to call you."

Not in the mood to get into the veracity of the statement, Reed pushed right by it. A return of Seesel's own tact, there no time to be wasted on pleasantries or banal back-and-forth.

"Is Chance Murphy there with you?"

A question that was met with a sharp intake of air, though nothing more.

Dead silence Reed did not have the patience for as he snapped, "Seesel! Is he there or not? Otherwise, finding his ass has to be my first priority right now."

Again, there was the clear din of air moving over the line. A response that this time was an exhalation before Seesel said, "He is. I called him earlier to give him a head's up about what was going on, and I guess it kind of freaked him out. Said he was afraid to go home, so he left work and just kept driving, ended up over here."

Much like the very first thing out of Seesel's mouth, Reed had no inclination to press him on what was just shared. Not the timing of it or who called who or even how Murphy knew where Seesel lived.

A bunch of questions that all paled compared to the fact that the young man had been found.

One less thing to worry about.

"We put in a call to Springfield PD earlier and asked them to put a car on the house," Reed said. "Have they shown up yet?"

"They have," Seesel said. "Right after Chance got here."

Why they hadn't called yet to inform Captain Grimes that Murphy was there, Reed couldn't be certain. An honest overlook or the young man hiding in the back bedroom or just the police not connecting the dots and figuring out it was information to be shared.

Options that were all equally likely, given what Reed saw out of them just a day earlier.

The only possibility that wasn't viable being that they had reached back to the captain and he hadn't let Reed know.

"Okay," Reed said. "One last thing. And don't you dare get pissy or heavy handed with me when I ask. Did you lean on Sheriff Alexander to make that little incident you told me about go away?"

Doing as instructed, Seesel replied, "No. The sheriff asked me if I knew anything about a cabin party, had heard any of my players talking about it at practice, and I told him no. Which was true.

"That's all there was, I swear."

The last time Reed spoke to Seesel, he got the impression the man was incapable of lying. Still in shock over what happened, he was reduced to his baser instincts, unable of being devious.

A sentiment Reed couldn't say remained, though still he had to believe what the man was saying.

Another unsuspecting victim, targeted through no – or at most, minimal – fault of his own.

"So that's what this is about?" Seesel asked. "Whatever happened that night?"

"It is," Reed replied. "Have Chance fill you in. In the meantime, neither one of you better so much as think about moving until you hear back from me."

Not waiting for Seesel to reply, Reed ended the call there. Swiping to clear the screen, he immediately dove right back into his recent log.

One of the last people he needed to speak to before moving, a moment later, Captain Grimes was on the line.

"You sitting at your desk?" Reed asked. An opening not meant to be nearly as pointed as with either of the prior conversations, this one simply for the sake of getting things moving.

A list of objectives both of them needed to act on immediately.

"What do you need?"

"We're sitting outside of Carly Mayes's apartment right now," Reed said. "I'll tell you the whole story at a later time, but suffice it to say, it is definitely the Hendricks clan, and they are definitely not done."

Going back through the list of things in his mind, he continued, "First thing, Chance Murphy is safe. He's with Matt Seesel in Springfield."

"He's-"

Grimes began to insert. A comment Reed cut off before it could become fully formed, having a good idea of what was about to be said.

Reiteration of the thought he'd had just moments before about how the news should have originated with Springfield PD, rather than Reed having to contact the people being protected himself.

"Yeah," Reed said, needing to push ahead so he and Billie could be on the move. Urgency that first began with the news about the youngest Hendricks sibling from Deke, climbing with each word shared by Mayes.

Anticipation that had made it difficult to sit still and work through the litany of phone calls, forcing himself to get all of the various pieces in motion before taking off.

"I guess he called Chance Murphy earlier to let him know to keep an eye out, kid freaked, turned his phone off and ran over there. Springfield PD is sitting outside as we speak."

In reply, Grimes gave the same throat click he always did. A signifier that he had heard and was jotting down notes accordingly.

That Reed could continue when ready.

"Like I said, we're outside of Mayes's apartment and just talked to Dean Morgan," Reed continued. "Both have police details sitting on them right now as well.

"I also spoke to Chief Duncan in New Albany, they found Joseph Hendricks's vehicle and cellphone and were able to harvest two numbers from it, but both have been disconnected. I told him about the other two siblings, and he agreed to pull back and keep watch, hope to nab them circling back.

"Between the victims already hit and Murphy, that leaves us with just the last two on the list of the seven deadly sins. Based on what Mayes just told me, it looks like the first of those is an Ava Kirkwood, at least that was her maiden name. Coshocton County Sheriff Broderick and his team are headed to check on her now."

"McMichaels and Jacobs are also on the road, moving that direction," Grimes inserted. A quick addition at mention of Coshocton, Reed having momentarily forgotten they had been sent to the Hendricks homestead to hunt for anything additional.

Anyone outside of the story Mayes shared who might also be a target, it now clear that their attribution of blame was not flawless.

Any information about where they might hide in the slim chance they went to ground after the arrest of their brother.

"Good," Reed said.

"You headed there next?" Grimes asked.

Barely was the question out before the screen of Reed's phone lit up. An incoming call from a number that wasn't saved, but instantly recognizable.

A sight that caused palpitations to rise through his chest, his heart rate ticking upward once more.

"Shit. Broderick is calling me now. That can't be good."

Chapter Seventy-Four

The Angel knew that this moment was coming. This exact instant when one of his siblings would begin to waffle and he would either have to go it alone or pick their asses up and drag them over the finish line.

Based on everything he'd seen the last six months – to say nothing of the previous twenty-eight years – he would have bet money that the one to lose their nerve would be The Tall Boy. A festering ball of emotion packaged in an oversized frame, the universe knowing before he was even born that he would be unable to defend himself and would need the additional size to insulate him from the world.

A veneer to keep others at bay, in whatever form that may take.

Six long months, The Angel had seen all the signs. Watched the way his brother stood in front of the spread in the basement, staring at each item as if he was committing it to memory, when in fact The Angel knew he was always searching for escape routes. Ways to get around what they had planned. Actions that would mitigate what they were about to do.

As if what they were receiving was anywhere near what they deserved.

Outside of the occasional barb to point out that none of this would even be necessary if The Tall Boy had done what he was supposed to while The Angel was away, The Angel had forced himself to keep his mouth shut. He'd absorbed all the questions his brother asked in silence. Pretended not to notice whenever The Tall Boy sought out the easiest assignments.

Things that were just as well, The Angel trusting himself far more to handle the difficult tasks than his sniveling brother.

All of that making the fact that it was sister, The Artist, who now seemed to be questioning things that much more unnerving.

His one real remaining ally in the world, suddenly having second thoughts.

"You ready?" The Angel asked.

Seated behind the steering wheel of her sedan, she stared at the single-story house down the street. A structure to match most of the others in the area, with white siding and a porch extended from the front, wooden columns holding it in place.

A place that was kept pristine during the summer months, but now that they were on the cusp between autumn and winter, was starting to look a bit shabby.

Misshapen leaves were heaped along the front of the porch, covering the junipers and lilies planted underneath. A trio of pumpkins had passed their expiration dates, their stems listing to the side.

Outdoor matters the owners had let fall by the wayside, their preferences resting indoors, as evidenced by the light spilling through the front windows and the smoke escaping the chimney, despite the late hour.

"Are we sure about this?" The Artist whispered.

Taking a moment to consciously swallow down the anger he was feeling, the angst he wanted to fling across the front seat, The Angel replied, "Nadine Hart has always been a night owl. You know that."

"Yeah, I know," she replied, "but that's not what I meant. Are we sure that our being here now, after-"

Again, the same feeling of repulsion rose within The Angel. Annoyance paired with the desire to swat her as he had their brother a couple nights before.

350

Or better yet, reach out and snatch the keys from the ignition, telling her to keep her ass there until he was done.

A damned tattoo gun couldn't be that hard to operate if she could do it.

"If not now, when?" The Angel said. Extending a hand, he waved it at the quiet block before them. A snapshot of the idyllic suburban crap they'd been staring at on television their whole lives, but never actually experienced. "There are no police parked outside. Nobody walking their dog or going for a run to see us.

"Hell, we're not going to get a better shot than this."

Pulling in a deep breath, The Artist followed the extension of his hand. Narrowing her gaze, she peered out ahead of them, checking the accuracy of his statement.

Facts there were no need for him to look up to confirm, his focus firmly on her.

"I just..." she muttered. "After what happened to our brother-"

"What happened to him, and mom, and our sister, is why we're here," The Angel said. A triple trump card that he had been careful not to play too early, knowing what the mention of their youngest sibling would do. "And if we don't finish this right now, you and I, then we wouldn't be doing right by any of them."

Chapter Seventy-Five

"We were too damned late. They got her," Sheriff Broderick managed to get out. A tone and delivery that were even more despondent than when he and Reed had stood on the front porch outside of Bertran Alexander's place earlier. "The sonsabitches got her."

Lifting his chin toward the roof of the sedan, Reed's eyes slid shut. His left hand tightened around the phone as his right curled upward, slipping along Billie's neck. Fingers furrowing through thick hair before pulling her inward, pressing the side of her skull against his.

Time and again, the first sentence Broderick had just said passed through his mind. A structure and sentiment that was largely correct, the man's only error in making it first-person plural.

They weren't the ones who were too late.

Reed was.

And now another young woman was permanently marred. Much like Carly Mayes, she was marked in a way that would leave scars both visible and internal, never to be scrubbed clean.

A violation of the highest form, seen each time they looked in the mirror. Felt every time they touched their forehead.

Noticed by every stranger they passed on the street.

"Shit," Reed muttered. Dropping the phone into his lap, he used the same hand to lash out at the steering wheel before him, mashing his palm into it in time with the same word coming out over and over. "Shit, shit, shit."

Peeling his eyes open, Reed again stared out at the street around him. A neighborhood that had all the signs of being peaceful and idyllic, seemingly unaware of the horror that had taken place earlier.

Was continuing to play out in places like it all over the region, always a step or two ahead of Reed and his partner.

"Is she...?" Reed asked, leaving the ending purposefully vague, allowing the sheriff to fill it as he saw fit.

An opening that led to the man jumping right to the most extreme, to be expected after what they encountered earlier. "She's alive, but it didn't look like it when we first got here. Found her lying motionless in the middle of the floor, had to call an ambulance and have them give her something to wake her up."

Exhaling slowly, Reed replied, "Damn it. We were close, just not..."

"Yep," Broderick whispered in return.

The sole reply of any kind for the better part of a minute as Reed tried to imagine another young woman marked somewhere. A fifth victim from the story Mayes shared just a short time earlier.

Another of the seven deadly sins, which one was now branded across her forehead far from mattering.

"You want to know the worst part?" Broderick eventually asked.

A question that made Reed cringe to even consider, letting a few more seconds pass before asking, "What's that?"

"The poor girl is seven months pregnant," Broderick answered. "Her husband took on a second job working nights over at the mill until the baby was born."

With just two short sentences, Reed understood the despondence in the sheriff's voice. Sorrow Reed couldn't help but feel, adding a growing stomach to the mental image he had just a moment before. An attack on essentially two people, threatening both the young woman and the child she carried inside.

Viciousness that was bad enough, made worse for Broderick by the fact that it was a second personal associate hit in as many days.

His predecessor, followed by a friend.

"Please tell me that part at least saved her from a beating," Reed whispered.

A sparing from even the lightened physical abuse received by Mayes, by virtue of her being pregnant, or on a tight timeframe, or whatever other reason.

Anything to let her at least sidestep that much.

"I don't know," Broderick admitted, a tinge of guilt adding to the sorrow. "I didn't think to lift her shirt and check if they wrote anything, either."

Not that it much mattered, a bit of magic marker nothing compared to the drugs in her system and the disfigurement lining her brow.

"Sheriff," Reed muttered, his left hand still clenched up tight. "Are you familiar with the Hendricks family? A mother Sarah who died six months ago. Daughter Mary, twin boys Joseph and James. Late twenties-early thirties."

"Know of them," Broderick said. "Always heard they were a little off, but having never interacted with them, didn't know if it was legit or your typical small-town gossip.

"Why? Are they next?"

"No, they're the ones doing it," Reed replied. "Every last word you've heard is legit."

There was no deciphering whatever Broderick said in reply. A mumbled string of cursing and threats and ideas that came out as little more than gibberish.

Mutterings Reed listened to for but a few seconds, ending things by saying, "A team of officers that I work with at the BCI are headed to the Hendricks farmhouse now. You and your team are more than welcome to meet them there."

Chapter Seventy-Six

Ava Kirkwood was ENVY. A piece of information Reed hadn't asked for but Sheriff Broderick offered anyway, handing it off as the last thing said before ending the call.

A closing before he and his young deputies took off, intent on making their way to the Hendricks homestead in time to meet Officers McMichaels and Jacobs.

A location that Reed was fully confident the arriving force could handle, no matter what they might find. A good chunk of the local sheriff's department seething with anger over repeated attacks to their own, coupled with the two men who had helped Reed bring in Joseph Hendricks earlier.

A combination of motivations that would be more than sufficient, especially considering Reed didn't really expect anybody to be there.

The time between attacks was already accelerating, sure to go even faster now that their brother had been brought into custody. One last desperate push to bring things to an end, wanting to close it out tonight before disappearing forever.

An option Reed was fairly certain they wouldn't reach for just yet, every indicator thus far being that they were going to see this through.

A message they were intent had to be fully shared, their own safety be damned.

Reaching to his lap, Reed took up the small spiral-bound notebook. Flipping back to the same page he'd been staring at for days now, he added one more name to the list.

Ava Kirkwood. ENVY.

Five of seven completed, leaving just two remaining.

"LUST and WRATH," Reed said, the sound of his voice bringing Billie a little closer. Lifting both feet onto the middle console between the front seats, she brought her muzzle well past Reed, her warm breath fogging the windshield in front of them.

Presence that Reed leaned into, tilting his head and shoulder against her, his focus still fixed on the list in hand.

"Chance Murphy has to be LUST," Reed muttered aloud. "Has to be. Which would make Nadine Hart WRATH."

Pulling his foot back inside the car, he slammed the door shut. A sudden loss of cool air and ambient noise, placing him and Billie inside a sealed environment.

Total quiet, allowing him to play back the story Carly Mayes shared one last time, recalling every detail mentioned about the girl. How she and Murphy had dated up until the start of the year. The way she didn't accept his stated reason, believing Anna was the real cause. Her joining forces with Kirkwood, inviting Anna and Mayes out to the party for the first time ever.

The facts that Mayes still couldn't remember a thing that happened, and a couple days later, a tape of Anna started making the rounds.

The very definition of wrath if Reed had ever heard it.

Flipping the notebook into the passenger seat, having stared at the damn thing for the last time, he reached out and turned on the ignition. Grabbing up his phone, he went again to the call log. Another in what felt an unending list that was nothing short of torturous as he sat behind the wheel, aching to be moving again.

A problem this particular contact was uniquely positioned to solve.

"Hit me," Deke answered.

"Can you get me an address for a girl named Nadine Hart?"

Chapter Seventy-Seven

Why The Angel felt the need to tie the man up, The Artist had not a clue, beyond maybe it just being something for him to do. A way to keep busy in the aftermath of the tussle that had taken place as they burst through the backdoor into the house, finding the man and their target not asleep, as most normal people should be at such an hour, but both sitting at the kitchen table.

Each wearing flannel pajama pants and baggy sweatshirts, they'd been seated with mugs of hot cocoa in front of them, a shared plate of cookies filling the gap in between.

A scene that The Artist would have found almost endearing in a different time and place. A young couple stealing away a few minutes together, ignoring the clock or whatever they might have to do the next day.

The kind of stuff The Artist had sure as hell never experienced in her life. If she hadn't walked in to witness it for herself, wouldn't have believed even existed.

A snapshot of a happy couple on their way to marriage, shattered by the unexpected intrusion.

Peeking through the back windows as they made their way around the house, The Artist's first inclination was to simply turn and walk

359

away. A final sign from the powers that be that they weren't meant to finish what they set out to do.

A message that should have already been made obvious by their brother being arrested – or worse – driven home one last time.

Turn around. Walk right back down the driveway.

Get in the car and drive away, never to return.

A course of action The Artist never got the chance to voice, beat to it by her brother beside her interpreting things in a very different way. His own particular lens, magnified by a factor of one hundred by recent events.

Anger and spite and whatever streak of evil that lived inside of him, all bubbling to the surface, telling him that what they were seeing wasn't wishing them to leave be, but to go faster. An extra victim to be added to the list, making the punishment they were there to mete out that much more severe.

An impending possibility that made him abandon all reason or self-preservation, bypassing the previous approach of knocking and drawing their targets out in favor of kicking in the damn door.

Desire and anticipation that had been threatening to consume him for months, finally overtaking him. The need to keep getting bigger chunks of the violence he'd long craved.

The visible shift in mindset after the arrest of their brother.

Bursting through the back door in a spray of sawdust and wood chips, the sudden entry had had the intended effect. Like prey spotlighted by a poacher, the couple had both sat frozen at the table, each with cookies in hand, their mouths and eyes wide.

Momentary paralysis that allowed The Angel to get across the linoleum floor, making it almost to the table before the man so much as moved. A head start that let The Angel land a couple of blows, already tilting things in his favor before his opponent was even able to bring his fists up before him.

The beginning of a fight that lasted longer than The Artist would have anticipated, spilling out from the kitchen and into the living room.

An optimal distraction to let her slip in a few moments later. An unknown and unexpected accomplice able to move on their real target while the woman stood framed in the doorway to the kitchen, both hands raised to cover her mouth, watching The Angel pummel her fiancé.

A frightened onlooker without the wherewithal to scream out or pick up her phone for help.

Even less, the awareness to avoid the syringe loaded with ketamine that The Artist jammed into her neck. One last target on a list going back years.

A final act before the two of them – and hopefully their brother – could disappear, leaving this entire disaster and everything that came before behind for good.

"Is that really necessary?" The Artist asked. Braced on both knees in the kitchen, her head was turned to peer back through the same open doorway that their target had stood in just a short time earlier.

Under her, there was no use bothering with the drop cloth. By her side, no rags or alcohol wipes.

The time for preventative measures was behind them. If The Tall Boy hadn't already fingered them, it was only a matter of time before the authorities pieced things together.

Pulling the knot on the confiscated extension cord he was using as a binder tight, his teeth coming together as a small grunt slid through, The Angel turned and glared at her. Fixing it in place, he rose to his feet and walked back her direction, each step sounding out as he stomped back toward her.

A stare he maintained until making it all the way into the kitchen, only then sliding it to the woman by their side.

"She's out. Let's get started."

Chapter Seventy-Eight

For quite possibly the first time since Reed and Billie left the bar after training a couple of days earlier, something went their way. A small break in the form of the address Deke provided for Nadine Hart being located in Powell, a suburb on the north side of Columbus.

Another of those to have graduated from Coshocton High and moved over to the greater Columbus area, no doubt in search of more opportunity or more people or, just, *more*.

Reasoning that Reed didn't bother trying to decipher, thankful only for the jump that it gave him and Billie. A location that was just shy of ten miles from Carly Mayes's apartment, considerably closer than trying to push all the way back east or even hit one of the many small bergs in between.

An impending site that had his pulse thrumming as he alternated glances between the road and his phone, jumping past Deke and Sheriff Broderick in the recent call log to the man he last spoke to just minutes before.

The same one who answered mid-ring with his standard, "Grimes."

"One last thing," Reed said.

Where he was on the list of items Reed had requested shortly prior, there was no way to be certain.

Tasks Reed trusted his captain would get to, neither one mentioning them as Grimes replied, "Ready."

"Deke is about to send you an address for Nadine Hart, who I believe is the seventh and final sin on the list. We're on our way now, but can you have Powell PD send over a cruiser to help us sit on the place? Or even better, get her the hell out of there?"

"Done," Grimes replied, pausing as if about to hang up before asking, "If she is seven, I take it..."

"Ava Kirkwood," Reed replied. "ENVY. Sheriff Broderick found her just a few minutes ago."

"Christ."

Bobbing his chin slightly in agreement, Reed glanced to the rearview mirror. A force of habit while changing lanes, the scant few cars that were on the road pushed aside by his lights.

"Yeah."

"Calling PPD now."

"Thanks," Reed muttered, ending the call there.

A way to clear the screen, bringing the GPS map back up before him. An overhead schematic that was much tighter than many he'd been staring at throughout the course of the investigation, this one conveying just a couple of miles.

A stretch that was mostly covered by the same highway they were on, pushing due north away from the outer belt before making a handful of turns into residential streets.

A gap he handled exactly as he had the trip to Carly Mayes' apartment, using the lights to push aside any vehicles, the time of night and thin crowd precluding the need for sirens. Warning chimes that could be heard from distance, Reed not wanting to give the remaining Hendricks family members the benefit of an alert.

The start of another chase like with their brother earlier.

If they were already there, he wanted to catch them before they had a chance to get away.

And if not, there was no point in announcing their presence to the entire neighborhood, spoiling the scene in case the Hendricks had intentions of showing up later.

Flicking his gaze from the screen to the road ahead, Reed wound his way through a series of successively smaller streets. Roads that went from the multi-lane freeway to a four-lane highway to a major thoroughfare going in both directions, separated by a turn lane in the middle.

A steady winnowing down that went to a standard two-way residential street before ultimately settling into a street much like the one in Westerville. Pavement just wide enough for a lone vehicle to pass through, winding between cars lining the curb on either side.

Vehicles that were firmly in the middle of the automobile spectrum, mostly consisting of sedans and mid-sized SUVs.

Means of transportation matching the homes sitting behind them, many with piles of leaves sitting by the curb or remainder pumpkins still resting on porches and stoops.

Details that Reed just barely took in, his repeated sideways glances more to check house numbers than to ascertain anything about the place he now found himself. A constant back-and-forth, matching their position on the screen to the world outside.

A gap they managed to steadily whittle down, pulling to a complete stop just two doors shy of their destination.

A spot close enough to get to within seconds, but far enough away not to be seen or heard approaching from right outside.

"Alright, girl," Reed muttered, the strained sound of his voice pulling out a single sound in reply from his partner.

A lone noise to let him know she was ready, the concentrated anticipation inside the vehicle leaving her aching for movement as well.

Sliding the sedan up nose-to-nose with a pickup truck parked inches from the curb, Reed reached out and twisted off the ignition. Not bothering to even pull the keys, he went straight for the glove box, drawing his weapon out.

Leaving the front cover on it sagging open, he pulled the gun over and did one quick check to make sure the magazine was full and the chamber loaded before pushing open the driver's door and stepping out onto the sidewalk

An exit matched by his partner behind him, spilling through the front seat and out onto the concrete.

Coiled energy wrapped in black fur that fell in alongside Reed, the two of them taking off together at a jog for the address Deke had given them. A one-story Craftsman-style house with wide columns holding up a front porch and a pitched roof rising above.

One of the few on the block with any inside lights still visible, every window along the front porch lit up from within.

Illumination dimmed by blinds drawn down, leaving only bright lines around the outside. Vertical rectangles that Reed put his focus on, staying the course until reaching the front corner of the lawn and then taking off at a diagonal across the grass.

Soft padding that absorbed any sound of their approach as they went straight for the closest edge of the wooden steps leading up onto the porch.

His strides already elongated by the pace of their jog, Reed leapt straight to the top step. One last foothold before reaching the floor of the porch, Billie still just a few inches from his side.

Drawing to a stop, Reed flexed his knees. A lowered stature while ignoring the tightness in his calf, his gun extended before him, the barrel aimed at the planks of the porch. Cocking his head to the side, he stood and listened, hoping for any sound of activity from within.

Voices or movement to match the lights burning bright.

Anything to indicate that the glow shining through the windows was due to Hart and whoever she lived with being night owls, and not the Hendricks clan hard at work inside.

Hearing absolutely nothing, Reed crossed one foot over the other. A slow creep sideways, pausing just long enough to check for any cracks around the edges of the first blind. Small slivers that might give him an indication of what was on the other side.

Some sign as to whether he should knock on the door and explain to Hart what was going on, or if he and Billie should burst through and save her from becoming the sixth victim.

Seeing nothing, Reed took two more steps to the side. A few more feet, bringing him to the outermost window of the home. The one that whoever pulled the blinds shut hadn't been as concerned about, stopping it just a couple inches shy of the sill.

A crack more than sufficient to let Reed peek inside at the bloodied man sprawled out on the floor, his hands tied to the sofa above his head.

Chapter Seventy-Nine

The Angel's knuckles stung from the repeated shots it had taken to put down the fiancé of their final target. The one who was inarguably the most important, not about to be let off the hook for her role in what happened.

The mastermind behind it all, letting a little high school angst ruin their sister's life.

And their mother's after that.

And now all of theirs, the price she was about to pay but a small fraction of the debt she owed them.

Flexing his fingers, he couldn't help but be reminded of his sister making the same gesture earlier in the day. A way of working out the soreness, no matter how vastly different their respective causes.

The Artist from squeezing her fingers together for hours on end, applying the markings that would finally pay retribution to those who did even worse to their beloved kid sister long ago.

The Angel, from having to go toe-to-toe with their target's significant other. A young man who clearly spent some time in a training facility, probably fashioning himself some sort of MMA aspirant.

A guy who had played some ball in high school or college and still saw the inflated twenty-year-old version of himself each time he looked in the mirror.

Thought he was tough enough to mix it up a little bit, making no effort to grab a weapon or to call the police, instead raising his hands before him. A sight that had nearly made The Angel laugh, a gym rat in a pair of pajama bottoms no match for someone who had been through what he had.

No matter how great the disparity in their respective sizes.

Fight training that far surpassed anything found in a strip mall, imparting above all else that there was no such thing as a fair fight. A maxim the guy now knew intimately as he lay sprawled in the corner of the room, a gash above his left temple sending a stripe of dark blood into his hairline, his hands extended overhead and tied to the base of the sofa with an electrical cord.

The results of a wicked series of shots to his ribcage to get him doubled over at the waist before The Angel grabbed him by the nape of the neck, driving his head into the coffee table. Hard contact that turned the man's legs to Jell-o beneath him, his knees buckling as he began to crumple.

A descent to the floor The Angel helped along, using the free fall to pound him into the table a second time. Momentum and gravity and The Angel's own angst that combined to split the soft skin along his brow, opening a gash more than an inch wide.

A crevasse from which bright red blood bubbled up, striping the side of his face and dripping to the floor below. A font that contributed to a spot on the hardwood that was nearly the size of a softball before The Angel eventually got him flipped over and dragged him a few feet to the side.

Better positioning to allow him to tie the man's ass up, ensuring that his slumber lasted just as long as the chemically induced sleep his fiancé was now enjoying.

A pair of soon-to-be-wedded assholes, both to eventually wake up with new scars.

More things they could share, like the cocoa and cookies they were enjoying when The Angel and his sister first arrived.

"Hey!" The Artist said, her body going rigid as she kneeled over their target on the kitchen floor. A word laden with urgency, despite the lowered tone employed.

A single syllable, hinting that it wasn't the first time she'd said it. Repeated tries to get The Angel's attention while he was lost in revelry, leaning against the kitchen counter and replaying the previous battle.

A blow by blow of what took place, replete with imagining how much more damage he could inflict if given the chance.

Feeling the slightest hint of palpitations rise through his chest, The Angel jerked himself out of his trance. His body tensed as he unfolded his arms, swinging them down to brace either palm against the counter behind him.

A starting block for him to push away from, ready to move.

"What?"

"I heard something," she replied, her voice still lowered. "I think someone's here."

Chapter Eighty

Reed never expected the front door to be unlocked. A rare oversight by the Hendricks siblings, not originally planning to go after Nadine Hart in her own home or feeling the pressures of a truncated timeframe in the wake of their brother getting caught.

An error that meant when Reed snapped his leg out and drove his heel through the wood separating the handle from the jamb on the front door, there wasn't nearly the resistance he was anticipating. A lack of a deadbolt that allowed the lone catch to give in easily, flinging the door inward and propelling him forward.

An excess of momentum that a couple of months before – or a couple of months in the future – would have been no problem. Moments when his left leg was fully healed and its strength back up to one hundred percent.

Times that were decidedly not in that instant, the combination of being off balance and his own momentum sending him toppling to the floor. An unceremonious crash onto the hardwood, spilling him across the walkway extended from the doorway through the center of the living room.

A makeshift partition, with the windows and television he'd just peeked through on one side, the sofa and the incapacitated victim on the other, the man's feet just inches from Reed's shoulder.

Surroundings Reed took in and filed away in an instant, his focus jerked away by the guttural roar reverberating from the backend of the home. A sound that preceded its source by only a moment, pouring through the open doorway into what Reed guessed was the kitchen beyond.

The place where two ladies were both on the floor, one splayed flat on her back, the other on her knees beside her, a tattoo gun clutched in hand.

A scene Reed caught only a sideways glimpse of as he rested on his hip before it was erased from view, blotted by a man with rosy cheeks and curly hair barreling toward him. Swinging into focus, he ran at a full sprint, arms both pumping.

Mouth open wide, he continued with the ongoing wail, letting the sound roll from him like a siren.

A man Reed recognized on sight, his features a bit more disheveled in person, but no doubt matching the cherubic form and shortened stature of the booking sheet Reed had seen earlier.

James Hendricks.

A person whose very name filled Reed with loathing, nearly causing him to raise the weapon gripped tight in his hand and begin unloading. One trigger pull after another, fully imparting the animosity he had for the man and the entire operation he was a part of.

An option that wasn't one for a variety of reasons, leading him to the next best thing.

"*Attack!*"

The reverberation of the door smashing into the wall and the man's carnal roar both still hung in the air as Reed unleashed the command. The same word he said to his partner on the training ground on Sunday, enhanced by adrenaline and the accumulated vitriol of every moment since.

Conglomerated emotion that caused it to roll from deep in his diaphragm, reverberating through the cavernous interior of the house, easily surpassing either of the existing sounds while adding a fourth to the mix.

The deep braying of Billie as she shot across the threshold dividing the porch from the living room. A rocket start to match what Reed had witnessed days before, sending her hurtling past him.

A blur of black fur and coiled energy, needing only a couple of strides to reach full speed before leaping.

Kinetic power that slammed into James, hitting him much harder than anything Kona had administered to Reed. A massive collision of man and animal, the slap of the two sides coming together echoing out, replacing the barking of Billie and the yell of James as they both careened sideways, writhing in air as they toppled into an end table.

An article of furniture that stood no chance against their combined weights, reduced to splinters as they crashed to the ground, their force sending reverberations through the floor.

Absorbed impact that spurred Reed back to moving, his pulse thundering as he pulled his elbows and knees both toward his core, raising up onto a base. All fours, enabling him to bring his feet up under him.

A frantic scurry to get up and get to his partner.

Make sure she was safe.

Put down James before he could harm anybody else.

Three feet away, the man he'd been chasing for days was fighting to do the same. A struggle to find balance while trying to free himself from Billie clamped onto his arm, her teeth buried into cloth and flesh.

Spastic movements that did more harm than good, both materials ripping with each jerk of his arm. Shredded cloth and skin that dappled the floor with blood beneath him as he reached for a chunk of the end table on the floor at his side.

A makeshift club that made it no higher than an inch from the floor before Reed was on him, lashing out with his right foot a second time in as many minutes. Another hard strike with no regard for his leg or his balance or anything else.

Scything his foot forward, Reed drove the toe of his shoe into James's cheek, splitting the skin and sending more blood and spittle against the wall as his head snapped the opposite direction.

Absorbed energy that made his opposite cheek slap against the floor before rotating back toward Reed, eyelids fluttering.

The beginning of unconsciousness that Reed saw the rest of the way through by raising the gun in his hand and driving the butt of it into the top of James's skull.

A knockout blow that caused the man's entire body to go limp, everything motionless save the arm still locked in Billie's grasp.

A chew toy Reed relieved her of, ordering her to release as he extended the gun before him with both hands and took two steps to the side. A quick movement returning him to the same sight he was looking at just moments before, neither lady in the kitchen having moved an inch.

"Mary Hendricks, put down that damn tattoo gun and step away from her with your hands up."

Chapter Eighty-One

"Worst part about it was, I really did like the girl," Chance Murphy said.

Of everything Reed had seen and heard over the last eight hours – or even the forty-eight before that – for some reason that one line stuck with him the most. A single sentence that was uttered as the young man sat across from him in the interrogation room on the third floor of the 8th Precinct, delivered there by escort of the Springfield Police Department.

One of many acts of cleanup that were performed in the wake of Reed and Billie apprehending the two remaining Hendricks siblings. Tasks that were split among a handful of different departments across the state, everybody working to process and clean away the mess that was made by the trio hellbent on revenge.

Sloppy, erratic vigilantism, a fair chunk of which wasn't aimed in the right place.

That part, Reed suspected, being why Murphy's comment stayed with him. Another on the tally such as his grandfather, Dean Morgan, and his coach, Matt Seesel, and even his old classmate, Carly Mayes, who had done nothing wrong.

They just bore the misfortune of being ancillary to an event that had been taken to extreme proportions by the Hendricks siblings, any need for factual accuracy be damned.

Now more than seven hours after loading Mary and James Hendricks into the rear of the Powell PD cruisers, and watching as the local paramedics treated Nadine Hart and her fiancé and transported them to the hospital for further care, Reed found himself back in the same exact chair where he had that conversation with Murphy. One last discussion to hopefully glean out a final lingering detail or two before heading downstairs to sit with Captain Grimes and Chief Brandt.

The final summation where they would snip away any remaining loose ends and compare notes on all that had transpired. A meeting to make sure everyone had the full and accurate tale before even thinking of approaching the governor's office.

No matter how many damned times the man called and asked for an update.

A number that Reed got the impression was well into double digits, based on the chief's demeanor and the few side comments she'd let slip before she and Grimes stepped into the observation room behind him.

An audience to his talk with Joseph Hendricks before he was moved to a more permanent location where he would await the start of his legal process in a few days.

While an infinite amount had transpired in the short time since the two were seated a few feet apart, Hendricks looked exactly as Reed remembered him. His exaggerated length balanced precariously on a seat much too small for him, he stared directly at the table between them.

Gaze fixed, his eyes were glazed, it almost indecipherable as to whether he was even fully cognizant of where he was or what was going on.

"Mary and James are both in custody," Reed opened. A return to the only topic that managed to evoke a response the last time they spoke, and as good a place as any to jump in.

A starting point that this time didn't have nearly the same effect, Hendricks's features remaining placid.

As Reed had come to expect they might.

"We apprehended them inside Nadine Hart's living room," Reed said. "WRATH, I presume?"

Again, he paused, waiting for any sort of response, before adding, "I mean, I'm only guessing, seeing as how we stopped them before they were able to finish. Same for Chance Murphy.

"The two most important people involved with what happened to Anna both got away, free and clear."

This time, there was the same flicker Reed noticed earlier. Movement behind the eyes that was unmistakable, Reed's previous thinking it was attributed to Mary and James when he referred to his siblings done in error.

A false assumption made on incomplete information, only in the time since realizing it was the thought of Anna that had penetrated Hendricks's veneer.

"At least, I'm guessing you all thought they were the most important, based on the faulty story you put together and splashed clear across your basement," Reed said.

Unlacing his hands atop the table, Reed dropped his left hand to his side. Fingers splayed wide, he ran it the length of Billie's back, feeling the underlying ridges of muscle and the occasional knob of vertebrae along her spine.

Slow and even strokes that she had long since stopped reacting to, accepting it as reassurance that their job was finished.

She had done well, entitled to any rest she could now siphon off for herself.

"The basic narrative is pretty straight forward," Reed said. "Your sister was the target of a couple of jealous high school girls. She was pretty and friendly and drew the attention of the wrong boy, so some popular girls who wanted said boy played a trick on her that went way too far.

"They drugged her and staged some lewd acts and released a video that humiliated Anna and made her leave school. It launched a brief investigation, caused your mother to do what any concerned parent would do, and ended all contact Anna had with the outside world until years later when she moved across the country to go to college.

"This all happened almost seven years ago to this day. An anniversary that you and your siblings planned everything around to give it a little extra emphasis. More than two years after she took her own life, and even six months after the passing of your mother and what must have been the explicit instructions to make everyone involved with what happened that night pay.

"Your brother had been out on parole for a while by then. You left your job coaching, your sister left her job as a high school art teacher in Indiana, and the three of you decided to unleash hell."

Aware of how fast he was going, the amount of information being pushed across the table, he paused.

Not to elicit a response from Hendricks, but to make sure he didn't miss what came next. The part that left Reed with a sour taste, sure to stay with him long after the case was fully wrapped and the Hendricks clan sent to various prisons for the foreseeable future.

"We might as well start with what you got right," Reed said. Holding the index, middle, and ring fingers of his right hand up before him in a pitchfork formation, he continued, "Three. Out of seven potential targets, you got three of them right."

Lowering his hand back to the table, he added, "Less than half. All that time spent surveilling and planning, and you guys scored less than fifty percent on the part that actually mattered."

An infinite amount more, Reed wanted to add. Extra comments about how people were now permanently marred both physically and psychologically. How lives were ruined over the faulty assumptions and gullibility of the Hendricks.

How their need to send a message with the seven deadly sins had them believing rumors and grasping at whispers that weren't true.

A host of things he had to consciously push aside, knowing that if he started to unload, there would be no stopping it. A deluge that would end with him on his feet, palms planted into the tabletop as he berated the man opposite him.

"And even that is being generous," Reed said. "We know Ava

Kirkwood and Nadine Hart were both interested in the boy who liked Anna, but we don't know how much of an active role they took in creating or posting the tape. If anything that transpired was their intention, or the actions of someone else who got overzealous.

"Same as we don't know if Sheriff Alexander really just brushed things under the rug, or if there wasn't the evidence to support digging further into things. If he talked to all parties and nobody came forward or they did what kids often do and simply lied to him.

"A whole bunch of questions that I'm guessing the answers to would make your batting average even lower, but we don't need to get into right now," Reed continued. "What we can talk about are the ones we know about for certain. Dean Morgan, the grandfather who thought he was giving his grandson some money for a deposit on college tuition.

"Matt Seesel, the high school coach who answered honestly when he told the sheriff he didn't know anything about a party at a cabin.

"Carly Mayes, who wasn't just some *drunk bitch*, as you guys ascribed her, but someone who was given the same drug as your sister to sideline her."

With every statement that poured forth from Reed, the fingers on his left hand began to move quicker. Speed to match the growing angst inside of him. Frustration at a handful of different things that had been growing for days, overriding the sheer exhaustion of having been awake over twenty-four hours and counting.

"Even Chance Murphy," Reed said, "who legitimately was interested in your sister, and much like Carly Mayes, didn't remember a damned thing about that night until he saw himself in the same video and had no idea his mother had asked for money from his grandfather, much less what it was used for."

Once more, the urge to keep going spiked in Reed. Desires to share more of what Murphy had sat in that very chair and explained to him. More ways that the Hendricks clan had messed up.

Threats of how easy the prosecution was going to be of three people all apprehended in the homes of an intended victim.

Thoughts that Reed let pass, there no need to rehash every single detail uncovered from the last three days. Minutiae there would be plenty of time for later, his only real intention in bringing Hendricks in being to lay the entire story out.

Give him the chance to push back on any discrepancies.

Make sure he was aware of the massive blunders that had been committed in recent days.

Falling silent, Reed sat and stared at the young man across from him for two full minutes. One hundred and twenty seconds that Reed counted off one at a time in his mind, waiting for Hendricks to verbalize a response.

Even for him to flick his focus upward, meeting Reed's gaze.

A narrow opportunity for him to react in any way that he let slip by, remaining fixed in position as Reed patted Billie on the back and pushed away from the table. Leaving his chair where it was, he turned for the door, making it as far as his hand reaching for the knob, before finally Hendricks spoke.

His first words since sometime before bolting out of Murphy's house, his voice thick with going unused for the last ten hours.

"Do you know why she killed herself?" he asked, the unexpected question sending pinpricks through Reed's core. Sensation he allowed to pass while keeping his back to Hendricks.

"Somebody in Boise found the video," Hendricks said. "It had been uploaded to one of those internet sites years before, and somehow someone at Boise State found it and thought it would be funny to circulate it."

Hearing the strain in the man's voice, the conviction with every syllable that was uttered, Reed rotated in place, turning to regard him square.

"It wasn't," he continued, red tendrils beginning to stripe the sclera of his eyes as he turned to match Reed's stare. "Five years and two thousand miles removed, that damned thing was still following her around. Just like she knew it always would.

"And she couldn't do it anymore."

Blinking away the film of moisture that lined his eyes, he added, "If you know who my mom was, have seen the things we've been tattooing on people, you know how important religion was to her. She believed in forgiveness. She was willing to overlook what happened before.

"But once they took Anna away from us, there was no forgiving that. Not ever."

Epilogue

"What the girl said was right," Deke opened. "There wasn't a lot on the video, but there was enough."

Stated without lead-in of any kind, Reed still knew exactly what his friend was referring to. A final piece that he had asked Deke to look into an hour earlier after speaking with Joseph Hendricks and hearing what had happened to cause his sister to take her own life.

An allusion to the video that Carly Mayes had told him about, that serving as the impetus for everything that happened to Anna Hendricks, and by extension all that had taken place in the time since.

A hunt that Reed had asked him to perform so they could see how widespread it was and if Bertran Alexander should have done more originally. A search he expected to take the better part of the day or longer, instead requiring barely more than an hour.

The unanimous decision between Reed, Chief Brandt, and Captain Grimes after finishing in the interrogation room earlier was that his conversation with Hendricks was sufficient to serve as a debrief for the time being. Completely laying out the narrative and more or less vetted by an active participant, they agreed that they had enough to present to the governor for the time being.

The first of what would likely be many conversations, the

remainder to take place after all involved had been able to get some rest and put a bit of distance behind them, allowing the assorted emotions attached to the case to settle.

Animosity over what happened to Anna Hendricks, and how her family had later responded to it. Guilt that so many innocent people had been branded before the culprits could be found.

Lingering frustration about how the case was brought to them in the first place.

Matters that they had all touched on briefly before parting just as the morning shift was starting to show at the station. New arrivals such as Officers Derek Greene and Julie Madsen, who had both waved to Reed and Billie in passing, but had the good sense to leave it at that, sensing the miasma of emotions enveloping them.

Palpable frustration cloaked in exhaustion, the combination serving as a silent excuse for them to slip away without any kind of extended interaction. A graceful exit with the intention of going home and falling into bed, the short time since split almost equally into thirds.

The first chunk was spent making the drive from the 8th Precinct back to the farmhouse, moving against the flow of morning traffic allowing them to go much faster than their counterparts heading into the city. Commuters stuck waiting at traffic lights or enmeshed in long queues, many slurping on coffee or staring ahead vacantly, looking as if they would rather be anywhere else in the world.

From there, Reed and Billie had both gone straight to the shower for the second part of the hour. A direct route through the house to begin the long process of washing the events of the last couple of days away, both literally and figuratively.

Dirt and sweat and even James Hendricks's blood that snaked through the six feet standing in the porcelain white tub, swirling around the drain before eventually disappearing. Residue that was much easier to scrub away than what Reed trusted would linger much longer.

Those same feelings of guilt and frustration, superimposed with what he witnessed from each of the many victims. People who would start by trying to wash away what was written across their torsos before moving on to try and do the same with the dark letters etched into their brows.

A process that they would take to their graves, the mere thought of it causing Reed's own skin to tingle. Sensation that he attacked with a washcloth and soap, standing under the hottest water he could tolerate and vigorously working at his own flesh until it was bright pink.

Efforts that might have been sufficient to strip away any accumulated grime, but still left him feeling unclean in a way he could only hope would pass with time.

Stepping out and toweling off, the remaining bit of the hour was allotted to sustenance for himself and his partner. An early breakfast or a very, very late dinner, depending on how one wanted to look at it.

Food that they both attacked, each devouring it in hulking bites. A meal that was just barely finished when Reed's phone had first sprung to life, Deke's name displayed across the screen.

One of just a very few people who always had direct access, Reed accepting it while letting Billie out through the backdoor.

"What her brother said was also correct," Deke continued. "Someone had put it up on a website for sharing homemade stuff around that time. Not one of the biggies, but the views it got was still more than enough."

The phone held out before him, Reed exhaled slowly through his nose as he stepped over the threshold and onto the deck behind his home. Cold floorboards that he could feel through the soles of his feet as he crossed to the rear edge, his gaze fixed on his partner working her way across the grass.

One last trip to relieve herself before they could both descend into the slumber they so desperately needed.

Sleep that Reed wasn't sure he would be able to find, his hope that the sheer fatigue gripping him would be enough to pull him under. A means to overpower the assorted thoughts swirling through his mind, this latest bit of data just one more chunk to be considered.

"Any way of knowing who posted it?" Reed asked.

"Yes and no," Deke replied. "I can see who the account belonged to, but it isn't active anymore, doesn't look like it has been in over a year.

"We can definitely drill down further, but my guess is it won't amount to much."

Again, Reed exhaled slowly, his mind trying to piece together how to best approach the matter. A topic that was probably best left for the legal system to decide, his own understanding of such things hazy at best.

New laws about public shaming and online sharing, to say nothing of the jurisdictional nightmare that would likely be attached to such a thing. Items he would push aside until sitting down for those future debriefs with Brandt and Grimes, nothing more to be done this morning.

All three Hendricks siblings were in custody.

The people responsible for the case first presented to him and Billie were behind bars, any further threat stopped for the time being.

A win, if such a thing could even be counted from all that had taken place.

"Also," Deke said, "I went ahead and pulled it down. Scrubbed it from a couple of other places as well.

"There's still a digital footprint for now in case we need it, but nothing is active anymore. Once this is all over, we'll wipe it out for good."

His brows rising in surprise, before Reed could relay as much, his attention was drawn down to the screen of his phone shifting before him. A flash of bright white before moving to black.

A visual that was followed in order by an audible click over the line, letting him know that he had another incoming call.

"I hope that's alright," Deke added.

"Absolutely," Reed replied, pulling his focus from the name stretched across the screen of his phone and putting it back on the conversation at hand. "I just didn't know you could do that."

Chuckling softly, Deke replied, "Someday, I'll have to give you a lesson on everything I can do, my friend."

A bit of mirth that Reed matched, allowing himself to smile for what felt like the first time in days. "I'd like that."

"For sure," Deke said. "Until then, I'll let you get that, and be sure to give my best to Miss Serena."

"I will," Reed said. An immediate response, followed by his smile fading just slightly. "Wait, did you-"

"Ha!" Deke replied. "Naw, that didn't take any computer wizardry, just a little common sense. Talk to you later."

"Talk soon," Reed replied. "Thanks again."

Ending the call there, Reed flipped over to the incoming line. A quick transition that was marked by the sound of the road in the background, hinting that Serena was already in the car and on her way to work.

An early start, offset by his and Billie's extremely late finish.

Schedules that seemed in opposition far more than they aligned recently.

"Morning," Reed said, lifting his focus from the phone to Billie slowly making her way back toward him. A dark silhouette still damp from the shower, the first rays of morning flashing against her wet fur.

"Hey there!" Serena said, her voice threaded with surprise. "After it got to the fifth or sixth ring, I figured you must have already gotten started for the day."

"Just ending the last one, actually," Reed replied.

"Oof," Serena answered, the sound of a blinker faintly audible in the background. "That's a long day."

"It was," Reed conceded, "but it's over now."

"The day, or the case?"

"Both," Reed said, watching as Billie covered the last bit of ground separating them and hopped up the couple of steps leading from the ground to the deck. Barely breaking stride, she headed on toward the back door, Reed turning in place to follow her.

The final act for both of them before falling into their beds, concluding what Serena had just rightly pointed out as a very long day.

"No bullet holes this time, right?"

"Nope," Reed said, following his partner into the kitchen and swinging the door shut behind them. "For me, or anybody else."

"Glad to hear that," Serena replied. "Though I have to admit, you needing a nurse last time wasn't the worst thing in the world."

The same faint smile Reed had been wearing while talking to Deke returned. A grin that lingered as he watched Billie thread her way through the chairs arranged around the table and lower herself onto the bed taking up most of the floor space beneath it.

An oversized mat of fleece and flannel that she sprawled herself atop, intent not to move for the foreseeable future.

"No, it was not," Reed agreed, leaving his partner to her rest as he passed through the living room and down the hall toward his bedroom. Bare feet padding over hardwood floors, everything still shrouded in shadow from the day just starting to awaken.

"I don't suppose that means you've had a chance to think about what we broached the other night, does it?"

"I have not," Reed admitted, entering the last doorway on the right and falling sideways onto his bed.

An unceremonious ending to a journey that seemed to have lasted for days, blessed rest finally at hand. "But I will. I promise."

Turn the page for a sneak peak of *The Cat, Reed and Billie Mysteries Book 12, or* download *now and* continue reading November 2023: dustinstevens.com/TCwb

Sneak Peek

THE CAT, REED AND BILLIE MYSTERIES BOOK 12

The white paper suit that The Cat was wearing crinkled with each step. Oversized legs that rubbed together as he moved forward, emitting a low whooshing sound. A faint baseline that was added to by the crunching of the frozen gravel beneath his feet. The low buzz of the tube lighting illuminating the interior of the barn behind him.

Elongated bulbs that backlit him, casting his shadow across the clearing. A distorted image that made his legs look like they were but a foot or two in length, while the rest of him spilled more than fifteen feet across the rutted stone. Small pebbles that were pockmarked both by his own feet and the tires of a handful of vehicles, most recently the aging Pontiac resting nearby.

Otherwise, there were absolutely no signs of life.

No additional sounds.

No visible lights in the distance or movements of animals moving through the forest pushed tight on either side.

Raising a hand to his head, The Cat peeled back the hood of the Tyvek suit. Ignoring the tug of the elastic band as it dragged across his mane of dark hair, he let it fall back between his shoulder blades.

Lifting his face toward the star-speckled sky above, he could feel the cold picking at the perspiration lining his scalp. Icy air that he drew into his lungs, letting it expand his chest, cooling him from within.

A calming balm that he drew in one time after another, using it to slow his heartrate.

Whether The Cat wanted to consider the day when he first arrived in Ohio four months ago as the start of things or if he preferred to go all the way back to the beginning, well before he could have possibly envisioned any of this, was moot. An anniversary date that he was well beyond considering. The kind of thing that lesser people might concern themselves with.

What did matter was that at long last, the interminable wait was finally over. The task he had set out for himself was about to begin.

His ascension to the mountaintop, the fulfillment of a dying wish that was bestowed upon him, was finally at hand.

A reclamation project of all that had been lost. A solidification of all that should be.

Forevermore.

Content that he was alone in the world, The Cat stepped away from the concrete pad serving as the foundation for the barn. Cutting a diagonal across the gravel lot, the sound of the suit he was wearing was blotted out by the crunch of stone beneath his feet. Soft scraping that carried through the night as he went directly to the driver's door of the aging vehicle and wrenched it open.

Reaching into the footwell, he pulled up on the trunk release, needing only a glance in the opposite direction to see the spring-loaded hinges had done as they were designed. The lid of the rear space was pointed upward, ready to accept his impending deposit.

A thought that couldn't help but bring a smile to The Cat's lips. An increase in pace as he retraced his path from just moments before and stepped into the barn to be greeted by a host of sights and smells.

A sensory onslaught that made the smile grow even larger. A sadistic grin that stretched across the lower half of his face, fed by the metallic tang of blood that flitted across his nostrils. The same copper-infused molecules that he could almost taste on his tongue.

Remnants of what he had spent the last hour doing inside the barn.

A pitstop in the middle of an evening that had started hours before, with just as much still left ahead.

A planned three-part sequence, each part more exhilarating than the one before. An escalation that pushed adrenaline into The Cat's system, causing him to move at a pace just shy of a jog. Long strides that chewed up the space, carrying him from gravel onto concrete.

A transition between surfaces that he barely noticed, his focus on the parcel enveloped in plastic in the center of the barren floor. An elongated bundle that he didn't bother to even seal, instead choosing to grab it by the flaps left free on either side.

Hefting the dead weight up from the floor, The Cat could feel the muscles in his arms and shoulders flex. His core tightened as he balanced the uneven package across his thighs and began to walk once more.

A third trip across the same path in as many minutes, swinging wide through the gravel to clear the side of the vehicle. A looping route, allowing him to nestle his offering into the open maw of the trunk.

A deposit made with care, ignoring the burn of lactic acid in his hands and forearms and the shortness of breath in his chest. Signs of exertion that he pushed aside as he tucked either end inside, making sure that it cleared the rim of the trunk hood.

Added effort now that would be more than worth it later.

One of a thousand different details already considered and committed to memory. Decisions predicated on ease and efficiency, right down to the bunched plastic left pointed skyward on either side. Makeshift handles that were ideal for wrestling the bundle into position.

And came with the added benefit of providing him a narrow viewing port to the contents. A thin window, enabling him to meet the lifeless stare of the girl tucked inside.

Bright blue eyes that he peered into, meeting her gaze as he reached upward and slowly lowered the trunk hood between them.

"I'm coming, I'm coming," Reed Mattox muttered as he half-jogged from the kitchen to the living room of his farmhouse. Arms pumping, he slid his stockinged feet across the carpet, ignoring the ongoing drone of the pair of announcers both splashed across the flatscreen television mounted to the wall beside him. Guys in suits and overcoats with perfectly coiffed hair and neon smiles, both clutching microphones.

The latest in what had been an unending line of studio hosts and analysts looking to build excitement for the impending game.

As if a contest with the given nickname of Bedlam needed any additional hype.

"I said I'm coming," Reed muttered, his comment and his attention instead aimed at the cellphone resting on the coffee table bisecting the television and his sofa. A small rectangle with the faceplate lit up, the sound of the University of Oklahoma's fight song spilling from the speaker.

A special ringtone reserved for exactly two people.

Snatching the phone up, Reed didn't so much as bother looking at the screen. Rotating on the ball of his foot, he turned back toward the kitchen and raised the device to his cheek.

"Boomer."

"Sooner!" his father shouted back at a decibel loud enough to cause Reed to jerk the phone back, even while a smile crossed his features.

"You're jumping the gun on me tonight," Reed said, crossing over the threshold from the living room into the kitchen. A transition marked not just by a shift from carpet to hardwood, but a dip in temperature.

A drop caused by the back door standing open a few inches to allow Reed's housemate and K-9 partner Billie to return whenever she was finished doing her business out in the backyard.

Final preparations of her own before they settled in for kickoff.

"Yeah, well, something tells me I'm not going to be much up for conversation during this one," Rhett Mattox replied.

Snorting loudly, Reed padded to the microwave resting atop the counter. Tugging open the door, he was greeted by a plume of steam carrying with it the scent of leftovers.

Remnants from a Thanksgiving feast the day before. Meat and potatoes and all the fixings, slathered with a generous covering of gravy. His first-ever attempt at preparing the meal entirely himself which had – if his friend Deek and his grandmother's reviews were to be believed – turned out reasonably well.

Enough so, anyway, to have earned a second go-round while watching the game.

"Oh, yeah? Just going to sit there and quietly enjoy the game, are you?" Reed asked.

His turn to snort in reply, his father asked, "Have you seen our pass defense? I'm sure I'll be saying plenty, I just wouldn't necessarily call it conversation."

With each word shared, his father's voice climbed. The start of an ascension that would no doubt be full-on yelling by the second or third possession. Impassioned critique aimed at the players, and the coaches, and the referees, and probably even the opposition's mascot.

Anywhere to fling his ire, should things not go the Sooners way. A weekly rite that Reed had seen going back decades, some of the tougher seasons during the nineties enough to send the family dog diving for cover under the bed.

"How about you?" his father asked. "You ready?"

"Fire is blazing, pregame is on, food just came out of the microwave," Reed replied. "Even Billie's getting ready, in the back-yard doing what she needs to as we speak."

Coughing out a laugh, Rhett replied, "Atta girl. How'd it go yesterday?"

"Good," Reed replied, sliding the plate from the microwave out onto the counter to cool. Leaving it in place, he stepped sideways to the fridge, adding, "Could have you used your help, though. Even after sending a bunch home with them, still have a ton of leftovers."

"Lef-tovers?" his father replied, purposely mispronouncing the word. "You mean, like food that you couldn't finish?"

"Yeah, yeah," Reed said. The start of a response that was cut short by an audible click sounding out over the line. The telltale noise of an incoming call that drew his attention, ending with him muttering, "Shit."

"What? Did they kick off without me?"

"No," Reed said. "Work is calling."

"Tell the governor you're too busy, Bedlam is about to start."

"I would," Reed said, "but this one isn't the governor."

"Oh," his father said, the same tinge of disappointment that Reed could already feeling creeping in threading through the word. "You want me to text you with score updates?"

"Maybe. I'll let you know."

"Okay, and before I forget, your mother wants to know what you're planning for Christmas."

"Ha!" Reed replied. "Tell her I haven't even thought about it yet."

Saying nothing more, Reed ended the call there. A quick shift, letting the mirth of a moment before fade as he switched to the incoming line.

"Mattox."

As if summoned on cue, the darkened silhouette of his Belgian Malinois partner appeared. A solid black canine resembling a wolf, she slid through the opening in the backdoor and presented herself just past the threshold.

An officer reporting for duty, even before the voice of Jackie - the dispatcher from the 8th Precinct of the Columbus Police Department where they were assigned when not working for the governor under the state's Bureau of Criminal Investigation – replied, "Hey, hon. I'm so sorry to be calling like this, but the evening shift guys got called to a break-in and you're the next ones up on call."

Keep reading *The Cat* November 2023: dustinstevens.com/TCwb

Thank You

Howdy, friends!

One of my all-time favorite Life-Of-A-Writer stories to tell is from roughly seven years ago, when I had just started dating someone new. After meeting her family for the first time, her mother got one of my books, read it, and then immediately called her daughter and whispered, "Um, about this new boyfriend of yours..."

(The book in question was *The Boat Man,* which set Reed and Billie up for this magical ride we've been on for so long, but let's face it, isn't for the faint of heart :)

The reason I bring this up now is, I can't help but wonder if some of you might have had similar thoughts while reading this one. A reaction that was very much by design, as in the early stages of putting the plot outline together, I kept circling back to ask myself, "What would be the most massive intrusion that one person could inflict on another? Something that couldn't be hidden. Couldn't be erased. Would send an unequivocal message for the rest of that person's life."

From that, I came up with the notion of a forehead tattoo, and then worked background to concoct a backstory that would warrant that kind of retribution.

Hopefully, what ensued made for an entertaining read, and is the sort of thing we never, ever see in real life.

Speaking of real life, please allow me to again take this opportunity to say thank you, both for reading this book and for supporting Reed and Billie the way you have. This entire series was first launched from a love of our furry friends, and that affection only deepens with each successive installment. Never did I imagine while watching a working K-9 team in an airport early one morning that this is where it would go, but I'm just as excited as you folks to see what the future holds for our favorite detecting duo.

(And for those of you who may be looking ahead, please keep an eye out for a new standalone novel, *Overlook,* out next – an excerpt of which is included above – followed by more later this year from HAM, the Zoo Crew, and maybe even a bit more Reed and Billie, just for fun ;)

Many thanks again, and until next time, happy reading!

Much love,

Dustin

Welcome Gift

Sign up for my newsletter and receive a FREE copy of my first bestseller – and still one of my personal favorites – *21 Hours:* dustin-stevens.com/DS21Free

About the Author

Dustin Stevens is the author of more than 70 novels, the vast majority having become #1 Amazon bestsellers, including the Reed & Billie and Hawk Tate series. *The Boat Man*, the first release in the best-selling Reed & Billie series, was named an Indie Award winner for E-Book fiction. The freestanding work *The Debt* was named an Independent Author Network action/adventure novel of the year and *The Exchange* was recognized for independent E-Book fiction.

He also writes thrillers and assorted other stories under the pseudonym TR Kohler.

A member of the Mystery Writers of America and International Thriller Writers, he resides in Honolulu, Hawaii.

Let's Keep in Touch:
Website: dustinstevens.com
Facebook: dustinstevens.com/fcbk
Twitter: dustinstevens.com/tw
Instagram: dustinstevens.com/DSinsta

Dustin's Books

Works Written by Dustin Stevens:

Reed & Billie Novels:
The Boat Man
The Good Son
The Kid
The Partnership
Justice
The Scorekeeper
The Bear
The Driver
The Promisor
The Ghost
The Family
The Cat

Hawk Tate Novels:
Cold Fire
Cover Fire
Fire and Ice

Hellfire
Home Fire
Wild Fire
Friendly Fire
Catching Fire

Zoo Crew Novels:
The Zoo Crew
Dead Peasants
Tracer
The Glue Guy
Moonblink
The Shuffle

Ham Novels:
HAM
EVEN
RULES
HOME
GONE

My Mira Saga:
Spare Change
Office Visit
Fair Trade
Ships Passing
Warning Shot
Battle Cry
Steel Trap
Iron Men
Until Death

Night Novels:
Overlook
Decisions

Twelve

Hobby Lobby Mysteries:
The Exchange
Badger Games

Standalone Thrillers:
Moonshine Creek
The Subway
The Ring
Peeping Thoms
One Last Day
Shoot to Wound
The Debt
Going Viral
Liberation Day
Motive
21 Hours
Scars and Stars
Catastrophic
Four

Standalone Dramas:
Quarterback
Be My Eyes
Ohana
Just A Game

Children's Books w/ Maddie Stevens:
Danny the Daydreamer...Goes to the Grammy's
Danny the Daydreamer...Visits the Old West
Danny the Daydreamer...Goes to the Moon
(Coming Soon)

Works Written by T.R. Kohler:

Dustin's Books

Hunter Series:
The Hunter
Street Divorce

Jumper Series:
Into The Jungle
Out To Sea

Bulletproof Series:
Mike's Place
Underwater
Coming Soon

Translator Series:
The Translator
The Confession

Made in United States
Troutdale, OR
11/03/2024